W9-CXN-610

Vernon God Little

Vernon God Little

DBC PIERRE

CANONGATE

First published in the United States of America in 2003
by Canongate Books, 841 Broadway, New York, NY 10003.

First published in the UK in 2003
by Faber and Faber Ltd

10 9 8 7 6 5 4

Copyright © DBC Pierre, 2003
The moral rights of the author has been asserted

ISBN 1-84195-460-8

Typeset by Palimpsest Book Production Limited, Polmont, Stirlingshire, Scotland
Printed in the United States of America by R. R. Donnelley Ltd, USA

www.canongate.net

Act I

Shit happened

one

It's hot as hell in Martirio, but the papers on the porch are icy with the news. Don't even try to guess who stood all Tuesday night in the road. Clue: snotty ole Mrs Lechuga. Hard to tell if she quivered, or if moths and porchlight through the willows ruffled her skin like funeral satin in a gale. Either way, dawn showed a puddle between her feet. It tells you normal times just ran howling from town. Probably forever. God knows I tried my best to learn the ways of this world, even had inklings we could be glorious; but after all that's happened, the inkles ain't easy anymore. I mean – what kind of fucken life is *this*?

Now it's Friday at the sheriff's office. Feels like a Friday at school or something. School – don't even fucken mention it.

I sit waiting between shafts of light from a row of doorways, naked except for my shoes and Thursday's underwear. Looks like I'm the first one they rounded up so far. I ain't in trouble, don't get me wrong. I didn't have anything to do with Tuesday. Still, you wouldn't want to be here today. You'd remember Clarence Somebody, that ole black guy who was on the news last winter. He was the psycho who dozed in this same wooden hall, right on camera. The news said that's how little he cared about the effects of his crimes. By 'effects' I think they meant axe-wounds. Ole Clarence Whoever was shaved clean like an animal, and dressed in the kind of hospital suit that psychos get, with jelly-jar glasses and all, the type of glasses worn by people with mostly gums and no teeth. They built him a zoo cage in court. Then they sentenced him to death.

I just stare at my Nikes. Jordan New Jacks, boy. I'd perk them up with a spit-wipe, but it seems kind of pointless when I'm naked.

Anyway, my fingers are sticky. This ink would survive Armageddon, I swear. Cockroaches, and this fucken fingerprint ink.

A giant shadow melts into the dark end of the corridor. Then comes its owner, a lady. As she approaches, light from a doorway snags a *Bar-B-Chew Barn* box in her arms, along with a bag of my clothes, and a phone that she tries to speak into. She's slow, she's sweaty, her features huddle in the middle of her face. Even in uniform you know she's a Gurie. Another officer follows her into the corridor, but she waves him away.

'Let me do the preliminaries – I'll call you for the statement.' She slides the phone back to her mouth and clears her throat. Her voice sharpens up to a squeak. 'Gh-*hrrr*, I am not calling you a moron, I'm explaining that, stuss-tistically, Special Weapons And Tactics can limit the *toll*.' She squeaks so high that her *Barn* box falls to the floor. 'Lunch,' she grunts, bending. 'Only salad, poo – I swear to God.' The call ends when she sees me.

I sit up to hear if my mother came to collect me; but she didn't. I knew she wouldn't, that's how smart I am. I still wait for it though, what a fucken genius. Vernon Genius Little.

The officer dumps the clothes in my lap. 'Walk this way.'

So much for Mom. She'll be pumping the town for sympathy, like she does. 'Well Vern's just *devastated*,' she'll say. She only calls me Vern around her coffee-morning buddies, to show how fucken tight we are, instead of all laughably fucked up. If my ole lady came with a user's guide it'd tell you to fuck her off in the end, I guarantee it. Everybody knows Jesus is ultimately to blame for Tuesday; but see Mom? Just the fact I'm helping the investigation is enough to give her fucken Tourette's Syndrome, or whatever they call the thing where your arms fly around at random.

The officer shows me into a room with a table and two chairs. No window, just a picture of my friend Jesus taped to the inside of the door. I get the stained chair. Pulling on my clothes, I try to imagine it's last weekend; just regular, rusty moments dripping into town via air-conditioners with missing dials; spaniels trying to drink from sprinklers but getting hit in the nose instead.

'Vernon Gregory Little?' The lady offers me a barbecued rib. She offers half-heartedly, though, and frankly you'd feel sorry to even take the thing when you see the way her chins vibrate over it.

She returns my rib to the box, and picks another for herself. 'Gh-*rr*, let's start at the beginning. Your habitual place of residence is seventeen Beulah Drive?'

'Yes ma'am.'

'Who else resides there?'

'Nobody, just my mom.'

'Doris Eleanor Little . . .' Barbecue sauce drips onto her name badge. *Deputy Vaine Gurie* it says underneath. 'And you're fifteen years old? Awkward age.'

Is she fucken kidding or what? My New Jacks rub together for moral support. 'Ma'am – will this take long?'

Her eyes widen for a moment. Then narrow to a squint. 'Vernon – we're talking accessory to murder here. It'll take as long as it takes.'

'So, but . . .'

'Don't tell me you weren't close to the Meskin boy. Don't tell me you weren't just about his only friend, don't you tell me that for one second.'

'Ma'am, but I mean, there must be plenty of witnesses who saw more than I did.'

'Is that right?' She looks around the room. 'Well I don't see anyone else here – do you?' Like an asshole I look around. Duh. She catches my eyes and settles them back. 'Mr Little – you *do* understand why you're here?'

'Sure, I guess.'

'Uh-huh. Let me explain that my job is to uncover the truth. Before you think that's a hard thing to do, I'll remind you that, stuss-tistically, only two major forces govern life in this world.

5

Can you name the two forces underlying all life in this world?'

'Uh – wealth and poverty?'

'Not wealth and poverty.'

'Good and evil?'

'No – *cause* and *effect*. And before we start I want you to name the two categories of people that inhabit our world. Can you name the two proven categories of people?'

'Causers and effecters?'

'No. Citizens – and *liars*. Are you with me, Mister Little? Are you *here*?'

Like, duh. I want to say, 'No, I'm at the lake with your fucken daughters,' but I don't. For all I know she doesn't even have daughters. Now I'll spend the whole day thinking what I should've said. It's really fucked.

Deputy Gurie tears a strip of meat from a bone; it flaps through her lips like a shit taken backwards. 'I take it you know what a liar is? A liar is a *psychopath* – someone who paints gray areas between black and white. It's my duty to advise you there are no gray areas. Facts are facts. Or they're *lies*. Are you here?'

'Yes ma'am.'

'I truly hope so. Can you account for yourself at a quarter after ten Tuesday morning?'

'I was in school.'

'I mean what period.'

'Uh – math.'

Gurie lowers her bone to stare at me. 'What important facts have I only now finished outlining to you, about black and white?'

'I didn't say I was in *class* . . .'

A knock at the door saves my Nikes from fusing. A wooden hairdo pokes into the room. 'Vernon Little in here? His ma's on the phone.'

'All right, Eileena.' Gurie shoots me a stare that says 'Don't relax' and points her bone at the door. I follow the wooden lady to reception.

I'd be fucken grateful, if it wasn't my ole lady calling. Between you and me, it's like she planted a knife in my back when I was born, and now every fucken noise she makes just gives it a turn. It cuts even deeper now that my daddy ain't around to share the pain. My shoulders round up when I see the phone, my mouth drops open like, duh. Here's exactly what she'll say, in her fuck-me-to-a-cross whimper, she'll say, 'Vernon, are you *all right*?' I guarantee it.

'Vernon, are you *okay*?' Feel the blade chop and dice.

'I'm fine, Ma,' now my voice goes all small and stupid. It's a subliminal plea for her not to be pathetic, but it works like pussy to a fucken dog.

'Did you use the bathroom today?'

'*Hell*, Momma . . .'

'Well you know you get that – inconvenience.'

She ain't so much called to turn the knife, as to replace it with a fucken javelin or something. You didn't need to know this, but when I was a kid I used to be kind of unpredictable, for 'Number Twos' anyway. Never mind the slimy details, my ole lady just added the whole affair to my knife, so she could give it a turn every now and then. Once she even wrote about it to my teacher, who had her own stabbing agenda with me, and this bitch mentioned it in class. Can you believe it? I could've bought the farm right there. My knife's like a fucken skewer these days, with all the shit that's been added on.

'Well you didn't have time this morning,' she says, 'so I worried that maybe – you know . . .'

'I'm fine, really.' I stay polite, before she plants the whole fucken Ginzu Knife Set. It's a hostage situation.

'What're you doing?'

'Listening to Deputy Gurie.'

'LuDell Gurie? Well, tell her I know her sister Reyna from Weight Watchers.'

'It ain't LuDell, Ma.'

'If it's Barry you know Pam sees him every other Friday . . .'

'It ain't Barry. I have to go now.'

'Well, the car still isn't ready and I'm minding an ovenful of joy cakes for the Lechugas, so Pam'll have to pick you up. And Vernon . . .'

'Uh?'

'Sit up straight in the car – town's *crawling* with cameras.'

Velcro spiders seize my spine. You know gray areas are invisible on video. You don't want to be here the day shit gets figured out in black and white. I ain't saying I'm to blame, don't get me wrong. I'm calm about that, see? Under my grief glows a serenity that comes from knowing the truth always wins in the end. Why do movies end happy? Because they imitate life. You know it, I know it. But my ole lady lacks that fucken knowledge, big-time.

I shuffle up the hall to my pre-stained chair. 'Mister Little,' says Gurie, 'I'm going to start over – that means loosen up some facts, young man. Sheriff Porkorney has firm notions about Tuesday, you should be thankful you only have to talk to me.' She goes to touch her snatch, but diverts to her gun at the last second.

'Ma'am, I was behind the gym, I didn't even see it happen.'

'You said you were in math.'

'I said it was our math *period*.'

She looks at me sideways. 'You take math behind the gym?'

'No.'

'So why weren't you in class?'

'I ran an errand for Mr Nuckles, and got kind of – held up.'

'Mr Nuckles?'

'Our physics teacher.'

'He teaches math?'

'No.'

'G-*hrrr*. This area's looking real gray, Mister Little. *Damn* gray.'

You don't know how bad I want to be Jean-Claude Van Damme. Ram her fucken gun up her ass, and run away with a panty model. But just look at me: clump of lawless brown hair, the eyelashes of a camel. Big ole puppy-dog features like God made me through a fucken magnifying glass. You know right away my movie's the one where I puke on my legs, and they send a nurse to interview me instead.

'Ma'am, I have witnesses.'

'Is that right.'

'Mr Nuckles saw me.'

'And who else?' She prods the dry bones in her box.

'A bunch of people.'

'Is that right. And where are those people now?'

I try to think where those people are. But the memory doesn't come to my brain, it comes to my eye as a tear that shoots from my lash like a soggy bullet. I sit stunned.

'Exactly,' says Gurie. 'Not real gregarious, are they? So Vernon – let me ask you two simple questions. One: are you involved with drugs?'

'Uh – no.'

She chases the pupils of my eyes across the wall, then herds them back to hers. 'Two: do you possess a firearm?'

'No.'

Her lips tighten. She pulls her phone from a holster on her belt, and suspends one finger over a key, eyeing me all the while. Then she jabs the key. The theme from *Mission: Impossible* chirps on a phone up the hall. 'Sheriff?' she says. 'You might want to attend the interview room.'

This wouldn't happen if she had more meat in her box. The dismay of no more meat made her seek other comforts, that's something I just learned. Now I'm the fucken meat.

After a minute, the door opens. A strip of buffalo leather scrapes into the room, tacked around the soul of Sheriff Porkorney. 'This the boy?' he asks. Like, fucken no, it's Dolly Parton. 'Cooperational, Vaine, is he?'

'Can't say he is, sir.'

9

'Give me a moment with him.' He closes the door behind him.

Gurie retracts her tit-fat across the table, turning to the corner like it makes her absent. The sheriff breathes a rod of decay at my face.

'Bothered folk, son, outside. Bothered folk are quick to judge.'

'I wasn't even there, sir – I have witnesses.'

He raises an eyebrow to Gurie's corner. One of her eyes flicks back, 'We're following it up, Sheriff.'

Pulling a clean bone from the *Bar-B-Chew Barn* box, Porkorney moves to the picture on the door, and traces a line around Jesus' face, his bangs of blood, his forsaken eyes. Then he curls a gaze at me. 'He talked to you – didn't he.'

'Not about this, sir.'

'You were close, though, you admit that.'

'I didn't know he was going to kill anybody.'

The sheriff turns to Gurie. 'Examine Little's clothes, did you?'

'My partner did,' she says.

'Undergarments?'

'Regular Y-fronts.'

Porkorney thinks a moment, chews his lip. 'Check the back of 'em, did you, Vaine? You know certain type of practices can loosen a man's pitoota.'

'They seemed clean, Sheriff.'

I know where this is fucken headed. Typical of where I live that nobody will come right out and say it. I try to muster some control. 'Sir, I ain't *gay*, if that's what you mean. We were friends since childhood, I didn't know how he'd turn out . . .'

A no-brand smile grows under the sheriff's moustache. 'Regular boy then, are you, son? You like your cars, and your guns? And your – girls?'

'Sure.'

'Okay, all right – let's see if it's true. How many offices does a girl have that you can get more'n one finger into?'

'Offices?'

'Cavities – holes.'

'Uh – two?'

'Wrong.' The sheriff puffs up like he just discovered fucken relativity.

Fuck. I mean, how am I supposed to know? I got my fingertip into a hole once, don't ask me which one. It left memories of the Mini-Mart loading-bay after a storm; tangs of soggy cardboard and curdled milk. Somehow I don't think that's what your porn industry is talking about. Not like this other girl I know called Taylor Figueroa.

Sheriff Porkorney tosses his bone into the box, nodding to Gurie. 'Get it on record, then hold him.' He creaks out of the room.

'Vaine?' calls an officer through the door. 'Fibers.'

Gurie re-forms into limbs. 'You heard the sheriff. I'll be back with another officer to take your statement.'

When the rubbing of her thighs has faded, I crane my nostrils for any vague comfort; a whiff of warm toast, a spearmint breath. But all I whiff, over the sweat and the barbecue sauce, is school – the kind of pulse bullyboys give off when they spot a quiet one, a wordsmith, in a corner. The scent of lumber being cut for a fucken cross.

two

Mom's best friend is called Palmyra. Everybody calls her Pam. She's fatter than Mom, so Mom feels good around her. Mom's other friends are slimmer. They're not her best friends.

Pam's here. Three counties hear her bellowing at the sheriff's secretary. 'Lord, where *is* he? Eileena, have you seen Vern? Hey, love the hair!'

'Not too frisky?' tweets Eileena.

'Lord no, the brown really suits you.'

You have to like Palmyra, I guess, not that you'd want to imagine her humping or anything. She has a lemon-fresh lack of knives about her. What she does is eat.

'Have you fed him?'

'I think Vaine bought ribs,' says Eileena.

'Vaine Gurie? She's supposed to be on the Pritikin diet – Barry'll have a *truck*!'

'Good-night, she damn near *lives* at *Bar-B-Chew Barn*!'

'Oh good Lord.'

'Vernon's in there, Pam,' says Eileena. 'You better wait outside.'

So the door flies open. Pam wobbles in, bolt upright like she has books on her head. It's on account of her center of gravity. 'Vernie, you eatin rebs? What did you eat today?'

'Breakfast.'

'Oh Lord, we better go by the *Barn*.' Doesn't matter what you tell her, she's going by *Bar-B-Chew Barn*, believe me.

'I can't, Pam, I have to stay.'

'Malarkey, come on now.' She tugs my elbow. The force of it recommends the floor to my feet. 'Eileena, I'm taking Vern – you tell Vaine Gurie this boy ain't eaten, I'm double-parked out front, and she better hide some pounds before I see Barry.'

'Leave him, Pam, Vaine ain't through . . .'

'I don't see no handcuffs, and a child has a right to eat.' Pam's voice starts to rattle furniture.

'I don't make the rules,' says Eileena. 'I'm just sayin . . .'

'Vaine can't hold him – you know that. We're gone,' says Pam. 'Love your hair.'

Eileena's sigh follows us down the hallway. My ears flick around for signs of Gurie or the sheriff, but the offices seem empty; the sheriff's offices that is. Next thing you know, I'm halfway out of the building in Palmyra's gravity-field. You just can't argue with this much modern woman, I tell you.

Outside, a jungle of clouds has grown over the sun. They kindle the whiff of damp dog that always blows around here before a storm, burping lightning without a sound. Fate clouds. They mean get the fuck out of town, go visit Nana or something, until things quiet down, until the truth seeps out. Get rid of the drugs from home, then take a road trip.

A shimmer rises off the hood of Pam's ole Mercury. Martirio's tight-assed buildings quiver through it, oil pumpjacks melt and sparkle along the length of Gurie Street. Yeah: oil, jackrabbits, and Guries are what you find in Martirio. This was once the second-toughest town in Texas, after Luling. Whoever got beat up in Luling must've crawled over here. These days our toughest thing is congestion at the drive-thru on a Saturday night. I can't say I've seen too many places, but I've studied this one close and the learnings must be the same; all the money, and folk's interest in fixing things, parade around the center of town, then spread outwards in a dying wave. Healthy girls skip around the middle in whiter-than-white panties, then regions of shorts and cotton prints radiate out to the edges, where tangled babes hang in saggy purple underwear. Just a broken ole muffler shop on the outskirts; no more sprinklers, no more lawns.

'Lord,' says Pam, 'tell me why I can just taste a *Chik 'n' Mix*.'

Fucken yeah, right. Even in winter the Mercury stinks of fried chicken, never mind today when it's like a demon's womb. Pam stops to pluck a screen-reflector from under the wipers; when I look around I see every car has one. Seb Harris rides through the haze at the end of the street, distributing them from his bike. Pam opens the thing out and squints at the writing: 'Harris's Store,' it reads, 'More, More, More!'

'Lookit that,' she says. 'We just saved us the price of a *Chik 'n' Mix*.'

Deep fucken trouble keeps my euphoria at bay. Pam just molds into the car. Her soul's already knotted over the choice of side-order, you can tell. She'll end up getting coleslaw anyway, on account of Mom says it's healthy. It's vegetables, see. Me, I need something healthier today. Like the afternoon bus out of town.

A siren wails past us at the corner of Geppert Street. Don't ask me why, they can't save any children now. Pam will miss this corner anyway – it's fucken traditional, look, there she goes. Now she'll have to cut back two blocks, and she'll say, 'Lord, nothing stays put in this town.' Reporters and camera people roam the streets in packs. I keep my head down, and scan the floor for fire ants. 'Far aints,' Pam calls them. Fuck knows what other fauna climbs aboard in the century it takes her to get in and out of the fucken car. *Wild Fucken Kingdom*, I swear.

Today everybody at the *Barn* wears black, except for the Nikes on their feet. I identify the different models while they box up the chicken. Town's like a club, see. You recognize fellow members by their shoes. They won't even sell certain shoes to outsiders, it's a fact. I watch these black forms scurry around with different-colored feet and, just like when anything weird screens through the Mercury window, Glen Campbell starts to sing 'Galveston' from Pam's ole stereo. It's a law of nature. Pam only has this one cassette, see – *The Best of Glen Campbell*. It jammed in the slot the first time she played it, and just kept on playing. Fate. Pam sings along with the same part of the song every time, the part about the girl. I think she once had a boyfriend from Wharton, which is closer to Galveston than here. No songs about Wharton I guess.

'Vern, eat the bottom pieces before they get soggy.'

'Then the top pieces will be on the bottom.'

'Oh Lord.' She lunges for the tub, but doesn't get past the refresher wipes before we turn into Liberty Drive. She must've forgot about Liberty Drive today.

Look at all the girls crying by the school.

Galveston, oh Galveston . . .

Another luxury wagon parks up ahead, with even more flowers, even more girls. It maneuvers slowly around the stains on the road. Strangers with cameras move back to fit it all in.

I still hear your sea waves crashing . . .

Behind the girls, behind the flowers are the mothers, and behind the mothers are the counselors; senior brownies at a petting zoo.

While I watch the cannons flashing . . .

Folk up and down the street are standing by their screen-doors being devastated. Mom's so-called friend Leona was already devastated last week, when Penney's delivered the wrong color kitchen drapes. Typical of her to go off half-cocked.

'Oh my Lord, Vernie, oh God – all those tiny crosses . . .' I feel Palmyra's hand on my shoulder, and find myself sobbing spit.

The picture of Jesus that hangs behind the sheriff's door was taken at the crime scene. From a different angle than I last saw him. It doesn't show all the other bodies around, all the warped, innocent faces. Not like the picture in my soul. Tuesday breaks through me like a fucken hemorrhage.

I clean my gun, and dream of Galves-ton . . .

*

Jesus Navarro was born with six fingers on each hand, and that wasn't the most different thing about him. It's what took him though, in the very, very end. He didn't expect to die Tuesday; they found him wearing silk panties. Now girls' underwear is a major focus of the investigation, go figure. His ole man says the cops planted them on him. Like, *'Lingerie Squad! Freeze!'* I don't fucken think so.

That morning crowds my mind. 'Hay-zoose, slow the fuck up!' I remember yelling to him.

A headwind worries our bikes on the way to school, weights them almost as heavy as this last Tuesday before summer vacation. Physics, then math, then physics again, some stupid experiment in the lab. Hell on fucken earth.

Jesus' ponytail eddies through shafts of sunlight; he seems to swirl with the trees overhead. He's changing, ole Jesus, turning pretty in an Indian kind of way. The stumps of his extra fingers have almost disappeared. He's still clumsy as hell though, and his mind's clumsy too; the certainty of our kid logic got washed away, leaving pebbles of anger and doubt that crack together with each new wave of emotion. My buddy, who once did the best David Letterman impression you ever saw, has been abducted by glandular acids. Sassy song and smell hormones must fume off his brain, the type that curdle if your mom senses them. But you get the feeling they ain't regular hormones. He keeps secrets from me, like he never did before. He got weird. Nobody knows why.

I saw a show about adolescents that said role models were the key to development, same as for dogs. You could tell whoever made the show never met Jesus' dad, though. Or mine, for that matter. My dad was better than Mr Navarro, until the end anyway, although I used to get pissed that he wouldn't let me use his rifle, like Mr Navarro let Jesus use his. Now I cuss the day I ever saw my daddy's gun, and I guess Jesus cusses his day too. He needed a different role model, but nobody was there for him. Our teacher Mr Nuckles spent all kinds of time with him after school, but I ain't sure ole powder-puff Nuckles and his circus of fancy words really count. I mean, the guy's over thirty, and you just know he sits down to piss. He spent all this time with Jesus, up at his place, and riding in his car, talking softly, with his head down, like those caring folk you see on TV. One time I saw them hug, I guess like brothers or something. Don't even go there, really. The point is, in the end, Nuckles recommended a shrink. Jesus got worse after that.

Lothar 'Lard-ass' Larbey drives by in his ole man's truck, flicking his tongue at my buddy. 'Wetback fudge-packer!' he yells.

Jesus just drops his head. I sting for him sometimes, with his retreaded, second-hand Jordan New Jacks, and his goddam alternative lifestyle, if that's what you call this new fruity thing. His character used to fit him so clean, like a sports sock, back when we were kings of the universe, when the dirt on a sneaker mattered more than the sneaker itself. We razed the wilds outside town with his dad's gun, terrorized ole beer cans, watermelons, and trash. It's like we were men before we were boys, back before we were whatever the fuck we are now. I feel my lips clamp together with the strangeness of life, and watch my buddy pull alongside me on his bike. His eyes glaze over, like they do since he started seeing that shrink. You can tell he's retreated into one of his philosophical headfucks.

'Man, remember the Great Thinker we heard about in class last week?' he asks.

'The one that sounded like "Manual Cunt"?'

'Yeah, who said nothing really happens unless you see it happen.'

'All I remember is asking Naylor if he ever heard of a Manual Cunt, and him going, "I only drive automatics." We dropped the biggest fucken load.'

Jesus clicks his tongue. 'Shit, Vermin, you always only thinkin bout dropped loads. Just loads, and shit, and girl tangs. This is real, man. Manual Cunt asked the thing about the kitten – the riddle, that if there was a box with a kitten inside, and if the box also had an open bottle of death-gas or whatever, that the kitten's definitely going to knock over at any moment . . .'

'Whose kitten is this? I bet they're pissed.'

'Fuck, Verm, I'm serious. This is a real-time philosophy question. The kitten's in this box, definitely gonna die at some moment, and Manual Cunt asks if it may as well be called dead already, technically, unless somebody's there to see it still alive, to know it exists.'

'Wouldn't it be easier just to stomp on the fucken kitten?'

'It's not about wasting the kitten, asshole.' You can tick Jesus off real easy these days. His logic got all serious.

'What's the fucken point, Jeez?'

He frowns and answers slowly, digging each word out with a shovel. 'That if things don't happen unless you see them happening – do they still happen if you know they're gonna – but don't tell nobody . . .?'

As the words reach my ears, the mausoleum shapes of Martirio High School slam into view through the trees. A bitty chill like a worm burrows through me.

three

Too fucken late. When you spot a jackrabbit it automatically spots you back; it's a fact of nature, in case you didn't know. Same goes for Vaine Gurie, who I spy in the road by my house. Storms clouds park over her patrol car.

'Pam, stop! Leave me right here . . .'

'Get a grip, we're nearly home.' Pam don't stop easy once she's going.

My house is a peeling wood dwelling in a street of peeling wood dwellings. Before you see it through the willows, you see the oil pumpjack next door. I don't know about your town, but around here we decorate our pumpjacks. Even have competitions for them. Our pumpjack is fixed up like a mantis, with a head and legs stuck on. This giant mantis just pump, pump, pumps away at the dirt next door. The local ladies decorated it. This year's prize went to the Godzilla pumpjack on Calavera Drive, though.

As Pam throttles back the car, I see media reporters up the street, and a stranger lazing next to a van in the shade of the Lechugas' willow. He moves a branch to watch us pass. He smiles, don't ask me why.

'That man's been there all morning,' says Pam, squinting into the willow.

'He a stranger, or media?' I ask.

Pam shakes her head, pulling up at my house. 'He ain't from around here, I know that much. He has a camcorder, though . . .'

Fuck, fuck, fuck goes the mantis, like it does every four seconds of my life. Gas, brake, gas, brake, Pam berths the car like a ferryboat. Fuck, fuck, gas, brake, I'm snagged in the apparatus of Martirio. Across the street, Mrs Lechuga's drapes are tightly pulled. At number twenty, ole Mrs Porter stares from behind her screen-door with Kurt, the medium-size black and white dog. Kurt deserves a place in the fucken Barking Hall of Fame, although he ain't made a sound since Tuesday. Weird how dogs know things.

Next thing you know, a shadow falls over the car. It's Vaine Gurie. 'Who do we have here?' she asks, opening my door. Her voice plays from deep in her throat, like a parrot's. You want to check her mouth for the little boxing-glove kind of tongue.

Mom scurries across our porch with a tray of listless ole joy cakes. She's in Spooked Deer mode. She looked this way the last time I saw my daddy alive, although Spooked Deer can mean anything from her frog oven-mitt being misplaced, to actual Armageddon. But her mitt's right there, under the tray. She heads down the steps past our willow, the one with her wishing bench under it. The wishing bench is quite a new feature around here, but already the damned thing's listing into the dirt. She pays no mind, and flounces up to Pam's car.

'Howdy pardner,' she says to me, dripping with that cutesy-shucksy Chattanooga-buddy-boy shit she started when I first showed evidence of having a dick. Feel the bastard shrivel now. I pull away, in vain because she chases me, covers me with spit and lipstick and fuck knows what else. Placenta, probably. All the while she smiles a smile you know you've seen before, but just can't put your finger on. Clue: the movie where the mother visits this young family, and by the end they have to grapple fucken scissors from her hands.

'Gh-*rrr*.' Vaine steps between us. 'I'm afraid your pardner here absconded from our interview.'

'Well call me Doris, Vaine! I'm almost a Gurie myself, I'm so cozy with LuDell, and Reyna and all.'

'Is that right. Mrs Little, let me explain where things stand . . .'

'Well these cakes are just singing out to be tasted – Vaine?'

'I'm afraid I don't make the laws, ma'am.'

'At least come up to the house – no point getting hot and ornery, we can straighten things out,' says Mom. I stiffen. You don't want Gurie poking around my room or anything. My fucken closet or anything.

'I'm afraid Vernon will have to come with me,' says Gurie. 'Then we need to take a look through his room.'

'Well, God, Vaine – he hasn't done any wrong, he *always* does like he's told . . .'

'Is that right. So far he's done nothing but lie, and when I trust him alone he absconds. We still can't account for him at the time of the tragedy.'

'He wasn't even there!'

'Not what he told us, he told us he was in math.'

'It was the time of our math *period*,' I correct. Print me a fucken T-shirt, for chrissakes.

'Then there's no need to worry,' says Gurie. 'If you have nothing to hide.'

'Well but Vaine, the *news* says it's open and shut – everybody knows the cause.'

Gurie's eyelids flutter. 'Everybody might know the *effect*, Mrs Little. We'll see about the cause.'

'But the *news* says . . .'

'The news says a lot of things, ma'am. The fact is we've run this county dry of body-bags, and I, for one, hold the opinion that it'd take more than a single, unaided gunman to do that.'

Mom stumbles to her wishing bench, abandoning her cakes to the side. She overbalances a little as the bench settles unevenly into the dirt. The fucken bench settles a different way every week, like it's indexed to her head or something. 'Well I don't know why everything has to happen to *me*. We have witnesses, Vaine – *witnesses*!'

Gurie sighs. 'Ma'am, you know how accessible the so-called witnesses are. Maybe your boy knew. Maybe not. The fact is, he absconded before our interview was over – people with airtight alibis just don't do that.'

This is how long it takes Pam to lever herself out of the Mercury. It grunts with relief as she lets go the frame. Fire ants catapult across the seat.

'I took him, Vaine. Found him near dead from starvation.'

Gurie folds her arms. 'He was offered food . . .'

'Fiddledy-boo, the Pritikin diet wouldn't even feed the nose on a growing boy.' One sweaty eye snaps to Gurie. 'How's it going, Vaine – the Pritikin diet?'

'Oh – fine. *Gh-rr.*'

That's Gurie stuck through like a bug. The crumpled-looking stranger with the camcorder catches my eye from under the Lechugas' willow, then looks at Vaine. He still has a smile without promise, a chalk smile that strikes me edge-ways, don't ask me why. Gurie pays no mind. She just fixes him in the corner of her eye. The guy wears tan overalls with a white dinner jacket, like ole Ricardo Moltenbomb, or whoever Mom's favorite was who had the dwarf on *Fantasy Island*. He eventually penguin-walks over the road, fixing his camcorder onto a tripod. It tells you he's either a tourist, or a reporter. Only way to tell reporters these days is by their names – ever notice how fucken bent your local reporters' names are? Like, Zirkie Hartin, Aldo Manaldo, and shit.

'So,' says Gurie, ignoring Moltenbomb. 'Let's get this child into town.' Child my ass.

'Well wait,' says Mom. 'There's something you should know – Vernon suffers from a kind of – *condition.*' She rasps it like it's cancer.

'*Heck*, Momma!'

'Vernon Gregory, you know you get that *inconvenience*!'

Jesus, fuck. My overbite grows a yard. Moltenbomb chuckles from the roadside.

'We'll take care of him,' says Gurie, wiping a hand on her leg. She nudges me down the driveway with her body; effective law-enforcement if you have ass-cheeks like fucken demolition balls.

'But he hasn't done any wrong! He has a *clinical condition*!'
Clinical condition my fucken ass.

Just then, Fate plays a card. The hiss of Leona Dunt's Eldorado
echoes up the street. The uterus-mobile from hell. It's full of
Mom's two other so-called friends, Georgette and Betty. They
always just drop by. Until Tuesday, Mrs Lechuga was the leader of
this pack; now she's indisposed until further notice.

Leona Dunt only shows up when she has at least two things to
brag about, that's how you know your position in life. She needs
about five things to go to the Lechugas', so we're junior league.
Fetus league, even. Apart from having the thighs and ass of a cow,
and minimum tits, Leona's an almost pretty blonde with a honey-
suckle voice you know got its polish from rubbing on her last
husband's wallet. That's the dead husband, not the first one, that
got away. She never talks about the one that got away.

Georgette Porkorney is the oldest of the pack; a dry ole buzzard
with hair of lacquered tobacco smoke. We just call her George.
Right now she's married to the sheriff, not that you'd want to
imagine them doing anything. And get this: just like the rhinos
you see in the wild on TV, she has a bird that lives sitting on her
back. It's called Betty Pritchard, Mom's other so-called buddy.

Betty just has this mopey face, and tags along saying, 'I know, I
know.' Her ten-year-ole is called Brad. Little fucker broke my
PlayStation, but he won't admit it. You can't tell him fucken anything; he has an authorized *disorder* that works like a Get Out of
Jail Free card. Me, I only have a *condition*.

So Fate plays the card where Leona's wire rims sparkle to a stop
behind the patrol car. Ricardo Moltenbomb, the reporter dude,
makes a flourish like a bullfighter, then steps aside as an acre of
cellulite drains onto the dirt we call our lawn. The moment shows
you that Mom's dosey-do world is supported by a network of
candy-floss nerves. Now watch them fucken melt.

'Hi, Vaine!' calls Leona. She leads the way on account of being
youngest, which means under forty.

23

'What, Vaine?' calls Georgette Porkorney. 'My ole man grow weary of you at the station?'

Mom takes the catch. 'Vaine's just doing a routine check, girls – come on up for a soda.'

'More trouble, Doris?' asks Leona.

'Well gosh,' says Mom. 'These cakes are perspiring!' Believe me, there ain't the life in those cakes to perspire.

Vaine Gurie preps her throat to speak, but just then Moltenbomb steps up to her with his camcorder and his alligator smile. 'A few words for the camera, Captain?'

An audience forms around them, consisting of Pam, Georgette, Leona, and Betty. Georgette's cigarettes appear. She's settling in. Betty's mope turns into a scowl, she steps back. 'You're not going to smoke on TV, are you – George?'

'Shhh,' says Georgette. 'I ain't on TV – *she* is. Don't piss me off, Betty.'

Deputy Gurie's lips tighten. She draws a long breath, and frowns at the reporter. 'Firstly, sir, I'm a deputy, and secondly you should consult the media room for updates.'

'Actually, I'm doing a background story,' says Moltenbomb.

Gurie looks him up and down. 'Is that right. And you are . . .?'

'CNN, ma'am – Eulalio Ledesma, at your service.' Sunlight strikes some gold in his mouth. 'The world awaits.'

Gurie chuckles and shakes her head. 'The world's a long way from Martirio, Mr Ledesma.'

'Today the world *is* Martirio, ma'am.'

Gurie's eyes dart to Pam. Pam's mouth jacks wide open like a kid in a fast-food commercial. The shape of the word 'TV!' shines out. 'Your Barry'll be so proud!' she says.

Deputy Gurie looks herself over. 'But I can't just go on like this, can I?'

'You're spotless, Vaine – get a grip,' tuts Pam.

'Is that right. G*h*. And precisely what am I supposed to say?'

'Relax, I'll lead you right in,' says Mr Ledesma. Before Gurie can object, he sets down his tripod, aims the camera at her, and steps in front. His voice ripens to melted wood. 'Once again we don the cloak of mourning – a cloak worn ragged by the devastating fallout of a world in change. Today, the good citizens of Martirio, Central Texas, join me in asking – how do we heal America?'

'Gh-*rr*,' Gurie opens her mouth like she has the fucken answer. No, Vaine, duh – he ain't finished.

'We start on the front line, with the people whose role in the aftermath of tragedy is changing; our law-enforcement professionals. Deputy Vaine Gurie – does the community relate differently to you at a time like this?'

'Well, this is our first time,' she says. Like, fucken *duh*.

'But, are you increasingly called upon to counsel, to lend moral as well as civil support?'

'Stuss-tistically sir, there are more counselors in town than officers of the law. They don't enforce laws, so we don't counsel.'

'The community is meeting the challenge, then – pulling together?'

'We have some manpower over from Luling, and the dogs are here from Smith County, sure. A committee in Houston even sent up some home-made fudge.'

'Obviously freeing valuable time for you to spend with survivors . . .' Ledesma motions me over.

Gurie falters. 'Sir, the survivors have survived – my job is to find the cause. This town won't rest until the cause of the problem is identified. And corrected.'

'But surely it's open and shut?'

'Nothing happens without an underlying cause, sir.'

'You're saying the community has to search inside itself, maybe face some hard truths about its role in the tragedy?'

'I'm saying we have to find the one who caused it.'

Twinkles stab Ledesma's eyes. He reaches for my shoulder and pulls me into the frame.

'Did this young man cause it?'

Gurie's chins recoil like snails shot with vinegar. 'Gh-*rrr* – I didn't say that.'

'Then why should the American taxpayer bankroll you to detain him, on the first day of his probable lifelong trauma?'

Other reporters move toward us down the street. Sweat brews on Gurie's face. 'That'll be all for now, Mr Lesama.'

'Deputy, this is the public domain. God Himself can't stop the camera.'

'I'm just afraid I don't make the laws.'

'The child has broken laws?'

'Well, I don't know.'

'You'll detain him just in case?'

'Gh-*r*.'

The frown on the sheriff's wife is almost down to her tits. Which is way down. Ledesma sizes her up, his tongue lolls restless in his cheek. Gurie tries to shuffle away, but he swings the camera like a gun.

'Perhaps you'll tell us the name of the sheriff who briefed you?'

The way Georgette Porkorney talks you wouldn't think she gave a shit about the ole sheriff. She gives one now, though. Her phone flies out of her bag in a shower of Kleenex.

'Bertram? Vaine's on TV.'

After a second, Gurie's phone rings in her pocket. 'Sheriff? No sir, I swear to God. Bandera Road? About two blocks from here. Dogs? Yes sir, right away.'

Ledesma folds up his camera and watches Vaine shuffle to her car, defeated. Then, as a crack of thunder chases the last shine from the pumpjack, he turns to me and winks in slow-motion. It has to be slo-mo for how fucken fast it is. I try not to smile. Or drop a load the size of fucken Texas.

'You owe me a story,' he mouths silently, pointing a short, puffy finger. I just nod, and follow my ole lady onto the porch with Leona, George, and Betty. She ushers them inside, then hangs back at the screen to see if ole Mrs Porter, childless Mrs Porter, out-of-the-spotlight Mrs Porter, is still watching from her doorway. She is, but she's pretending not to. Kurt the dog's watching, though. He don't care to pretend.

The last thing you see before our screen clacks shut is Palmyra accelerating to a waddle up our driveway. She passes Gurie, and jabs a finger at the stain around her badge.

'Uh-oh, Vaine – barbecue sauce.'

In a black and white world, everything in my room is fucken evidence against me. A haze of socks and underwear riddled with secret dreams. My computer has history to wipe from the drive, like the amputee sex pictures I printed for ole Silas. He doesn't have a computer, see. Silas is a sick ole puppy – don't even go there, really. He trades stuff with us kids in return for pictures, if you know what I mean. I make a note to wipe the computer, or 'Perform some Virtual Hygiene,' as Mr Nuckles would say. My eyes crawl around the rest of the room. Last week's laundry sits in a pile by my bed, Mom's lingerie catalog is under it; I have to return it to her room. And hope like hell she never tries to open page 67 or 68. You know how it is. Then there's my closet, with the Nike box in back. Inside are two joints, and two hits of LSD. Don't get me wrong, I'm only holding them for Taylor Figueroa.

Muddy light breaks through the gloom outside my window. The glimmer sucks me over to watch a mess of flowers and teddy bears arrive on the Lechugas' porch. Now it looks like Princess Debbie's place, or whoever the princess was who died. It's all just in a pile, still wrapped. So you know the Lechugas paid for it. Nobody else sent flowers for Max, that's the sadness of the thing. Pathetic, really.

I'm studying this whole tragedy routine, in back of my jellified brain. The Lechugas have to send themselves teddy bears, for instance. Know why? Because Max was an asshole. Saw-teeth of damnation I feel just thinking it, waiting for fiery hounds to unleash mastications and puke my fucken soul to hell. But at the same time, here's me with water in my eyes, for Max, for all my classmates. The truth is a corrosive thing. It's like everybody who used to cuss the dead is now lining up to say what perfect angels of God they were. What I'm learning is the world laughs through its ass every day, then just lies double-time when shit goes down. It's like we're on a Pritikin diet of fucken lies. I mean – what kind of fucken life is this?

I drag the crusty edge of a T-shirt over my eyes, and try to get over things. I should clean up my mess, seeing as everybody's so antsy, but I feel like smeared shit. Then a learning jumps to mind, that once you plan to do something, and figure how long it'll take, that's exactly how long Fate gives you before the next thing comes along to do.

'Vern?' Mom hollers from the kitchen. '*Ver*-non!'

four

'V*er-non?*'

'Do what?' I yell. Mom doesn't fucken answer. A typical mother thing, they just monitor the notes of your voice. If you ask them later what you said, they don't even fucken know. Just the noises have to sound right, like, dorky enough.

'Ver-*non.*'

I close my closet door, and step down the hall to the kitchen, where a familiar scene plays around the breakfast bar. Leona's in the kitchen with Mom, who's messing with the oven. Brad Pritchard is on the rug in the living room, pretending you can't see his finger up his ass. Everybody pretends they can't see it. See the way folks are? They don't want to smutten their Wint-O-Green lives by saying, 'Brad, get your fucken finger out of your goddam anus,' so they just pretend it ain't there. Same way they try and avoid the sting of mourning around this ole town. They can't, though, you know it. Their ribs are pressed tight with the weight of grief. The only hopeful sight is Pam, beached on dad's ole sofa at the dark end of the room. A Snickers bar appears from the folds of her moo-moo.

I go to the kitchen side of the bar, where Leona's still working up to her brags; she has to empty Mom out first, so her voice slithers up and down, 'Oh how *neat, wow,* Doris, oh *great,*' like a foam sireen. Then, when Mom's all boosted up, she trumps her.

'Hey, did I tell you I'm getting a maid?'

Mom's mouth crinkles. 'Oh – *hey.*'

Hold your breath for the second thing. George blows ultra-slim cigarette smoke over Betty as they pretend to watch TV; their ultra-mild smiles come from knowing how many things there are.

Mom just frets over the oven. Gives her somewhere to stick her fucken head if no more things turn up. A bug of sweat crawls down her nose, 'Thk,' onto the brown linoleum.

'Yeah,' says Leona, 'she starts when I get back from Hawaii.'

The house sags with relief. 'Well gosh, another vacation?' asks Mom.

Leona flicks back her hair. 'Todd would've wanted me to do *nice* things, you know – while I'm *young*.' Like: yeah, right.

'Hell, but I can't believe today,' says George from the living room. That signals the end of the brags.

'I know, I know,' says Betty.

'You think things have gone as far as they can go, then – *boom*!'

'Oh golly, I *know*.'

'Six pounds if it's an ounce, and I only saw her last week. Six pounds in a *week*!' George weaves a trumpet of smoke around the words. Betty waves them away with her hand.

'It's that diet, all those carbs,' says Leona.

Pam grunts darkly in back.

'I know,' says Betty. 'Why didn't she stick to Weight Watchers?'

'Honey,' says George, 'Vaine Gurie's lucky to stick to the seat of her damn shorts. I don't know why she tries.'

'Barry threatened her,' says Pam. 'She has a month to ditch her flab, or he's gone.'

George points her mouth into the air, so the words will fly over her head to Pam. 'Then forget Pritikin – she needs the *Wilmer* Plan.'

'But Georgette,' says Mom from the kitchen, 'the Wilmer didn't work for *me* – not yet, anyway.'

Leona and Betty level eyes at each other. George coughs quietly. 'I don't think you quite got the hang of it, Doris.'

'Well, I guess I'm still trying it out, you know . . . Anyway, did I tell you I ordered the side-by-side fridge?'

'Wow,' says Leona, 'the Special Edition? What color?'

Mom's eyes fall to the floor. 'Well – almond on almond.'

Look at her: flushed and shiny with sweat, hunched under her brown ole hair, in her brown ole kitchen. Deep inside, her organs pump double-time, trying to turn bile into strawberry milk. Outside, her brown ole life festers uselessly around the jokey red bow on her dress.

I prompt her from the laundry end. 'Ma?'

'Well there you are – go ask that TV man if he'd like a Coke, it must be ninety degrees outside.'

'The one dressed like Ricardo Moltenbomb?'

'Well he's much younger than Ricardo Montalban – isn't he, girls? And better-looking . . .'

'Hnf,' says Pam.

George leans out of her chair to catch Mom's eye. 'You're going to ask a total *stranger* inside, just like that?'

'Well Georgette, we Martirians are known for our hospitality . . .'

'Uh-huh,' snorts George. 'I didn't see many of those cheerleaders up here, after their bus broke down that time.'

'Well but this is different.'

All the girls except for Pam exchange lip-tightenings. George clears her throat a little.

Brad Pritchard finishes with his ass. Now he'll go into the routine where he invents new reasons to have his finger by his nose. As I slip through the kitchen door, I catch his eye, point to my ass, then suck my finger.

'M-*om*,' he squeals.

Beulah Drive is spongy with heat. I wander over to a lemonade stand some kids have set up on number twelve's driveway; they ask fifty cents for information about the reporter, so I wander back, and check the red van under the Lechugas' willow. My nose flattens to the rear glass. You can see a lunchbox behind the seat, with half a brown apple in it. Some wires on the floor. A chewed-up ole book titled 'Make It In Media'. Then you see Ledesma's head rested on a pair of ole boots. He splays naked across a canvas mat inside, eyes closed, muscles heavy and slick.

He jackrabbits when I spot him.

'*Shit!*' He jerks up onto an elbow, rubbing his eyes. 'Big man – come round to the door.'

I tap a stray teddy onto the Lechugas' lawn, and move around to the side. A blast of sweat hits me when the door opens. The guy's face is waxy. Definitely over thirty. I can tell my ole lady likes him, but I ain't so sure.

'You live in the van?' I ask.

'Tch – the motel's full. Anyway, it gives my corporate Amex a break.' A bunch of glass phials tumble across the floor as he grabs his clothes.

'Mom says you can come up for a Coke.'

'I could sure use your bathroom. And maybe a bite to eat.'

'We have joy cakes.'

'*Joy* cakes?'

'Don't ask.'

Ledesma grabs a handful of the tiny bottles from the floor, stuffing them into a pocket as he stretches into his overalls. He studies me through quick, black eyes. 'Your mom's stressed today.'

'This is one of her better days.'

He gives a laugh like asthma, 'Hururrr, hrrr,' and slaps me on the arm. Kind of slap my dad used to give me, when he was feeling friendly. We move back over the road and up the driveway, but Ledesma stops by the wishing bench to adjust his balls. Then he shakes his head, and looks at me.

'Vern – you're innocent, right?'

'Uh-huh.'

'I don't know why it gets to me, tch. All this shit raining down on you, I can't help thinking – what kind of fucking life is this?'

'Tell me about it.'

He puts a hand on my shoulder. 'I'd be prepared to help.'

I just stare at my New Jacks. To be honest, intimate moments aren't my scene at all, especially when you just saw a guy naked. Next thing you know you're in a fucken TV-movie, quivering all over the place. I guess he senses it. He takes his hand away, tweaks his crotch again, and leans against the wishing bench, which sharply tilts away.

'Shit,' he says, pulling back. 'Can't you stand this somewhere flat?'

'Yeah, like – back at the store.'

He laughs. 'You should tell your story, little big man, clear your name – the world loves an underdog.'

'What about the spot we just did, with Deputy Gurie?'

'Tch – camera wasn't running.'

'Get outta town.'

'Call it a favor – between underdogs.'

'You're an *underdog*?' Mrs Porter's door opens as I say it; Kurt's nose snuffles out.

'Only underdogs and psychos in this world,' says Ledesma. 'Psychos like that fat-assed deputy. Think about it.'

I don't think long. You have to quiver on TV, it's a fucken law of nature. You have to quiver and be fucken devastated all the time. I know it for sure, and you'd know it too if you saw Mom watching Court TV. 'See how impassive he is, he chopped up ten people and ate their bowels but he doesn't show a care in the world.' I personally don't see the logic in having to quiver if you're innocent. If you ask me, people who don't eat your bowels are more likely to be impassive. But no, one learning I made is that juries watch the same shows as my ole lady. If you don't quiver, you're fucken guilty.

'I don't know,' I say, turning to the porch.

Ledesma hangs back. 'Don't underestimate your general public, Vern – they want to see justice being done. I say give them what they want.'

'But, like – I didn't do anything.'

'Tch, and who knows it? People decide with or without the facts – if you don't get out there and paint your paradigm, some-one'll paint it for you.'

'My *what*?'

'Pa-ra-dime. You never heard of the paradigm shift? Example: you see a man with his hand up your granny's ass. What do you think?'

'Bastard.'

'Right. Then you learn a deadly bug crawled up there, and the man has in fact put aside his disgust to save Granny. What do you think now?'

'Hero.' You can tell he ain't met my nana.

'There you go, a paradigm shift. The action doesn't change – the information you use to judge it does. You were ready to crucify the guy because you didn't have the facts. Now you want to shake his hand.'

'I don't think so.'

'I mean figuratively, asshole,' he laughs, punching out six of my ribs. 'Facts may seem black and white by the time they hit your TV screen, but professional teams sift through mountains of gray to get them there. You need positioning, like a product in the market – the jails are full of people who didn't manage their positions.'

'Wait up, I have a witness, you know.'

Ledesma heads up the porch steps. 'Yeah, and Deputy Lard-ass is so interested. Public opinion will go with the first psycho who points a finger. You're butt-naked, big man.'

We creak through the screen into the cool of the kitchen. Mom's here, all wiped dry with her frog mitt, a smudge of joy cake on one cheek. The other ole flaps are in the background acting natural.

'Ladies!' says Lally, grinning. 'This is how you lounge, while I'm outside like a slave?'

'Oh, Mr Smedma,' says Mom.

'Eulalio Ledesma, ma'am. Educated people call me Lally.'

'Well can I get you a Coke, Mr Lesma? Diet, or diet-decaf if you prefer?' Mom loves it when important people call by, like the doctor and all. Her lashes flutter like dying flies.

Lally hoists his ass onto the kitchen bench, makes himself comfortable. 'Thanks, just water for me – and maybe one of these cakes. Actually I have something exciting to share with you ladies, if you're interested.'

'Wake me when it's over,' mutters Pam in back.

Lally pulls out the glass bottles, filled with like piss. 'Siberian Ginseng Compound.' He jams one into my hand, winking. 'Better than Viagra.'

'Hee, hee,' go the girls.

'So, Lally,' says Mom, 'do you sleep in the van, or . . .?'

'Right now I do – motels are full between here and Austin. I hear some generous townsfolk are taking in guests, but I haven't come across them yet.'

'Well, ahem,' Mom looks down the hall. 'I mean . . .'

'Doris, you're not going to let Vernon drink that stuff, are you?' It's George's distraction technique, look at it. It gives me mixed feelings. I mean, I'm glad she interrupted my ole lady from inviting Ledesma to stay. But now everybody's attention snaps to me.

'Oh, it's harmless,' says Lally. 'Great stress-buster.'

George watches me fondle the phial. Her eyes narrow, which is a bad fucken sign. 'Like you're *real* stressed, Vern. Got a job for the summer?'

'Nah,' I say, downing the ginseng. It tastes like dirt.

'Doris, you hear the Harris boy bought a truck? Paid cash for it too, a Ford truck. *All* the boys I know have summer jobs. Course, they all have *haircuts* too.'

'It ain't a Ford,' says Brad from the floor.

'Bradley,' says Betty, 'I wish you wouldn't say "ain't".'

'Pluck off.'

'Don't you talk to *me* like that, Bradley Everett Pritchard!'

'Goddam *what*? I said "*Pluck*" for chrissakes, I mean, *shit*!' He spits and squirms across the rug, then stomps up to Betty and smacks her in the gut.

'*Bradley!*'

'Pluck off, pluck off, PLUCK *OFF!*'

35

I just stay quiet. Lally looks over, sees my eyes fixed longingly up the hall. He gulps his ginseng and says, 'I appreciate your help, big man – maybe your room would be a better working environment.' He turns to Mom. 'I hope it's no problem – Vern agreed to collate some local data for me . . .'

'Oh, no problem Lally, gosh,' says Mom. 'Quickly, Vern! Hear that girls? It's a job for Lally, he's colliding data for Lally!'

I scurry away like a pack of rats. 'Only job he'll get looking like that,' says George. 'Guilty-looking hair, if you ask me. And those shoes don't help none either, same shoes as that psycho Meskin . . .'

Fuck her. I kick a pile of laundry, and slam my bedroom door. What I'm seriously considering, in light of everybody's behavior, is just to evacuate through the laundry door; hop a bus to Nana's, and not even tell anybody. Just call up later or something. I mean, the whole world knows Jesus caused the fucken tragedy. But because he's dead, and they can't fucken kill him for it, they have to find a skate-goat. That's people for you. Me, I'd love to explain the sequence of events last Tuesday. But I'm in a bind, see. I have family honor to think of. And I have my ma to protect, now that I'm Man of the House and all. Anyway, whoever points a finger at me, just for being a guy's friend, has some deep remorse coming. Tears of fucken regret, when the truth comes marching in. And it always comes, you know it. Watch any fucken movie.

I still hear everybody through my bedroom door, talking like bad actors, the way they do. 'It's a challenging time for everyone,' says Lally.

'I know, I *know*.'

'And Vaine's pushing things so hard,' says Leona. 'Can't she sense our grief?'

George barks a cough. 'My ole man's pushing *Vaine* hard – he gave her a month to pump some life into her conviction average, or she's history.'

'You mean he'd throw her off the force,' asks Mom, 'after all this time?'

'Worse. He'd probably make her Eileena's assistant.'

'Oh my God,' says Leona, 'but Eileena's like – the *receptionist*. That's as low as *Barry's* job!'

'Lower,' Pam chuckles darkly.

You hear a quiet gap. That means everybody's sighing. Then Mom goes, 'Well this is sure a big month for Vaine. And I can't say it's going too well, the way she's handling Vernon and all.'

'Tch,' goes Lally. 'Maybe the dogs'll shed some light.'

'Dogs?' asks Leona.

'Sniffer dogs, from Smith County.'

'Well but, what can *dogs* do now?' asks Mom.

'Can I call you Doris?' asks Lally. His voice drops a tone. 'You see, Doris, people are asking how anyone in their right mind could orchestrate such a rampage. They're starting to wonder if drugs were involved. If rumors about a drugs link are correct, these specialist dogs will tie it up as fast as cock a leg.'

'Well *good*,' huffs Mom, 'I feel like calling them over here right now, and putting a stop to this ridiculous business with Vernon.'

I take the drugs out of the shoebox in my closet, and drop them into my pocket. The joints leave my hand wet. Kurt barks outside.

five

To be fair, the rumors about ole Mr Deutschman didn't say he'd actually dicked any schoolgirls. Probably just touched them and shit, you know. Real slime though, don't get me wrong. He used to be a school principal or something, all righteous and upstanding, back in the days before they'd bust you for that type of thing. Maybe even before talk shows, back when you'd just get ostracized by word of mouth. He probably used to get his hair cut at the fancy unisex on Gurie Street, with the coffee machine and all. But not anymore. Now he slinks through the valley behind the abattoir, to the meatworks barber shoppe. Yeah, the meatworks has its own barber on Saturdays. It's just ole Mr Deutschman and me here this morning. And Mom.

'Well don't listen to Vernon, the unisex usually takes off a lot.'

Her head-scarf and shades supposedly make her invisible. The invisible twitching woman. Me, I wear the reddest T-shirt you ever saw, like a goddam six-year-old or something. I didn't want to wear it. She controls what you wear by keeping everything else damp in the laundry.

'Well go ahead, sir, it'll only grow back.'

'Hell, Ma . . .'

'Vernon I'm only trying to help you out. We'll have to find you some decent shoes too.'

Sweat starts to pool in my ass. The lights are off, just one ray glows sideways through the door onto these green tiles. The air reeks of flesh. Flies guard two historical barber chairs in the middle of the room; white leather turned brown, cracked and hardened to plastic. I check them for arm clamps. I'm in one, Deutschman is in the other; his hands creep around under his gown. He seems happy to wait. Then a whistle blows outside, and the meatworks' marching band assembles on the gravel in the yard. 'Braaap, barp, bap,' band practice starts. One majorette I see through the door is about eighty-thousand years ole, her buns smack the backs of her legs as she marches. My eyes flee to a TV in the corner of the room.

'Look, Vernon, he doesn't have arms or legs, but he's neatly groomed. And he has a *job*, look – he even invests on the stock market.'

They ask the kid on TV what it feels like to be so gifted. He just shrugs and says, 'Isn't everybody?'

The barber mostly slashes mid-air; two halves of a fly hit the deck. 'Barry was here. Said there could be a drugs link.'

'A drug slink, yes,' says Mr Deutschman.

'A drugs link, or another firearm.'

'Another farm, uh-huh. I heard it was a panty cult – you hear it was a panty cult?'

On balance, today sucks. You don't want to be here if they find any drugs. So I'm here with two spliffs, and two acid pearls in my pocket; nasty gels, according to Taylor, like your mind would projectile-exit your nose if you took one. I tried to ditch them on the way down, but Fate was against me. Fate's always fucken against me these days.

Load my pack, and lope away is what I'll do; all crusty and lonely, like you see on TV. Ditch Taylor's dope, and lope away. More successfully than last night, with Lally and the world's media camped outside. I only got four steps away from my porch before they came a-sniffing. Now they think I take out the trash in my backpack. Last night was long, boy, long and shivery with ghosts and realizations. Realizations that I have to act.

'Vaine's coming down with they dogs,' says the barber. 'I'll tell her we need a SWAT team, with some of they automatic guns, that rip the meat off offenders' bodies, not any ole dogs.' Click, slash; he evens up my skull. I scan the floor for ears.

'Meat's better'n dogs,' says Deutschman.

'Sit still, Vern,' says Mom.

'I have stuff to do.'

'Well, Harris' store might take you on.'

'What?'

'For a job, you know – Seb Harris even bought himself a truck!'

'That ain't what I'm talking about. Anyway, Seb's dad just happens to own the whole store.'

'Well, you're the man of the house now, I'm counting on you to make good. All the boys I know have jobs, that's all.'

'Like which boys, Ma, like just who?'

'Well – Randy and Eric?'

'Randy and Eric are dead.'

'Vernon Gregory, I'm just saying if you want to prove you're all grown up it's about time you got wise to the way things work in this world. Be a *man*.'

'Yeah, *right*.'

'And don't you get smart either, in front of everybody. Don't let's end up like that other time after I found *those underpants*.' Deutschman's hand twitches under his gown.

'*Damn*, Momma!'

'Go ahead, cuss your mother!'

'I ain't cussing!'

'My *God*, if your *father* was here . . .'

'Here's Vaine,' says the barber. I spin out of the chair, ripping the gown off over my head.

'Well go ahead, Vernon – go right ahead and humiliate your mother, after all that's happened to me.'

Fuck her. I bang out through the screen into the sun. Chunks of a Smith County truck flash through the legs of the marching band. Martirio may be a fucken joke, but you don't mess with the boys from Smith County. Smith County has armored personnel carriers, for chrissakes. Trombones spit glare, horns throw back pictures of me puckering, melting, shrinking into the bushes at the steep end of the compound.

Hot grasses heckle my face on the way up the hill; skeeterhawks twitch through the air, but dust is too bored to rise up. One cloud hangs in the sky, over my empty, desperate body. My ole lady won't run after me. She'll stay back, tell all my slime to the boys, so they can wear a knowing smile next time they see me. Underpants my ass. And there's no drugs link, is there fuck. Jesus never had the damn money. See Hysteriaville here? Science says there must be ten squillion brain cells in this town, but if you so much as belch before your twenty-first birthday they can only form two thoughts between them: you're fucken *pregnant*, or you're on *drugs*. Fuck it, I'm outta here. Life's simple when I'm angry. I know just what to do, and I fucken do it. Underpants my fucken ass.

I'll tell you a learning: knife-turners like my ole lady actually spend their waking hours connecting shit into a humongous web, just like spiders. It's true. They take every word in the fucken universe, and index it back to your knife. In the end it doesn't matter what words you say, you feel it on your blade. Like, 'Wow, see that car?' '*Well it's the same blue as that jacket you threw up on at the Christmas show, remember?*' What I learned is that parents succeed by managing the database of your dumbness and your slime, ready for combat. They'll cut you down in a split fucken second, make no mistake; much quicker than you'd use the artillery you dream about. And I say, in idle moments, once the shine rubs off their kid – they start doing it just for fucken *kicks*.

I stop dead. Something crackles around the bend on the track. It's the red van, spinning a trail of fluff-balls down the hill. Like somebody with oldtimer's disease, who doesn't remember what's good for them, I glance at my T-shirt. 'Ping,' it jackrabbits to Lally. He stops with a crunch, forcing down the electric window with the flat of his hand. Tappets mark time with my heart, tic, tic, tic.

'Big man!'

I wave, like I'm in the freezer section at the fucken Mini-Mart or something. I should drop the drugs where I stand, but the dogs are close by. They'd know. Anyway, I ain't that decisive in life, not with all this grief on board, not with my anger evaporated. It fucken slays me. Van Damme's your man if you want the drugs dropped right here.

Lally calls me over. 'See those cops? They came from your place – jump in.'

Ginseng clinks around the floor as we cut a fresh trail toward home.

'Where's the rest of your head?' Lally slicks down his eyebrows in the mirror. You can tell the mirror hasn't pointed at the road awhile.

'Don't ask,' I say.

'You going somewhere?'

'Surinam.'

He laughs. 'How'd you get down here? I didn't see a car this morning . . .'

'We walked.' I'm supposed to say Mom's car is in the shop. But it ain't in the shop. The car paid for the new rug in the living room, the one Brad wipes his fingers on.

'What do you think the cops want?'

'Search me.'

'Tch.' Lally shakes his head. 'Things won't get any easier, you know. Take my advice – I could cut a report by sundown, it could air by tonight – Vern? I think it's time to tell your story. Your real, true story.'

'Maybe,' I say, slouching low in the seat. I feel Lally watching me.

'You don't even have to appear, I can patch it together from clips of friends and family. Camera's loaded, big man. Just say the word.' I hear Lally's offer, but just sit wishing Marion Nuckles would tell *his* damn story. He knows I'm clean, he was there. I can't believe I get all the heat – me, who has family secrets to watch out for – while he lounges around in goddam silence. I mean, what's *he* holding back?

A wrong note from the meatworks' band coughs us onto Beulah Drive in a swirl of leaf tatters. A baby marketplace has grown around the pumpjack since I've been gone. One stall sells Martirio barbecue aprons, just like Pam's. Next to it, some media men pay a buck a hit for some fudge from Houston. One of the fudge sellers gloomily puts on an apron. The apron sellers gloomily munch fudge. My face goes Porked Monkey. It's the face for when life around you travels in fucken dog years, but you stay frozen still. For instance, a whole mall grows around the pumpjack, but I'm here with the same problems I went out with this morning. I just look down, herd ginseng with my foot.

'Take one,' says Lally.

'Say what?'

'Take some ginseng, keep your strength up.'

As he says it, I notice the ginseng is the same shade of piss as the acid pearls in my hand. Dogs would never smell through the ginseng. I reach down for a bottle, but Lally brakes to avoid a stray teddy under the Lechugas' willow; I overbalance, the dope cigarettes fall from my hand.

Lally switches off the engine, looks at the joints, picks one off the floor, sniffs it, and grins. Then he looks at me. 'Tch – you could've just said you didn't want to share.'

'Uh, they ain't mine actually.'

'Not for long, anyway,' he says, frowning into his mirror.

I spin around to see the Smith County truck nose onto Beulah Drive, a block behind us. Velcro fucken ant-farms seize my gut.

'Here, give them to me,' says Lally. He lifts himself up, and stashes the joints through a tear in the seat.

'Thanks – I'll be right back.' I fly across our lawn, into the house, and up the hall to my room, where I pick the cap off the ginseng. I take Taylor's LSD pearls and poke them into the bottle. They blend right into the piss, and the cap replaces like new. I drop the bottle into the Nike box, next to my padlock key, and hide it back in my closet. As I stroll onto the porch, all nonchalant, cooled by a sweat of relief, I see Vaine Gurie, Mom, and a Smith County officer arrive in the truck. Air-conditioning blows their hair like seaweed underwater, except Mom's, which blows more like one of those tetchy anemone things. Lally sits quiet in the shade of the Lechugas' willow. I guess he turned out okay, ole Lally, in the end. 'A good egg,' as the once-talkative Mr Goddam Nuckles would say.

Fate suddenly plays its regular card. Leona's Eldorado sashays past the pumpjack, full of musty, dry wombs and deep, bitter wants. Mom withers. The fucken timing of these ladies is astounding, I have to say, like they have scandal radar or something. They foam out of the car like suds from a sitcom washing machine, except for Brad, who stays in back. He's eating a booger, you can tell. Betty Pritchard gets out and starts to strut around the lawn like a fucken chicken.

'I think I need the bathroom – I just can't be sure with this infection.'

Leona and George take the high ground by our willow. 'Hi, Doris,' they wave. I almost make it back into the house, but Vaine Gurie unfolds faster than you'd expect from the cab of the truck. 'Vernon Little, come down here please.'

'Another setback, Doris?' asks Leona, hopefully.

'Well it's nothing, girls,' says Mom. 'There's some fudge inside.'

'We don't have long,' says Leona, 'they're coming to lay the sunken patio at three.'

'Well, I thought it was the people with my Special Edition,' says Mom, scuttling over the dirt. 'I saw the car, and thought the new fridge was here . . .'

'Ma?' I call. She doesn't hear.

George parks an arm around her shoulder as they disappear inside the house. 'Honey, of course they'll come after him if he insists on looking like that – that haircut's the *pits*.'

The screen clacks shut, Mom's voice trails away into the dark. 'Well I couldn't sway him, you know how boys are . . .'

'Vernon,' says Gurie. 'Let's go for a little ride.'

I search her face for signs of uncovered truth, imminent apology. None appear. 'Ma'am, I wasn't even there . . .'

'Is that right. Makes it difficult to explain the fingerprints we found then, doesn't it.'

Picture a Smith County Sheriff's truck with me inside, sitting quiet on a road between three wooden houses. Bugs chitter in the willows, oblivious. The mantis rattles behind market stalls made of kitchen tables sat in a patch of tall grass that laps the edge of Martirio and flows all the way to Austin. Then Brad Pritchard appears at my window; nose to the sky, finger pointed at his shoes.

'Air Maxes,' he states. 'New.'

He stands with his eyes shut, waiting for me to blow a fucken kiss, or break down weeping or something. Asshole.

I lift my leg to the window. 'Jordan New Jacks.'

He squints momentarily before pointing at my Nikes. 'Old,' he explains patiently. Then he points at his. 'NEW.'

I point at his, 'Price of a Barbie Camper.' Then at mine, 'Price of a medium-range corporate jet.'

'Are not.'

'Are fucken too.'

'Enjoy jail.'

His shuffle across the lawn turns into a scamper up the porch steps. A single raised finger shines back at me through my own front doorway, until the screen cracks shut in front of it. Then, just as the officers start the truck, the screen swings open again. My ole lady bursts out, and hurries down to the road.

'Vernon, I love you! Forget about before – even *murderers* are loved by their families, you know . . .'

'Heck, Ma, I ain't a murderer!'

'Well I know – it's just an *example*.'

Lally shoots me a stare from his van, motioning like a camera with his hands. 'Just say the word!' he yells.

Mom stands helpless in the road behind us, and parks her chin on her chest. Her lips prime up for tears. The pain of it ploughs me over, inside out. I spin to see Lally through the back window as he rushes to her, puts a hand to her shoulder. Her ole soggy head leans toward it. He slides his shoulder under to absorb her tears, then stands tall, and stares gravely at my truck disappearing.

I can't take it. I lunge across Gurie and holler back through her window with all the air in the fucken world: 'Do it, Lally – *tell 'em the fucken truth.*'

Jail is sour tonight. Dead like the air between your ass and your underwear when you're sitting down. A TV buzzes somewhere in the background; I listen out for a news-flash about my innocence, but instead the weather report theme plays. I hate that fucken theme. Then a voice bangs down the corridor. Footsteps approach.

'Don't you let me find them burgers gone, I mean it. Sure, right, it's Dr Actions Diet Revolution now, huh. All your noise about Prettykins, and now – don't tell me – it's a fuckin burger diet, right? Sure, fuckin protein, uh-huh. What? Because there *is* no other news except your fuckin barn of an ass . . .'

The man stops outside my cell. Light through the grille outlines a fuck-you pout crowded with teeth. *Barry E Gurie – Detention Executive*, says the badge. He sees me awake, and presses the phone into his neck.

'You ain't pullin your rod in there are ya, Little? You ain't chokin your chicken all day and night, are ya?' He laughs this smutty laugh, like Miss goddam Universe just sucked his boy or something. Even at long range his breath hits you like a solid block, just slithers down your face leaving a trail of onion-relish and lard. What a disgusting human being, I swear. If this is how much of an asshole everybody's going to be, about such a devastating fucken issue, then I better get the hell out of town. Maybe even out of Texas. Just until they get the story straight. Nana's ain't even fucken far enough, the way folk are behaving right now.

Barry continues his rounds, lingering for the rest of the night down by the TV. I lay back onto the bunk in my cell, and drift into the important and scary business of my future. Remember that ole movie called *Against All Odds*, where this babe has a beach-house in Mexico? That's where I can run. Mom can visit after things die down. There she is, sobbing with joy, ole spanky-cheeked Doris Little, who could be played by Kathy Bates, who was in that movie *Misery*. Tears of pride at the excellent sanitation, and at my decent, orderly life. See how it works? It's the future now, young Vernon has been vindicated. Now he's buying her a clay donkey, or some of those salad utensils Mrs Lechuga makes such a big deal about. The salad utensil seller would say to me, 'You want the same kind Mrs Lechuga got, or you want the *Deluxe* edition?' There's a fucken point up Mrs Lechuga's ass. See? That's definitely my new plan. I like the food just fine, burritos, and cappuccinos and whatever. They say money's cheap down there, hell – I could really make good. Folk must live in those beach-houses, for real.

But the pessimist in me says, 'Kid, forget vacations, what yez need is a cake wid a fuckin bomb in it.' My pessimist has a New York accent, don't ask me why. I ignore it. The question of the babe needs thought; you never see guys running alone, admit it. Who to take is Taylor Figueroa. She's in Houston now, in college or something, on account of being older than me. But she's the fox to take. Moist air stirs me through the bars of my cage, and in my mind it becomes a shunt of hormone from the lip of her skirt. I'll take that girl to Mexico, see if I don't. Now that I'm grown up, now that I've been to jail and all. I wasn't close to her at school, even though we nearly made out once. I say nearly because, fucken typical of me, I had her on a plate and I let her go. You're just never taught when to be an asshole in life. There was this senior party that I wasn't invited to, and Taylor was there, face as soft as panties, just her big wet eyes seeped out. She left the party and crashed on the back seat of a Buick in the Church parking lot, where I just happened to be with my bike. She was wasted. She called me over. Her voice was sticky like freshly bitten cake. Some drugs fell out of her clothes onto the ground by the car. I picked them up. She said to keep them for her, in case she passed out or whatever. I kept them too, you know it. Boy was she fucken bent though. She started saying my name, and writhing around the back seat of the car. Don't even ask me who drives a fucken Buick at our school, but she added some value to his back seat. I helped unpeel her shorts a little, 'So she could breathe' – her words, not mine – I didn't even know you could breathe from down there. Brown Wella Balsam hair licked her body all the way down to her buns, where gray cotton tangas peeped out; clefted heaven in workaday dew. She was wasted, but conscious.

So guess what your fucken hero did, take a shot. Vernon Gonad Little went into the party and sent her best friend out to mind her. I never got a finger to her panties, even though I was close enough to catch the lick-your-own-skin-and-sniff-it disease that wastes me today; fucken hauntings of hollows between elastic and thigh, tang ablaze with cotton and apricot muffin, cream cheese and pee. But no, duh, I went inside. I even kind of strode in, like a TV doctor, all fucken mature. It fucken slays me, she was right there. I tried to look her up again, but Fate deployed the shutdown routine you get whenever you miss a ripe opportunity in a dumb way. A billion reasons she can't be located, and fucken blah, blah, blah. So much for Taylor Figueroa.

Tonight, though, my hand is her mouth. Every stroke of my boy brings her cotton closer, burrows vents for her fruit-air to escape and waste me. Mexican fruit-air, boy, if I have my way. As I abandon myself to the dream, muffled wisps of the TV-news fanfare travel the corridor like an infection. Then a prisoner snorts with laughter.

six

'You touch bag? Make fingerprince?' This is what Mr Abdini asks me. Don't even ask me the rest of his name.

'Fingerprints? Uh – I guess so.' I'm uneasy enough today, without having to meet folk like this.

Abdini is fat the way an anvil is fat, but his face is probably swept back by the velocity of his talking. He's my attorney. The judge appointed him. I guess nobody else works Sundays around here. I know you're not allowed to say it anymore, about other places being different and all, but, between you and me, you can tell Abdini is the product of centuries of fast-talking and double-dealing. Ricochet Abdini, 'Bing, ping, *ping*!' He's dressed in white, like the Cuban Ambassador or something. A jury would convict on his fucken shoes alone, not that his shoes are my biggest problem. They're the least of my fucken problems, know why? Because if you take a bunch of flabby white folk, of the kind that organize bake-sales and such, and put them in a jury, then throw in some fast-talker from God-knows-where, chances are they won't buy a thing he says. They can tell he's slimy, but they're not allowed to officially *do* anything, on account of everybody has to pretend to get along these days. So they just don't buy what he says. It's a learning I made.

Therefore, Mr Something Fucken Abdini Something stands sweating in my cell, getting ready to say 'Therefore' probably. His eyes bounce across a file in his hand, which is all about me. He grunts.

'You tell me whappen.'

'Uh – excuse me?'

'Tell me whappen in school.'

'Well, see, I was out of class, and when I came back . . .'

Abdini holds up a hand. 'You went batroom?'

'Uh – yeah, but that wasn't . . .'

'Very impotent evidence,' he hisses, scribbling in the file.

'No, see, I was . . .'

Just then the guard clanks at the door. 'Shh,' goes Abdini, patting my arm. 'I fine out. You don tsetse fly today. We try bail.'

Barry ain't around this morning; another guard escorts us through the sheriff's back door, and down the alley behind Gurie Street. Abdini said there couldn't be any media in court today, on account of me being a juvenile. Anyway, everybody's at the funerals. 'An option holding limited appeal,' as the now-dumbstruck Mr Asshole Nuckles would say. It's bitterly hot today; unusual this early in summer. And quiet like when you hold your breath, though you can still sense cotton dresses over on Gurie Street, and kids jumping through sprinklers. Typical Sunday things, but with the damp fizz of tears about them. They come with their own wave of sadness.

Three buildings along from the sheriff's office stands Martirio's ole whorehouse, one of the Wild West's most beautiful buildings. The fun gals are gone though, now it's next to the courthouse. The only gal left is Vaine Gurie, a whole barrel-load of fucken laughs. She waits for us at the back. Her eyebrow rides high today. I'm led up some stairs into the mostly empty courtroom, where the guard maneuvers me into a small wooden corral, with a fence around it. It's almost possible to be brave in here, if you add up your Nikes, your Calvin Kleins, your youth, and your actual innocence. What shunts you over the edge is the smell. Court smells like your first-grade classroom; you automatically look around for finger-paintings. I don't know if it's on purpose, like to regress you and freak you out. Truth be told, there's probably an air-freshener for courtrooms and first-grade classrooms, just to keep you in line. 'Guilt-O-Sol' or something, so in school you feel like you're already in court, and when you wind up in court you feel like you're back in school.

You're primed for finger-paintings, but what you get is a lady behind one of those sawn-off typewriters. Court, boy. Fuck.

I look around while everybody shuffles papers. Mom couldn't make it, which ain't such a bad thing. I learned that the authorized world doesn't recognize the knife. Your knife is invisible, that's what makes it so convenient to use. See how things work? It's what drives folk to the blackest crimes, and to sickness, I know it; the thing of everyone turning the knife just by saying hello, or something equally innocent-sounding. The courts of law would shit their pants laughing if you tried to say somebody was turning the knife just with their calendar-dog whimpers. But here's why they'd laugh: not because they couldn't *see* the knife, but because they knew nobody *else* would buy it. You could stand before twelve good people, all with some kind of psycho-knife stuck in them that loved-ones could twist on a whim, and they wouldn't admit it. They'd forget how things really are, and slip into TV-movie mode where everything has to be obvious. I guarantee it.

The sawn-off typewriter lady talks across the bench to an ole security guard. 'Oh my, it's a fact. We had a copy of that same catalog, me and my girls.'

'No kidding,' says the guard, 'that same one, huh?' His tongue pushes some spit around his mouth. That means he's picturing whatever she just said. He shunts some spit around, picturing it for a moment, then he says, 'Don't forget the judge has girls too.'

'That's a fact,' says the typist.

They turn to stare daggers at me. The typist's daggers come wrapped in Kleenex, I guess so they don't get shit on them. I just stare at my Nikes. Things have gone beyond a fucken joke. You just know the justice system ain't set up for folk like me. It's set up for more obvious folk, like you see in movies. Nah, if the facts don't arrive today, if everybody doesn't apologize and send me home, I'll jump bail and run over the fucken border. *Against All Odds*. I'll vanish into the cool of tonight, see if I fucken don't, hum cross-country with the moths, with my innocent-headed learnings and my ole panty dreams.

'All-a rise,' says an officer.

A bright-eyed lady with short gray hair and bifocal glasses glides behind the tallest desk. *Judge Helen E Gurie* says the sign. Her swivel chair rattles politely when she sits. The Chair of God.

'Vaine,' she says, 'it'd have to be one of your cases, now wouldn't it?'

'Gh-*rrr*. We have a suspect, Judge.'

Abdini stands. 'We apply pearlymoney herring, your honor.'

The judge squints over her glasses. 'A preliminary hearing? Wait one darned minute, I draw both your attentions to the Texas Family Code – this is a juvenile matter. Vaine, I sure hope you observed the provisions for service of process that apply in this instance.'

'Gh-*r*.'

'And why is no record of interview filed with the complaint?'

Just now the main door creaks open behind me. Sheriff Porkorney scrapes into the room and takes off his hat. Vaine stiffens like a bone.

'We hoped a particular piece of evidence would come in first, ma'am,' she says.

'You *hoped* the evidence would come in? You hoped it would just *fly right in*? How long has this young man been in custody?'

'Gh . . .' Vaine's eye flicks back to the sheriff. He just stands by the door, arms folded, real quiet.

'Good Lord!' Judge Gurie snatches a paper from her desktop. 'You're seeking *indictment*?' She removes her glasses, fixing a stare at Vaine. 'And fingerprints is all you have?'

'Let me explain, ma'am, that . . .'

'Deputy, I doubt you'll cook up a grand jury on one set of prints. Won't even defrost 'em.'

'It's more than one set, your honor.'

'Doesn't matter how many you have, they're all from the same exhibit, the sports bag. I mean – *please*. Maybe if it was a *gun* . . .'

'Ma'am, some new information came into the public domain last night, which I thought . . .'

'The court isn't interested in what you *thought*, Vaine. When you take the pointed end of a stick and wake this whole tangled process up with it, we want to hear what you damn well *know*.'

'Well, the boy also lied, and he ran away from his interview . . . gh . . .'

Judge Gurie clasps her hands like a first-grade teacher. 'Vaine Millicent Gurie – I remind you the child is not on trial here. Given the particulars before me, I'm inclined to release your suspect and have a damn long talk with the sheriff about the quality of procedure reaching this bench.'

Her gaze penetrates Vaine's every hole, however many that is. At the back of the room, the sheriff's lips tighten. He puts on his hat and creaks back out through the door. I don't know about where you live, but around here we teach life's hard lessons with our lips.

Abdini stands. 'Objection!'

'Pipe down, Mr Abdini, we have other attorneys on call,' says the judge.

Gurie lifts her eyebrow. 'Your honor, this new information, you know . . .'

'No, I do not know. What I know ain't a whole lot so far.'

The typist and Gurie exchange a glance. They sigh. The ole court officer immediately turns to frown my way. 'She ain't seen it yet,' the guard behind me says under his breath. Everybody tightens their lips.

'What is going on here?' asks the judge. 'Has this court slipped into a parallel universe? Have I been left behind?'

'Ma'am, some new facts came to light – we're following them up right now.'

'Then I'm going to release your suspect until you can show me some particulars. I also expect you to apologize for all this trouble.'

A high-voltage tremor cracks through me, of hope, excitement, and ass-naked fear. You think I'm going to stick around for the so-called justice system to get its shit together? Am I fuck. Buses leave Martirio every two hours for Austin or San Antonio. The automatic teller machine with fifty-two dollars in it, from Nana's lawnmowing fund, is a block from the Greyhound station. Which is five blocks from here.

The typist sighs, and tightens her lips some more. Then she leans up to the bench and cups a hand to the judge's ear. Judge Gurie listens, frowning. She puts on her glasses and looks at me. Then at the typist.

'When's the next report? Lunchtime?'

The typist nods; one righteous eye darts to Vaine. The judge reaches for her hammer. 'Court is adjourned until two o'clock.'

'Bam.'

'All-a rise,' says the guard.

Men hardened by the friction of learning, steel men of savvy quietly applied, crusty ole boys of rough-hewn glory, probably smoke a lonely cigarette in their cells during lunch breaks from court. They probably don't have to talk to their moms.

'Well Vernon, what I mean is, do you have your own room, or did they put you with other – you know, other *men* . . .?'

Barry stands leering by the phone, eyes puckered into goats' cunts. It seems Eileena's eyebrows perch high this lunchtime too, as far as her wooden hair allows. I don't know about where you live, but around here we take the moral high ground with our eyebrows.

'Well you know,' says Mom, 'you hear about the nice boys, the clean boys, always getting – you know, you hear about bigger men, hardened criminals, always getting the nice boys and . . .'

After God-knows-how-many years of life in this free country she doesn't have the tools to just say, 'Have you been taken up the ass yet by some lifer?' That's how pathetic things are. Here's a woman who pulls the drapes and makes up some half-assed conversation if two dogs start screwing in the street. Yet, for all I know she

54

probably takes a fucken fire-hydrant up the ass every night, just for kicks. Boy, I tell you.

Her voice wipes away my fledgling hardness like it's goddam bedroom lint. What kind of fucken life is this? Light through the window calls me, sings of melted ice-cream on the sidewalk outside, the ghost of little tears nearby. Summer dresses full of fresh air, Mexico down the way. But not for me. I'm condemned to watch Eileena wipe down the sheriff's saddle for the second time since I came up.

I find myself wondering if the sheriff's saddle usually gets so much attention, and if it does, why it ain't worn away to nothing. Then I see the room has a TV. Eileena's eye snaps to it.

It's the lunchtime news. You hear the fanfare of trumpets and drums, then the face of an asshole appears in the far distance, staring through the back window of a departing Smith County Sheriff's truck.

'Vernon, I have some bones to pick with you,' says Mom.

'I have to go now.'

'Well Vernon . . .'

'Click.'

My eyes latch onto the screen. A breeze rustles cellophane on the Lechugas' teddy farm, then snags a wire of Lally's hair and floats it off his head. The pumpjack squeaks rhythmically under his voice. 'This proud community takes a decisive step from the shadow of Tuesday's devastation, with the arrest of a *new player* in the deadly web of cause and effect that has brought the once-peaceful town to its knees.'

'Ain't see me on my fuckin knees,' says Barry, straddling a chair.

'To his neighbors, Vernon Gregory Little seemed a normal, if somewhat awkward teenager, a boy who wouldn't attract attention walking any downtown street. That is – until today.'

Lush pictures fill the screen, of crime-scene tape dancing under a blackened sky, body-bags punctuating drag-marks of blood, moist ladies howling pizza-cheese bungees of spit. Then a school photo of me, grinning.

'I definitely saw changes in the boy,' says George Porkorney. You can see her cigarettes hidden behind the fruit-salad plant on the breakfast bar at home. 'His shoes got more aggressive, he insisted on one of those skinhead haircuts . . .'

'I *know*,' says Betty in back.

Cut to Leona Dunt. Her handbag needs to be a yard taller for how big the word *Gucci* is written on it. 'Wow, but he seemed like such a regular kid.'

Black, disordered xylophone music joins the soundtrack as the camera bumps up the hallway to my room. Lally stops by my bed to face the camera. 'Vernon Little was described to me as something of a loner; a boy with few close friends, given more to playing on his computer – and reading.' The camera takes a vicious dive into the laundry pile by the bed. Out comes the lingerie catalog. 'But we find no Steinbeck, no Hemingway in Vernon Little's private library – in fact, his literary tastes run only to this . . .' Pages flap across the screen, sassy torsos cut me that once tugged chains of shameful sap through my veins. Then we hit page 67. Flapping stops. 'An innocent prop,' asks Lally, 'or a chilling link to the confused sexuality implied by Tuesday's crimes?' Twisted violins join the xylophone. The shot pans over my computer screen to the file marked 'Homework'. 'Click.' Cue the amputee sex pictures I saved for ole Silas Benn.

'Well golly,' says Mom. 'I had no *idea*.'

Lally sits beside her on my bed, cranking his brow into a sympathetic A-frame. 'As Vernon's mother, would it now be fair to number you among the victims of this tragedy?'

'Well, I guess I am a victim. I really guess so.'

'Yet you maintain Vernon's innocence?'

'Oh God, a child is always innocent to his mother – well even *murderers* are loved by their families you know.'

Some fucken powerdime shift. Lally lets it sit there. Even Barry Gurie knows it's all over, he just sighs out of his chair and says, 'Time to go down.' He steadies me to the door, but I turn for the blow I know is coming. Things could've been different if I'd learned to spell earlier, if I'd just been a smarter, more regular kid. But as things turned out, I was almost seven before I could spell *The Alamo*. So there's no title at all on the finger-painting I gave Mom when I was five. Just a bunch of stick-corpses and a shitload of red.

'Well, you can see he was just a normal little boy, in almost every way.'

'All-a rise.' The court officer detours around my computer, and a boxload of other shit that turned up on the courtroom floor. Mom's panty catalog has a table all to itself. Even my ole finger-painting is here, but they don't seem to have bothered with my Nike box. The ozone in court has a new, unhealthy crunch to it.

'Mr Abdini,' says the judge, 'I trust your client understands he is being arraigned – I draw your attention to the various issues of waiver that might apply.'

Abdini cocks his head. 'Your honor?'

'The matter will proceed to indictment, sir. Might be time for you to act.'

'Ma'am,' I say, 'this whole thing can be cleared up with a call to my witnesses, my teacher and all . . .'

'Shhh,' hisses Abdini.

'Counsel, please inform your client that he's not on trial here. Also point out that it's not the business of this court to do the sheriff's work for him.' She sits back for a moment, then turns to Vaine.

'Deputy – you *have* checked alibi witnesses?'

'I'm afraid the last witness, Miss Lori-Bethlehem Donner, passed away this morning, Judge.'

'I see. What about the boy's teacher?'

'Marion Nuckles didn't mention the suspect's whereabouts at the time of the tragedy.'

'He didn't mention, or you didn't ask?'

'His doctors say he won't be able to talk until the end of March next year. We couldn't get more than a few words, ma'am.'

'Well dammit Vaine. What were those words about?'

'Another firearm.'

'Oh good Lord.'

Vaine nods, tightening her lips. She can't fucken stop herself glancing at me as she does it.

'We apply bail your honor,' says Abdini.

'Is that right,' says Gurie. 'Judge, the boy has a history of absconding, from before he was even in trouble . . .'

Abdini throws out his arms. 'But little man is part of family home, with plenty things in the house – why he won't stay?'

'It's a single-parent family, Judge. I don't see how a woman on her own can override the will of a teenage boy.' She ain't seen the fucken knife in my back.

'It's nothing short of tragic,' says the judge. 'Every child needs a man's hand. Is there no way to contact the father?'

'G*h* – he's presumed deceased, Judge.'

'Oh my. And the boy's mother couldn't make it to court today?'

'No, ma'am – her car is under repair.'

'Well,' says Judge Gurie. 'Well, well, well.' She leans back into her throne and makes a church with her fingers. Then she turns to me. 'Vernon Gregory Little, I'm not going to turn down your application for bail at this time. But neither am I going to release you. In light of the facts here presented, and commensurate with my responsibility to this community, I am remanding you in custody pending a psychiatric report. With reference to any rec-ommendations in that report, I may consider your application at a later date.'

'Bam,' goes the hammer.

'All-a rise,' says the officer.

Muzak plays near the cells tonight. It fucken lays me out and buries me alongside my friends. It goes: '*I beg your par-den, I*

58

never promised you a rose gar-den.' Hot weather always brings these fucked ole tunes, always in the background, in fucken mono. Fate. Like, notice how whenever something happens in your life, like you fall in love or something, a tune gets attached. Fate tunes. Watch out for that shit.

I lay on the bunk and imagine this tune playing at a Greyhound terminal. In the TV-movie of my life, I'd be the crusty, mixed-up kid, all rugged and lonely, older than my years; dragging long shadows to hop a bus out of town, a bus with Mexico written on it. 'Pssschhh,' the crusty ole driver opens the door of his motor-coach, and smiles like he has a secret, that everything turns out fine. The kid's boot steps out of the dirt. His guitar swings low. A cowgirl with blond hair and Levi's sits alone, halfway down the aisle, probably wearing blue cotton panties under. Bikinis, or tangas. Probably bikinis. Nothing crusty about her. See what I mean? It's this kind of strategic vision that separates us from the animals.

My ole lady calls, but I can't make my imagination deal with her. I have until fucken Wednesday to do a little dreaming. That's when the shrink can see me. I survive two and a half days with Jesus' leaden soul in the shadows, and three rubber nights a-twanging with soundbites of his death. In the end, I pass the time practicing faces for the psychiatrist. I don't know if it's better to act crazy, or regular, or what. If the shrinks on TV are anything to go by, it'll be fucken hard to find out, because they just repeat every damn thing you say. If you say, 'I'm devastated,' they go, '*I hear you saying you're devastated.*' How do you deal with that? All I know is what I learned last week, that a healthy life should feel spongy, like a burrito. This Tuesday night, the first-week anniversary of the shootings, my life feels like a fucken corn chip.

I hear Barry's keychain swinging up the corridor, clink-a-clink. He stops by the grille of my door, out of sight, just breathing and clinking. He knows I'm waiting for him to say I have a call. But he starts to walk away, then shuffles back again. See?

'Little?' he finally says.

'Yeah, Barry?'

'That's Officer Gurie to you. You ain't porkin the preacher in there are ya? You ain't tossin the ham javelin all night long, thinkin of your Meskin boy? Grr-hrr-hrr.'

Fuck him to death. He walks me upstairs to the phone, and I fantasize about ramming his baton up his goddam ass. Not that he'd probably even feel it.

The weeping sax from the TV weather plays in the office, just to cheer me up. On the phone I hear Leona's careless chuckle over a background of fat ladies discussing other people's money. The weather plays at their end too. I get it in fucken stereo. Then comes the skidmark of my ole lady's voice.

'Vernon, are you *all right*?'

Her sniffling feels like she physically has her tongue in my ear, like an anteater or something. Makes me want to puke and bawl at the same time, go fucken figure. Here's why she's going for gold, let me tell you: it's because now I'm not only in *jail*, but I might be fucken *crazy* as well. What a bonanza for her if I'm fucken *crazy as well*. Then her problem would be that she already spent her best whimpery moves; like, she'd have to shred a tit or something, just to keep up with the Unfolding Tragedy of Her Fucken Life. Out of kindness, I absorb the maximum number of sniffles before speaking.

'How could you do that to me, Ma?'

'Well I only told the *truth*, Vernon. Anyway young man, how could you do all *this* to *me*?'

'I didn't do anything.'

'Well, famous actors put toothpaste under their eyes to help them cry. Did you know that?'

'Say *what*?'

'I'm just telling you for court, in case you look too impassive. You know how impassive you can look.'

'Ma – just don't talk to Lally anymore, okay?'

'Hold on,' she takes her mouth from the phone, 'it's all right

60

Leona, it's the fridge people.' You hear questioning noises in back, about the time of night, then Mom comes on the line again. 'Well it's *ridiculous* – I've waited *days* for you people!'

'Goodnight, Ma.'

'Wait!' She presses her mouth to the phone, whispering. 'Vernon – it's probably best not to mention anything about the, er . . .'

'Gun?'

'Well yes, probably best to keep it between us, you know?'

My daddy's gun. If only my ole lady had let me keep it at home. But no. The fucken gun gave her the tremors. I had to stash it far from the house, way out in the public domain. Nuckles must know it's there. Jesus must've used it as a wild card, must've mentioned it to stop him following, to make him think there was an arsenal stashed away. But then Jesus died. Took the information, the context, all our innocent boyhood times with him. Took the truth with him.

Just my gun's left behind, with all the wrong fingerprints on it. Left behind, just waiting.

Act II

How I spent my summer vacation

seven

The sign on the shrink's door says: 'Dr Goosens.' What a crack. *Goosens.* Whoever invented the Cold Light of Day sure went to fucken town on it, boy. On the ride over here I had a truckload of ideas about how to act crazy, maybe pull some Kicked Dog, some Spooked Deer and all, like Mom does. I even thought I could maybe drop a load in my pants or something, as a last resort. It's a slimy secret, I know it. I even loosened my asshole in case it came to that. But now, in the cold light of day, I just hope I flossed enough.

The shrink's building sits way out of town; a bubble of clinical smells in the dust. A receptionist with spiky teeth, and a voicebox made from bees trapped in tracing paper, sits behind a desk in the waiting room. She gives me the fucken shiver, but the jail guards don't seem to notice her at all. I have an urge to ask her name, but I don't. I can imagine her saying, 'Why, I'm Graunley Stelt,' or 'Achtung Beed,' or something way fucken bent. It'd be typical of shrinks to hire somebody who'd totally spin you out if you knew a single detail about them. If you weren't edgy when you came in, you would be after you met the fucken receptionist.

'Bloop,' an intercom hoots behind her desk.

'Didn't you get my email?' asks a man.

'No, Doctor,' says the receptionist.

'*Please* monitor the systems, there's no point upgrading our technology if you don't monitor the *systems.* I emailed you *three minutes ago* for the next patient.'

'Yes, Doctor.' She taps at her keyboard, scowls at the monitor, then looks at me. 'The doctor will see you now.'

My Nikes chirp over black and green linoleum, through a door, and into a room with supermarket lighting. Two armchairs sit by a window; an ole stereo rests beside one of them, with a notebook computer on top. At the back of the room stands a hospital bunk on wheels, with a towel over it. And there's Dr Goosens; round, soft, butt-heavy, and as smug as a Disney worm. He smiles sympathetically, and waves me to an armchair.

'Cindy, bring the client's file, please.'

Check my fucken face now. *Cindy!* It slays me. Now I'm just waiting for her to say, 'Groovy, Wayne,' and bounce through the door in a little tennis skirt or something. She doesn't though, not in the cold light of day. She trudges past in socks and sandals, and hands a file to Goosens. He thumbs through the pages and waits for her to leave the room.

'Vernon Gregory Little, how are you today?'

'Okay, I guess.' My Nikes tap each other.

'Alrighty. What can you tell me about why you're here?'

'The judge must think I'm crazy, or something.'

'And are you?' He gets ready to chuckle, like it's obvious I ain't. It might help if the judge thought I was bananas, but looking at Ole Mother Goosens just makes me want to tell him how I really feel, which is that everybody backed me into a nasty corner with their crashy fucken powerdimes.

'I guess it ain't up to me to say,' I tell him. It doesn't seem enough though; he stares and waits for more. As I catch his eye, I feel the past wheeze up my throat in a raft of bitter words. 'See, first everybody dissed me because my buddy was Mexican, then because he was weird, but I stood by him, I thought friendship was a sacred thing – then it all went to hell, and now I'm being punished for it, they're twisting every regular little fact to fit my guilt . . .'

Goosens raises a hand, and smiles gently. 'Alrighty, let's see what we can discover. Please continue to be candid – if you open yourself up to this process, in good faith, we won't have a problem at all. Now, tell me – how do you *feel* about what's happened?'

66

'Just wrecked. Wrecked dead away. And now everybody's calling *me* the psycho, I know they are.'

'Why do you think they might be doing that?'

'They need a skate-goat, they want to hang somebody high.'

'A scapegoat? You feel something intangible caused the tragedy?'

'Well, no, I mean – my friend Jesus ain't around, in person, to take any blame. He did all the shooting, I was just a witness, not even involved at all.' Goosens searches my face, and makes a note in his file.

'Alrighty. What can you tell me about your family life?'

'It's just regular.' Goosens holds his pen still, and looks at me. He knows he just found a major bug up my ass.

'The file notes that you live with your mother. What can you tell me about that relationship?'

'Uh, it's just – regular.' The whole subject drags a major tumor out of my ass, don't fucken ask me why. It just lies there on the floor, throbbing, glistening with gut-slime. Goosens even leans back in his chair, to avoid the heaving tang of my fucken family life.

'No brothers?' he asks, wisely steering east. 'No uncles, or – other male influences in your familial network?'

'Not really,' I say.

'But you had – friends . . .?' My eyes drop to the floor. He sits quiet for a moment, then reaches over to rest a hand on my leg. 'Believe me, Jesus touched me too – the whole affair touched me deeply. If you're able, tell me what happened that day.'

I try to dodge the spike of panic you get when you hear yourself fixing to bawl. 'Things had already started when I got back.'

'Where had you been?' asks Goosens.

'I got held up, running an errand.'

'Vernon, you're not on trial here – please be specific.'

'I needed the bathroom on the way back from an errand Mr Nuckles sent me on.'

'The school bathroom?'

'No.'

'You took a leak outside school?' He leans his head over, as if the information might splat in his face.

'Uh – not a leak, actually.'

'You had a bowel movement, outside school? At the time of the tragedy?'

'Sometimes I can be kind of unpredictable.'

Silence fills the forty years Fate gives me to recognize the import of things. This would never happen to Van Damme. Heroes never shit. They only fuck and kill.

A shine comes to Goosens's eyes. 'You told the court this?'

'Hell no.'

He blinks and folds his arms. 'Forgive me, but – forensically, doesn't a fresh stool, situated away from the scene of the crimes – automatically rule you out as a suspect? Fecal matter can be accurately dated, you know.'

'I guess that's right, huh?' You can tell Goosens is giving me extra service. He's only supposed to suck information for the court, but here he is, prepared to take a chance and give me a revelation along the way. He clamps his lips tight, to hit home the significance of it all. Then his eyes fall.

'I hear you say you're kind of – unpredictable?'

'It's no big deal,' I draw circles on the floor with a Nike.

'Is it a diagnosed condition – sphincter weakness, or suchlike?'

'Nah. Anyway, I almost don't get it anymore.'

Goosens runs his tongue over his upper lip. 'Alrighty, so tell me – do you like girls, Vernon?'

'Sure.'

'Can you name a girl you like?'

'Taylor Figueroa.'

He chews his lip, and makes a note in the file. 'Have you had physical contact with her?'

'Kind of.'

'What do you remember most about your contact with her?'

'Her smell, I guess.'

Goosens frowns into the file, and makes another entry. Then he sits back. 'Vernon – have you ever felt attraction towards another boy? Or a man?'

'No way.'

'Alrighty. Let's see what we can discover.'

He reaches for the stereo and presses 'Play'. A military drum beats out, softly at first, but growing in power, threatening, like a bear coming out of a cave, or a bear going into the cave, and you're in the fucken cave.

'Gustav Holst,' says Goosens. '*The Planets* – Mars. This'll rouse some glory in a boy's soul.' He walks to the bed and smacks it with the flat of his hand. The powerdime takes a reckless shift.

'Get undressed for me, please, and come lie up here.'

'Un-dressed?'

'Sure – to finish the exam. We psychiatrists are medical doctors first, you know – don't confuse us with your everyday psychologists.'

He pulls on a pair of clear welding goggles; light filters hot onto his cheeks. Folding my Calvin Kleins takes a while, in order to stop loose change falling from the pocket. Even though my loose change is in a plastic bag at the sheriff's office. Brass stomps black and twisted over the drums from the stereo as I climb onto the bed. Goosens points at my underwear.

'Off, please.'

A thought comes to me; it is that a breeze on the butt, in the presence of supermarket lighting, should only be felt by the dead. I'm a naked fucken animal. But even naked animals need bail. Especially naked animals need it.

'On your stomach,' says Goosens. 'Spread your legs.'

'Ta-t-t-t, TA-TA-TA.' Musical hellfire accompanies the touch of two fingers on my back. They trace a line down my body, then turn into hands, and grab both cheeks of my ass.

'Relax,' he whispers, spreading my cheeks. 'Does this make you think of Taylor?'

'TA-TA-TA, TA-T-T-T!'

69

'Or – something else?' His breathing quickens with the march of his fingers, they trace a tightening circle around the rim of my hole. A line of violent cussing forms in my throat. The bail thought stops it.

'Doctor, this don't seem right,' I say. What a fuckhole, I swear. I should jam a table-leg through his fucken eye, make him grunt like a tied hog. Jean-Claude would do it. James Bond would do it with a fucken cocktail in his hand. Me, I just squeak like a brownie. He takes no fucken notice anyway. A cool finger invades me as the music explodes to a climax. I grunt like a tied hog.

'Al-*righty*, one for Jesus. Just relax, this next procedure won't hurt a bit – in fact, don't be embarrassed if you experience arousal.' He grabs a pair of steel salad tongs, adjusts his goggles, and lowers his face to my ass.

'*I don't fucken think so*,' I quiver, spinning upright. Cobwebs of spit fly from my mouth. Goosens recoils, forearms held up like a surgeon.

He slowly reaches for the towel on the bed, and wipes his middle finger. Huge gingery eyes stare through the goggles. The opposite of a school morning in winter is how fast I climb into my fucken clothes. I don't button my shirt, I don't tie my laces. I don't fucken look back.

'Think carefully, Vernon,' says Goosens. 'Think very carefully before jeopardizing your bail application.' He stops to sigh a moment, and shake his head. 'Remember there are only two kinds of people in your position: glorious, powerful boys, and prisoners.'

Music whips twisters behind me as I scramble out through the waiting room. Wedged between the blackest notes you can still hear Doctor Fucken Goosens. 'Okay – *alrighty* . . .'

I sit under a personal cloud in back of the jail van, like a sphinx, a sphinxter, to the beat of that rude orchestra music by Goosestep Holster. It does nothing to erase memories of the shrink, and his fucken ass-banditry. I try not to think what his report will say. I just watch the scenery pass by my window. Dead products dot the roadside on the way back to town: an abandoned shopping cart, a sofa skeleton. Under a tree sits a busted TV, empty of wacky antics. Pumpjacks poke dirty fingers into the landscape, but we drive past all of it, including the sky and the distance, ignorant of the fence wire that twangs a straight line to Mexico.

Mexico. Another coupon tacked onto the pile I'll redeem when I get some power in my fucken life. Look around this life and all you see is folks' coupons tacked everywhere, what they'll do *if*, what they'll do *when*. Warm anticipation for shit that ain't even going to happen.

'Kid,' says one of the guards, 'you ain't haulin your stalk back there, are ya?' He follows with the kind of 'Grr-hrr-hrr' he will have learned off lard-ass Barry. I swear these guys must share that one joke around, ole Barry must give fucken smut classes after work or something. Snatches of their talk filter back to me.

'Uh-huh, Vaine Gurie petitioned the county for a SWAT team.'

'Over the sheriff's head?'

'Uh-huh. Barry upgraded their in-surance same fuckin day.'

'He told you that?'

'Tuck says.'

'Tuck What's-his-name, at the morgue? What's he know about Barry's in-surance?'

'Tuck *sells* goddam in-surance. Dropped Amway to *sell* fuckin *in-surance*.'

'No shit.'

I sense a learning: that much dumber people than you end up in charge. Look at the way things are. I'm no fucken genius or anything, but these spazzos are in charge of my every twitch. What I'm starting to think is maybe only the dumb are safe in this world, the ones who roam with the herd, without thinking about every little thing. But see me? I have to think about every little fucken thing.

*

As I sit, then lay, then pace, then sit again in my cell, waiting for my next court appearance, time, being an agent of Fate, slows way the fuck down. Thursday eats Wednesday, and Jesus' last breath drags ten days into the past, towing Nuckles's silence behind it, as if he was never even there, like the truth was my shadow alone. To stretch things even further, Mom calls to say Lally has been contracted to shoot another report from Martirio. It's typical of where things are at with Fate, slowing time down all over the place, calling the weirdest fucken people Cindy. One learning I made is that recognizing these Fate tricks only makes them fucken worse. Even as I pass on to you these amazing life insights, I curse you with making them fucken worse. Because once you know about them, you fucken wait for them to happen.

The day of my court appearance is hot and soupy. I sense dogs across town, chilling under window-mounted air-conditioners, letting any ole cat pass by, and cats letting any ole rat pass by, and rats – probably too fucken lathered to even want to pass by. I'm the only one passing by, in fact, on my way to the classroom. I mean, courtroom.

'All-a rise.'

Court froths with sighs and the stench of hot clothes this Friday. Everybody stares at me. 'Oh Lord,' as Pam would say. Pam might come by later, but Mom can't make it. Faces disfigured with memories of black blood and gray skin dot the crowd. Kin of the fallen. Mr Lechuga stares death-rays at me, and he ain't even Max's real daddy. Lorna Speltz's mom is here, like a damp kind of turtle. I get waves of sadness, not for me but for them, all mangled and devastated. I'd give anything for them to be vastated again.

Vaine is gone, her table is occupied by a shiny man wearing black and white. Judge Gurie catches his attention. 'Mr Gregson, I take it you're appearing for the State?'

'One hundred percent correct, ma'am – all the way to the district court.' Perky fucker.

The judge picks Goosens's file off her desk and waves it at the prosecutor. 'I have a report on the defendant's state of mind.'

'We vigorously oppose bail, your honor.'

'On what grounds?' asks the judge.

The prosecutor fights a smile. 'In common parlay – the kid's stole more damn chain than he can swim with. We're afraid he'll go down with it, and we'll never see him again!' A chuckle runs through the court. It stops at the judge, who scowls at Goosens's file, then turns to Abdini. 'Any further submissions in respect of this application?'

Abdini stops fussing at his table and looks up. 'Is family boy, have many interest . . .'

'I know all that,' the judge flaps her hand, 'I mean anything new, like the – digestive condition mentioned in this report, for instance.'

'A-ha, the toilet . . .' says Abdini, mostly to himself.

'If your honor pleases,' says Gregson, 'we'd object to the court doing the defense's homework for them.'

'Very well. They clearly haven't been instructed, so I'll leave the clues at that.'

'Also, ma'am, we'd like to enter a statement from the witness, Marion Nuckles,' says Gregson.

The judge's eyebrows become airborne. Breathing dies in the room. 'I was told no statement could be taken until March next year!'

'It's a transcript of digital media taken at the crime scene, Judge. A reporter from CNN sourced it for us, in the public interest.' Motherfucker Lally flashes to mind. Makes you wonder which poor suck he's fucking over right now.

'Well that's very public-spirited of them. Is the defendant's alibi supported by the witness?' asks the judge.

'Not our brief, your honor. Our statement concerns the possible whereabouts of another firearm – I'm sure we all agree, that casts a serious light on the prisoner's bail application.'

Judge Gurie puts on her glasses, reaching for the document. She

73

scans it, frowning, then lays it down and peers at the prosecutor. 'Counsel, the actual murder weapon was found at the outset. Are you saying you can link a *second* gun to these crimes?'

'Very possibly, ma'am.'

'Do you have that gun?'

'Not as such, but officers are investigating.'

The judge sighs. 'Well, it's obvious neither of you has seen the psychiatric report. In the absence of hard evidence, I'll be ruling on the basis of this assessment.'

An itchy silence falls over the room, measured in tens of thousands of years. The crowd divides its attention between me and the bench, all the while juggling the decent, downtown skills that let them soak it up without looking like they're at a traffic accident and fucken enjoying it. They juggle those skills with their eyebrows.

Judge Gurie sits still for a moment, then surveys the court. It freezes. 'Ladies and gentlemen, I think it's fair to say we've had enough. We're fed up – outraged! – at these continual damned breaches of our rightful peace.' Applause erupts; some asshole even whoops like a TV audience. You wait for the chant, 'Gu-rie! Gu-rie! Gu-rie!'

The judge pauses to straighten her collar. 'My decision today takes into account the feelings of the victims' families, as well as those of the wider community. I also acknowledge that, despite the defendant's stable, if not very affluent background, he is a standing candidate to stand trial as an accessory to these crimes.' The typist looks over at my corral, probably to boost the polish on her own dumb kids. None of them in jail today, no sirree. 'Vernon Gregory Little,' says the judge, 'in light of the disorder identified in this report, and taking into account submissions by both counsels – I am releasing you . . .'

'My babies, my poor dead babies,' squeals a lady at the back. Outrage spews through the room.

'Silence! Let me *finish*,' says the judge. 'Vernon Little, I am releasing you into the care of Dr Oliver Goosens, starting Monday, on an outpatient basis. Failure to comply with the doctor's schedule of treatment, in any way whatsoever, will result in your further detention. Do you understand?'

'Yes, ma'am.'

She stretches over the bench and lowers her voice. 'One more thing – if I were defending, I'd seriously consider expanding on this, ehm – bowel thing.'

'Thank you, ma'am.'

I'll be damned. I burrow through the mess of onlookers and float out of the courthouse into the sun, just like that. Reporters buzz around me like flies at a shit-roast. I'm full of feelings, but not the ones I dreamed of. Instead of true joy, I feel waves; the kind that make you look forward to the smell of laundry on a rainy Saturday, the type of drippy hormones that trick you into saying I Love You. Security they fucken call it. Watch out for that shit. Those waves erode your goddam bravery. I even get a wave of gratitude for the judge – go fucken figure. I mean, Judge Gurie's been good to me, but – expand on the bowel thing? – I don't fucken think so.

'How do we find your turds?' they'd ask. 'Why,' I'd say, 'my logs are over there, in the den behind the bushes – right there, next to the goddam gun y'all are looking for.' To be honest, the gun ain't such a big deal. The fingerprints *on* the gun are my fucken problem. Thinking about it brings a whole new set of waves. I decide to ignore them, for my own safety. You just can't afford waves when you have to be in Mexico by daybreak.

The Mercury sits with two doors open, dripping ants all over Gurie Street. Mrs Binney, the florist, almost has to stop her brand-new Cadillac to get past. Mrs Binney doesn't wave today. She pretends not to see me. Instead she watches Abdini decoy some reporters on the steps, and floats right by with a fresh mess of tributes for the Lechugas' front porch.

'We happy we allow home to continue our young life,' says Abdini, like he's me, or we're fucken brothers or something. 'And we cantinue inbestigation into whappen that terryball day . . .'

I got me some learnings in court, I have to say. The way everybody acts, court is like watching TV-trailers; a shade of this movie, a bite of that show. The one where the kid gets cancer, and everybody speaks haltingly. The one where the rookie cop decides whether to be a bag-man for bribes, or to blow his crusty partner's cover. I personally wouldn't recommend playing that one, though; everybody ends up being on the take, like even the mayor. And don't fucken ask what show I got stuck with. 'America's Dumbest Assholes' or something. 'Ally McBowel.'

The Mercury bitches under Pam's sandals. That's because she uses both pedals at once. 'No point *having* a brake pedal if your foot's a mile away on the other side of the car,' she'll tell you if you ever bring it up. I only brought it up once. 'Might as well throw the darned pedal out the door.' Camera people scatter as we lunge up Gurie Street. I see the TV pictures in my mind, the shot of my ole mutton head looking back from the Mercury.

'But, what kind of *meals* did you get?' asks Pam.

'Regular stuff.'

'But like, what? Like, pork 'n' beans? Did you get dessert?'

'Not really.'

'Oh *Lord*.'

She spins the car into the *Barn* drive-thru. One good thing about Pam's TV-movie; you know how the thing's going to end. That's the kind of life I want, the life we were fucken promised. A fuzzy ole show with some flashes of panty and a happy ending. One of those shows where the kid's baseball coach takes him camping, and teaches him self-respect, you've seen that show, with electric piano notes tinkling in the background, soft as ovaries hitting oatmeal. When you hear that piano it means somebody's hugging, or a woman is crumpling her lips with overwhelming joy, down by a lake. Boy, the life I could have with the right music behind me. Instead I watch Liberty Drive screen through the window, with *Galveston* playing in back. We pass the place where Max Lechuga sucked his last breath. He said some words, but you couldn't hear them. Heat comes to my eye, so I spark up a distraction.

'Ma home?' I ask.

'Waiting on the fridge delivery,' says Pam.

'You're kidding.'

'Humor her, she's going through a lot. No harm in just waiting.'

'That'll be one long wait.'

Pam just sighs. 'You'll be sixteen in a few days. We won't let anything spoil your birthday.'

I cushion myself in this familiar ole cream; family, with all its flavors of smell. I've only been gone a week, but my ole routines seem like a past life. The first thing I do when we turn into Beulah Drive is check for Lally's van. I try to see past a knot of reporters in the road, but then the Seldome Motel's new minibus pulls up by the Lechugas' teddy farm. Strangers lean out, take pictures, bow their heads, then the van pulls away toward the mantis market. Lally's space under the willow is empty.

'Take these fries to your ma,' says Pam through a mouthful of drumstick.

'Not coming in?'

'I have pinball right now.' Playing pinball is healthy, according to Pam.

Reporters jostle me all the way to the front door. I slip inside, locking the door behind me, then just hang, soaking up the familiar whiff of ketchup and wood polish. All's quiet inside, except for the TV. I go to leave the fries on the breakfast bar, but just as I reach the kitchen, I hear a noise up the hallway. Like a sick dog. Then comes a voice.

'*Wait* – I'm sure I heard the door . . .'

It's Mom.

'God, *unghh, ugh*, Lalito, Lally – *wait*!'

eight

'Doris – I think the Special Edition arrived!' Here's Betty Pritchard.

My heart ain't even restarted before these ladies turn up. The fridge? I don't fucken think so. Georgette Porkorney clomps onto the porch by the kitchen door. Mom always leaves that fucken door open. Even now, when she's balling Lally up the hall.

'Look!' says George. 'They're pulling over at Nancie Lechuga's!'

'I know, I *know*! *Doris!*'

My Nikes tense in their shame. I stare at the painting beside the laundry door. A clown holds up a fucken umbrella, and bawls one big tear underneath. Mom calls it art.

'Hi, Vern,' says Leona, stealing a fry. 'Stress binge?'

I forgot about Mom's fries. Now the bag's squished in my fucken hand. I park it on the breakfast bar, next to a greeting card with a cartoon baby on it. '*It's Wuv!*' says the baby. I look inside the card and see a love poem from Lally to Mom. There ain't puke enough in the world for today.

When everybody is assembled with a view of the hallway, Mom steps out of her room and ripples toward us in a filmy pink robe. An alien scent drags behind her. 'Well hi, baby, I didn't expect you back.' She pelts me a hug, but as she does it, her left tit flops free and smacks me on the arm.

'Doris, they're trying to deliver the fridge to Nancie's!' says Betty.

'Wow, this is *exciting*,' says Leona. 'Weird, too, because I wasn't even going to stop by! My new consultant's installing the toning station today, and I still have new tenny-runners to buy . . .'

Three whole brags. My house is fucken Baconham Palace, all of a sudden. The reason steps into the hallway, wearing a blue robe with gold detail, and new Timberlands on his sockless feet. He throws his arms wide. 'It's Martirio's Angels!'

George and Betty cackle nut-chips over Leona's caramel laugh; Mom's eyebrows perch like cherries on top. Nobody will ask why Lally's suddenly dicking my ma, the truth of things will just get wiped over with cream-pie lies. Don't fucken ask me about this love people have of saying things are fine when they ain't fucken fine at all. Lally's toothbrush in my bathroom ain't fucken fine at all. He avoids my eyes as he walks through the kitchen, like I was nobody, as if fucken nothing; he breaks open one of his ginseng bottles, tweaks his balls, and keeps right on grinning.

'Hurry, Doris,' says George. 'It's the Special Edition, go say something!'

'Well, I'm not even *dressed*.'

'Maybe I'll drive to Houston,' says Leona. 'Buy some gymwear too . . .' It's a record-breaking fourth thing. Mom just smiles powerfully, and cozies back into Lally's arms.

'Shit, Doris, *I'll* go tell them,' says George. 'They're unloading the damn thing already, look!' I crane to the kitchen window; sure enough, a JC Penney's truck is parked in front of the Lechugas'. A teddy bear lays pinned under the back wheel.

'Well but, *wait* . . .' says Mom.

There used to be a horse that could do math on stage. Everybody thought the horse was so fucken smart, he would tap the answer to math questions with his hoof, and always get it right. Turns out the horse couldn't do math at all, could he fuck. He just kept tapping until he felt the tension in the audience break. Everybody relaxed when he'd tapped the right number, and he felt it, and just stopped tapping. Right now Lally takes a cue from the tension in the room, just like the horse that did math on stage.

'Tch – the Special Edition?' he says. 'Babe, after they screwed you around so long I called and cancelled that order. I'm sorry – we'll take a drive to San Antone, I need some more ginseng anyway.'

'Well, oh my.'

'But, you ordered almond-on-almond, didn't you?' asks George. 'Look, they're unloading a new almond Special Edition side-by-side into Nancie's!'

'What a day,' says Leona. Her face goes blank trying to suck back the fourth brag. Too late now, honey chile.

My eyes trudge over the breakfast bar, past the power bill you can see tucked behind the cookie jar, and into the living room, grasping at any straw of human dignity. Then Brad walks in, wearing a brand-new pair of Timberlands. Fucken 'Bang!' goes the door. He hoists his nose and heads straight for the TV. He'll go sit on the rug and lip-read the beeps on the *Springer* show, I guarantee it.

My face caves in. This is how I'm being grown up, this is my fucken struggle for learnings and glory. A gumbo of lies, cellulite, and fucken 'Wuv'.

I turn to go to my room, but Lally grabs my head. He makes like he's mussing my hair, but he's actually holding me back. 'Little big man – let's go share some thoughts.'

'Well sure,' says Mom, 'you retire for men's business – I'll fix a brew and fill the gals in on a certain somebody's diet.'

'What,' asks Leona, 'she went back to *Weight Watchers*?'

'The *Zone*,' says Mom.

I'm tuned out by the time Lally nudges me to the dark end of the living room. I get sat at Pam's end of the sofa, the end closest to the floor. He spreads himself at the high end, and studies my shoes with a frown.

'Tch, I can't tell you what you've put your mother through. Can you imagine if I hadn't been around to pick up the pieces?'

Is he fucken kidding or what? He's been here seven days, and now he's like my fucken blood? I just stare at the rug. A fucken yard of it dies.

'To say we're challenged, Vern, is to put it very mildly.'

I climb off the sofa. 'They're your damn pieces.'

'What was that?' He grabs my arm.

'Fuck *off*,' I say.

He slaps me with the flat of his hand. 'Fuckin cuss at me.'

The noise draws Brad over, shuffling on his ass. Lally tightens his grip on my arm.

'Lalito, how do you want your coffee?' calls Mom.

'Hot and sweet, like my woman.' Lally flashes Brad a smile, and winks. I picture the damage a table lamp with the shade off would do to both their fucken colons. Lally pulls me close and starts to speak softly. 'I hear talk of a firearm. You hear about another firearm?'

I just stay quiet.

He watches me for a moment, then hoists his eyebrows high. 'Remind me to call Dr Goosens.' He waits for a reaction, but I stay impassive. He waits a little longer, then settles back into the sofa and starts to scratch out the Dallas Cowboys label my dad sowed into the arm. 'It's not too late to shift the paradigm, Vern. In fact, if the paradigm doesn't shift, the story will die. Nobody wins if the story dies. I'm waiting to hear if I've been commissioned for a whole series, in depth. Could cross over into feature rights, web events. We could turn your situation around three hundred and sixty degrees . . .'

'Learn some fucken math.'

'Well look!' Mom walks in with the coffee. 'He's only twelve and he has a hundred million dollars! An e-mailionaire, look guys!'

It's *America's Youngest Millionaires* on TV. The ladies drift over like farts.

'Small fry,' says Brad. 'My first billion's in the bag.'

'Attaboy, Bradley!' says George.

Eyes move to the screen like sinners to fucken church. 'A *millionaire* before he was *ten*,' says the reporter, 'Ricky is now well on the road to his *second hundred million dollars*.' The way he says 'doll-larrs' you'd think he'd dipped his fucken tongue in molasses, or something. Pussy or something. Ricky just sits there like a spare prick, in front of the Lamborghini he can't even drive.

When they ask him if he feels great, he just shrugs and says, 'Doesn't everybody?'

'What an *incredible* boy,' says Mom. 'I bet his *mother's* on cloud *nine*.'

'A billion dollars,' sighs Leona. Her feet turn in like a little girl, and she leans over to whisper loud in Brad's ear, 'Remember who did all the driving in your humble years!'

A warm, fuzzy moment takes hold of the room. Then everybody's eyes settle on me. I pull away from Lally and head up the hall.

'Aren't you staying for *Millionaires?*' asks Mom.

I don't have an answer. I just blow some air through my cheeks and shuffle away, to fucken Mexico, via my room.

'C'mon, big man,' calls Lally. 'I'm only funnin.' I let his words thud lonely on the rug behind me.

'Wow, Nancie must've bought a new fridge,' says Leona as I reach the hall. She's good that way, Leona, how she keeps things moving along. I guess all these ole fakes are good that way, with their fucken pre-programmed coos and sighs and bullshit. One learning you should know: ladies like this can't deal with silence.

I lock my bedroom door and stand still on the other side, scanning the empty holes Vaine Gurie left in my mess. My disc player is still here, with a few discs around it. I grab an ole Johnny Paycheck compilation and load it, cranking the volume way up. Clothes fly out of the closet into my Nike backpack. Even a jacket flies in, because you never know how long I'll be gone. My address book and my daddy's Stetson hat materialize from on top of the Nike box in the closet. I spy an ole birthday card from Mom amongst my chattels, with dumb-looking puppy-dogs on it. It brings a wave of sadness, but it won't stop me.

When I'm all packed, I pause to listen at the door, mapping the voices in the living room. 'Hell no,' says George, from her usual chair. 'Nancie's still running on Hank's insurance.'

'Well I don't know why they hem and haw about my Tyler's

payout,' says Mom. She's on her way back to the kitchen for cake, you can tell. 'I mean, it's been nearly a year.'

'Honey – they need a body, *you* know that,' says George.

I grab my pack, heave up the bedroom window, and jump out into the shady lea of the house. It's directly in line with Mrs Lechuga's window across the street, but her drapes are still pulled tight, and the media hangs mostly on the driveway side. I carefully pull down the window behind me, then run under the biggest willow, to the back fence. Who lives on the other side is a wealthy couple; at least their house is painted wealthy. It means they spend less time spying through their screen, not like Mrs Porter. Wealth makes you less nosey, in case you didn't know. I climb over the fence, scare a hiss out of their cat on the other side, and scoot across their lawn to Arsenio Trace, the last street on this side of town. Everything's calm, except for some loser selling watermelon at the dead end of the road. I turn away from him, pulling the hat brim low over my forehead, and lope toward town, real normal, even with a new kind of limp I invent to the tune of sprinklers along the way, 'Mexico, Mexico, Mexico, fsk, fsk, fsk.'

Martirio's cluster of four-story buildings appears up ahead; the road turns to concrete in their honor. A crowd gathers in front of the Seldome Motel, must be to catch a glimpse of some network stars. I hear Brian Gumball is down here, doing a live show. I ain't stopping to check, though. Food stalls sizzle at the side of the motel, but I content myself with the thought of enchiladas when I get over the border. I guess Taylor likes enchiladas, not that I ever asked her. It's one of the things I should've asked her, but never did. Tsk. It bums me to think how few things Taylor has actually said to my face; like, maybe twenty-nine words, in my whole fucken life. Eighteen of those were in the same sentence. A TV scientist wouldn't give great odds of a college girl running away in the heat of the moment with a fifteen-year-old slimeball like me, not after a relationship spanning twenty-nine words. But that's fucken TV scientists for you. Next thing they'll be telling you not to eat meat.

Willard Down's used-car lot shimmers on the corner of Gurie Street, looking faded since he cancelled his 'Down's Syndrome – Prices Down!' campaign. He cancelled it on account of little Delroy Gurie. A flash of red catches my eye at the back of the lot. It's Lally's van, with a seventeen-hundred-dollar tag on the windscreen. Then, next thing you know, Fate puts Vaine Gurie in the Pizza Hut opposite my bank. She sits by the window, hunched over a wedge of pizza. Sitting by the window ain't a sharp idea for a diet fugitive, but you can see the place is overflowing with strangers. I stop and fumble in my pack, watching her through the corner of my eye. Strangely, I get a wave of sadness watching her. Fat ole Vaine, stuffing emptiness into her void. Her eating strategy is to take six big bites, until her mouth's crammed to bursting, then top up the gaps with little bites. Panic eating. Here's me yearning for Mexico, there's Vaine hogging herself slim, just another fragile fucken booger-sac of a life. I stare down at my New Jacks. Then back at Vaine; detached, sad, and furtive. I mean, what kind of fucken life is this?

I can't risk going to the ATM right now. I turn my face away, and just keep walking to the Greyhound yard. I can check the timetable, hang out until the coast is clear. Heat shimmers clean at the end of the street, a pair of Stetsons wriggle through it. Dirk's Eatery passes on my right, with all the specials painted on the window, and a couple of die-hards bent over their grits inside. The dog out front doesn't look at me when I pass. He just twitches an eyebrow, you know how they do.

I limp into the Greyhound waiting room, all casual. A few other folk are here, nobody beautiful though, no cowgirls or anything. Next bus to San Antonio is in twenty minutes. She might already be on the bus, the cowgirl. Trying to blend into the place, I line up behind two Mexican ladies at the ticket counter. They talk in Spanish. It gives me a buzz, I have to say, that and the spicy smell of their clothes. It makes me picture my new beach-house, with

Taylor's laundry hung out on palm trees to dry, her panties and all. She's probably naked in the house because her panties are all out to dry. Bikinis in the sun. Or tangas. Probably bikinis.

I chase some spit with my tongue, and watch an ole man at the back of the room flick through the *Martirio Clarion*, our so-called paper. The skin of his face hangs down in pockets, like he has lead implants. Character, they call it. It ain't character, though; you know it's feelings. Erosion from waves of disappointment and sadness. One thing I learned from watching folk these last days is that waves are mostly one-way; you collect them over a lifetime, until finally the least fucken thing makes you bawl.

I get quite comfortable, standing in line with my musings. Then the man's paper flops open to a picture of me. 'Guilty?' asks the headline. The room turns icy. My eyes bounce, and I swear I see a flash of Jesus' casket being wheeled in to catch the San Antonio bus. I shut my eyes, and when I open them there's no casket. But I expect it, back in my soul. That, or some fucken shit. You know Fate.

Inch by inch, I shuffle behind the Mexican ladies toward check-in. My bravery has ebbed away. I decide to try my New York accent on the man at the ticket counter, just ask him some question; that way, if anybody comes looking for me later, he'll say, 'Nah, I only saw some kid from The Apple.' The ladies finish and move away. The clerk stops tapping at his keyboard, and looks up. My mouth opens, but he doesn't look at me, his eyes shoot over my shoulder.

'Howdy Palmyra,' he says.

Pam's shadow falls over me. 'Hell, Vernie, what're you doing down here?'

'Uh – looking for work.'

'Lord, a boy can't work on an empty belly – c'mon now, I'm on my way past the *Barn* to your place . . .'

Fuck. Everybody in the place looks up to watch Pam drag me out by the hand, like a goddam kid. The man with the newspaper nudges somebody next to him, and points. I feel the noose of this fucken town tighten around my throat.

nine

'The dogs will also uncover firearms, and other devices,' says the sheriff on TV. 'So if a weapon is found, it'll just be a matter of matching the fingerprints.'

'And if you get a match – case closed?' asks the reporter.

'You bet.'

Mom switches off the TV on her scurry back to the kitchen. 'Lord, Vernon, please don't go to the Tragedy Sale in those shoes, you heard what everybody thinks. *Please*. I can't believe there isn't a pair of Tumbledowns in your size around town.'

'Timberlands, Ma.'

'Whatever. Look, here's the pastor now. I know it's not much of a job, but, as Lally says, it's important to show the community you're making good.'

'But I didn't *do* anything – *damn!*'

'Vernon Gregory!' says Lally. 'Don't argue with your mother.'

He wears this fancy suit today, with a tie and all. Suddenly this fancy fucken suit appeared.

I just want to fucken die, go back to jail, to the warmth of Barry and his crew of madcap funsters. Last night was a long night at home, real fucken long. To cap it off, Kurt started barking again. I swear the barking circuit that orbits town every night starts and ends with fucken Kurt. For such a nerdy dog, I don't see how he got to be president of the barking circuit. It ain't like he's a fucken rat-wheeler or anything.

Lally sucks down a ginseng, and nuzzles Mom. 'Hey,' he grunts, 'remember what we talked about? If I get the series, we'll fill this house with Special Edition fridges.'

Her lips tighten. 'Well I don't know what happened to that

order, now it looks like Nancie got one. Anyway, if you saw her old refrigerator you'd know why. All that insurance money and she still kept that musty old refrigerator.'

'Shhh,' whispers Lally. 'We got a new speakerphone, didn't we? Now you don't even have to hold the receiver!'

I get waves about it all. My ole lady was never Honey Bear like this with my daddy. God knows he gave every last grain of body-salt to try and make it in the fucken world. It just wasn't enough, in the end, I guess. The day he got his first thousand dollars, the neighbors must've got ten. Aim for a million bucks, you suddenly need a billion. I upgraded my computer, but it wasn't enough. No matter what, it ain't fucken enough in life, that's what I learned.

The preacher steps over the porch and maneuvers his flab past the kitchen screen. 'This glorious Saturday smells of joy cakes,' he booms. I swear the Lord giveth and just keeps fucken givething to Pastor Gibbons.

'They're hot and perky, Pastor,' Mom whisks the napkin off a tray of pessimistic-looking bakes, offering it up like it was a feel of her tits twenty years ago. Gibbons' new Timberlands chirp a trail across the linoleum.

He grabs a cake, then turns to smile at me. 'And you're my deputy for the day?'

'That's your boy,' says Lally, 'he'll give a hundred and fifty percent.'

'Awesome, I'll put him on the bake stall – we're hoping to raise ten grand today, for the new media center.'

Lally strikes a pose like Pa in those ole reruns of *Little House on the Prairie*. 'This town sure is teaching a thing or two about community spirit, Pastor.'

'God knows the Tragedy Committee has worked miracles to bring some good out of the devastation,' says Gibbons. 'Word is, one of the networks might even put us national today.' He pulls focus from infinity to Lally's face. 'Wouldn't be – your people, would it, Mr Ledesma?'

Lally smiles the smile of a doting God. 'I'll certainly be giving you some camera time, Pastor, don't you worry. The world will be yours.'

'Oh my,' Gibbons does the coy padre off that ole army hospital show. 'All right, Vernon,' he says, nudging me toward the door. 'The Lord helps those who help themselves . . .'

'See you there,' says Mom.

Lally follows us onto the porch. As soon as we're out of Mom's sight, he grabs my ear and twists it hard. 'This is the way forward, little man – don't blow it.'

Son of a stadium full of bitches. I rub my ear on the way to the New Life Center; the pastor listens to the radio as he drives, nose up to the windscreen. He doesn't talk to me at all. We pass Leona Dunt's house, with the fountain in front. Her trash is out four days early again. That's to help you take stock of all the rope-handled boutique bags, and razor-edged boxes barfing tissue and ribbon. You could sell her a fucken turd if it was giftwrapped, I swear.

The Lozano boys are out hawking T-shirts on the corner of Liberty Drive. One design has 'I survived Martirio' splattered across it in red. Another has holes ripped through it, and says: 'I went to Martirio and all I got was this lousy exit wound.' Preacher Gibbons tuts, and shakes his head.

'Twenty dollars,' he says. 'Twenty dollars for a simple cotton T-shirt.'

I slouch low in my seat, but not before Emile Lozano sees me. 'Yo, Vermin! Vermin Little!' he whoops and salutes me like a fucken hero or something. The pastor's eyebrows ride up. Thanks, fucken Emile. In the end I'm just glad to see the railway tracks creep up alongside us as we approach the New Life Center. The radio is pissing me off now, to be honest. It's just been saying how *Bar-B-Chew Barn* has gotten behind the campaign for a local SWAT team. Now it's making noise about the hunt for the second firearm. They don't say exactly where they're fixing to hunt; like, they don't say they're specifically going to hunt around Keeter's or anything. If they were going to hunt around the Keeter property, you'd think they'd say it.

The New Life Center is actually our ole church. Today the lawn and carpark have been turned into a carnival market, a laundry-day of tousled whites flapping under the sun. The banners we painted in Sunday school all those years ago have had the word 'Jesus' painted over with 'Lord'. I help the pastor unload the car and carry stuff to a cake stand right next to the train tracks. He installs me there, as caretaker of the cake stand, and – get this – I have to wear a fucken choir gown. Vernon Gucci Little, in his unfashionable Jordan New Jacks, with fucken choir gown. After ten minutes, the morning freight train lumbers past my back, honking all the while. It never honks if you don't stand here in a fucken choir gown.

You don't know how full my head is of plans to disappear. The crusher is that I got identified by Pam at the bus depot, so they'll just be waiting for my face to show up again. Truth be told, they probably installed a fucken panic button or something, In Case of Vernon. Probably connected it to Vaine Gurie's ass. Or Goosens's pecker or something. It means I'll have to cross country to the interstate, maybe find a truck on its way from Surinam, or a driver who hasn't seen the news, a blind and deaf driver. Plenty of 'em out there, if you listen to Pam.

As the sun pitches high and sharp, more folk wander into the market. You can tell they're making an effort not to seem drained and bleak. Drained and bleak is what town's about these days, despite the joy cakes. They ain't setting the world on fire with sales, I have to say. Everybody keeps a safe distance from the joy cakes. Or from me, I guess. Mr Lechuga even turns his desk away from me, over by the prize tent, where he's selling lottery tickets. After a while Lally and my ole lady arrive. You can't actually see them yet, but you can hear Mom's Burt Bacharach disc playing somewhere. It cuts through the gloom like a pencil through your lung. Nobody else would have that disc, I fucken guarantee it, with all these jingle singers going, 'Something big is what I'm livin for,' all tappetty-shucksy, bubbly silk pie, just the way she likes. A typical stroke-job of musical lies, like everybody grew up with back then, back when all the tunes had a trumpet in them, that sounded like it was played through somebody's ass.

'Well hi Bobbie, hi Margaret!' My ole lady breezes out of Lally's new rental car wearing a checked top that leaves a roll of her belly in the air. I guess she quit mourning already. She also has sparkly red sunglasses. All she needs is a fucken poodle to carry, I swear. The vacuum in her ass no longer sucks her hair into a helmety perm, now it hangs wanton and loose.

Lally wanders up to my stall and prods a joy cake. 'Turnover?'

'Four-fifty,' I say.

'The smiles on these cakes aren't even facing the right way – come on, Vern, lure the bucks in – these aren't the only cakes in the world, you know.'

'Thank fuck for that,' I want to say, but I don't. You'd think I had though, for the fucken daggers he stares at me. Then he just strolls away.

'Nice gown,' he snorts over his shoulder.

Mom lingers back. 'Go ahead, Lalito, I'll see you at the sizzle.' Her eyes flick over the crowd, then she sidles up to me like a spy. 'Vernon, are you *all right*?' That's my ole mom. I swell with involuntary warmth.

'I guess so,' I say. That's what you say around here if you mean 'No'.

She fidgets with my collar. 'Well, if you're sure – I only want you to be happy.' That's what you say around here if you mean 'Tough shit'. 'If you could just get a job,' she says, 'make a little money, things'd be fine again, I know they would.' She squeezes my hand.

'Mom, with Eulalio around? *Please . . .*'

'Well don't deny me my bitty speck of happiness, after all that's happened! You always said be *independent* – well, here I am, asserting my *individuality* as a woman.'

'After what he did to me?'

'After what he did to *you*? What about what *you* did to *me*? This is something special with Lally, I know it is. A woman *knows* these things. He already told me about an amazing investment company – over ninety percent return, virtually guaranteed. That's how much they offer, and he told *me* about it, not Leona or anyone else.'

'Yeah, like we have money to invest.'

'Well, I can take out another loan, I mean – *ninety percent*!'

'With that snake-oil merchant?'

'Oh baby – you're *jealous*,' she licks her fingers and rubs a trail of spit across an imaginary smudge on my cheek. 'I still love you the most you know, golly, I mean . . .'

'I know, Ma – even murderers.'

'Hi Gloria, hi Cletus!' She leaves me with a kiss, then sashays east up the stalls, dragging my soul in the dust behind her. Don't even ask me what the laws of fucken nature say about this one. I mean, you see reindeer and polar bears on TV, and you just know they don't get alternating rage and sadness over their fucken loved ones.

Next thing you know, my goddam heart stops beating any-way. Just clean fucken stops in its tracks, the whole damn thing. I immediately fucken die. There, less than ten feet away, steps Mrs Figueroa – Taylor's mom. God, she's beautiful too. The waistband on her denims throws a shadow on her skin, which means there's space in there. Just the up-thrust of her butt keeps her jeans up. Not like my ole lady, who just about needs a fuck-en military harness. My mouth quivers like an asshole, trying to say something cool to win her over, to get Taylor's number. Then I see a fucken choir gown on my body. By the time I look back up, the meatworks' barber has stepped in front of her. He doddles through the crowd towards the beer stand, dressed like he's at a fucken funeral or something.

He bumps into my stall on the way. 'Sorry, miss,' he says to me.

Mrs Figueroa laughs, to finish me off. Then she's gone. The barber catches another ole guy's eye across the beer stand. 'I'm gettin a posse up,' he calls, 'to hep the Guries find that weapon. Cleet, if you're interested, we're headin out in about an hour.'

'Where'll we meet?'

'Meatworks – bring the kids, we'll barbecue after the hunt. We're gonna cover the trail through Keeter's – word is, the teacher Nuckles said somethin about a gun out there, afore he went haywire.'

Jeopardy. I have to get to Keeter's. My eyes search the market for a window of opportunity, but all I see are drapes in the form of Lally, Mom and the goddam pastor. Then I just keep fucken seeing them; with Betty Pritchard, without Betty Pritchard. At Leona's champagne stand, away from Leona's champagne stand. I tingle cold in the heat for a whole hour, then another. Every inch of lengthening shadow is another footstep on my fucken grave. Georgette Porkorney arrives. Betty comes to meet her, they walk past my stand.

'Look, he's just so *passive*,' whispers George. 'Of course he'll fetch trouble if he stays so *passive* . . .'

'I *know*, just like that, ehm – Mexican boy . . .'

George stops to do a double-take at Betty. 'Honey, I don't think passive's the word, in light of everything.'

'I *know* . . .'

The only relief comes with Palmyra; she musses my hair and slips me a Twinkie. Finally, at two o'clock, the pastor goes into the prize tent with Mr Lechuga.

'Bless you all for supporting our market,' a loudspeaker blares. Clumps of people move towards the tent. You can see Mom, Lally, George, and Betty on the far side of the lawn, mooching by Leona's champagne stand. You can't actually see Leona, but you know she's there because Mom throws back her head when she laughs.

'And now,' says Gibbons, 'the moment you've all been waiting for – the grand prize draw!' Everybody turns towards the tent. My window opens.

'Hey dude!' I call a passing kid, of the kind that can't close their lips over their braces, like they have a fucken radiator grille for a mouth or something. 'Wanna job for an hour?'

The kid stops, looks me up and down. 'Not in a freakin dress I don't.'

'It ain't a dress, duh. Anyway, you don't have to wear it, just mind these cakes awhile.'

'How much you payin?'

'Nothing, you get a commission on sales.'

'Flat or indexed?'

'Indexed to what?' Like, the kid's only fucken ten years ole, for chrissakes.

'*Vol*-ume,' he sneers.

'I'll give you eighteen percent, flat.'

'You for real? These stupid cakes? Who ever heard of a *joy* cake anyway, I never heard of no *joy* cake.' He turns to walk away.

'And here's the winning ticket,' says Gibbons. '*Green forty-seven!*' A sluggish frenzy breaks through the tent. The kid stops, and drags a mangled pink ticket from his pocket. He squints at it, like it might turn fucken green. Then Mom's voice occurs.

'Well, oh my Lord! Here Pastor, *green forty-seven*!'

The ladies and Lally clot around her, cooing and gasping, and hustle her into the tent. Boy is she boosted up. My ole lady never won anything before.

'Dude!' I call metal-mouth back.

'Twenty bucks flat, one hour,' he says over his shoulder.

'Yeah, like I'm Bill Gates or something.'

'Twenty-five bucks, or no deal.'

'Here's the lucky winner,' says the pastor, 'of this sturdy, pre-loved refrigerator, generously donated, without a thought for their own grief, by the *Lechugas* of *Beulah Drive*.'

That's the last you hear of my ole lady's voice. Probably forever. What you hear is just Leona.

'Oh – *wow*!'

'Thirty bucks,' the kid says to me, 'flat, one calendar hour. Final offer.'

I'm hung out to fucken dry by this fat midget, who could just about net crawdads with his fucken mouth. Or rather, I would've been hung out to dry if I was even coming back to pay him. But I ain't coming back. Today I'll give the gun a wipe, grab my escape fund from the bank, and blow the hell out of town. For real.

'It's ten after two,' says the kid. 'See you in one hour.'

'Wait up – my watch says quarter after.'

'It's fuckin *ten* after – take it or leave it.'

Whatever. I rip the gown off and stuff it into a box under the table, then I run crouched alongside the railroad tracks toward the green end of Liberty Drive. Preacher Gibbons's voice echoes down the line behind me. 'Speaking of refrigerators, did y'all hear the one about the rabbit?'

Glancing over my shoulder, I see Mom run crying to the restrooms behind the New Life Center. But I can't afford any waves. I have to grab my bike and fly to Keeter's. Strangers mill around Liberty Drive corner, next to a new sign erected in front of the Hearts of Mercy Hospice. 'Coming Soon!' it reads. 'La Elegancia Convention Center.' A real ole man scowls from the hospice porch. I pull my head in and start to cross the street, but a stranger calls out to me.

'Little!' I speed up, but he calls again. 'Little, it's not about you!' The dude must be a reporter. He breaks from a group of roaming media, and steps up to me. 'The red van that used to park next to your house – you seen it around?'

'Yeah, it's at Willard Down's lot.'

'I mean the guy that used to drive it . . .'

'Eulalio, from CNN?'

'Yeah, the guy from Nacogdoches – you seen him?'

'Uh – Nacogdoches?'

'Uh-huh, this guy here – the repairman.' He pulls a crumpled business card from his shirt pocket. '*Eulalio Ledesma Gutierrez*,' it reads, '*President & Service Technician-In-Chief, Care Media Nacogdoches.*'

The stranger shakes his head. 'Bastard owes me money.'

'O Eulalio, yo! Lalio, yo! Lalio, share this fucken challenge now.' That's what I sing on the ride out to Keeter's. I feel Jesus with me in the breeze, happier than usual, not so deathly, maybe because I finally got a fucken break. I'm going to call the number on this card, and get the slimy lowdown on Yoo-hoo-lalio. Then, when that reporter turns up at home later, for his cash, everybody will discover the fucken truth. It means I can leave town knowing my ole lady's okay. This business card is all the artillery I need. What I learned in court is you need artillery.

Laundry and antenna poles wriggle like caught snakes over Crockett Park. This is a neighborhood where underwear sags low. For instance, ole Mr Deutschman lives up here, who used to be upstanding and decent. This is where you live if you *used* to be less worse. Folks who beat up on each other, and clean their own carburetors, live up here. It's different from where I live, closer to town, where everything gets all bottled the fuck up. Just bottled the fuck up till it fucken explodes, so you spend the whole time waiting to see who's going to pop next. I guess a kind of smelly honesty is what you find at Crockett's. A smelly honesty, and clean carburetors.

The last payphone in town stands next to a corrugated metal fence on Keeter's corner, the remotest edge of town. If you live in Crockett's, this is your personal phone. Empty land stretches away behind it into the folds of the Balcones Escarpment, as far as you can imagine. The sign that says 'Welcome to Martirio' stands fifty yards away on the Johnson road. Somebody has crossed out the population number, and written 'Watch this space' over it.

That's fucken Crockett's for you. Smelly honesty, and a sense of humor.

I lean my bike against the fence and step up to the phone. It's twenty-nine minutes after two. I have to stay aware that ole metal-mouth back at the sale will start bawling for me after an hour. I wipe the phone mouthpiece on my pants leg, a thing you learn to do up this end of town, and call up CMN in Nacogdoches. CMN – *CNN* – Get it? Fucken Lally, boy. New York my fucken wiener.

The number rings. A real ole lady answers. 'He-llo?'

'Uh, hello – I'm wondering if Eulalio Ledesma works there?'

You hear the ole gal catch her breath. 'Who is this?'

'This is, uh – Bradley Pritchard, in Martirio.'

'Well, I only have what's left in my purse . . .' Coins clatter onto a tabletop at her end. You sense it ain't going to be a quick call.

'Ma'am, I'm not calling for anything, I just wanted . . .'

'Seven dollars and thirty cents – no – around eight dollars is all I have, for groceries.'

'I didn't mean to trouble you, ma'am – I thought this was a business number.'

'That's right – "*Care*" – I had cards printed for Lalo, "*Care Media Nacogdoches*," that's the name he chose. You tell Jeannie Wyler this was never a tinpot operation – we moved my bed into the hallway to make space for his office, to help him get started.'

Mixed feelings I get. Like Lally falling off a cliff chained to my nana. 'Ma'am, I'm sorry I troubled you.'

'Well, the president isn't here right now.'

'I know, he's down here – you must've seen him on TV these days?'

'That's in very poor taste young man. Why, I've been blind for thirty years.'

'I'm real sorry, ma'am.'

'Have *you* seen him? Have *you* seen my Lalo?'

'As a matter of fact, he's staying at my – uh – friend's house.'

'Oh heavens, let me find a pen . . .'

Another bunch of stuff clatters down the line. I stand here and wonder how you read and write when you're blind. I guess you etch lines that you can feel with your fingers, like in clay or something. Or cheese, carry cheese around all the time.

'I know it's here somewhere,' she says. 'You tell Lalo the finance company took everything, they wouldn't wait another second for payment on the van, and now the Wylers are suing over their video camera. Imagine that! – and I was the one who talked them into repairing it in the first place. Those cameras don't fix themselves overnight you know, that's what I told her. I just wish everything wasn't in my name . . .'

She finds the cheese, and I give her my phone number. My early joy has melted now, with the serious reality of things. I say goodbye to the lady and ride away towards the escarpment, to find the gun. Jesus rides with me in spirit. He stays silent. I've changed the course of Fate, and it weighs on me heavy.

Bushes on Keeter's trail are bizarre, all spiky and gnarled, with just enough clearing between them so the unknown is never more than fifteen yards away. Not many creatures come this far into Keeter's. Me and Jesus are the only ones I know. Last time I saw him alive at Keeter's, he was in the far distance.

Ole man Keeter owns this empty slab of land, miles of it probably, outside town. He put a wrecking shop by the ole Johnson road, *Keeter's Spares & Repairs* – just a mess of junk in the dirt, really. He doesn't even run it anymore. When we say Keeter's around here, we usually mean the land, not the auto shop. You might see some steers on it, or deer; but mostly just bleached beer cans and shit. The edge of the universe of town. Martirio boys suck their first taste of guns, girls and beer out here. You never forget the blade of wind that cuts across Keeter's.

In the thick of the property lies a depression in the ground, sixty-one yards across, with wire and bushes matted around it. At the steepest end is an ole mine shaft. The den, we call it. We rigged up a door with some sheets of tin, and put a padlock on it and all.

It was our headquarters, during those carefree years. That's where I took a shit the other day, the day of the tragedy, if you need to know. That's where the rifle is stashed.

It's two thirty-eight in the afternoon. Hot and sticky, with fast-moving clouds bunched low across the sky. I get to within two hundred yards of the den and hear a hammer-blow. Something moves in the bushes up ahead. It's ole Tyrie Lasseen, who runs *Spares & Repairs*, sinking markers into the ground. He's dressed in a suit and tie. He jackrabbits before I can hide.

'Okay, son?' he calls. 'Don't be touchin nothin, could be dangerous.'

'Sure, Mr Lasseen, I'm just cruising . . .'

'I wouldn't recommend you cruise around here, maybe you better head back to the road.'

Tyrie is the kind of Texan who takes his time telling you to fuck off. He shuffles three steps towards me, and wipes some sweat from the top of his head. His eyes crinkle like barbed wire snagged with horsehair, and his mouth hangs open a little. Ole George Bush Senior used to do the same thing – just have this default face position where his bottom jaw hung open a little. Like these guys listen through their mouths or something.

'Sir, I'm just passing through to the San Marcos road, I won't touch anything at all.'

Mr Lasseen stands there and listens, through his mouth; his tongue lolls like a snake inside. Then these rusty sounds slither onto the breeze. 'The San Marcos road? The *San Marcos* road? Son, I don't recommend takin this way to the San Marcos road. I recommend you head on back to the Johnson road, and ride around it.'

'But, the thing is . . .'

'Son, the best thing I recommend is to get yourself back onto the Johnson road. I recommend that, and don't be pokin around here no more – this'll be a restricted area just now.' His jaw drops even lower, to hear any stray comeback, then he throws a finger at town. 'Go on now.'

Weeds blow across the trail home, corrugated metal sheets flap, and with their creaks come the sound of dogs barking. I have only one chance left to reach the gun. When Lasseen is safely out of sight, I edge my front wheel off the track and rocket through the wilds in an arc that will take me around him, to the back of the den. Bushes squat lower on this part of Keeter's, joined by tall grasses and chunks of household debris. I nearly smash into a nest of toilet bowls, abandoned in the undergrowth like some kind of vegetarian pinball machine. As I slalom through them, I see a *Bar-B-Chew Barn* cap up ahead. Voices waft down on a breeze.

'Who cares about ole *nature*,' says a kid.

'It's not *just* nature, Steven – there might be a *gun*.'

It's the meatworks posse. I know it even before the marching band strikes up. I lay down the bike and huddle into the nest of bowls, trying to gauge the distance between me and the dogs working their way from the town side. It's four minutes to three. Kids start to surround my position. I crouch low.

'Bernie?' says a little voice.

'*Wha?*' My nerves half electrocute me to fucken death.

I spin my head around. Behind a bush at my back crouches Ella Bouchard. She's a girl from Crockett's, who used to go to my junior school. Believe me, you don't want to fucken know.

'Hi, Bernie,' she says, shuffling closer.

'*Shhh*, willya! I'm tryin to rest a little here, *God*.'

'Looks like you're hidin out to me, that's what it looks like, to me anyway . . .'

'Ella – it's real urgent that nobody disturbs me right now – okay?'

Her smile falters. She watches me through big blue eyes, like doll's eyes or something. 'Wanna see my south pole?' Her dusty ole knees part a little, a flash of panty shines out.

'Shit, come *on*, willya? *Hell*,' I blow extra air out of my cheeks with the words, like a Democrat or whatever. I still look, though.

It's automatic with panties, don't tell me it ain't. Ole cotton there, stretched gray, like fucken airplanes use her to land on.

'Can I just hang out – Bernie?' She closes back her legs.

'*Shhh!* Anyway, my name's not even Bernie, *duh*.'

'It is *too* Bernie, or somethin like that, it's Bernie or *somethin* like that.'

'Listen – can't I owe you or something? Can't we hang out another time?'

'If it's true, and for actual real, maybe. Like when?'

'Well I don't know, just sometime, next time or whatever.'

'Promise?'

'Yeah I promise.'

I feel her breath lapping at my face, Juicy-Fruit breath, hot and solid like piss. I turn my back, to invite her to crawl away, but she doesn't. I can tell she's staring.

'Fucken *what*?' I say, spinning around on her.

She throws a weak smile. 'I love you Bernie.' Then, with a thump of plastic sandal, and a swish of blue cotton, she's gone. It's five minutes after three. Your eyes automatically check when it's time for deep shit, in case you hadn't noticed.

'Okay team, stop here for the first item in your snack-packs!' yells a lady. 'That's the item with the *red* label, the *red*-label item only.'

'Don't go there, boys,' you hear Tyrie Lasseen call in the distance. 'That's an ole mine shaft, stay well away.' Relief scuds through me as Tyrie warns them away from the den. Then another cluster of voices comes near.

'Todd,' says a lady, 'I told you to go before we left the meatworks. Just use one of these bushes, nobody can see.' You hear a dorkball squeak something in back, then the lady says: 'Well you ain't gonna find one out here, this ain't the *mall*, in case you hadn't noticed.'

We don't even have a fucken mall, by the way. Notice how folks always throw in that extra smart-assed thing when the media's around. They just pick the first fucken thing to say, like the mall or whatever.

'Use those toilet bowls, over there,' calls some asshole in a fake girl's voice.

'Hey, yeah,' says a lady, 'I saw some toilet bowls around here somewhere – maybe that'll help you pretend.'

'Wait up!' says Ella Bouchard. 'You better not use them potties – snakes sleep in 'em.'

'Oh my God,' says the lady. 'Todd, wait! I better come with you.'

They crackle through the bushes into my nest. I stand out of the dirt and pick up my bike, casually, like I'm in the freezer section at the Mini-Mart or something.

'It's the psycho!' says the kid.

'Shhh, Todd, don't be silly,' says the lady. She turns to me. 'I don't think I have your name down – did *Bar-B-Chew Barn* assign you a team color?'

'Uh – green?' I say.

'Can't be green, it can only be a color from their logo.' She pulls out her phone. 'I'll call Mrs Gurie and check the list – what's your name again?'

'Uh – Brad Pritchard.'

'*Brad Pritchard?* But we already have a Brad Pritchard . . .'

There comes a wet rustle from the bushes, like a dog eating lettuce, then Brad tiptoes into the clearing with Mini-Mart bags tied over his Timberlands. He points out a cloud with his nose. 'That's nouvelle; having the convict look for his own gun.'

'Vaine?' says the lady into her phone. 'I think we need some assistance.'

I jump onto my bike and hit the pedals hard. Dirt spews across the clearing.

Girls giggle, camera tool-belts rattle, and in amongst them as I ride away, ride like the fucken wind itself, you hear Brad Pritchard faking a dumb girl's voice. 'Hey, *Bernie* – wanna see my *south pole?*'

I spin twisters along the track to town. My only option is to hit the fucken road. Right away. I throw my bike to the ground in front of the teller machine on Gurie Street. I love my bike, but I just crash it the fuck down. It ain't a fancy bike, but it's strong, and used to belong to my grand-daddy, back when the town still only had two roads. I crash it down. That's the kind of twisted shit this life has in store for you, guaranteed.

I put my bank card into the machine, and tap in the code – 6768. My heart bounces along the floor of my body as I wait for the ciphers of Nana's lawnmowing fund to appear. After nine years, a message jumps to the screen.

'Balance – $2.41,' it says.

ten

I have no option but to spin home and grab stuff to pawn or sell. It's after four when I reach the house, willing it to be empty. Empty. Like: yeah, right. Lally's rental car is out front. I enter like a ghost through the kitchen screen. At first everything's quiet inside. Then there's a knock at the front door. An air-dam of perfume collapses into the hall. I freeze.

'Shhh, Vernon, I'll get the front door.' Mom scuttles over the rug like a hamster.

'Do-*ris?*' the kitchen screen opens behind me. Leona wafts in, flouncing her hair.

'Shhh – Lally's *sleeping!*' hisses Mom.

Get that. When my daddy used to doze on the sofa after a few beers, she'd put on high heels and clomp around the kitchen, just to wake him up. I swear to God. She'd *pretend* to be doing stuff that required clomping, but she wasn't actually doing anything at all. She'd clomp back and forth for no reason, instead of just saying 'Wake up'. That was in the days after he hit me, after things went kind of sour.

A bedspring creaks up the hallway. Mom gently opens the front door to the reporter Lally owes money to. 'Afternoon, ma'am, is Eelio Lemeda here?'

'Lally? Well, he's here, but he's indisposed right now – can I tell him who called?'

'I'll wait, if you don't mind.'

'Well he shouldn't be much longer.'

The toilet flushes deep in the house. The bathroom door bangs, and Lally stomps down the hall. 'Vanessa, have you seen my therapy bag?'

'No, Lalito – anyway, I think you're all out of your gin-sling things.'

Fucken *Vanessa*? I search her face for clues. One thing you notice is her cheeks are all proud and peachy, like when she eats ice-cream in important company. Her eyelashes flutter double-time.

'Van*essa*?' says Leona.

Mom blushes. 'Well I'll explain just now.'

She hides another final notice from the power company behind the cookie jar, then goes to fuss over Lally, who only has his robe on, you can just about see his cock flapping all over the place. If you had a fucken electron microscope you could just about see it. He strides into the kitchen with this smile full of teeth, and grazes a hand to Leona's butt as he passes. She gives a wiggle.

'Lally,' says Mom, 'there's someone at the front door for you.'

'For *me*?' His smile stiffens. Joy wells up in my heart. As he turns to the door, I tackle Mom into the corner of the kitchen.

'Ma, go check Lally's visitor – fast! Go on now!'

'Well Vernon, what on earth's gotten into you? That's Lally's private business.'

'No it ain't, Ma, quick – it's real important.'

'Oh, Vernon – *cope* for God's sake.' She flashes her creamiest-pie smile as George and Betty clack into the kitchen, in the middle of one of their typical conversations.

'Honey, no way,' says George, 'just being a shareholder doesn't mean he has to buy that whole ridiculous SWAT thing of Vaine's. Can you imagine? She can't even keep her damn flab under control, let alone a team of gunmen!'

'I know, I know.'

I try to shunt my ole lady up to the front door, to witness Lally's shame, but her skin-tight pants don't make her any lighter; she won't budge at all.

Lally opens the door to the man. 'Don't tell me – you're on a recovery mission.'

'Yeah, if you can spare it,' says the guy.

'Here you go, fifty dollars – and thanks.'

Now Mom grabs me by the shoulders – fucken *me*, no less – and spins me into the corner. 'Vernon, don't tell your nana, but I had to raid the lawnmowing fund to help Lally. His camera equipment wiped the code from his Visa card. I'll put it back as soon as my loan is approved.'

'Ma, I *needed* that money . . .'

'Well Vernon Gregory, you know that's Nana's lawnmowing account, and it's supposed to be earning interest for your college fund.'

'Yeah, like you get a whole *pile* of interest off fifty dollars.'

'Well I know it's not much, but it's all I have – just a mother on my own.'

Lally finishes with the reporter, but he doesn't come inside. Does he fuck. Instead he stands on the porch and hollers: 'Park in the driveway, Preacher – the girls won't be leaving for a while.' He leaves the front door open, and swaggers into the kitchen, passing me by without a glance.

'Lally, I forgot to mention,' says Mom, 'a lady called for you, from the network I think.'

'A lady?' Lally's hand twitches over his crotch.

'Uh-huh, she sounded very senior – she'll call back later.'

'She didn't leave a name?'

'Well she said it was your office – I told her to call back.'

One of Lally's eyes snaps to me. A quivery eye. Then he grabs Mom around the belly and says, 'Thanks, Vanessa – you're indispensable.'

'Van-*essa*?' say the ladies.

Mom swells. 'Well, I can't tell you much now – can I, Lalito?'

'Suffice to say,' says Lally, 'the network was impressed with her appearance the other day. No promises, but we could be seeing a lot more of her – when the right strategies are in place.'

'I'll always be the same old Doris to you girls, though, you know I won't change a bit, deep down.'

Check Leona. Her mouth flaps empty of words for a moment, then she goes, 'Wow, it's weird because, did I tell you guys my new dialogue coach is sending my reel to the networks? Right after I get back from Hawaii – *God*, that's so *weird*, isn't it . . .?'

Mom just snuggles back into Lally's arms. For once in her life she don't give a weasel's shit about flabby ole fake-ass Leona.

'*Vanessa Le Bourget*,' Lally says into my ole gal's ear. 'Boor-*jay*,' he croons, like the cartoon skunk off TV, the one that always tries to fuck the cat. Mom just about shits on the floor when she hears it. Leona nearly bursts out fucken bawling. Lally's on a roll. I just let him roll. 'Tch, I can't wait to share you with the crew back in New York, you'll just love those guys.'

'Well don't be impatient, Lalito, everything has its time. Meanwhile you'll have everything you need, even though it's just lil' ole me, in this itty-bitty town.'

'You can say *itty* again – damn hole doesn't even have a sushi bar!'

'Not like Nacogdoches,' I say.

'Nacog-*doches*?' says Betty. Lally shoots me the devil's eye.

'Bwanas tardies,' booms the pastor, stepping through the door like he's a fucken Meskin all of a sudden. Bwanas tardies my fucken ass.

'C'mon in, Preacher,' says Lally. 'Can I fix you a loosener?' Lally's eye doesn't scan my way anymore. His eye has a new scanning pattern.

'Thanks, but no,' says Gibbons, 'I have to get that refrigerator moved into the media center – it's a mighty fine donation, I can't thank y'all enough.'

'Vernon, perhaps you'll explain to the pastor why you abandoned his charity stall today,' says Lally. Tension turns the air in the room to crystals.

'I got a stomach ache.'

'Surely,' he says, 'a person bailed for murder would do better to . . .'

106

'I'm not even on bail for murder, I'm a goddam *accessory* to Jesus Navarro's murders – *fuck*!'

Lally leans in like a whip and smacks the back of my head. 'Control yourself!'

I fill with acid blood. Mom starts to bawl in the corner, making it as difficult as possible for the ladies to maneuver her to the sofa.

'Such *aggression* in that boy,' says George. 'He was bound to fetch trouble, with so much aggression.'

'I know, *I know* – just like that, ehm – other boy . . .'

A dizzy feeling comes over me as I hit the ring-end of my fucken tether. I pull Lally's business card out of my pocket, and hold it up in the air. 'Everybody – I called *Yoo-lalio's* office today, and guess who answered? His blind *momma*, who just had her house emptied by the finance company on account of his van repayments.' Lally's eyes turn to coal. 'Now she's facing a lawsuit over the camcorder he *stole*. Did you know he's actually a TV repairman, who works out of his momma's bedroom in Nacogdoches?'

'Oh *please*,' says Lally. He squeezes his balls but forgets to let go.

I glance over the bar. The ladies are way perked up. Land of Daytime Milk and Honey for them. I pose dramatically, hoganger makes me do it. 'You think I lie? I guarantee his mother's gonna call here just now, hunting his ass. I guarantee it. Just ask her the story.' A smile comes to my face, know why? Because Lally's turning white. Everybody stares at him as he leans into the corner, wiping his face with his hand.

'Tch, that's *preposterous*. The evil lies coming from this child's mouth.' He takes a heavy breath, then turns and spreads his arms to the ladies. 'Hands up who ever heard of a features reporter moonlighting as a repairman?' Everybody shakes their heads. 'And why might that be?'

'Well, because – there's more *money* in reporting?' sniffs Mom. 'He wouldn't *need* to repair TVs, with all that extra *money*.'

'I rest my case.'

'Wait up,' I say, 'I didn't say he moonlighted as anything – he's just a repairman with a whole pile of trouble left back in Nacogdoches. Look at his card, go on.'

'Ladies,' says Lally, 'this is ridiculous. Do you know how many Ledesma Gutierrezes there are in this country? And have you ever seen me repair a TV?'

'No,' they say.

'Have you ever seen me *on* TV, presenting a feature report?'

'Well sure,' they say, motioning the pastor to join in. 'We were in it with you!'

'Thank you,' says Lally. He turns to stare at me. 'And now, in light of everything we've just heard, and, frankly, for our own protection – I'm calling the police.'

'Oh no, Lally, *please*,' says Mom.

'Sorry, Vanessa – I'm afraid it's my duty. The boy needs urgent help.'

Then, just as my world starts to slip through my fingers, Fate plays a humdinger. The phone rings. Mom gasps to a halt, mid-fucken-sob. Everybody freezes.

'I'll get that,' says Lally.

'I don't think so,' I say, diving for the phone. 'Mom, come take this call.'

My ole lady hunches off the sofa, all shiny around the nose and eyes, and does her finest victimmy shuffle to the phone table. She looks around at everybody, especially Lally, before picking up the phone. A pleading kind of look she gives Lally, real Kicked Dog. Then her voice smoothens like cream. 'Hello? Mr Ledesma, well sure – may I say who's calling?' She hands the phone to Lally. 'It's CNN.'

I grab it back. 'Mrs Ledesma?'

'*Vernon!*' snaps Mom.

'Remember me? From Martirio . . .?'

'*Who is this?*' asks the young New Yorker on the phone. Lally snatches the receiver and turns to the wall.

'Renée? Sorry about that – things are a little crazy down here.

I got the series? Fan-*tastic*!' He raises a thumb to the ladies. 'Conditional on what? Not a challenge, we still have the firearm piece, the suspect, and the townsfolk coming to terms with their grief. It can spin-off in a thousand directions.'

'Well you know,' whispers Mom to the ladies, 'I couldn't decide between *Vanessa* and *Rebecca* . . .'

'I was coping with *Doris*,' grunts George.

Lally finishes the call. He dangles the receiver over the cradle, taking a moment to gaze at everybody. The ladies stare into his eyes, Pastor Gibbons toys in his pocket. Then Lally drops the handset, 'Crack', cups his balls through his robe, and strolls to the middle of the room. 'Before we open the champagne, I guess we have a rather more – human challenge to share.' His eyes snap to me. 'Pretty outlandish behavior we saw there, Vernon. Damn scary, actually, in light of everything.'

'Fuck you to hell,' I say.

'Vernon *Gregory*!' snaps Mom.

Lally pushes a little spit around his mouth. 'Simple compassion dictates that it's time to turn this boy over to someone who can help. If we cling when he needs professional care, we may only damage his chances of recovery.'

'*You're* the one who needs care,' I say. '*Lalo*.'

'You *are* under a psychiatric order, after all.' He pauses to chuckle, to reminisce. 'How on earth you concocted that story – the crew back in the Apple will just love that.' He checks his watch. 'Come to think of it, they're probably down at *Bunty's* right now.'

Mom hisses a footnote to the ladies. 'They have this bar called *Bunty's*, you probably heard of it – *Bunty's*?'

'Or at the *Velvet Mode*, for melon slammers,' says Lally. 'I might have to give them a call. Right after I contact the sheriff.'

'Well Lally, *please*,' says Mom. 'Can't we just wait till morning, I mean, he had a stomach ache – he does have this, er – condition . . .'

The phone rings. Everybody's face lights up, as if more big deals will trickle down the line. But Lally tightens. This is where the horse would stop doing math on stage. I reach for the handset. He beats me to it.

'Le Bourget residence?' He tries to flash a good ole boy's grin to the ladies, but a quiver beats him to it. 'I'm sorry, you must have the wrong number.' His breathing quickens.

I dive around his legs and hit the speaker button. Mrs Ledesma's voice wails out.

'Lalo, oh my God, Lalo? I ran out of groceries, Lalo, please . . .'

Lally's lips dance uncontrollably, his eyes flash across the room. 'Oh – oh it's you,' he trembles.

'How could you leave me so long,' cries the lady. '*Es que no queda nada Eulalio, hasta mi cama se lo han llevado . . .*'

'Tell us in English!' I yell toward the phone. Lally's foot whips off the floor, dislodging me backwards onto the rug. He switches off the speaker.

'Oh you poor souls,' he says into the phone. 'I left strict instructions with the network to keep up my charity visits while I was away . . .' I go for the speaker button again, but he keeps me at bay with his leg. 'Yes, I know, sweetheart – but mental illness can be cured, that's why I contribute, that's why I share myself with your cause – you and all the other beautiful ladies at the home . . .'

I reach the far side of the phone table on my belly, but Lally quickly says goodbye, and slams down the phone. It rings again. He rips the cable from the wall. All breathing in the room gets canceled, along with platelet aggregation and whatever else your body does for kicks.

Lally turns to face everybody. 'I guess I have – something to share.' I squint through a waterline of smoke, to the dark of the sofa where the ladies sit, riveted. Their knees stick tight together. 'Some time ago, I decided to share my resources with the less fortunate.'

'Amen,' says the pastor softly.

Lally's face falls. 'I surprised myself – I'd been so ambitious, so wrapped up in *Me*. Then I became involved with real people – real problems.' He pauses to dab a finger at the corner of his eye. 'The voice you just heard is one of my ladies – one of my Sunshine Souls.'

'Wow, she sounded so *together*,' says Leona.

'Shhh, Loni, *God*,' says George.

'Tragic, isn't it?' says Lally. 'Confined through no fault of her own. They all are.'

'Bull-*shit*,' I say.

'Vernon Gregory, that's *enough*,' says Mom.

'Were you – *supporting* them?' asks George.

Lally sighs. 'Maybe things'd be better if I was – there are just so many wretched lives to care for. And I have so little to give . . .'

'No, son,' scalds the pastor, 'you're giving the greatest gift of all – Christian love.'

Lally shrugs helplessly. 'If you see me a little short of cash – you now know why. I just feel so guilty having anything at all.' His eyes crawl over the sofa, snuggling into the ladies' pouts, sliding down their weeping lashes, before collapsing on the floor. He shakes his head. 'I guess the real tragedy is – they now know where I'm staying.'

It takes a full second for Spooked Deer to take hold of Mom. She twitches. 'Well – why is that tragic?'

He flicks a glossy eye at me, sighs. 'The home's strictest rule is non-disclosure of carers' identities. If they found out about this, I could be prevented from giving in future. I don't know if I could survive a month without visiting my special girls. It means – I'll have to move along.'

There's a stunned silence. Then my ole lady implodes. 'Well God, Lally, *no*, I mean – *no*, *God* . . .'

'I'm sorry, Doris. This is bigger than the two of us.'

'But we can disconnect the phone, change the number . . . Lalito? You can't walk out after this whole month of bliss.'

'*Week* of bliss,' corrects Lally. 'I'm sorry. Maybe if Vernon hadn't called the home, maybe if he didn't harbor such a grudge – but no. Things'll only get more challenging after I call the sheriff.'

'Shoot,' says George, 'I'd call him myself if he wasn't tied up at the *Barn* meeting.'

Trickles then torrents of blood and vein soak through the bottom of Mom's legs, her brownest organs sweat through her pores. In the end just these pleading eyes poke up, the eyes of a well-kicked dog. Squished Kitten even.

Leona watches her quiver become a sob, then turns to Lally. 'There's space at my place.'

'My *God*,' he says. 'The pure charity of this town . . .'

Mom's eyes pop. 'Well, but, but, the home might find you *there*, as *well* – that woman, she could just as easy find you at Leona's as here . . .'

'I'm unlisted,' says Leona with a shrug. 'I have call-screening and closed-circuit security.'

Mom's eyes fall to the tan-line where her wedding ring once sat. 'Well but Vernon could just as easily give that number to the patients, you saw his behavior – couldn't you, Vernon, just give Leona's number to the home . . .?'

'Ma, the guy's a goddam psycho, I swear to God.'

'Well see? He could call them right now, see his attitude? I think Lally and I should take a room at the Seldome for a while . . . Lalito? And do all those other things you want to do, around town . . .?'

'Tch, the Seldome's full.'

'Well but they'd always find space for *me*, I mean, I was *married* at the Seldome.'

Leona picks her bag off the sofa and fishes in it for her keys. 'Offer's open.'

My ole lady's already halfway across the room. 'What's the Seldome's number?'

Lally reaches out to stop her. 'Doris – that's not all.' He fumbles in his shirt pocket and pulls out two crumpled joints. 'Vernon didn't do such a good job hiding these.'

'*Cigarettes?*' asks Mom.

'Illegal drugs. You'll understand now why I can't be associated with the boy.' He throws the spliffs scornfully onto the coffee table, leaning past me to whisper, 'Thanks for the story.'

In the background you hear Leona's car keys drop into George's lap. 'I guess I'll ride with Lally. Take the Eldorado when you're ready – it'll need some gas.'

'*We* have a spare room,' says Betty. 'We haven't used Myron's studio since he died.'

Lally and Leona clack out through the screen into a dirty afternoon. A promise of rain on dust puffs through the door behind them. To Mom I know it smells of their sex.

'I'll be back for my stuff,' calls Lally. Mom's skin has all melted together. Her face drips down her arms onto her lap.

I run a step after him. 'How'd you know it said Gutierrez on the card, motherfucker? How'd you know it said Ledesma *Gutierrez*, when you didn't even look at the card?' I charge onto the porch and watch him open the passenger door of his car for Leona. Then you see the Lechugas' drapes twitch open a crack. Leona flaps a little wave towards it, from behind her back. The drapes close.

I'm a kid whose best friend took a gun into his mouth and blew off his hair, whose classmates are dead, who's being blamed for it all, who just broke his mama's heart – and as I drag myself inside under the weight of these slabs of moldy truth, into my dark, brown ole life – another learning flutters down to perch on top. A learning like a joke, that kicks the last breath from my system. The Lechugas' drapes. It's how Mom's so-called friends coordinate their uncannily timed assaults on my home. They still have a hotline to Nancie Lechuga's.

eleven

I stand on the porch this Sunday evening and try to force Mexico to appear in front of me. I tried it all day from the living-room window, but it didn't work. By this time tonight I imagined cactus, fiestas, and salty breath. The howls of men in the back of whose lives lurked women called Maria. Instead there's a house like Mrs Porter's across the street, a willow like the Lechugas' and a pump-jack next door, dressed as a mantis; pump, pump, pump. Vernon Gridlock Little.

'Lord God in heaven *please* let me have a side-by-side, let me open my eyes and it be there . . .'

Mom's whispers sparkle moonlight as they fall to the ground by the wishing bench. Then Kurt barks from Mrs Porter's yard. Kurt is in trouble with Mrs Porter. He spent all day on the wrong side of the fence from the Hoovers' sausage sizzle, and eventually destroyed Mrs Porter's sofa out of frustration. Fucken Kurt, boy. His barks cover the creaking of planks as I step off the porch. It's a well-upholstered barking circuit tonight, on account of the *Bar-B-Chew Barn* hayride. A hayride, gimme a break. We don't even have fucken *hay* around here, they probably had to buy it on the web or something. But no, now it's the traditional Martirio Hayride.

'Oh Lord God, bring Lally back, bring Lally back, bring Lally back . . .'

It's been a long day. Cameras pinned me in the house since Lally left yesterday. Now they went to cover the hayride. Mom senses me approaching her willow; she sobs louder, and gets a hysterical edge to her voice, to make sure I don't miss the implication of things. A large flying bug scoots behind the mantis as I step close.

'Wishing bench is airborne this end,' I say, to break the ice. 'Like the dirt's caving in underneath.'

'Well Vernon just *shutup*! – you did this to me, all this – all this *fucking shit*.'

She cussed me, boy. Hell. I study her ole hunched body. Her hair is sucked back into a helmet again, and she wears her regular toweling slippers with the butterflies on top, their rubber wings torn off by the white cat she used to have, before the Lechugas ran it over. I'm compelled to reach out and touch her. I touch her where the flab from her back dams under her armpit, and feel the clammy weight of her ole miserable shell, all warm and spent. She cries so cleanly you'd think her body was a drum full of tears that just spill out through the holes.

I sit down beside her. 'Ma, I'm sorry.'

She gives an ironic kind of laugh, I guess it's ironic when you laugh while you sob. After that she just stays sobbing. I look around at the night; things are liquid-clear, warm and dewy, with a snow of moths and bugs around the porch lights, and distant music from the hayride.

'Papa always said I'd amount to nothing.'

'Don't say that, Ma.'

'Well it's true, look at me. It's always been true. "Just plain ungainly," Papa used to say, "Ornery and ungainly." Everyone was head of the cheerleading squad, and homecoming queen, and class president. Everyone was Betty, all sparkling and fresh . . .'

'Betty *Pritchard*? Gimme a break.'

'Well Vernon, you just know *everything*, don't you! Betty was class president in the fourth grade you know, and had all the bubbly parts in school plays – she never cussed or smoked or drank like the rest of us; bright as sunshine, she used to be. Until she started getting beaten black and blue by her father, whipped till she bled. So while you're all critical, and know everything about everyone, just remember the rest of us are only human. It's *cause and effect*, Vernon, you just don't realize – even *Leona* was relaxed and sweet, before her first husband went, you know – the other way.'

'The one that died?'

'No, not the one that died. The first one, and out of consideration you shouldn't even ask.'

'Sorry.'

She takes a breath, wiping her eyes with the palm of her hand. 'I lost a few pounds for the prom, though. I proved Papa wrong, just that once. Den Gurie asked me to be his date – *Den Gurie*, the *linebacker*! – I slept under the shawl of my prom dress all week.'

'There you go – see?'

'He picked me up in his brother's truck. I almost fainted from excitement, and from hunger, I guess, but he told me to relax, said it'd be like spending a night with my kin . . .' Mom starts to hiss from the back of her throat, like a cat. It's another way to weep, in case you didn't know. The early part of a strong weep.

'So what happened?'

'We drove out of town, sang songs nearly all the way to Lockhart. Then he asked me to check the tailgate on the truck. When I climbed out, he drove away and left me. That's when I saw the hog farm by the road.'

A bolt of anger takes me, about the fucken Guries, about the ways of this fucken town. The anger cuts through waves of sadness, cuts through pictures of young Jesus, the one who nailed himself to a fucken cross before anybody else could do it. That's why this town's angry. They didn't get a shot at him. But they don't have anger like I have anger brewing up. Anger cuts through a wide range of things. Cuts like a knife.

After a second, I feel the dampness of Mom's hand on mine. She squeezes it. 'You're all I have in the world. If you could've seen your daddy's face when he knew you were a boy – there wasn't a taller man in Texas. All the great things you were going to be when you grew up . . .' She narrows puffy eyes into the distance, through Mrs Porter's house, through the town, and the world, to where the cream pie lives. The future, or the past, or wherever it fucken lives. Then she shoots me this brave little smile, a genuine smile, too quick for her to pull any victimmy shit. As she does it, violins shimmer into the air across town, like in a movie. Even Kurt hangs silent as a guitar picks its way out of the orchestra, and a Texan voice from long ago herds our souls up into the night. Christopher Cross starts to sing 'Sailing'. Mom's favorite tune from before I was even born, before her days fell dark. Type of song you listen to when you think nobody likes you. She gives a broken sigh. I know right away the song will remind me of her forever.

It's not far down to paradise, at least it's not for me
And if the wind is right you can
sail away
And find tranquility . . .

Fate tunes. This one breaks my fucken heart. We sit listening as long as we can bear it, but I know the song has sunk a well into Mom's emotional glade, and I guess mine too. Dirty blood will gush high just now. The piano brings it on.

'Well,' she says. 'George said she can only decoy the sheriff until tomorrow. And that isn't even counting the thing about the drugs.'

'But at least I'm innocent.'

'Well Vernon, I mean, *huh-hurr* . . .' She gives one of those disbelieving laughs, a hooshy little laugh that means you're the only asshole in the world who believes what you just said. Notice how popular they are these days, those kinds of fucken laughs. Go up to any asshole and say anything, say, 'The sky is blue,' and they'll wheel out one of those fucken laughs, I swear. It's how folk spin the powerdime these days, that's what I'm learning. They don't shoot facts anymore, they just hoosh up their laughs, like: *yeah, right.*

'I mean – surely the damage is done,' she says. 'You *did* have that awful catalog, and now these illegal drugs . . .'

117

Awful catalog, get that. Her closet is probably full of that lingerie, but now it's an awful catalog. I skip the catalog and move on to the drugs. 'Heck, plenty of dudes are into that stuff – anyway it ain't even mine.'

'Well I know, that catalog was *mine* – what on earth got into you? Was it something the Navarro boy put you up to?'

'Hell no.'

'I don't like to speak badly, but . . .'

'I know, Ma, Meskins are more *colorful*.'

'Well I only mean they're more – flamboyant. And Vernon, they're *Mexicans*, not Meskins, have some respect.'

The conversation is nano-seconds away from including the word 'panties', something you should never hear in conversation with your mom. Knowing her, she'd probably say 'underpants' or something. 'Interior wear', or something way fucken bent. A new resignation settles over me, that I can't run out on my ole lady while she's like this. Not right away, not tonight. I need to reflect, alone.

'I think I'll take some fresh air,' I say, stretching off the bench.

Mom opens out her hands. 'Well what do you call this?'

'I mean at the park or something.'

'Well Vernon, it's nearly eleven o'clock.'

'Ma, I'm being indicted as an accessory to murder for chrissakes . . .'

'Well don't cuss at your mother, after all I've been through!'

'I ain't cussing!'

There's a pause while she folds her arms, and hunches her shoulder to wipe an eye. Clicking night bugs make it seem like her skin is crackling. 'Honestly, Vernon Gregory, if your *father* was here . . .'

'*What did I do?* I'm only trying to go to the *park*.'

'Well I'm just saying *grown up* people make *money* and *contribute* a little, which means getting up in the morning – I mean, there must be a thousand kids in this town, but you don't see them all at the *park* in the middle of the night.'

Thus, quietly, and with love, she reels me out to the end of my tether, to that itchy hot point where you hear yourself committing to some kind of fucken outlandishness.

'*Yeah?*' I say. '*Yeah?* Well I've got live and direct *news* for *you*!'

'Oh?'

'I wasn't even going to *tell* you yet, but if this is how you're gonna be – I already talked to Mr Lasseen about a job, so, *hey*.'

'Well, when do you start?' A smile's shadow passes over her lips. She knows I just cut lumber for a cross. The motivation behind her higher-than-Christ eyebrows gives me the fire to carry it on.

'Tomorrow, maybe.'

'Doing what?'

'Just helping out, you know.'

'Well I used to know Tyrie's wife, Hildegard.' She ups the ante, makes me think she'll bump into Tyrie's wife. But I hold my course, I say anything not to lose another knife game. My ole lady doesn't lose at knife games. She ain't lost this one yet. 'Well what about Dr Goosens? I'll die if I see the police around here again . . .'

'I can work mornings.'

'What will Tyrie Lasseen think, if you don't do a full day's work?'

'I already fixed it with him.'

'Well you can pay me a little lodging then, now that you're so *grown up* and all.'

'Oh, sure, you can have most of it – *all* of it if you want.'

She sighs like I'm already behind with my rent. 'The power company comes first, Vernon – how quickly will you get paid?'

'Uh – I can probably get an advance.'

'Without any working history?'

'Oh sure,' I say, squinting into the sky. 'So *now* can I go to the park?'

She blinks dreamily, her ole innocent eyebrows rise up to heaven. 'I never said you *couldn't* go to the park . . .'

Needless to say, there is no fucken job. I stand insulated from my world by the buzzing tequila-ozone of what I just did. Lies scatter around me like ants.

'Well I guess I'll have to make lunches for you now,' says Mom.

'Nah, I'll come home for lunch.'

'From Keeter's? But that's *miles* away.'

'Twenty minutes, it takes me.'

'Oh goodnight, it's almost twenty minutes by *car . . .*'

'Nah – I know all the shortcuts.'

'Well maybe I better call Hildegard Lasseen and see what they expect, I mean it's *ridiculous*.'

'Okay, I'll take lunch.'

'Y'all die and nobody told me?' Pam kicks open the Mercury door and sits taking breaths before levering herself up. Something as big as a goddam bullfrog jumps out through her legs, I swear. 'Vernie, come help ole Palmyra with these bags – I've been calling your damn number since Adam & Eve.' She drops some sacks onto the driveway, then struggles over to the willow, pulling back the branches like drapes. Mom sits sniffling underneath.

'Lalito's gone,' she sniffs.

'Took his time about it,' says Pam. 'C'mon now, this food's getting soggy.' She begins the long haul up to the porch. I gather the *Bar-B-Chew Barn* sacks, and linger beside her.

'Vernie, look!' she says, pointing into the sky. I look up. 'Tsh,' she slaps my belly. She even makes the little sound, 'Tsh,' like a cymbal. It's just a thing we do, me and Pam. 'C'mon, Doris, or I'll call Lolly and tell him about your *herpes*.'

'*Shit*, Palmyra, *God*.'

Thunderclaps of laughter ripple through Pam's flesh. My ole lady struggles to keep her misery, squirms and wrassles with herself on the bench. In the end, she gets mad and scuttles up to the porch. 'You're just too damn perky – it's *important* to hurt sometimes.'

'Want me to push ya down the stairs? Haugh, haugh, haugh.'

'Well for *God's sake*, Palmyra. Anyway, we don't want your damn food.'

'Haugh, haugh, haugh. You should've seen Vaine at the hayride, she put away more corn than a truckload of empty Meskins.'

'But Atkins diet is supposed to be *protein* . . .'

'Barry's out for the night.'

'Oh?'

'A few of the posse owe him a beer. He found a gun yesterday, at Keeter's.'

twelve

It ain't my idea to leave before dawn. My ole lady decided to visit Nana, that's why the house stinks of hairspray. You know why she's leaving early: so nobody sees her scurry through town on foot. All she wants is for them to see her arrived, all hunky-dory. Not scurrying. It's a learning I made since the car went.

'Well I just can't believe there isn't a pair of Tumbledowns around town, I mean, I'll have to try down by Nana's.' She gives off breathy noises, and flicks her fingertips through my hair. Then she takes a step back and frowns. It means goodbye. 'Promise me you won't miss your *therapy*.'

An electric purple sky spills stars behind the pumpjack, calling home the last moths for the night. It reminds me of the morning when ole Mrs Lechuga was out here, all devastated. I try not to think about it. Instead I look ahead to today. Going to Keeter's is a smart idea; if anybody sees me out there, they'll say, 'We saw Vernon out by Keeter's,' and nobody will know if they mean the auto shop, or the piece of land. See? Vernon Gray-matter Little. In return, I've asked Fate to help me solve the cash thing. It's become clear that cash is the only way to deal with problems in life. I even scraped up a few things to pawn in town, if it comes to that. I know it'll come to that, so I have them with me in my pack – my clarinet, my skateboard, and fourteen music discs. They're in the pack with my lunchbox, which contains my sandwich, the two joints, and a piece of paper with some internet addresses on it.

As for the joints and the piece of paper, I heard the voice of Jesus last night. He advised me to get wasted, fast. If at first you don't succeed, he said, get wasted off your fucken ass. My plan is to sit out at Keeter's and get some new ideas, ideas borne out of the bravery of wastedness.

I ride down empty roads of frosted silver, trees overhead swish cool hints of warm panties in bedclothes. Liberty Drive is naked, save for droppings of hay, and *Bar-B-Chew Barn* wrappers. In this light you can't see the stains on the sidewalk by the school. As the gym building passes by, all hulky and black, I look the other way, and think of other things.

Music's a crazy thing, when you think about it. Interesting how I decided which discs not to pawn. I could've kept some party music, but that would've just tried to boost me up, all this thin kind of 'Tss-tss-tss,' music. You get all boosted up, convinced you're going to win in life, then the song's over and you discover you fucken lost. That's why you end up playing those songs over and over, in case you didn't know. Cream pie, boy. I could've kept back some heavy metal too, but that's likely to drive me to fucken suicide. What I need is some Eminem, some angry poetry, but you can't buy that stuff in Martirio. Like it was an animal sex doll or something, you can't buy angry poetry. When you say *gangsta* around here, they still think of Bonnie & fucken Clyde. Nah, guess what: I ended up keeping my ole Country albums. Waylon Jennings, Willie Nelson, Johnny Paycheck – even my daddy's ole Hank Williams compilation. I kept them because those boys have seen some shit – hell, all they sing about is the shit they've seen; you just know they woke up plenty of times on a wooden floor somewhere, with ninety flavors of trouble riding on their ass. The slide-guitar understands your trouble. Then all you need is the beer.

Silas Benn has an ole washing machine for a letterbox. You have to watch out for it, because it's behind some trees as you approach his place from this end of Calavera Drive. I mention it because someday you might want to swing into Silas's driveway at speed. Watch out for the fucken washing machine. It's just one of the weird things about ole Silas. I know it's early to visit, but he always leaves his living-room light on, for security I guess, and it gives you the chance to say, 'Heck, Silas, I saw your light on.' He's wise to that ole line, but he still plays along. I nudge my bike up his driveway, and walk around to his bedroom window, tapping on the pane in the usual way. Then I stand back and hold my breath. A chink opens in the drapes. I tread softly to the back door. After some scrapes and rattles, Silas opens up and peeks out through crusty eyes.

'Pork my henry, son, what kinda time d'ya call this?'

'Heck, Silas, I saw your light on . . .'

'Ya dint see my damn *bedroom* light on. Dog-gone it, hell to berries . . .' Silas didn't have time to strap on his leg. He just hangs on a kind of crutch. Silas had a leg amputated, see.

'Sie, I got some real big business to run past you.'

He rustles through his robe for his glasses. 'Lemme see, whatcha find for me today . . .'

'Well y'see, that's the thing – I don't have any *hard* stuff, like on paper and all, on account of they took my computer away.'

'So what the . . .?'

'See, I have this plan how you can get all the pictures you want, hundreds of 'em – today even, when Harris's opens.'

'Aw hell, son, shill my wincer – ya dragged me up fer *nothin*?'

'Look,' I say, unfolding the sheet of paper. 'See these internet addresses? That's where all those hard-core pictures are kept, for free – even the *Amputee Spree* stuff that you really like. With these instructions, you can go by Harris's store, take the booth with the computer, and print out all you want. No kidding. With this list, you'll never have to pay for pictures again.'

'Shit, I don't know – I never got with them com-puder machines.'

'Forget it, it's easy. Everything you have to do is written here.'

'We-ell,' he says, stroking his chin. 'How much ya want fer it?'

'A case.'

'Git outta here.'

'No kidding, Sie, this list can save you a truckload of beer over the summer. A goddam truckload, at least.'

'I'll pay a six-pack.'

'We-ell,' I hesitate. You have to hesitate with Silas. 'We-e-ll. I don't know, Sie, plenty of kids'll wanna kill me, after I bust the business like this.'

'Six-packa Coors, I'll go git it.' He swings away into the house like a one-legged monkey. You can't drink till you're twenty-one around here. I ain't twenty-one. Good ole Silas always keeps some brews in stock, to trade for special pictures. Us Martirio kids are like his personal internet. He's our personal bar.

By seven-thirty this Monday morning I'm sat in a dirt clearing behind some bushes at Keeter's, sucking beer and waiting for ideas about cash. From where I sit you can watch the sun piss orange around the rims of those ole abandoned toilet bowls. I have my beers, my joints, and Country music pumping deep into my brain. I'm ready to howl like a coon-dog. I use it all to try and plot my position in life. There's me here, and Mexico down there. Taylor Figueroa in between. All I have to figure out is the rest of it. 'Get to the Nub of Things,' as Mr Nuckles used to say, back when his goddam mouth worked. To be honest, the only new information that comes to me is a whole swarm of lies about my so-called job. Take note of what happens in a lie-world like this; by the time you're in this deep, and you've invented an imaginary job, with an imaginary start time, and imaginary pay, and put your loved-ones through the sandwich routine, and 'Oh my God should I call Hildegard Lasseen,' and all – it doesn't matter anymore whether you admit the lie, or just get fucken busted doing it. People go, 'But he was so *credible*.' They start to realize you introduced them to a whole parallel world, full of imaginary shit. It's a pisser, I know it, I don't blame them at all. But it's like suddenly you qualify for membership in the fucken Pathology Zone, even though those same people immediately turn around and go, 'Can't make it, Gloria – my folks just flew in from Denver.'

Nah, my slime's so thick, it ain't worth coming clean at all. Take good note; Fate actually makes it *harder* to admit slime, the farther in you get. What kind of system is that? If I was president of the Slime Committee, I'd make it *easier* to come clean about shit. If coming clean is what you're *supposed* to do, then it should be made more fucken accessible, I say. I guess the shiver that really comes over me is that I just handed everybody the final nail for my cross. All they needed, on top of everything, was a credible lie. You can just see my ole lady on TV when they break the news, don't tell me you can't. 'Well but I even stayed up to pack his *sandwiches* . . .'

I fumble a lighter from my pocket, and spark up a joint. I ain't going by Goosens's today. Fuck that. My ole lady's safe with Nana. I'm going to find a way out of here.

'Bernie?' It's Ella Bouchard. She stops behind a bush at the edge of my clearing, and moves her lips the opposite way to what I hear in my ears, which is crawfish pie and filet gumbo.

Just let me say, in case you think I'm secretly in love with Ella, that I've known her since I was eight. Every boy in town knew Ella since they were eight, and none of them are secretly in love with her. Her equipment ain't arrived. You guess it maybe ain't coming either, when you look at her. Like her equipment got delivered to Dolly Parton or something. Ella's just skinny, with some freckles, and this big ole head of tangly blond hair that's always blown to hell, like a Barbie doll your dog's been chewing on for a month. Nobody yet figured out how to deal with Ella Bouchard. She lives with her folks, along the road from Keeter's Spares & Repairs. Her folks are like hillbilly types that don't move their arms when they walk, and just stare straight ahead all the time. The kind that repeat everything eighty times when they talk, like, 'That's how it was, yessir, the way it was was just like that, just like that, the way it was.' Probably explains why Ella's kind of weird too. Cause and effect, boy.

'Hi, Bernie.' She enters the clearing slowly, as if I'll run away. 'Whatcha doin?'

'Just hanging out.'

'Whatcha doin *really*?'

'Just hanging out, I toldja – you shouldn't even be here.'

'You're getting fuckin loaded and fuckin wasted off your ass. Anyway, you fuckin *promised*.'

Such a foul mouth on a girl probably shocks you. Then you must think: foul-mouthed girl, at Keeter's, alone with Bernie. Okay, yes, a bunch of us boys got our first whiff of nakedness from Ella Bouchard. It cured us of any horniness we might've had; you couldn't name the flavors of ice-cream it looked like she strained through her pants some days. Like, she probably set us back years in our sexual development. She just wanted to cuss, spit, and fart with us, and I guess the only currency she had was her ropey ole body. I know you're not allowed to say it anymore, about certain girls and all, but off the record, Ella was born with it. She'd always be the one doing messy tumbles on the lawn, legs flying open all over the place. Her underwear would always shine your way. When aliens land in town, Ella will be out front with her fucken dress up, I guarantee it.

She takes another step into my space, and looks down at me. 'Fuck, Bernie, you're just like an alcoholic.'

'My name's not Bernie, and I'm not just like an alcoholic.'

'What's your name then? It's something like Bernie, I know that . . .'

'No, my name's nothing like Bernie, not in the minimum.'

'I'll go ask Tyrie what the name of the guy is who's over here smoking weed and drinking beer.' She gets that fabulous edge that girls get to their voices, the edge that spells oncoming Tantrum From the Bowels of Hell, that says, 'I'll scratch the heavens down around you and suck the fucken air from your lungs and spit you to fucken hell and you know it.'

'Name's *John*, okay?'

'No it ain't, not John, it ain't John, it ain't John at all, not *John* . . .' You can tell right away she spends too much damn time around her folks.

'Ella, I don't want to make a big deal out of anything today, okay? I'm just trying to chill on my own, and just figure some shit out – okay?'

'Not called John you ain't, not with a name like John, uh-uh, you ain't John, no *way* . . .'

'Well – whatever, okay?'

'I knew it was Bernie. Can I have a beer?'

'No.'

'How come?'

'Because you're only eight.'

'I ain't too so *eight*, I'm nearly fuckin *fifteen*.'

'Still too young to drink alcoholic beverages.'

'Well fuck, *you're* too fuckin young to drink – and *smoke weed*, fuck.'

'No I ain't.'

'Yes you *are*! How old are you?'

'Twenty-two.'

'You are *not*, you are fuckin *not* twenty-two.' All this goes to illustrate the First Rule of dealing with edgy people. Don't, under any circumstances, get talking to them.

After a minute of clicking her teeth, and of me ignoring her, Ella starts to mess with the hem of her dress. She makes these noises, like a stroked snake or something, and goes, 'Fuck, it's *hot* out here.' Then she raises the hem up her legs, to where they start thickening and softening into thigh. You can tell she swiped this behavior right off some TV-movie. I hope it's not wrong to say it, but it's like watching a Japanese person barn-dancing, the credibility of it, I fucken swear.

'Ella, *c'mon* will ya?!'

No, here comes the dress on its way up her legs. I just grab my pack and start to stash everything back inside. So she turns to me, real polite. 'I'll go to the shop and scream. I'll tell Tyrie what you did to me, after all that weed and beer, Bernie.'

A learning grows in me like a tumor. It's about the way different needy people find the quickest route to get some attention in their miserable fucken lives. The fucken oozing nakedness, the despair of being such a vulnerable egg-sac of a critter, like, a so-called human being, just sickens me sometimes, especially right now. The Human Condition, Mom calls it. Watch out for that fucker.

I drop my pack and make a deal with Ella. It lasts until the ninth sip of the beer that we share. I know it's the ninth because she counts them. 'Every sip together makes our feelings grow,' she says.

And strangely, for a nano-second before the ninth sip, I do kind of start to begin commencing to like Ella, don't ask me why. I get a few waves about how fucked-up she must be, and how she just wants someone to pay attention to her. I'm loaded, I admit it. But for a flash I even kind of take to her, with her ole straw hair blowing across her face, and the smell of warm bushes around. My hand even brushes against her leg, making silk hairlets stand up. She wriggles until a wedge of underwear shows up on the dirt. But at the same moment the breeze grates this smell off her legs, like salami or something, and I pull right back. I try not to wrinkle my face up, but I guess I kind of do, and she sees it. She tucks herself back into a knot.

'Bernie, how come you don't fool around? You a *pillow-biter* or *what*?'

'Hell no. I just think you're too young, that's all.'

'Guys a whole lot older than you want to fool around with me.'

'Yeah, *right*. Like who?'

'Like Danny Naylor.'

'*Yeah, right*, I don't fucken think so.'

'Yeah he does, him and a whole shit-loada other guys.'

'*C'mon*, Ella . . .'

'Mr Deutschman'd even *pay* for it, I know that, I know that too well, *too* damn well.'

'Fuck, Ell, Mr Deutschman's around eight hundred years ole.'

'It don't matter, he's older'n you, and he'd still pay for it.'

'*Yeah, right*. Anyway, how do you know? You been over there and *asked* him?'

'I went by there once and he gave me a Coke, and touched me a little, on my ass . . .'

Don't even think it. A man has his honor, you know.

At the end of the day, I take all the gullies and back roads home, and keep my eyes lively to any roving cops or shrinks. I'm glad Mom's at Nana's – she'll have company, and food in her belly, if only macaroni cheese. I missed my date with Goosens, and have to leave town, see. I just couldn't abandon Mom if she was home sniffling, no way. That's how I'm programmed. By the time I get home, I'm ready to call Nana's and tell Mom the job didn't work out – really come clean, as a final gesture. Then, when I step inside my house, I hear an unmistakable set of squeaks and sighs. The wind falls out of my sails and stays at the door, like your dorky buddy on his first visit to your place. My ole lady's here. Bawling. I stand quiet, as if she'll ignore me. She doesn't though, and this is where her routine gets quite transparent, actually, because she clears her throat, loudly, then uses that energy to launch into a bigger, better bawl. It breaks my fucken heart. Mostly because she has to resort to these transparent kind of moves to get attention.

'What's up, Ma?'

'Shnff, squss . . .'

'Ma, what's up?'

She takes hold of my hands, and looks up into my eyes like a calendar kitten after a fucken tractor accident, all crinkly, with spit between her lips. 'Oh, *Vernon*, *baby*, oh *God* . . .'

A familiar drenching feeling comes over me, like when the potential exists for serious tragedy. One thing I take into account, though, is that my ole lady always *wants* my blood to run cold; she bawls more convincingly the longer I know her, because my blood-freezing threshold goes up. This far down the road, she even fucken hyperventilates. My blood is icy.

'Oh, Vernon, we're *really* going to have to pull together now.'

'Momma, calm down – is it about the gun?'

Her eyes brighten for a moment. 'Well no, actually they found *nine* guns on Saturday – *Bar-B-Chew Barn* disqualified the prize winners for planting guns along the route, there's all *kinds* of hell to pay in town today.'

'So what's the problem?'

She sets up bawling again. 'I went to cash the investment this morning, and the company was gone.'

'*Lally's* investment?'

'I've been calling Leona's all day, but he's not there . . .'

This so-called investment was with one of those companies with names chained together, like 'Rechtum, Gollblatter, Pubiss & Crotsch'. If you want to know who the *real* psychos are, take any guy who names a business to sound like a lawyer's company, and is still surprised when folk won't turn their back to him.

'Power's being disconnected tomorrow,' says Mom. 'Did you get the advance? I've been counting on your advance, I mean, the power's only fifty-nine dollars for goodness sake, but then when the deputies came . . .'

'Ma, slow up – *deputies* came?'

'Uh-huh, around four-thirty. They were okay, I don't think Lally said anything yet.'

'So what'd you tell them?'

'I said you were with Dr Goosens. They said they'd check you at the clinic tomorrow.'

The Lechugas' teddy farm seems ole and squashed when I wake up next morning. Another Tuesday morning, two weeks after That Day. The shade under their willow is empty. Kurt is quiet, Mrs Porter's door is closed. Beulah Drive is clean of strangers for the first time since the tragedy. June is barely underway, but it's as if summer's liquor has evaporated, leaving this dry residue of horror. At ten-thirty the phone rings.

'Vernon, that'll be the power company – when can I tell them you'll have your advance from work?'

'Uh – I don't know.'

'Well, do you want me to call the Lasseens and see what the hold-up is? I thought they promised it to you on your first day . . .'

'I'll have it tonight, tell them.'

'Are you sure? Don't say it if you're not positive, I can call Tyrie . . .'

'I'm sure.' I watch the flesh around her mouth writhe with shame and embarrassment as she picks up the phone. My head runs a loop of Ella's words at Keeter's. 'Mr Deutschman'd even *pay* for it.' Proof that my mind hooked onto the idea, is that I pretended not to be interested. I just changed the subject. That's how you know the demon seed was planted.

'Well hi Grace,' says Mom. 'He says he'll have it tonight, definitely. No, he's starting late today – he's studying marketing dynamics for work. Oh fine, just fine – Tyrie's real happy with his progress – says he might even get promoted! Uh-huh. Uh-huh? No, no, I've spoken to Tyrie personally, and he's definitely getting paid – Hildegard's an old friend, so it's not a challenge. Oh really? I didn't know you knew her. Oh, well – tell her hi.' Mom's eyes sink back into her sockets, she turns dirty red. 'What? Well if you could just hold them back until after lunch, I'd really appreciate it. The truck left already? Uh-huh. But if I give them cash when they get here, can't you stop them from . . .?'

Blood splurches like paste from both ends of my body, caking hard in grotesque spike formations that only happen to liars and murderers, and that my ole lady can see from the phone. Thoughts dance through my head that shouldn't be there. Simonize the Studebaker, for instance. Mom puts down the phone. Her eyes cut me loose in a raft.

'The disconnection truck already set off for the day,' she says. Razorfish slash the fucken raft. Mom's eyebrows lean up on one elbow to watch. 'I better call Tyrie.' She fumbles through the phone-table drawer for her address book. I stay on my stomach in front of the TV. Save me falling back down here when I'm fucken dead.

In between snatches of my video research, the news plays on TV. 'Overshadows events in Central Texas,' says a reporter, 'with official sources confirming this morning's tragedy in California as the worst of its kind so far this year. Condolences and aid continue to pour into the devastated community . . .'

'Vernon, do you have the *Spares & Repairs* number?'

'Uh – not right here.'

I don't look up. I hear you can get big money selling your kidneys, but my brain's stressed from wondering where to sell them. Maybe the meatworks. Who fucken knows. My only other plan, plan B, is the desperate plan. I browse through my daddy's ole videos for tips. For cream pie, actually, truth be told. *Close the Deal* is here, one of his favorites. One thing about my dad, he had every kind of plan to get rich.

'Here it is – Hildy Lasseen,' says Mom. She shuffles back to the phone, and picks up the receiver. An important-sounding fanfare accompanies her, as the TV jumps from global to local news.

'Mrs Lasseen doesn't work at the yard,' I say. 'That's just their *home* number.'

'No, the *Spares & Repairs* number is here too.' She starts to dial. All you hear is the TV in back.

'Don't write Martirio off yet,' says a reporter, 'that's the message from the team behind a new multimedia venture inspired by the struggle of our brave citizens – a venture its founder claims will spread the gospel of human triumph over adversity to every corner of the globe.'

'Martirio is already synonymous with sharing,' says Lally. Mom squeaks. She throws down the phone. 'Many a crucial lesson about loss, about faith, and justice, can still be shared, be made a gift of – a gift of hope and compassion to a needy world.'

'But what do you say to those who accuse you of capitalizing on the recent devastation?' asks the reporter.

Lally's eyebrows sink to their most credible level. 'Every tragedy brings lessons. Hardship is only repeated when those lessons

133

aren't learned. What we propose is to share our challenge, share the benefits of our struggle, in the hope that others can avoid those hard lessons for themselves. If we can save just one life, wherever it may be – we'll have been successful. Also remember that, being an interactive project, individuals across the planet will be able to monitor, influence, and support Martirio in its efforts, twenty-four hours a day, via the internet. I don't think anybody would call that a bad thing.'

'Fair enough, but with the tragedy now behind us – do you really think there's still a market for a lifestyle show from what is, after all, only the barbecue sauce capital of Central Texas?'

Lally throws out his arms. 'Who says the lesson's behind us? The lesson is still to come, we have perpetrators to be brought to justice, causes to be found . . .'

'But surely the case is open and shut?'

'Things may appear so from a media standpoint,' says Lally. 'But if we share the expertise of my partner in the venture, Deputy Vaine Gurie, we'll discover things aren't always as they appear . . .'

Mom whimpers. 'Lalito . . .?' She stretches her fingertips out to the screen.

'So,' says the reporter, 'you won't be relocating to California for the experiment, in light of today's tragic events?'

'Certainly not, our investment is here. We believe the good citizens of Martirio will shine in their challenge, with the generous backing of the *Bar-B-Chew Barn* corporation of course, and in conjunction with the Martirio Chamber of Commerce.'

Leona's hamster-petting eyes leap to the screen. 'Wow, how do I feel? It's just such a challenge, I never presented a show before . . .'

Mom's hand snaps back to her body. We both turn to the kitchen window. Under the rattle of the pumpjack, you hear the Eldorado on its way up the street. 'Vernon, I'm not home if those fucking girls come up here – tell them I'm at Nana's, or no, better – tell them I'm at *Penney's* with my gold Amex . . .'

'But, Ma, you don't even have . . .'

'Just *do it*!'

She scurries up the hall like a blood clot, as Those Girls bounce into the driveway. The bedroom door slams. It's too fucken much for me. I just continue to flick through Dad's videos. *Cash Makes Cash*, and *Did You Ever See a Poor Billionaire?* I have to learn how to turn slime into legitimate business, the way it's my right to do in this free world. My obligation, almost, when you think about it. What I definitely learned just now is that everything hinges on the words you use. Doesn't matter what you do in life, you just have to wrap the thing in the right kind of words. Anyway, pimps are already an accepted thing these days, check any TV-movie. Lovable even, some of them, with their leopard-skin Cadillacs, and their purple Stetsons. Their bitches and all. I can go a long way with what I already learned this morning from my daddy's library. Products and Services, Branding, Motivation. I already know I'll be offering a Service. I just have to Position and Package the thing.

'Doris?' George lets herself through the kitchen screen. Betty follows. 'Do-*ris*?'

'Uh – she ain't here,' I say.

Leona wafts through the door behind them. 'I bet she's in her room,' she says, shimmying right up the fucken hall. Suddenly I feel like one of those TV-movie secretaries when some asshole barges into the chairman's office, 'Sir, you can't go in there . . .' But no, fucken guaranteed, Leona barges into Mom's room.

'Hey, *there* you are,' she croons, like they just met at the Mini-Mart. 'Did y'all hear – I got my own show!'

'Wow,' sniffs Mom.

'You ain't got it yet, honey,' hollers George from her armchair. 'Not until Vaine raises the capital to partner up.'

'Oh *goodnight* Georgie, she'll get it – she just got her own *SWAT team*, for God's sake.'

'Uh-huh, and then appointed lard-bucket Barry to it, who's only a damn *jail guard*. I just hope by "SWAT" they mean "SWAT flies".'

'Heck, you're just miffed because the *Barn* went over the sheriff's head.'

'Sure, pumpkin, like I'm *sooo* devastated,' says George. 'I'm just sayin, a SWAT team don't qualify Vaine for goddam internet broadcasting, and it certainly don't give her the cash.' She pauses to suck half a cigarette into her chest. 'And anyway – our lil' ole tragedy just got shot off its damn perch.'

Leona stomps back out of Mom's room, and throws her hands on her hips. 'Don't you throw cold water on my big day, Georgette-Ann! Lalo says they won't have time to set up the *infrastructure* in California, not if we move fast.'

'We-ell.' George launches a finger of smoke at the ceiling. 'We-e-ell. I'll just try not to blink, in case I miss ole Vaine movin so fast.'

'Look, it's gonna happen – *okay*?!'

'Take one helluva new twist, is all I'm sayin.'

'*George* – Lalo just happens to be aware of that fact, *wow*!' The thrust of the last word flicks Leona forward at the waist. She stays there awhile, to make sure it sticks. Then she chirps back into Mom's room. 'Hey, did I tell you we're setting up Lalo's office in my den?'

Mom scurries into the hall. 'Well I guess we've got time for one coffee, before I go to Penney's. Vern, isn't it time for work?'

'Hey,' says Leona, 'I can drop him.'

'Loni, stop it,' says George.

'But – he'll get there faster . . .'

'Le-ona! It's just not fair.' George excavates a tunnel to Mom through her cigarette smoke. 'Honey, I hate to tell you, but Bertram's sending someone to get the boy. The shrink turned him in.'

'Well, but – Vern's making *money* now, why, he's getting *five hundred dollars*, just today . . .'

Leona shakes her head. 'You shouldn't've told her, George.'

'Oh sure, so you could take him via Lally, and film the arrest. Doris is our goddam *friend*, Leona.'

Mom's face peels off her head and hangs in tatters from her chin. 'Well, but . . .'

I just get up off the floor. 'Either way, I should go brush my hair.'

'Well, there, see? He's a changed young man, with a high-powered job and all.'

I leave the ladies and slide up the hall, via Mom's room, to reload my backpack. I pack my address book, my jacket, and some small clothes. My player, and some discs. I remove the clarinet and skateboard. I don't think I'll be going past town anymore. I grab the pack and head out through the laundry door, without a word to the Forces of Evil. You can still hear my ole lady from the porch, struggling to pump cream into her pie.

'Well I have to get to San Tone for the new fridge, and I'm getting a quote on one of those central-vac systems too, that plug right into anywhere in the house – I guess it's time to think about myself for a change, now that Vern has a career.'

From the bottom of the porch stairs I see a power company truck idling past the pumpjack, studying house numbers along the road. It jackrabbits to me, and starts to pull over. I just creak away on my bike.

thirteen

Nobody will look twice at us, I'm pretty sure of that. A boy and a girl on a bike. A boy in regular jeans, and a tangled blonde in a bluebonnet-blue dress. No smells on us, just like TV. I have my pack with me, so it could even look like we're selling things. Selling things is a good excuse around here.

'Guess what?' yells Ella into my eardrum.

I stop by the side of the Johnson road to instruct her how to be a bicycle passenger without killing the driver. She lifts her dress to show me her clean white underwear. I only half pay attention, because it seems a troubled afternoon to me; gusts come threaded with thunder, and the horizon behind Keeter's is lit by a single strake of gold. Ella doesn't notice omens, you can tell she's just getting a kick out of today. Probably because she's in a business adventure with me. Fucken Ella, I swear to God. We're going to split the booty, although she says she ain't in it for the money. That's how fucken weird she is.

I get some waves about it. For all I know, Deutschman could be trying to quit schoolgirls, he could be on the schoolgirl wagon, taking one day at a time and all. And now – heeere's Ella. I make an effort to think more like my dad's videos. I mean, the client has an Unfulfilled Need, so – here's a Timely and Caring Service. What's more, part of our Extensive After-Sales Service is that nobody will ever know. It's a Market Gap, for chrissakes. But my conscience still calls me from Brooklyn. 'Nah, Boinie,' it says. 'Yez openin up a whole can a woims for da guy.' Then I think of Mom at home. Probably with the power off, probably getting laughed at, on account of her poverty, and her lack of fucken pizzazz. Localized smirking from douche-bag Leona. I'm committed.

The bike whirrs between flaky shacks and trailer-homes, down streets without edges, until the light almost disappears from the sky. We come to a cheap wooden house, of the kind you can build in a weekend, painted clean, though, with a neat little lawn, and tidy edges of bricks and gravel. Ole Mr Deutschman's place. We crunch past a clay figure of a sleeping Mexican, and carefully lay the bike in the gravel beside the house. Mr Deutschman ain't expecting us. This is known as Cold Calling, in the trade. I take hold of Ella's shoulders to give her a final briefing.

'Ella, it's just look and touch, okay? Nothing heavy – okay? Call me if he goes too far.'

'Chill out, Bernie – I'm the one with the poles, *remember*?'

God she's fucken scary sometimes. The plan is for her to be shy and sweet, and leave the initiative to him. Like: yeah, right. I told her not to even open her mouth if she could help it, but that's asking a whole shitload from Ella, you know it.

She crunches around to Mr Deutschman's door while I crouch in the gravel, out of sight. I pretend to rummage in my backpack. A couple of fat raindrops smack me like birdshit. Typical fucken Crockett's. Then I hear the door open. Deutschman's voice warbles out.

'Who's this here?' he says, all kindly and ole. He has the voice quality of genuine oleness, like he swallowed a vibrator or something.

After I hear them go inside, I unload my pack and crunch around to the door, scanning the street for neighbors. There's nothing to see, except an ole parked Jeep, and not much to hear except wire twanging in a gust. I try Deutschman's front door – it opens. I hold my breath until Ella's voice chimes out from deep in the house.

'Mama buys them because cotton's supposed to be – *wow*, your hands are *cold* . . .'

Game on. I close the door behind me, and creep into the living room. A new smell imprints on my brain; the smell of ole pickled dreams, like organs in a jar. Other people's house-smells hit you harder when you're not supposed to be there. I move down this narrow hallway toward Ella's voice, past the bathroom, where other industrial smells hang. Then a car turns onto the road outside. I dampen the sound of my heart with my hand until it hisses away up the street; the car that is, not my fucken heart. I shuffle forward again.

Deutschman and Ella are in the room at the end of the hallway. The door stands ajar. I flatten myself against the wall, and crane for a peek through the gap. Mr Deutschman sits on one of those hard ole beds that you just about need a ladder to get up to. The bedclothes are symmetrically draped under his symmetrical ass, which makes a neat little crinkle on top. Next to the bed is a polished wooden table, where a lamp stands on a knitted doily. A wallet, a Bible, and a black-and-white picture in a heavy brass frame sit alongside. A friendly lady shines out of the picture, with clear, trusting eyes, and curly, woolen hair that blows alongside blossoms in a breeze. You can tell that breeze blew a long time ago. On the other side of the room is one small window that overlooks junk in the back yard, including a rusty kind of love-seat.

Ella stands at the end of the bed with her dress held under her chin. 'Ha! That *tickles* – wait up, you wanna see my south pole – or my *north* pole?'

She pulls her panties down to her knees; doesn't inch them down, sexily or anything, but fucken yanks them, smiling like you just found her in the Mini-Mart. See what I mean about Ella?

'My, what's this here?' Deutschman's fingertips tremble onto her bare ass, his breathing gets jerky.

I take a deep breath too. Then I jump in with Mom's Polaroid. Snap!

'The psycho!' says Deutschman. His lips seem to quiver in mid-air, then his head slumps onto his chest, with shame I guess.

'Mr Deutschman, it's okay,' I say. 'Mr Deutschman? We're not here to make any trouble, the young lady is here by choice, and I'm just here with her. You understand?'

He raises dull eyes at me, and swallows some silent words. Then he looks back at Ella. She cocks her head like a game-show hostess, and fixes him with a grin. *God* she's bent, I swear.

'Mr Deutschman,' I say, 'I'm real sorry to barge in like this, I mean no disrespect. But, y'see, you and I have special needs, we can help each other out.' Deutschman hangs his mouth open, listens like a Texan. 'See the young lady here? I bet you'd like to spend some time with her. Your needs'll probably get well satisfied.' I copy the salesmen in Dad's videos, who always spread their hands out and chuckle, like you must be the dumbest fuck in the world if you don't see how easy things are. 'A little cash is all we need, in return for everything. Your joining fee today could be three hundred dollars, for instance – one flat, easy payment – and I'll leave the two of you to hang out some more. I won't even come back at all. And Mr Deutschman, you can have this picture, and we'll never come by again, or say a word. That's our solemn promise to you, ain't it, Miss?'

Ella puts her hands on her hips, grinning like a Mouseketeer, with her drawers around her knees. Deutschman stares at the floor awhile, then reaches for the wallet on his bedside table. He empties it of banknotes, and hands them to me without a word. A hundred and sixty dollars. My heart sinks.

'Sir, is this all you have? Just this money here?' I look down at him, all ole and shaken, and my heart sinks some more. I open out the wad of cash and peel a twenty off the top. 'Here, sir, we don't want to clean you out or anything.'

Some fucken criminal I make. He takes the note without even looking up. What suddenly stings me, though, is this: Ella's getting all the attention she craves, and getting *paid* for it. Deutschman's using up some stale ole cash, and getting the kicks he probably dreamed about his whole adult life. My ole lady's getting peace of mind about my so-called job, and a new little income. And all I get is the privilege of juggling this big ole mess of lies and fucken slime. The thing has me so bummed I just want to get the fuck out.

'I'll leave you two alone now,' I say, turning to the door.

When I reach the door though, I hear Deutschman groan behind me. I spin around to see him sliding onto his feet. Ella's panties fly back up her legs.

'Don't stop,' says Lally from the window. He turns from the camera to call over his shoulder, 'Leona – come see what we got for the show!'

I grab Ella, her dress half-scrunched into her panties, and pull her out to the hallway, fumbling and dropping Mom's camera along the way. Deutschman clatters into the bathroom ahead of us, eyes and mouth jammed open. I flick the photograph to him through the door.

'Destroy it, sir, and whatever you do – don't talk to that guy.'

Floorboards bounce as we charge to the front door and out over the steps. We're met by raindrops flying sideways through the porchlight, weaving at us like angry sperm. I yank Ella around the corner in a spray of gravel, to where my stuff is tucked in the shadows. And there stands Lally with his camera.

'Whoa, kids – wait up.'

I take Ella's shoulders and shove her away. She spins toward the road, one arm flailing, the other still adjusting the ass of her panties through her dress. Lally swaggers over to my pack, planting himself between me and the bike. He gives his balls a luxurious grope.

'My but you're such a career man these days.'

A thousand cusses jump to mind, but none of them come out. Instead I fix his leer in my mind, lower my head, and launch myself into his guts. '*Dhoof!*' he flies back onto the bike, the camera spins through the air, then glances off his head with a crack.

'*Sack* of *shit!*' He unpeels his spine from the bike's frame and takes a swipe at my ankle. 'Wanna play in the real world, cocksucker?' he snarls.

I snatch up the camera and rip out the cartridge. Then I take aim at him with my leg, and kick for all my life's worth. I connect hard, and he crashes back across the bike, dazed and bloody, in a shower of gravel.

'Wow, Lalito,' calls Leona, still out of sight behind the house. 'Your star just saw a *spider* back here – is this how the job's *supposed* to be?'

I haul up my backpack and sprint onto the road. Ella breaks cover from behind the parked Jeep across the street, lunging for my free hand. I pull her head-first into the dusk and we steam down the road, hand-in-hand, chased by fast-moving clouds.

'Lalo,' says Leona behind us. 'Be honest, now – as a name, do you prefer *Vanessa* or *Rebecca*?'

Our heartbeats trail us along rows of warped shacks, past makeshift porches dangling yellow light, into creekbeds, over bluffs; we suck air like jet-engines until we're spent. Lally will be back on the road by now, searching. Pissed as hell. And the law won't be far behind him. Feel the powerdime glow hot.

'*Fuck*,' puffs Ella when we finally stop.

I kneel next to her in the bushes behind her house. From here you can see down an overgrown alley that runs between her back fence and the shack next door. At the end of the alley, you can just make out the Johnson road. Keeter's, and the escarpment beyond, roll deep and black behind it. As my breath settles, I hear the first crickets, and the pulse of rustling grasses in the wind. Moist air from Ella's mouth strokes my face. I turn to look back through the bushes, where the outermost lights of Crockett's twinkle. In amongst the quiet you hear a soft bustle from town, then a car approaching. A learning comes over me gently, warm like a stroke. It is that I have seven fucken seconds to plan the rest of my life.

'Ell, I have to trust you with something important.'

'You can trust me, Bernie.'

'We got a hundred and forty dollars. That's seventy apiece.' I pull the cash from my pocket, and rifle through it for a ten-dollar bill. I stuff the ten into my pocket, passing the rest to Ella. 'Can you take sixty of this to Seventeen Beulah Drive? Can you do that for me? You'll have to tie up your hair, change your clothes, and sneak down there like a shadow. Can you do that?'

'Sure I can.' She nods like a little kid, you know how they nod too much. Then she stares at me through shining eyes. 'What're *you* gonna do?'

'I have to disappear awhile.'

'I'll come with you.'

'The hell you will. They'd catch us in a second.'

She presses her lips shut, and stares some more. I swear she's like your cat or something, how she just stares. A truck growls along the Johnson road. I tense until it passes. Ella just keeps staring. Then a door bangs in the middle distance, and a lady's voice screeches out.

'E-*lla*!'

Ella's face drops. I guess this was a real adventure we had just now; you can tell it broke the ice with Ella Bouchard. I squeeze her hand, for recent ole times' sake, and pick up my pack. 'If you see my ole lady, tell her I'm sorry, and I'll be in touch. Or, no, better – don't tell her anything, just slide the cash under the door. Okay?' I stretch out of the grass, but Ella's hand intercepts me at the leg. I look down at her face. It suddenly seems configured to make brave decisions in life, like willpower soaks through her pores or something. She leans up to my mouth and plants a clumsy kiss.

'I love you,' she whispers. 'Stay clear of Keeter's track, they's settin up that SWAT thing tonight.' She reaches for my hand and stuffs all her cash into it, all but my mom's sixty dollars. Then she springs to her feet and swishes away down the alley like a cotton ghost.

'Eee-*lla*!'

'*Comin*!'

I still feel her spit on my lips. I wipe it on my arm. As I melt into the dark on the escarpment side of the road, I see a figure bobbing through the light at Keeter's corner. It's Barry Gurie's unmistakable fat head. He ain't rushing. The hiss of a car approaches from the other direction. Lally's car. I run before its lights sweep the road.

Act III

Against all odds

fourteen

Martirio twinkles like a nest of fireflies from the land above Keeter's. You can see the new sign at the Seldome Motel, and one corner of *Bar-B-Chew Barn* is visible, alongside the radio mast. If you squint, you can see the working spine of town, a centipede's legs of pumpjacks lit up along Gurie Street – fuck, fuck, fuck. I trace the spine as far as I can, down to Liberty Drive, at least. My town is beautiful from up here. It's as if a star shines for every creature in the constellation of Martirio, and a few more shine besides. There's just one tiny black spot at the northern edge of town, where no star shines at all. That'll be home.

Waves are coming. My survival instinct wore off when I left the Johnson road. Now, stamping Lally's video into the fucken ground, I can taste the salt of waves. They come with pictures of Mom in her darkened kitchen, scraping up any ole crumb of hope, to parlay into pie. But all she scrapes is bullshit. It slays me. She'll be muttering, 'Well at least he has a job, and we still have his birthday to look forward to.' But I'm halfway to the escarpment, on my way to goddam Mexico. Probably forever.

It's a little before ten. I can reach the highway in a couple of hours, then maybe hitch a ride, or catch a bus or something, down to San Antone. I take a last look at Martirio sparkling across the flats, my universe for all these long years. Then I set off toward the hills, all crusty and alone. My coping mechanisms open up to some cream pie. Remember that ole movie, with the beach-house? Plenty of folks must do that, for real. Nothing says you have to be a particular kind of person to do that. I imagine Mom coming down, after things blow over. I buy her some souvenirs. Maybe I send a maid back with her; she can jam that up

Leona's fat ass. A learning: deep shit sweetens your plans like crazy.

It's midnight when the first headlights flicker through the branches by the highway. To be honest, I don't even know which way is south. My ole man thought Scouts was for sissies, so I don't even know which fucken way is south in life. Instead of trying to figure it out, I call some Glen Campbell to mind, to help me lope along, crusty and lonesome, older than my years. 'Wichita Lineman' is the song I call up, not 'Galveston'. I would've conjured Shania Twain or something a little more sassy, but that might boost me up too much. What happens with sassy music is you get floated away from yourself, then snap back to reality too hard. I hate that. The only antidote is to just stay depressed.

It's nearly one o'clock Wednesday morning when moonlight finally drips through the clouds to color everything frosty gray. Texas is so fucken beautiful. If you ain't here already, you should come. Feel free to skip Martirio, that's all. Herds of trucks and cars pass on the highway, but none of them look like they'd stop. I mean, I know they won't stop if I don't get up and stop them, don't get me wrong. I just don't like my chances. A better idea is to wait for a bus, which has an established tradition of stopping. I settle in the crook of a bend in the highway, pull my jacket from the pack, and fashion a backrest against a bush. I sit and wait, and turn some learnings over in my head.

Where TV lets you down, I'm discovering, is by not convincing you how things really work in the world. Like, do buses stop any-where along the road, to pick up any kind of asshole, or do you have to be at a regular bus stop? You see plenty of movies where some crusty dude stops a bus in the middle of the desert or some-thing. But maybe that only applies in the middle of the desert. Or maybe only the drivers who saw those movies will stop. This all scuttles through my head, and starts to warp into other kinds of movies, like the one with the black devil-car that has a vendetta against this guy. I feel my hair wisp in the breeze, the grasses and bushes wisp around me. Just nature and me, wisping, while the devil-car has this vendetta.

A chill wades through my skin to wake me. It's after five in the morning. I hear the roar of a bus on the highway, and hoist my pack up to the roadside. A motorcoach hammers around the bend, glowing cool and cozy inside. I flap my arms, and make like I just arrived from the scene of an urgent reason to travel. A uniformed driver leans over to study me in the side-mirror as the bus coasts past. Then, 'Pschhsss,' he pulls over and stops, two hundred yards down the highway. I fly towards those tail-lights.

The door puffs open. 'You in trouble?' asks the driver.

'I have to get to San Antonio.'

'Martirio's only a few miles away, you should pick up the next service there – I can't just stop on a whim, y'know.'

'Yeah, but – I'm stuck out here, and . . .'

'You're *stuck* out here?' he looks around. 'We have like pre-determined stops, you can't just hail the service any old where.' I shoot him these puppy-dog eyes, and he eventually says, 'I'd have to charge you the whole fare, like from Austin – thirteen-fifty.'

I climb aboard without even checking where the cowgirl's sitting, or even if there is a cowgirl. I just gulp down the aura of crumpled bedclothes, of travelers messy with chippings of sleep, and shuffle to an empty row at the back. My adrenal gland coughs as we move away, half expecting Lally to appear, or Ella's mom, or some kind of shit. I don't even want to think what, because Fate always pays attention to what you think, then slams it up your fucken ass.

'Drrrrrr,' the motorcoach hits the road, and after nameless miles I hang suspended on the knife-edge of a doze, my brain like crystal grits. Then we pass a field of manure or something, the type of smeary tang your family pretends not to notice when you're in the car with them, and it suddenly floods my senses with Taylor Figueroa. Don't ask me why. I sense her in a field by the highway. She's down on all fours behind a bush, naked except for blue synthetic panties that strain hard into her thigh-vee, and glow dirty ripe. I'm there too. We're safe and comfortable, with time on our hands. I surf her upholstery with my nose, map her sticky heem along glimmering edges to the panty-leg, where the tang sharpens like slime-acid chocolate, stings, bounces me back from her poon. In my dream I bounce back too far. Then I see we're in a field of ass-fruit, and suddenly I don't know if it's Taylor's scent, or just the field I can smell. I scramble back to her cleft, but the edges have vanished. The forbidden odor dissolves into the body-heat and aftershave of the bus. I wake up snorting air like crazy. She's gone. Empty distance rolls past the window.

I sit up straight in the seat, hoping to fool myself into normality. But the waves start tumbling in, tidal waves of horror on the back of this beautiful dream. Now bright images of Jesus form around me. He doesn't look at me. He looks away, and takes the barrel into his mouth, tastes its heat. Around him, milky eyes dot the school yard like flowers, jerky eyes getting slower, fading dead away. Boom. Fractured air oozes coughs and gurgles, the hiss of desperate clotting, of vital last messages nobody hears. Mr Nuckles the teacher is here too, his face trimmed with bubbles of young blood. The memories are back. I shoot disorderly tears for the fallen, for Max Lechuga, Lori Donner, and everybody, and I know I'm fucked for the rest of the journey, maybe for the rest of my life, fucked and nailed through the eye of my dick to the biggest cross. How could they think I did this? I hung out with the underdog, moved out of the pack, that's how, and now I fill his place, now anything original I ever said or did has turned a sinister shade. I understand him for the first time.

'You all right?' asks an ole lady, approaching down the aisle. I must be gasping like a fish or something. She brings her hand to my face, and I meet with it like it was the hand of God.

'I'll be okay,' I say through a curtain of spit. She withdraws her hand, but my face follows it, without instructions from me, aching for another touch.

'I'm so sorry you have troubles. I'm right over here – if you need some company, I'm right over here.' She pulls herself back to her seat.

An angel from heaven, that ole lady, but I can't feel a thing except pain and darkness, the darkness of purgatory. I bury my face in my hands, and sit shaking with hurt, praying for some kind of hopeful distraction. Then, I swear on my daddy's grave, Muzak starts to play in the bus. Just a welling violin note at first.

Sailing, take me away . . .

It's light when we roll into San Antone, but too early to be busy. I'm as hungry as a loose dog. My eyes are still gritty with salt. I skulk around the terminal restroom until eight o'clock, then I go to the phones to call Taylor Figueroa's folks. I just feel empty, drained of my life juices. The current logic is this: if I can get Taylor's number, and take the first step into my dream, it'll boost me up, maybe even enough to call home and explain things. If I don't get Taylor's number, then I'll have so little left to lose that I'll call home anyway, because I won't care about being boosted up.

I punch in the number. A thought comes as I do it, that maybe my ole lady became best friends with the Figueroas overnight, and is over there drinking coffee, or bawling, more likely. You know how Martirio is. It's shit, because my ole lady never went to the Figueroas' in her life. But you know how Martirio is. The number rings.

'Peaches,' Taylor's mom answers in a cool, deep voice.

'Mrs Figueroa? This is a friend of Taylor's – I lost her number and wondered how I could get in touch.'

'Who's speaking?'

'Uh – just an ole school buddy, like, from school.'

'Yes, but who?'

'Oh, it's – Danny Naylor here, excuse me.' Big fucken mistake. Her voice immediately gets all relaxed and intimate.

'Well *hi*, Dan, I didn't recognize you at all – how's life treating you up at A&M?'

'Oh, great, great, I'm loving it, actually.'

'I saw your mom at the New Life market the other day, and she tells me you're coming down for the bluebonnet cookout.'

'Oh, sure – you know me.' Sweat runs down my fucken back, my vision gets metallic, like I just downed forty cups of coffee.

'Hooray,' she says. 'I'll be seeing your mom at the committee meeting tomorrow, I'll let her know you called, and that you're fine.'

'Oh, great, thanks a lot.'

'And I just *know* Tay'll be pleased to hear from you – hold on, I'll get you her number.'

Now there's a fucken thing. 'I just *know* Tay'll be pleased?' I get a sudden twist of the knife over that. Typical of asshole Naylor to horn in on my thing. Like, he only ever had one good joke in his whole school career. It makes me want to go, 'Yeah, I'll just update her on my genital cancer,' or something. Fucken Naylor, boy.

'Here it is Dan, she's still down at UT Houston – I know she has a lunch date, so you'll catch her then, if not right now.'

I list the number under 'T', and under 'F', in case I get amnesia, then I write it across the cover of the address book as well. 'Thanks Mrs Figueroa – you take care now, and give my love to Mom.'

'Sure, Dan – see you at the cookout.'

I hang up the phone, shaking my head from the dumbness of it all. You can picture Danny arriving at the cookout and going, '*What* fucken call?' Or everybody finding out he died in a line-dancing accident a week ago, or something. I just take the fucken cake, boy. I mean, there must be some highly twisted gangstas out there, really hard cases and all, but I bet they never got involved in a dorky piece of slime in their lives. Like, I bet ole Adult Hitler, a nasty piece of action, never had anyone looking out for him at the cookout because he called pretending to be Danny Fucken Naylor.

Having Taylor's number makes me look like I've got Attention Deficit Disorder, or whichever one it is where you freeze on the spot, or do mime acts or whatever. I devise a facial expression to cover it, frowning like I'm calculating Pi to eight billion decimal places. Underneath my new expression, I run all the thoughts that would've made me look stupid. Like the thought that my ole lady will be up by now. Probably being fucken defibrillated already, or whatever it is when the paramedics yell 'Clear!' I shuffle to the terminal doors, where a bus schedule is displayed. Buses leave regularly to Houston, which means I have plenty of time to call my ole lady. And buses from Houston leave regularly to Brownsville and McAllen, down by the Mexican border. I'm tempted to buy two tickets to the border, and just present one to Taylor, like a wedding ring or something. But my brain says no, don't even buy one yet. Chill for a second. Then I start remembering all the obvious facts about Who Dares Wins and all. Like, maybe the fact I don't take a ticket means I won't get her to come. I end up frozen at the fucken door, re-calculating Pi.

Say, for instance, two guys want to drag Taylor Figueroa to Mexico right away. One brings her roses, and says he has this plan to go to Mexico, and would she like to come along. The other dude turns up with a quart of tequila, a joint, and two tickets to the border. He doesn't show her the tickets right away, but says, 'I have hours to live – help me kill the pain.' He gets her wasted in three minutes flat, sucks her tonsils out of her throat, then pulls out the tickets and says, 'Ten minutes till the cops arrive and take you in as an accessory – let's jam.' Which one does she go with? You know the fucken answer, I don't have to tell you. And let me say, it ain't all on account of one being nice, and one being a slimeball. It's because one of them *knew* she would come. As Americans, we know this to be true. We *invented* fucken assertiveness, for chrissakes. But in amongst all the books and tapes, in between that whole assertiveness industry – and I don't mean how to fast-talk people, and increase sales and shit, like, that's a whole other industry on its own, I mean in the industry where you end up knowing like day is day that something's going to happen for you – you *never once* hear how to *actually fucken do it*. Like, for my money, just thinking positive doesn't cut the ice at all. I've been thinking positive all year, and fucken look at me now. My ole lady thinks a new refrigerator will turn up on her doorstep, but you ain't seen the fucker yet.

I limp back to the phones. I ain't sure Taylor will come along. In fact, if I'm really honest, I guess I feel she won't. She has a lunch date, and her life is all separate, and full of sunny-smelling skin and panty lace. I just have grisly fucken reality, uninvited, with its smell of escalator motors and blood, and whirrs and beeps that suck away your shine. Dreams are so damn perfect, but reality just always tugs the other way. The fact that our two lives will rub together for the time it takes to say hello doesn't automatically mean sparks will fly. The best you can probably expect is that her peachy-lace life gets smeared with booger-slime. It's enough to make you bawl. Specially because now I'm in the wrong frame of mind for it to happen. There's the learning, O Partner: that you're cursed when you realize true things, because then you can't act with the full confidence of dumbness anymore.

In the end I just piss myself off. I pack up my goddam philosophical activity set, and pull a quarter from my pocket. I toss it. It comes down heads, which means call her in Houston immediately. I pick up the phone, and punch in her number.

fifteen

'Hello?' The voice is liquid ass in panty elastic.

'Taylor, hi – it's Vern.'

'Wait up, I'll get her,' says a girl. 'Tay! *Taylor* – it's Vern.'

'*Who*?' calls a voice in the background.

Then you hear giggles. I fucken hate that. Your chances with a girl fall sharply in the vicinity of giggles. Learning: never try to deal with more than one girl at a time.

She finally clatters onto the line. 'Tayla.'

'Uh – hi, it's Vern.'

'*Vern*?'

'Vern Little – remember me?'

'Vern *Little*? Like, gee . . .' As she speaks, you hear the other girl in quiet hysterics nearby.

'You might've seen me on the news, Vernon Gregory Little – from Martirio?'

'Like, I'm real sorry – I heard about the massacre and all, but I usually only, like, watch cable, you know?'

'*Anal Intruder Channel*,' squeals the other girl.

'Fuck *off*, Chrissie, *God*.'

'Uh – well, I'm the messy-haired dude, from outside the senior party that time – I kept back some stuff of yours . . .'

'Oh hey, *Vern*. I'm *sorry* – you took care of me that night, like, boy, did I overdo it or *what*!'

'Hell, no big deal,' I say. In the background you hear her kick the other girl out of the room. Pause for giggles while she does it.

'Well it was really, like – *anything* could've happened to me, you know?' I push some spit around my mouth, imagine some things that could've happened to her. 'So how'd you get my number?' she asks.

'It's a long story – thing is, I'm coming over to Houston, I thought maybe we could grab a coffee or something.'

'Gee, Vern, I'm like, wow, you know? Maybe next time?'

'But, what about lunchtime, or something?'

'See, my cousin's coming over, and it's just like, whatever, a girl thing, you know? Anyway, it's real sweet of you to call . . .'

She utters the winding-up words, just like that. Then comes an awkward gap as she waits for the corresponding ending from me. A spike of horror makes me gamble.

'Taylor, listen – I just got out of jail, I'm on the run. I wanted to tell you some stuff before I disappear, you know?'

'Holy *shit*, like – what happened?'

'I can't really talk on the phone.'

'*God*, but you seemed like, wow, you know, such a quiet guy.'

'Maybe not so quiet, as it turns out. Not so damn quiet anymore.'

'*God*, but you're only, like – fourteen, no?'

'Uh, seventeen actually, now, these days. So yeah, I guess I must've just snapped, against the injustice and all.'

'*Oh my God . . .*'

I stand at the phones, flick my eyes around the terminal, and wait for the bait to drop. I wait in the name of all the conclusive knowledge, collected throughout the history of the world, that says girls just can't resist bad boys. You know it, I know it. Everybody knows it, even if you ain't allowed to say it anymore.

'Vern, maybe I could, like – whatever, you know? I mean it's like, *God*. D'you know the Galleria in Houston?'

'Not a whole lot.'

'See, I have to be at Victoria's Secret around two – I could, like, catch you out front, on Westheimer or whatever.'

'*Victoria's Secret?*' I trample my tongue.

She giggles. 'I know, it's so *embarrassing* – I'm supposed to be, like, *underwear* shopping, I can't believe I just invited you.'

156

'I'll wear shades.'

'Whatever,' she says, laughing. 'Are you, like – in a car?'

'I'll take a cab.'

'Whatever, look – there's like this inflatable octopus out front of the Galleria, some kind of promotion – I'll keep an eye out around quarter of two.'

See how things work? First I'm like a skidmark on her mouthpiece, and she wants to wind up the call. But see what happens now I'm in *trouble*. See the awesome power of *trouble*. Trouble fucken *rocks*.

The Houston bus costs twenty-two bucks. I'm hungry, but I only have forty-four bucks fifty left. Getting both of us to Mexico will cost more than that. When my bus pulls into Houston, just before one o'clock, I head to the phones and look up 'Cash' in the yellow pages. My music has to go. A cab drives me miles away, to a pawnbroker where I get offered twenty-five bucks for my two-hundred-dollar stereo, which I accept because the taxi meter is running, and already cost me ten bucks, which I had to pay up-front as soon as the driver knew we were going to a fucken pawnbroker. I also get offered twenty-five cents apiece for my discs. I sneer at the pawnbroker, and he gets mad. Real red ass on the pawnbroker, actually, as we say down here.

Then the cab drives me along this fancy set of highways, past big reflector buildings, to the Galleria. I try not to imagine what Taylor'll be wearing, or how she'll smell. Better not to get fixated on anything that leaves room to be bummed if it's not true. I might focus on those same shorts from before, then find her in jeans or something, and lose the wind out of my sails.

I distract myself by watching the driver. He's a career driver, whose body and ass are permanently molded into the shape of the seat. He seems okay, kind of big and whiskery, with a relaxed smile. Reminds you of Brian Dennehy, from those ole movies, like with the alien eggs in the pool. A bunch of us at school used to wish Brian Dennehy could be our dad, same way we wished Barbara Bush could be our granny. Not like my snotty ole nana. But my ole man was still alive when I saw those movies, and I felt I kind of betrayed him by wishing Brian Dennehy could be my dad. Maybe that percentage of negative energy contributed to his death. Who knows?

The cab turns onto Westheimer, which is like four Gurie Streets stapled together. I try not to be conscious of my pulse, but it goes up anyway. There's no fucken cure for that, by the way. In movies, your pulse goes up when you want it up – out here it just does its own thing. Your fucken pulse is the death of cool. I take some deep breaths as this humongous mall appears alongside us; a large blow-up octopus sways on some ropes by the sidewalk. My balls crawl up my throat.

'Right there, by the octopus,' I tell the driver.

The figure of a young woman stands by the road. I slouch low, hoping she doesn't see me yet. I hate it when you go to meet somebody, and they spot you twenty fucken miles away, and just stay staring at you. You feel like your steps bounce too much, or your shoulders are too dangly or something. You hold the same dumb smile.

It's Taylor Figueroa. She's in a short khaki skirt. Her legs and arms flow warm and careless under sparkling brown hair. Her eyebrows flash up when she sees the cab. I feel sick to my fucken stomach.

'That'll be seven-eighty,' says the driver.

The cool of her smell hits me as soon as the door opens, but the cab seat is so low and busted that I make it look like climbing Mount Everest to get out. Taylor freeze-frames her smile while I haul my pack across the eastern face of the fucken cab. Then I drop my wallet in the road. She folds her arms while I scramble for a banknote, and hand it to the guy.

'That's seven-eighty,' says the driver, 'and this is only five.' He holds the bill out the window like it's a turd.

Sprinklers of sweat pop up on my forehead. I fumble through my pocket for change, but the pocket's so tight I can hardly get my hand in at all. Van Damme would rip the back of his hand off rather than squirm like this, he'd punch the driver's fucken lights out. I finally just pass the guy a ten from my billfold.

'Keep the change,' I tell him, all nonchalant. Taylor leans over to kiss my cheek, but stops again, mid-air. The goddam driver waves a banknote out the window.

'Don't forget your five.'

'I said *keep* the change.'

'You sure? Thanks, thanks a lot . . .'

Fuck. Now Taylor's embarrassed. I'm embarrassed, and half fucken bankrupt, and at the end of it all, Taylor just scratches the kiss right out of the scene. I catch a closer blast of her perfume though, which has a hook in it, the barb of a real woman, in the sense of more complicated panties, probably silk, full cut, with lace panels and all. Maybe in a blue half-tone, or a kind of flesh tone. I'm slain by her.

'Hi,' she says, leading me past the octopus. 'You robbed a bank, huh?'

'Yeah – see this backpack?'

I just sound weary now, like a regular smeghead on a flat Houston day. Sweat drips from my nose. Taylor looks me over. Her deep brown eyes narrow.

'You okay?'

'I guess so.'

I just sound like I have no desire left to impress anybody, but in this new depression a curious thing happens. A life thing. What happens, I think, is that we establish a real kind of contact, like in a movie or something. She just saw me make a complete asshole of myself, and she knows I know it. And it's as if she relaxes some, and I relax along with her. Like the horse stopped having to do math on stage. It accidentally makes me genuine, I guess, and exposes me as an ole fuckaway dog, all beat up to hell. She leads me quietly into the mall, respecting the swirling ink of trouble, and other people's tears, around my soul.

159

'So what's up, you dirty boy?' she teases on the escalator.

'Shit, I don't know where to start.'

'I'll drag it out of you.' She slips her dry little hand into my bunch of wet finger-meats, and coaxes me through the crowd. 'We'll check for my cousin, then maybe grab a juice, get private.'

A juice. Grab a private juice. What a woman. I watch her neat little buttocks stretch the fabric of her skirt, left, right, left, without a panty-line in sight, not to the naked eye. I'm so fucken in love with her I can't even picture her panties.

We reach the lingerie store, where all this hard-core, shiny kind of underwear is displayed out front. I'm not so interested in all that burlesque kind of stuff, to be honest. Simple cotton bikinis for me, like a girl wears when she doesn't expect you to go there. I look around at the women in the store. You can tell they fucken pray for you to go there.

'I don't see her,' says Taylor, craning over the displays. 'Typical. You want to go talk? I'll understand if you don't . . .'

'Sure, but you'll have to keep some pretty heavy secrets. I'll understand if you can't.' Girls just love secrets.

'Whatever.' She wrinkles her bitty nose. 'Like, I don't need to know where the bodies are buried or anything.' She flashes her teeth, and walks me to a fancy-looking cafeteria across the concourse.

'Hell, there's no bodies or anything,' I say.

As she docks her ass onto a barstool, I notice she's not totally airbrushed after all – a couple of her teeth are crooked, and you can detect a recent zit under her make-up. I melt like a wad into Kleenex. She's so fucken real, so *here*.

'So, like – are you guilty?' she asks.

'Nah, I don't figure.'

'Is it, like, robbery or something?'

'Murder.'

'*Eek*,' her face crumples like she just stepped in puke. 'Don't you think it'd be better to, like, stay and fight it out?'

160

'Nah, the way things're stacked, I have to disappear awhile.'

Her eyebrows scrunch in sympathy. What I realize as I melt into her syrup is that I have to steer talk away from the slime, and start to build a platform of excitement to tempt her along. Order tequilas or something, kiss her on the mouth.

'Tay,' I frown, 'this might seem sudden, but – I have to ask you something real important.'

Her face stiffens, like faces do when there's an incoming choice of shit. Right away I know it's the wrong approach.

'Cash?' she goes. 'Like, if you need a loan . . .'

A waiter turns up. 'What can I get y'all?' Taylor and my eyes take a moment to separate.

'I'll have a guava licuado,' she says.

'Uh – make it two,' I say. Tequilas my fucken ass. After the waiter leaves, I try another angle. 'Heck, Tay, I'm being real selfish here – I didn't even ask how *you're* doing . . .'

She rattles both my hands. 'You're *killing* me, like, *God*. I'm just here, finishing this thing, I tried out for TV but didn't get casted yet – just like, *whatever*, you know?'

I smile, and suck warmth from the moment to mold into a platform of romance. Then she flicks back her hair and drops her eyes.

'And I'm seeing this *doctor*, can you believe it? He's an older guy, obviously, but I'm like *sooo* in love – he's the reason I'm shopping today, him and my cousin's new man are such *panty-pooches.*'

I start to hear her through a distant echo-tunnel, you know how you do. Then Mom's voice scurries from my mouth.

'Hey – *wow*.'

'*God*, I can't believe I just *told* you that! Anyway he drives a Corvette, like an original Stingray whatever, and in November we're doing Colorado for my birthday . . .'

'Hey, *wow*.'

O-so-soft-and-gentle-on-your-skin Fate now makes me die squealing for every pixel of her being, and with each turn of her smile, every token of how remote my dream is from her mind, I fucken die knowing this is barely the germ of an infection for a thousand miserable deaths.

Then Taylor stands off her stool, and waves up the concourse. 'Hey, there's my cousin – Leona! *Loni!*' she calls. 'Over here!'

Jesus fuck. It's Leona Dunt from back home. I don't know if Lally's with her. *Fuck.* I explode off my stool, snatching up the backpack. Leona stands posing by the lingerie store, she hasn't looked over yet. 'What's up?' Taylor asks me.

'I have to run.'

'But – what were you going to ask me?'

'Please, please, please, don't breathe a word of this to Leona.'

'You know *Leona?*'

'Yeah, *please.*' My Nikes fire me onto the concourse.

'*Vern!*' she calls, as I vanish into the crowd. I glance over my shoulder and capture her image forever; she's there like a lost kitten, lips open, eyebrows scrunched. 'Be careful,' she mouths silently. '*Call* me.'

I fester and decompose in the back of a Greyhound bus bound for McAllen, under the tumor light, the twisted lava-lamp of sky, just a shell of meaningless brand names, a shelter for maggots and worms. Vernon Gone-To-Hell Little. And I didn't call my mom at all, you guessed it. I didn't even eat all day. All I did was hammer myself to a cross.

Screen One in my brain plays endless warm close-ups of Taylor. I try not to watch, I try to stay in the lobby and avoid it. But the thing's right there, doing big rotations of milky ass. Screen Two runs that other timeless classic, *Mom*, or, *Honey I Butt-Fucked the Family*. I ain't trying to watch that one either. All I watch is a double-exposure of my ole goofy face in the window, as infinite distance rolls by outside; spongy, darkened distance, like rug-lint balls on wet graham cracker. Power lines and fence posts read past like sheet music, but the tunes are fucken shit.

This is the scenario when I get the day's clincher, the one I forgot to expect. A song gets attached to Taylor. Just when you think you're dicked to the maximum extent of natural law, something always comes up that you forgot about. I know the routine from here. Everybody knows deep down there's no way to kill a Fate song once it's stuck. They're like fucken herpes. The only way to wash them out is to buy the song and play it day and night, until it doesn't mean anything anymore. Only forty gazillion years it takes. Everybody knows it, but I don't remember being taught that little pearl back in school, about the destructive power of Fate songs. Correct me if maybe I was absent that day, or if that was the day I spent cleaning the yard on account of liberating frogs from the lab. No, as I remember it, we were too busy trying to assimilate fucken Surinam to be taught anything of actual value to our lives, like Fate songs for instance.

I hear Taylor's song through the 'Tss, tss, tss' of a guy's earphones, a couple of rows up. 'Better Man' is the tune, by Pearl Jam. I don't even know the words to the song, but you can bet I'll spend the next eighty years in hell making every line fit my situation. Even if it ends up being about fucken groundhogs in space or something.

Worst of all, it ain't even a pure sex song. No dirty little bass riffs running up and down the back, swinging and plucking; nothing masturbation can relieve. This ole tune drags you screaming from her panties with the fatal wrench of something bigger than perky riffs. Anodized, gritty wanting and yearning. The deathly heem of love.

A sob pops in my throat. I choke it, and look around for a harmless visual distraction, but all I see is a stocky young woman with a baby, a few seats up. The baby is pulling the woman's hair, and she's faking this look of terror.

'Oh *no*,' she says, 'how can you do that to *Mommy*?'

She pretends to bawl, but the baby laughs and gurgles like a psycho, and pulls even harder. I'm witnessing a fresh knife being laid into a brand-new soul. A training dagger. A maternity blade.

163

Here's his mom quietly opening up the control incision, completely innocent in her dumbness to the world.

'Oh no, you've *killed* Mommy, Mommy's *gone*!' She plays dead.

The little guy giggles for a minute, but only that long. Then he senses something's wrong. She ain't waking up. He killed her, she abandoned him, just like that, over a pull of hair. He pokes her with his finger, then he gets ready to bawl. And there you have it: he takes the handle in his own tiny hands and pulls in his first blade, right up to the hilt. Just to bring her back. And sure enough, with the splash of his first tear, she wakes right up.

'Ha, ha, I'm still here! Ha, ha, it's *Mommy*!'

Ha, ha, that's the Scheme of Things.

'Drrrrrrr,' the motorcoach fangs into a violet dusk, a bitter projectile full of knives and Vernon. I know I'm just being sour about shit. Tell me I'm just being sour about shit, on account of everything. I know it. But I just get this feeling in my head, like the Voice of Ages that says, 'This is no way for a young man to spend his learning years.'

Taylor will have finished shopping by now. She's probably already in this fucker's Stingray, with her skirt up around her waist. As I picture it, her grown-up panties become skimpy just to finish me off. Now they're reckless bikini numbers, tight and fast, with a tiny bow on the waist elastic. They slash and slice me. A wet patch the size of a dime glistens on her mound, and if you take a silky buttock in each hand, lift her off the seat, and snuff your face up close, you only whiff the bittiest thumbtack of tamarindo jerky, just a pin-prick. That's how squeaky clean she is, even on a hot lathery day like today. Squeaky clean, like a doll. Oh Taylor, oh fucken Tay.

The unexpected thing when the bus rolls into McAllen is the stillness. The driver switches off the engine, the door goes 'Pschsssss,' and the world just parks. It's nearly eleven o'clock and there's a new silence, loud with the creasing of clothes, as I rise out of the seat. It's like waking from a fever, specially after all these venomous thoughts. I follow other unfolded travelers to the front of the bus, where a smoky breath meets me at the door. Maybe a tang of freedom. The border is less than ten miles away.

I savor the glassy crunch of my New Jacks on the concrete, and with it grows a feeling that at least I'm still alive, still have my arms and legs, and the dreams that fucken kill me. And twenty-one dollars and thirty cents. The mostly empty bus terminal shines a promise of comfort, so I shuffle over to look for a coffee, or maybe a sandwich, anything to stop my bowel cells from applying for other jobs in the body. A Mexican boy sweeps the floor by the doors, and two ole ladies doze on chairs next to some boxes tied with rope. Upholstery weeps flea-powder and farts. Then my eye catches a TV at the back. It's the news. My brain says, 'Don't fucken go there.' I fucken go there.

'New shock for the Central Texas community of Martirio,' says the screen. Red and blue lights flash off the slick of a recent shower. Vaine Gurie stumbles up a driveway near the edge of town. She wears a tracksuit, and shields her face from camera lights. Another big woman helps her through a screen-door, then turns to the cameras.

'Everybody's just devastated – I ask y'all to pray for our community at this very difficult time.'

Cut to daylight. Crime tape flaps wearily across the Johnson road, around where my journey began last night. Lally enters the frame, walking towards the camera. His arm is in a sling. 'I was lucky to escape the scene. With a broken collarbone, and serious cuts and bruises, I can only be thankful I was here to witness a crime that dispels all doubt as to the cause of recent events in Martirio.' The stringy man from the morgue hovers over a corpse wrapped in plastic. Troopers haul it behind Lally to a waiting van. 'Barry Enoch Gurie was not so lucky. His body fell less than a hundred yards from the practice range of Martirio's elite new SWAT team – a team he was to have joined only hours after he was brutally gunned down with his own weapon.'

A picture appears of Barry as a cadet, shiny-eyed, hoping blindly into the future behind the camera lens. Lally returns with a deeper scowl. 'I was an unfortunate witness to the shots, shots that cut short the life of a man who overcame childhood autism to become a glowing star in law management, an officer described by colleagues and townsfolk alike as a true human being. As federal forces descend upon the stricken district, attention now turns to the whereabouts of confirmed killer Vernon Gregory Little . . .'

My school picture appears, followed by footage of me leaving the courthouse with Pam. Then a stranger in thick glasses comes on, wearing overalls and rubber gloves. 'The forensic environment is near perfect,' he says. 'We've already identified the tread of a sports shoe – an unusual kind of shoe for these parts – and there's evidence of tracks being covered up around the body's resting-place.'

Lally returns. 'The task of securing the state's borders and highways will continue long into the night – authorities warn the suspect may be armed, and should not be approached . . .'

I slap a stone eye around the terminal. The janitor sweeps half-heartedly in front of the restrooms. Behind a counter, a ticket clerk taps listlessly at his keyboard. I take a measured walk between them to the doors, then aim for the dark of the road and run, fly back to the highway.

I cross the highway at the darkest point, and pound along its shadow side, invisible, just two clear veins throbbing slime and lightning. Up ahead a road sign points to Mexico. Traffic trickles past it. I don't even know how far I have to go, I just run till I'm dead, then limp till I can run again. It's after midnight when the sparks die under my feet. I slow to a shuffle, and strangle a hiss in my throat. Waves loom at my back, crested waves which instead of foam spill flies, flies I have to kill, thoughts of defeat in a grubby swarm. Jesus comes with them, waving, but he's engulfed, drowning, gulping flies that join with the night to claim all his colors, return him to black. I stop, the way a rock stops that never moved. My head hangs buzzing in the dark, and when I raise it up, after a century's pause, I see a glow up ahead. I stumble forward, and see the glow become a glare, a kind of high-beam extravaganza in the middle of nowhere.

'International Bridge – Puente Internacional,' says a sign. '*Mexico.*'

From here the border looks like Steven Spielberg built it, a blast of arctic light framed in darkness. I pull on my jacket, though it ain't cold at all, and attempt to slick back my hair. I stride the last few hundred yards of home.

Lines of trucks stretch into the dark on the other side of the bridge, cars heavy with people pass through the middle. There's plenty of traffic on foot, even now, and no sign of a roadblock, except for the regular border checkpoints. I step onto the bridge knowing I step into my dream, pinning its fucken hem with my foot, for me to climb aboard. The redemption, the souvenirs, the lazy panties in fragrant sunshine.

You can already tell one thing: the clean concrete highway ends at the borderline, it's a different country after that. Tall, small people flow around me like tumbling store-displays, chubby types in denim carve between them, with all the confidence of home. Mexicans. The faces seem cautious, like you might interrupt a promise made to them. The hem of their dream hangs over this bridge too, that's why. You can taste it. I pass by an ole man wearing Ray-Bans, a *Baywatch* cap, a *Wowboys* jacket, fluorescent green Nikes, and carrying a Nintendo box tied with *South Park* bedsheets. Makes me stand out like a fucken shaved wiener, even aside from being six inches taller than everybody.

Checkpoint buildings sprawl on the Mexican side, officials in uniform stop cars and search them. I stand up my jacket collar, and try to lose myself in the flow of people. I nearly make it too, until I hear this voice.

'*Joven*,' calls a Mexican officer. I start to scuttle. '*Joven – Mister!*' I look around. He holds up the flat of his hand.

sixteen

The border officer takes his time strutting over from the check-point. His skin is darker than a lot of folks down here, and strings of gray-black hair are greased onto his mostly bald head, like with axle grease or something. Kind of a gross little dude, actually.

'Passport please,' he says. He looks pretty serious about things, and on top of everything he now has these gold teeth. Black eyes scald me.

'Uh – passport?'

'Yes, passport please.'

'Uh – I'm *American*.'

'Driver license?'

'Well – no, I'm an *American*, visiting your beautiful country and all . . .'

He stares at me. He's going to default to some nasty official type of shit, I can smell it coming.

'Follow me,' he says, and marches me back to the main building.

Inside smells of shoe polish. It's a kind of *Jurassic Park* for office supplies, with all these ole desks, and Chinese-restaurant kind of chairs, lit by lonely-looking supermarket lighting. A fan clicks in one corner. The effect is something between a courthouse and one of those public-health waiting rooms you see on TV, specially for the number of ole Mexican ladies in here. Don't fucken tell any-one I said that, though. I'm not crazy about the effect of it. The official ushers me to a desk, and sits behind it, all straight-backed, like he's the president of South America or something, like the borderline is the crack of his fucken ass.

'You have identification?' he asks.

'Uh – not really.'

He creaks back into his chair, spreading his hands wide, like he's about to point out the most obvious fact in the fucken universe. 'You can't enter Mexico without identification.' He tightens his mouth across, for the Most Obvious Fact effect.

Some lies form an orderly line at the back of my throat. I decide to go for tried and tested horseshit, which, if you're me, is the Dumb Kid routine. I cook up some family, fast. 'I have to meet my parents, see? They came down earlier, but I had to stay back and come down later, and now they're over there waiting, like, they're probably worried and all.'

'You parents on vacation?'

'Uh, yeah, we're going on vacation, you know.'

'Where you parents?'

'They're already in Mexico, waiting for me.'

'Where?'

Fuck. It's fatal when you get a guy like this, take note. How it works is that he'll narrow my bullshit down, make it slither to the spout end of the funnel of truth. See how the lie can start out all vague, like, 'Yeah, they're in the northern hemisphere,' or something? Well now he'll narrow it down, and narrow it down, until you end up having to give a goddam room number. Where the fuck are my parents?

'Uh – Tijuana,' I say, nodding.

'Ti-*juana*?' He shakes his head. 'This the wrong way for Tijuana – is the other side of Mexico.'

'No, well that's right, but they came the other way, see, and I was over here, so I have to go across and meet them. You know?'

He sits with his face pointed down, but his eyes pointed up, the way folks do when they don't buy your story. 'Where in Tijuana?'

'Uh – at the hotel.'

'What hotel?'

'The, uh – heck, I have it written somewhere . . .' I fumble with my pack.

169

'You don't enter Mexico today,' says the official. 'Better call you parents, and they come for you.'

'Well it's kind of late to call now – I was supposed to be there already. Anyway, I thought our two countries were in a pact or something, I thought Americans could walk right over.'

He shrugs. 'How I know you American?'

'Hell, you just have to look at me – I mean, I'm American all right, sure I'm American.' I hold out my hands, trying to copy the Most Obvious Fucken Fact effect. He leans forward onto his desk, and levels his eyes at me.

'Better call you parents. Tonight you stay in McAllen, tomorrow they come for you.'

I do the only possible thing at this end of the funnel of truth. I pretend he just gave me a really smart idea. 'Hey, yeah – I'll use the phone and get my parents over, thanks, thanks a lot.'

I limp to an ole phone on the wall, and pretend to put coins in it. Then I fuck around in my pack like a total dork-hole. I even pretend to talk on the goddam phone. Really, it's this kind of shit that brings up the whole psycho argument. After chewing the fat with my so-called parents, I sit on an empty stretch of bench, drifting into this endless purgatory while the fan squeaks like a sackful of rats. I sit until three in the morning, then three-thirty, horny for cool bedsheets. You know the one voice in your head that makes sense, like your internal nana or whatever? Mine just says, 'Grab a burger and cop some Zs, until it all makes a little more sense.'

I'm distracted by a flash of red at the window. Then blue. A patrol car pulls up outside. Troopers' hats appear. American troopers. I twitch off the bench, and shuffle past a wrinkled ole man who dozes against a filing cabinet. He could've fucken been here since he was a boy. In desperation, I go back to the official's desk. He stands talking to another uniformed Mexican. They turn to me.

'Sir, *señor* – I really need to cross the border and get some sleep. I'm just an American on vacation . . .' Through the corner of my eye I see another trooper pass by the window. He nurses an assault rifle at the entrance, and says something to his partner, then a Mexican officer arrives and talks to them both. The troopers nod, and step away.

'You parents coming?' my officer asks me.

'Uh – they can't make it right now.'

He shrugs and turns back to his partner.

'Look,' I say, 'I'm just a regular guy, you can check my wallet and everything . . .'

A different kind of shine comes to his eyes. He motions for my billfold. I hand it over. He pulls out my cash-card, arranging it on the desk with an official flourish, then he sits, takes the billfold to his lap, and checks out the twenty-dollar bill.

'This all the money you travel with?'

'Uh – that and my card.'

He picks my card off the desktop and turns it gently in his fingers, pausing at the side that says 'VG Little'. He chews his lip. I get a sudden inkling that Mexico might have different Fate than home. What I think I see in his black eyes is a shine that admits we're ole dogs together in a lumpy game. A shine of conspiracy. Then, in a jackrabbit flash, he palms the twenty out of my wallet into his desk drawer.

'Welcome to Mexico,' he says.

The famous actor Brian Dennehy would stand quiet, narrow his eyes right now, with unspoken respect for the secluded dealings of men. He might rest a hand on the guy's back and say, 'Give my love to Maria.' Me, I snatch up my pack and fuck off. The troopers are thirty yards away on the American side, talking on their radios. I turn the other way and vanish into the night of my dream.

Picture a wall of cancer clouds sliced clean across the border, cut with the Blade of God, because Mexican Fate won't tolerate any of that shit down here. Intimate sounds spike the tide of travelers, the new brothers and sisters who spin me south down the highway like a pebble, helpless but brave to the wave.

Reynosa is the town on the Mexican side of the bridge. It's big, it's messy, and there's a whiff of clowns and zebras in the wings, like any surprise could happen, even though it's the dead of night back home. Night doesn't die in Mexico. If the world was flat, you just know the edge would look like this. Natural law is suspended here, you can tell. Border traffic starts to break up in the town, and I leave the highway to zigzag through shadowy side streets, until I come to an alley where stalls tumble with music, and food glistens under naked lightbulbs. One kid at a food stall accepts a buck in coins for some tacos, which don't even smudge my throat on the way down. The food exhausts me. I sloosh back out of the alley like a knot of melted cows, and travel for another hour before logic catches up with me. I know I have to put some distance between me and the border, but I'm fucked without cash, and dead on my feet. Jesus wisps around me in fragments, maybe happy to be home in the land of his blood, maybe vengeful for the foreigners that killed him. I beg him for peace.

I find a dark nook by the edge of town, a bunker between houses, with a view of empty chaparral beyond, and settle against a wall to spin some thoughts. One house window has a curtain that waves in the breeze. As soon as their fucken dog quiets down, Taylor's body gets wrapped in the curtain like a Goddess, her tones flash milky through the lace bunched between her legs. Then she's in the dirt with me. Her hair is wild on the first day of our escape together; we lick and play into an anesthetic sleep, just conscious of life collapsing around us in grainy pieces.

I wake late next morning, Thursday, and find myself in a strange place, sixteen days after the moment that ripped my life in two. I know I have to find money to carry on. I could try Taylor, but first I need to be sure she didn't squeal on me to fucken Leona Dunt. I also have to call home and straighten things out, but

Mom's phone will probably be bugged, and anyway, on thirty American cents I ain't calling fucken nobody. I pick up my backpack, and lope to the highway out of town – Monterrey is one of the places it heads to. I'm glad to move on. I mean, Reynosa may have ended up having an Astrodome, or a petting zoo or something, but between you and me, I fucken doubt it.

Dirty trucks tilt down the highway, with all kinds of extra lights and antennas, like mobile cathedrals or something. I follow them on foot for now. I just want to be alone with my waves. I shuffle, then lope, then limp all day long until my shadow starts to reach for the far coast, and blobs of cactus grow mushy with evening light. I come to a bend in the road that dips downhill, and I get a feeling it's like the borderline to my future. Up ahead is night, but behind me there's color in the sky. It brings a shiver, but a senior thought says: leave the future to Mexican Fate.

As the sky unfurls a drape of stars, important omens arrive. A truck idles past with four million hood ornaments, lit up like JC Penney's Christmas tree, and painted with sayings everywhere. It doesn't snag my attention until it's past me, and I see the mudflaps at the back. Painted on each one is a lazy road that snakes between a beach and a grove of palm trees. My beach. Before I can scan the palm trees for panties, the truck pulls onto the wrong side of the road, and coasts downhill toward lights burning in some shambly buildings at the roadside. I guess that's a Mexican turn signal, just moving your vehicle onto the wrong side of the road. Learning: when you see traffic splattered over the front of a Mexican truck, you know it was fucken indicating. I run after it down the hill.

'*El alacrán, el alacrán, el alacrán te va picar . . .*' Music twangs out of a bar next to a gas station. The truck parks by the bar, and I watch the driver climb down from the cab. He's smaller than me, with a bunch of growth on his face, and a hefty mustache. He takes off his hat to slide into the roadhouse, cool and straight, like he's wearing guns. Then, when he's nearly inside, he gives his balls a squeeze. A little boy jumps from the truck behind him. I shuffle into the building without touching my balls. Nobody seems to mind. Inside, the air's tinged with muddy cooking oil from an alien kitchen. The driver stands at a rough wooden bar, and looks around at some tin tables where a couple of other dudes sit hunched over their beers. The bartender is Mexican-looking, except that he's white with red hair – go fucken figure.

The kid scampers to a table near a wall-mounted TV. Everybody else checks me out as I move to the bar with an idea in my head. A cold beer turns up for the truck driver. I pull a music disc out of my pack, point to it, then to the beer. The bartender frowns, looks the disc over, then thumps a cold bottle down in front of me. He hands the disc to the driver; they both nod. I know I should eat before I drink, but how do you say 'Milk and fucken cookies' in Mexican? After a minute, the men motion for my pack, and gently rummage through the discs. Their eyes also make the inevitable pilgrimage to the New Jacks on my feet. Finally, whenever a beer turns up for the truck driver, the bartender automatically looks at me. I nod, and a new beer shows up. My credit's established. I introduce myself. The truck driver flashes some gold through his lips, and raises his bottle.

'Sa-*lud*!' he says.

Don't fucken ask me when the first tequila arrived. Suddenly, later in life, glass-clear skies swim through the open side of the bar, with stars like droplets on a spider's web, and I find myself smoking sweet, oval-shaped cigarettes called *Delicados*, apparently from my own pack. I'm loaded off my ass. These guys' mustaches are up where their hair should be, and huge fucken caves are *howling* underneath, full of gold and tonsils, just *look* at them, singing their hearts out. Other folk join in, one of them even kneels. The whole night is snatches of humdinger, me and the boys, yelling, laughing, playing bullfights, pretending to be iguanas – I swear you'd load your drawers if you saw this one guy, Antonio, being a fucken

174

iguana. Dudes hug and bawl around me, they become my fathers, my brothers, my sons, in a surge of careless passion that makes back home seem like a fucken Jacuzzi that somebody forgot to switch on.

It must be the same oxygen in the air, the same gravitational suck as back home, but here it's all heated up and spun around until nothing, good or bad, matters more than anything else. I mean, home is fucken crawling with Mexicans, but you don't get any of this vibe where I come from. Take Lally; what difference is there in his genes that he ended up so fucken twisted? His ole man probably did iguana impersonations, in his day. Nah, Lally caught the back-home bug. The wanting bug.

Thoughts travel with me to the urinal, which I find is piled high with spent green limes, like they use in their drinks down here. I don't say it deodorizes a hundred percent, like you'd probably need them on the floor, and up the walls, but there's definitely a lemon-fresh effect, to boost up your thoughts. As I spray the limes, I realize there's a kind of immune system back home, to knock off your edges, wash out the feral genes, package you up with your knife. Like, forgive me if it's a crime to even say it, but remember my attorney, ole Abdini? They don't seem to have washed many of his genes out. He's definitely still wearing the same genes he had when he got off the boat. Know why? Because they're make-a-fast-buck genes. Our favorite kind.

Down here, in another space and time, I spend a night among partners with correctly calibrated Mexican genes.

An aneurysm wakes me Friday morning. I'm curled up on the floor behind a table. A brick in my head smashes into the back of my eyes when I look around. I give up, and try to focus instead on a rough, lumpy-looking wooden cross on the wall above my head. My Nikes hang from it.

'*Mira que te esta esperando* Ledesma,' says the truck driver from the bar.

'*Cual* Ledesma *cabrón*,' says the bartender.

'*Que* le des ma*mones al nabo, buey.*'

The driver drops a big ole load. You hear him spit on the floor. I sit up, and spy the boys at the bar straining to focus on the TV. I turn to the screen just as Lally's image is replaced by my school photo. Machine-gun bursts of Spanish rattle over the top. The boys don't seem concerned.

'*¿Que le ves al güero?*' says the barman.

'*Si el güero eres tu, pendejo.*'

'*Ni madres.*'

'*Me cae – tas mas güero que la chingada, tu.*'

I know '*chinga*' is the fuck word, I learned that at school. There must be a few ways to spin it, but '*chinga*' is definitely the mothership of local cussing. Don't even ask me the rest of it. The bartender picks up three shot glasses, wiping each one with the tail of his shirt, and lines them up on the bar. I watch my picture shrink into a corner of the TV screen, while a map of Texas assembles underneath. Photos of strangers scatter across it. Glowing red dots appear, like throbbing pain sites on an aspirin commercial. Places I must've been sighted. Lubbock, Tyler, Austin, San Antonio.

No dot appears at Houston, though. God, I love that girl.

Suddenly, the driver's kid runs out of a back room, and switches channel to some cartoons. I tremble off the floor and make my way to the bar, island-hopping between tables for support. Then I notice something familiar about the bartender. He wears my fucken shirt. And my jeans. I turn to see if it's true about my Nikes, my soul, now hanging from another man's cross. It's fucken true. I stare at the bartender, and he points to my trouser pocket. I look down at myself, past a T-shirt with 'Guchi' printed on it, to some orange pants dangling loose above sandals with ole tires for soles. My body is a fucken shrine. I check the pants pockets. Two hundred pesos in local bills are stuffed inside. Vernon Gates Little, boy. Mexican Fate.

The boys serve up a shot they say will cure me. It stings, and as

176

I drink it, a sunbeam bursts into the room, a blinding shaft that frames the crucifix on the wall, and lights up memories of last night. Pelayo, the truck driver, is driving me south, to his home state of Guerrero. To the mud-flaps.

He lifts his kid into the truck as I stumble to the gas station to buy a phonecard. I check the mud-flaps as I pass. Heaven, boy. Between them are painted the words, 'ME VES Y SUFRES.' My vesty surfers, or something. Wait till I tell Taylor.

She answers after five rings.

'Tayla.'

'Tay, hi, it's Vern.'

'What, who? Wait up . . .' Bumping noises come down the line, a man's voice rumbles, then quiet, like she moved into a closet or something. 'Yeah – who?'

'Vern.'

Dead fucken quiet for around a decade, then she comes back, real close to the receiver. 'Oh my *God*.'

'Tay, listen . . .'

'Like, I can't believe I'm talking to a *serial killer*.'

'Shit, I ain't no killer . . .'

'Yeah, *right* – they have bodies mounted up all the way to Victoria!'

'Get outta town,' I say. 'That can't be right.'

'But, like, you killed *some* people, right? *Something* happened – right?'

'Tay, please listen . . .'

'Oh, babe. Poor tortured babe. Where *are* you?'

'Mexico.'

'God, have you seen back home? It's like Miami Beach, the whole town's wired for cameras, with live web access, twenty-four seven. The company that set it up floated shares and bought *Bar-B-Chew Barn* – my dad submitted a proposal for a sushi bar, right where the unisex used to be! If it comes off, I'm moving back to manage it – can you believe it?'

I watch credits drip off my card like ketchup off a local fly. 'Tay, I'm at a public phone . . .'

Pulsating music and crowd noises break onto the line. You hear the man's voice, then Taylor yells back: 'It's *my* friend from outta town – *okay*?!' The door slams. She takes a deep breath, like a backwards sigh. 'Sorry, I'm, like, real vulnerable right now.'

'Hell, I don't want to . . .'

'You need cash, right? I have, like, six hundred put away for my vacation.'

'It'd save my fucken life.'

She sniffles, then her voice drops a tone. 'You talkin dirty to me, killer?' I swell in my new polyester pants. 'But, hey – where to wire it? Did you stop somewhere? And what if they, like – you know . . .'

'Shit, I guess that's right.'

'Vern, call me from wherever, like a city, or a big hotel – I'll check with Western Union.'

Her Fate song rings in my ears as I put down the phone. Six hundred bucks will probably *buy* a fucken beach-house down here. I'm boosted up. I get smart, and decide to call Pam. The line clicks. I swat flies while she hoists a ton of arm-fat to her head.

'He-llo?'

'Pam, it's Vern . . .'

'Oh my *God* – *Vernie*? We're *devastated* – where *are you*?'

I detect Mom in the background. I should've known it, they're probably on their nine-millionth burrito by now. Her sniffle wavers up to the phone, but Pam fends her off. 'Are you eating properly? Don't tell me you're not *eating*, don't tell me *that*, oh Lord . . .'

Mom snatches the receiver. 'Vernon, it's *Mommy*.' She immediately breaks into a runaway bawl. My eyes soak up with tears, which she feeds off, working up an even raunchier bawl. It's hard, this fucken moment in time.

'Ma – I'm just real sorry.'

'Well Vernon, the detectives say things'll be easier if you just come back.'

178

'I don't think I can do that.'

'But all this *death* Vernon, where *are* you? We know you were sighted near Marshall this morning . . .'

'Ma, I didn't kill nobody, I ain't running for that. I just have to make good, see? I'll maybe go to Canada, or Surinam or somewhere.' Bad fucken move. Mothers automatically detect the missing word in any multiple choice situation.

'Oh *Vernon* – Mexico? Oh my *God*, baby, *Mexico*?'

'I said Canada or Surinam, Ma.'

'Well but the longer you stay away, the more trouble will be waiting for you, don't you see that? Vernon? Mr Abdini says you have a defense, he's been poking around, he found some clues and all, and when Lalito moves back we can be a real family again, just like before.'

'You ain't still waiting on Lally . . .'

'Well but that old woman at the home never called back, so why not? Vernon? It's love, a woman *knows* these things.'

'Mom – when did you last speak to Lally?'

'Well he's very busy, *you* know that.'

I snort in an ironic kind of way. I guess it's ironic, when somebody passes off total bullshit as reality. Points drip off my phonecard as if they're points in my soul; I feel like I'll expire when they run out. I make a note to try and keep some points, in case they end up being cross-linked to my soul. Another learning about deep shit: you get real fucken superstitious.

'Where *are* you? Just tell me that – Vernon?'

'Ask him when he last *ate*, Doris.'

'Mom, these credits are gonna run out – what's important is that I'm fine, and I'll call when I get settled.'

'Oh *Vernon*.' She starts bawling again.

I badly want to leave her some cream pie, tell her about my beach-house, and her visit and all. But I just fucken can't. I just kill the call.

seventeen

'Ay, ay, ayeeeeeee, *Lu*-pita! Ay, ay ayeeeeeee . . .'
Tunes scratch out of the radio as we roll south in the truck, Pelayo, the kid, Jesus the Dead Mexican, and me. 'A veritable hotch-potch,' as bastard Mr Nuckles would call us. You'll drop a load when you hear the local hoe-down music; big ole polkas with guitar, bass, and accordion, and all these guys going 'Ay, ay, ay,' and shit. Even better is the station-breaks; announcers holler echoes like they're calling a fucken boxing match. I sit as high as a God on the passenger side of the truck, squinting through the slit of glass between an overgrown dashboard shrine of the Virgin, and a fringed curtain with baby soccer balls hanging off it. Pelayo's kid is in a game with me. His name is Lucas. Every time I look at him, he looks away real fast. So I keep him in the corner of my eye, train him to expect my eyes to move slow, until he's lulled into that pattern; then I suddenly cut back and catch him staring. Ha! He blushes like crazy, and buries his face into his shoulder. For some reason I get waves from this little game, I really do, a flock of butterflies in my heart and all. Don't get me wrong, I'm still an asshole. I haven't gone The Other Way, or anything. But, just honestly, it's like one of those Simple Things in Life, that folk always talk about, but you never know what they fucken mean. Imagine a regular ten-year-old doing this, back home. I don't fucken think so. He would've already primed some cusses, just *in case* you fucken looked at him.

We heave deep into the guts of Mexico, past Matehuala and San Luis Potosí, where greener scenery blends with my hangover to weave frosted dreams, of home, and of Taylor. I try to push away the silken threads, the octopus flesh writhing, flashing purple and red, puffing tang-spray and honey, so I can air the musty, uphol-stered ole thoughts, lavender-smelling thoughts I get every day about the dead. Thoughts too big to even shiver at, thoughts just calmly there, to stay forever, like flounces on the satin in your cas-ket. The thoughts combine with the climb into Mexico City to bring soundbites of everyone I know, crying behind their fly-screens, 'Devastated, devastated, devastated, the nightly news, the ni-ghtly *newwws*, the *Nigh*-tly *Nooze* . . .' until in my mind, I'm chased through skies of churning bile by a black and putrid vor-tex that swirls across whole states, whole fucken countries, just to gash me, hook out my guts, pulsating, and stomp them with boots and spurs, like a nest of baby rattlers, 'Get *that* end! *Stomp! Cut* that fuckin bastard, he's still movin!'

Vernon Godzilla Little.

By midnight on this foreign Friday in June, a permanent shiver hangs around me. I leave my flesh and bones at the northern edge of Mexico City, and just the noodles of my nervous system drive with me south. We only nearly get killed a dozen times. When we finally pop out of the city, we're in a dangerous condi-tion to be driving. Just like everybody else around. Alpine forests we drive through, dodging humongous motorcoaches lit up like space shuttles, down to tropical places that give way to areas of rock and cactus, and empty noise on the radio. Everything adds up to make me edgy. I expect to see Dr Goosens's secretary out here, or the meatworks' marching band or something. I try to keep the dream weaving in my head, a thread of Taylor, a thread of beach, a thread of 'Sailing'. But the weaving gets harder, the threads get matted and replaced by veins. 'Devastated, devastated, *devastated* . . .'

We finally stop in a town where they must have a fly farm. I fight with some flies over a sweaty hot-dog, until one gets stuck in the mustard. Mexican flies are slow. I look around. The place is just like the TV-movie where these casino gamblers are in death's lobby, waiting to see if the elevator's going up or down. You expect nightclub pianists' bones in a display case somewhere, I swear. There's Muzak, needless to say. Muzak, and evidence of rats. Then, when I step into the hot, dishwashy dawn, to take a leak before retiring to the truck, a fucken scorpion scuttles towards me. The omens just ain't clear anymore.

Acapulco spreads out in a pattern just like Martirio: saggy, colored underwear districts on the outskirts, sharpening through Y-front and sensible-shoe zones to the center, where silk speed shines tight. The edges show up as we climb the last hill before the coast. Pelayo has to leave his load in Acapulco before heading to his village, farther north. Smells tag our progress into town. We should soon reach the Medicated Pet Soap district, then travel through the Old Spice, and Herbal Essence zones, if it's anything like home. Right now we pass a zone where you just jam a finger up your ass and sniff it.

The road winds out of the hills until blue ocean unfolds in the distance. Acapulco is this huge round bay, with hotels and hotels and hotels. I have to find the biggest one, and call Taylor. I realize the risk of being recognized will grow, because I've heard about this place before, which means tourists will be here from home. Acapulco I've heard of, and Coon-Can, or wherever fucken Leona went one time. I start to feel the shiver breathing down on me. I scan the distance for the correct-looking hotel to call from, but deep in my soul I'm hoping I don't see it. That's how your mind operates, to avoid the shiver, fucken look at it. My face even acts like I'm scanning the bay, my eyes squint, and my lips push out with the concentration of looking for the correct hotel. I even play games with myself, like: if I see a blue sign on the street, I'll get Pelayo to stop. But I know if I see one, my brain will find some excuse why I can't stop. Then the game'll go: if I see a sign with the color green on it, I'll double-definitely stop. I just take the fucken cake, boy, fuck.

Pelayo solves it by pulling over at a little roadside bar, behind the main boulevard. We haven't eaten since our death-dog, and now Saturday is well underway. Pelayo stops on the sidewalk by the bar, and just looks at me. He senses I have to melt back into my dry-cleaned world awhile. He makes me understand that if I want a ride to his town, I should meet him here in two hours, after he's unloaded the truck. An awkward membrane grows between us as he says it. As if he knows my natural habitat is in one of these towers full of wealthy people. He knows he'd be like a fucken gardener in one of these places, if so much. His eyes grow shy from the truth of things, and for the moments past of our unusual friendship. He slaps my back, and turns to the bar with his invisible guns. Lucas turns too, with confused eyes. So much for Vernon Gonzalez Little.

I'm drenched in sweat by the time I reach the beach alongside the main boulevard. It's fancy. It doesn't cost anything to walk on the sand, so I take off my shirt, and my flappy ole Firestone sandals, and start to look American again. Two security guards watch me head for this massive hotel. They wave when I look at them, just another American dweebo, they must say. I spit back my hair and eyebrows, and strut into the hotel like I'm wearing guns, just like Pelayo learned me. The lobby is about the size of fucken Dallas–Fort Worth airport, marble floored, with beautiful lobster-people gliding around. *Awesome* place. A bellhop holds the elevator doors open for me, and I ain't even near them.

'Going up, sir?' he asks.

I try not to drop a load, but it's fucken hard. I see myself at that place last night, with the flies, and the nightclub pianist's rotting corpse, and today it's like I'm waiting for hula-girls to suck my boy, I swear. Leona Dunt could only dream of coming to this fucken place. An American family sweeps past me into the elevator, dressed like Tommy Hilfiger on a golfing convention; it's a mama with a tense ole man, and the traditional two kids – a good one and a bad one. Type of folk who get lighthearted over dinner-music, and start talking about their feelings, to show how liberated they are. Your fucken cutlery drawer on parade.

'Now, Bobby, remember what we said – you know the deal,' says the mom.

'*Yeah*, Bobby,' says the dad in back, like a fucken sock puppet. The girl hoists her eyebrows.

'But I don't *feel* so great,' says Bobby.

'We planned the bay cruise days ago, and it's already paid for,' says the mom.

'*Days* ago,' says Dad.

The kid just sulks. The ole lady tightens her lips. 'Forget it, Trey, you know what he's like. Let's just hope it doesn't turn out like the *other time*, after we spent *all that money* on *scuba lessons* . . .'

World-class knifing, I have to say. And just one smug face left, on the girl.

I saunter toward smells of sausage and coffee, looking for a public phone. Outside, I see a huge patio laid out with a buffet. I stupidly pick up a menu. The cheapest thing on it costs more than a fucken helicopter joyride. Then a waiter starts to hover, so I keep walking towards some bathrooms that are in a service area by the pool. I pass a real-life psycho on the way, too; an up-and-coming one. This fat little dork is standing next to another kid in the pool, being a real pal, while his little sister dive-bombs the water around them. Then, out of earshot of his buddy, the fat kid snarls at his sister: 'I told you to jump *on* him, not *near* him . . .' A future senator, guaranteed.

I pass some lounge chairs facing the bay, with boats and parachutes gliding past them, and the squeak of bitty children in the surf nearby. I start fantasizing that some kid starts drowning right in front of me, and I jump in and save him. In my mind, I rehearse what I'd tell the reporters, and I even see the newspaper headlines spinning up. 'Juvenile Hero Pardoned,' and shit. After a minute, it's the fucken president's kid I'm saving. The president weeps with gratitude, and I just shuffle away. See me? All this drags through my head like a fucken rusty chain.

To snap myself out of it, I go find a phone on the street outside the hotel. I punch in Taylor's number.

'Glassbadanbow?' says a kid. He's handing out flyers by the road.

'Say *what*?'

'Jew like croose in Glass badan boat?'

'Tayla,' the phone answers. I wave the kid away.

'Mexico calling,' I say.

'Hi, killer.'

Something's wrong, I can tell. I get a pang to curl her up around me, her and her safe, deodorized world, where her biggest problem in life is getting bored, or smelling Glade around the house. Probably her biggest personal secret is eating boogers. She's been bawling just now, you can tell.

'Everything okay?' I ask.

Taylor gives a sniffly laugh. 'I'm just like, what the fuck, you know? This damn guy I was dating . . .'

'The doctor?'

'The so-called doctor, yeah. I just want to run away, *God* . . .'

'Know how you feel.'

'Anyway, where are you?' she asks, blowing her nose.

'Acapulco.'

'Dirty dog. Lemme see the map – are you, like, by the beach?'

'Yeah, on the main boulevard.'

'That must be the Costera Miguel Aleman – there's a Western Union agent at a place called *Comercial Mexicana*.'

'I'll make it up to you, Tay.'

'But listen – it's Sunday tomorrow, and I can't get the cash till Monday. The agent's open till seven Monday night, so if you go at six . . .'

'No sweat,' I lie, watching the last credits drip off the screen.

'And babe,' she says. Beep. The line goes dead.

*

The fucken *Love Boat* is here. I swear to God, from those ole shows my mom watches, with the horny cruise director, and Captain Stupid and all. It has the Wella Balsam kind of logo on the funnel. Star-studded Acapulco, boy.

I pull my head into the cab as the bay falls away behind us. Pelayo's truck bangs over some hills, then heads north along this TV-movie coastline, with coconut trees, whole fields of them. The beach ain't as white as *Against All Odds*, and the water ain't as blue, but hey. A lagoon runs alongside us for part of the drive, right out of *Tarzan* or something. We even pass through a military roadblock, with a fucken machine-gun nest, no bullshit. My intestines pump, but they end up just being kids, these soldiers, like cartoon ants, in oversized helmets.

After a few hours, we leave the road and turn down a track toward the sea. The track ends with some logs sunk into the beach, and jungle backed up behind. It's a minuscule town, of slummy wooden houses, with pigs, chickens, and grizzly-looking dogs around. Not even slummy, more like out of *National Geographic*. Fucken paradise. Pelayo parks behind a store that's held together with Fanta signs, and a porch of dry palm leaves. Two men lay in hammocks there, sucking beer. A flock of kids gather as we pile out of the truck. You can tell Pelayo's the dude around here. He's probably like the Mr Lechuga of town, except human. Now I'm the alien in his world. He takes trouble to make me feel at home, snapping at the kids to get away, and calling up a beer from the store. I just stand quiet, nose up to the breeze, listening to a dictionary full of new bugs. Ungawa wakashinda, I swear. Pelayo opens the beers with his teeth, and proudly walks me to a covered patio on the beach. Two older men sit at a table, and an ole lady leans behind a makeshift bar.

A naked kid suddenly brushes past her, trying to spear a wounded crab on the sandy concrete. He finally stabs it clean through the back, '*Yesssss!*' he says, stopping to pull back an imaginary lever with his fist. Pelayo kicks the crab out of my way, and sweeps me to a table by the beach.

A crowd of bottles gathers on the table. Toward evening, a young dude turns up who speaks some English; a lean, smart-looking guy called Victor, with braces on his teeth – something you don't see much down here. He tells me how important it is for him to get ahead in life, so he can bring wealth into the village and all. Makes me feel like the lowest fucken snake. He translates the words painted between the mud-flaps on the truck. 'You see me, and suffer,' they mean. '*Me ves, y sufres.*'

When I first show signs of being loaded, the boys offer me oysters as big as burritos, right out of the sea. Fucken forget it. I ate one when I was a kid, and it felt like something I sucked down the back of my nose. They even offer me the oysters at a time when I have a booger-plug ready to suck down my throat. Without thinking, I point at my nose while I suck it down, then pull a face, and point at the oyster. They drop Acapulco-sized loads over that. They can't look me in the face for an hour after, for the fucken loads they drop. Typical of me to introduce slime to paradise.

After a tequila, as lions and tigers stir under this silicon-clear evening, I try to explain the beach-house dream, the mud-flaps, and Fate. I'm a little loaded. *Fucken* loaded, actually. But as soon as I start to talk about it, Victor and Pelayo take my arm and lead me up the beach, through the palms, where bats now orbit, to a place ten minutes away, where the jungle almost pushes you into the sea. Kids follow us, shining in and out of the surf. Then Victor stops. He points through the fading light, and I squint to follow his finger across the sand. There, all locked up, almost hidden in the jungle, sits an ole white beach-house. My place.

The boys say it's okay to camp here until Monday. Maybe longer. Maybe for fucken ever. After they totter home up the beach, I sit on the balcony of the house, let the evening filter off the sea and through my soul. Suddenly all the different waves inside me alloy into one tune, with feathers of my original dream dancing the edges of this new symphony; my ole lady down here, checking out the neat sanitation, reflecting on how good things got. I may have to change my name, or become Mexican or something. But it's still *me*, without any trace of slime around. I look out over the garden of this place, onto the beach, and see Taylor there running around in her panties, brown like a native.

I spend all Sunday in this Valhalla, lazing with my dreams. When I wake Monday morning, a hot, wet wind blows across me, and my boy is like fucken reinforced cement, like he's chipped off Mount Rushmore. My hand's nowhere near him, he's just being guest of honor at his own little parade. I look around to see the sky clouded over, and shabby gray pelicans swoop and dive into the surf. The heads of coconut trees swish and move around at the speed I wish my life would go, cool and smooth. For the first time in a while, there's that little edge of gladness to be waking up this morning. Today's my birthday.

Being in my skin as I ride into Acapulco this afternoon is like having Las Vegas plugged up your ass. I'm sixteen, and Las Vegas is plugged up my fucken ass. I'm on my feet before the bus even gets into town, buzzing with potentialities; tropical fish and birds, banana leaves, monkeys, and sex. The beach-house. Turns out it belongs to an ole fruit farmer behind the village, who doesn't use it at all. Victor thinks I could probably stay there for free, if I tended it.

The boulevard in Acapulco is sticky this evening, colored lights blare as big as ideas along its length. Victor loaned me a straw hat, to soften my coconut-tree hair, and oyster-shell ears. I catch my reflection in the window by Comercial Mexicana; Huckleberry Finn, boy. I put on my guns before entering the store, to compensate for the hat, I guess, then just strut around in a circle, like a dog deciding where to lay down. I eventually spot the Western Union counter, with folk waiting around it, including shiny red and white folk from home. An attendant sees me right away.

'Uh – I'm expecting a wire from Houston, Texas.'

'Name?' asks the clerk.

My face starts to calculate Pi. 'Uh – I ain't sure who she sent it to . . .'

'You have the password?' asks the guy. Fuck. I feel more people line up behind me.

'I better call and get it,' I say, shuffling away from the counter.

Folk look at me strangely, so I keep on shuffling, right out of the store; out of the freezer, back into the fucken oven. I have to get hold of Taylor. Maybe she didn't send it, once she knew about the password. I have no points left on my phonecard. I can't even call Pelayo. Vegas sputters and dies in my ass.

I walk up the boulevard until I find a phone. I don't know if it's like TV, where you can call anybody collect, from anywhere. I decide to call her collect. Sweat flows between my mouth and the operator when I talk. She speaks English at least. Then sweat runs between my ear and the operator when she tells me you can't call this mobile number collect. When I hang up the phone, sweat dammed on top of my ear crashes onto my fucken shoulder, then runs crying onto the road. Probably back into the fucken sea after that.

It pisses me the hell off, actually, that all the well-raised liars and cheats will go to their regular beds tonight, with no greater worry than what they can screw out of their folks tomorrow. Me, I'm stuck in Surinam with a bunch of criminal charges forming an orderly line back home. Anger fuels me back to the store, up to the agent's desk. Nobody else is around right now. The clerk looks up.

'I can't find the password,' I tell him.

'What's your name?'

'Vernon Little.' I wait for his eyebrows to blow off his fucken head. They don't. He just studies me for a moment.

'How much you expecting?'

'Six hundred dollars.'

The guy taps at his keyboard, checks his screen. Then shakes his head. 'Sorry, nothing here.' I pause for a moment, to calculate the depth of my fuckedness. Then the agent's eyes rivet to something over my shoulder.

I'm suddenly grabbed around the waist. 'Freeze!' says a voice.

eighteen

My ass jumps into my throat. I break the grip around my waist and spin toward the entrance, legs coiled like springs. Shoppers stop and stare.

'Happy Birthday!' It's fucken Taylor.

I spin a full circle, looking for the heavies who must be here to get me. But it's only Taylor. The clerk at the wire agent's counter smiles as she wraps an arm around my waist, and leads me shaking from the store.

'You didn't wait for the wire details, like the password, *dummy*,' she says.

'Uh-huh, so you hopped a fucken plane.'

'*Language*, killer!'

'Sorry.'

'Well I couldn't leave you stranded. Anyway, I'm bummed back home, and this is my vacation money – I hope you don't mind sharing. Here's three hundred, and we'll work the math out later . . .'

'I'll try to cope. How'd you know it's my birthday?'

'Hell-*o*? The whole *world* knows it's your birthday.'

The reality of what's happening starts to tingle in my brain. Taylor's here. I found a beach-house, and Taylor's here, with money. One thing to be proud of: I don't respond to the flood of joy-hormones, the one that makes you want to sniff flowers, or say I love you. I contain myself like a man.

'Wait'll you see where we're staying,' says Taylor, dragging me along the street. 'If they'll let you in – you look like an *Indian*.'

'You got a hotel?'

'Twin room, so you better behave – serial killer you.'

I become heavier for her to pull. 'Wait up – I found somewhere to stay you won't believe – on a beach, with jungle . . .'

'Eew! With, like, *spiders* and *bugs*? *Eew!*'

'You never saw *Against All Odds*?'

'I already paid for the room, Vern, like, *God*.'

Whatever. As we walk, I remember I have to keep enough trouble around me to not give a shit how I act with her. You can only really be yourself when you have nothing left to lose, see? That's a learning I made. It may sound dumb, but it ain't easy when your dreams roll up. Take note, you can feel jerksville lurking in back. And as we know, just by thinking it, you suffer it worse. The learning: potential assholeness when a dream comes true is relative to the amount of time you spent working up the dream. $A=DT^2$. It means I could even fucken puke.

She's wearing white shorts, I can't tell yet if there's a visible panty-line because they're kind of crinkled. Maybe one of the crinkles has formed over the topography of her panty-line. She also has a peach-colored T-shirt with a little Scorpio logo on it, and a stiff kind of jacket that she wears over the top. Her long brown limbs are perfectly attached to her body. I kind of frown at the jacket, though. She sees me and smiles.

'The plane was like a refrigerator.'

It's almost dark when we reach her hotel, one of the bigger ones. She pulls me into the lobby, where all these folk start looking at us. My shoulders hunch. Everything suddenly looks alien, like some kind of store display, with me the only one moving. Except I ain't even moving, not at all. I just become silent.

Taylor collects her key, then her voice goes into overdrive, or underdrive, more like it. 'C'mon upstairs – you'll like it – *c'mon*.'

I look at her perfect nose and skin and hair. She smiles a crooked little smile, a horn smile, and takes my hand. Actually, she takes my fingers first, just the ends of them, and caresses them all the way up to my palm. I get electric fucken shocks to my boy. We climb into an elevator car and ride up to her room. Nice room she has, with a view over the whole bay. Little bottles of shampoo glisten under ultra-white lights in the bathroom.

'Welcome home,' she says. She pulls some tequila miniatures out of the mini-bar, while I just stand here like a spare prick, then she curls up on the bed closest to the window. Somewhere in the composition of the air-conditioning is a licked-skin smell that brings a plague of fruity tangs to mind, damp edges of elastic crusted by sand and sea; salt lips pouting musk and vinegar. I scatter them, and move to the bed. Her sunny-smelling hair makes it seem like a regular day on vacation; fluffy, normal and free – I guess like your sixteenth birthday should feel. But my ole lady will be home, thinking it's my birthday, and trying to shut things out of her mind. She probably bought my cake while I was still there, just to start looking forward to it. I picture a lonely cake on the table, with my mom sobbing over it. 'Lord, you'll make it *soggy*!' Pam would say. Even the truth of things, like that she'd probably be at the *Barn* with Pam, even that makes me sad. Taylor must pick up some of this backwash, because she throws a tequila at me.

'Snap out of it.'

I fumble the catch. 'Tay – you're here to see I ain't committing any murders. You're a witness – right?'

'Whoa, back up. I don't want to even, like – you know? I'm just here for whatever.'

'But if a court, I mean if . . .'

'You ain't *quitting*, are ya, killer? She pats the bedclothes by her thigh. Come to Tay-Tay, you bad boy.'

Taylor raises her bottle, and we slug our tequilas down. I lie back on the bed like I'm wearing guns. She crawls half off the bed to grab some beers, and as she does it, her ass strains into the air. Panty-line. Bikinis. I'm fucken slain. In my dreams we're always alone, stuck tight together, somewhere secluded and safe, but never anywhere fancy like furnished rooms. Always just in a gap in some bushes, or in a field, where she absorbs me like an ameba, all kiss-smell, and thighs, and lips blow-drying the sweat on my skin. Part of the dream includes a kind of yearning to be in a room, all locked up with her, but I never am. Until now.

After four drinks, I'm laid back on one elbow feeling like it's my birthday. Drinks are wonderful that way. Taylor kicks off her leather sandals, one of them flies behind the TV. She runs a finger around the lip of her bottle, and studies me through vixen eyes.

'Vernon, tell me all those things you did.' Her voice is like a little girl's.

What did I say about trouble? She rolls closer until there's an inch of breath between us, alcohol haze with a far-away hint of cheese. We don't touch at all, but hang suspended, sucking chemical data like trembling dogs. Then comes a shock from the tip of her nose, wire touching wire. We melt into each other's mouths, my hand finds the round of her ass, surfs it, a finger charts an edge of panty – doesn't pick, or lift – just teases and glides, moving higher, feeling the climate change around her rudest rebellion, all for Vern.

'Violent, nasty boy,' she says. 'Tell me you killed for Tayla.'

Her whisper becomes a thread in the lace, fibrous and baking with desperate heat. She squirms out of her shorts, kicking them onto the floor by the mini-bar. Panties – The Final Frontier. I lower my face as the creases on her mound disappear, taut glory unfurling, pressing into my touch, forcing my hand flat to squeeze nectar through the silk, lagoons that trickle over the elastic and run down her thigh.

'Death-bug – *God*, murder – *uuugh, God* . . .'

She tries to close back her legs, wriggles hard, but she's lost, I'm on fire, committed even more now she's shy of her musky damp. I pull aside her weeping panty to face a delta writhing with meats, glistening with sweat carrying spicy coded silts from her ass; olives, cinnamon dust and chili blood. She gives up, beaten, without a secret left in the animal world. Her knees bend up and she takes in my tongue, my finger, and my face, she cries and bucks, horny ridges, ruffles, and grits suck me up, suck me home to the stinking wet truth behind panties, money, justice, and slime, burning trails through my brain like acid through butter. Pink Fucken Speed.

'Ugh, *fuck!* Tell me what you did to those people, tell me you *loved* it.'

I don't make a sound.

'Tell me! Tell me you killed!'

She starts to tighten her legs, draw away, and I whisper until she relaxes, and pulls me back to her vee. I've heard about these kinds of girls.

'Did you, Vern, did you do all that for me – for us . . .?'

I feel a fatal oscillation on the head of my man, press him into the bedclothes, rub the stitching across his veins. 'Yeah,' I moan. 'I did it for you.' I keep whispering, but a new reality seeps into me, heavy like the beginnings of an infection. Suddenly her pout turns to rubber, her breeze to raw shrimp and metal-butter. Something ain't right. She scoots to the edge of the bed. Her cleft sneers through the silk of her panties as she bends over one last time. I know I've had the last of Taylor Figueroa. My world dissolves under my belly with a jet like stung snakes squirted out through their own eye-holes. Then quiet. Just a slow ocean moving slowly, and spit-curry after-poon drying cold on my face. Taylor pulls up her shorts, ties her sandals, flicks her hair in the mirror.

'Okay!' she says into the breast of her jacket.

The door opens and four men walk in. I shield my eyes from the glaring camera lights. 'Vernon Gregory Little?' asks one. Like – duh.

I could handle everybody in the lobby staring at me, if only one of them was Taylor. She doesn't stare, or even look. She crouches next to a smiling technician, and listens to an earpiece connected to wires in her jacket.

Then she giggles into a microphone. 'It's so *exciting*. You really think I can anchor the show? Like, *God*, Lalito . . .'

I'm led away from her crouching ass, an ass barely dry with my spit and my dreams. Her careless laugh follows me from the lobby. People around the hotel entrance fall silent when I come through in hand and leg cuffs. You can actually hear indoor palms rustling in the air-conditioning, that's how quiet things get. Quiet and icy-cold, I don't have to tell you. A plane is waiting at the airport. Right away you know some money got invested in the story. Like, it'd be hard to tell some anchorman it was all just a big mistake. Anchormen across the land would drop mountainous loads if you tried to tell them that. I struggle to work up some cream pie. But I can't, can I fuck. Instead I choke on aviation perfume, and the 'Goodbye' sound of jets whining, like when Nana used to go up north. Across the way, you can see stressed passengers shuffling to immigration without a thought in their heads except the shine on their mall-brand luggage. Me, I'm tied in a metal tube with two marshals who choose conversations according to how well they contrast with the fucken shit I'm in. Talk about their car, a steak dinner, a ball game. One of them farts.

I just sit and watch a flashbulb on the tip of the wing light up the dark outside. After a couple of hours of flashes, which is a lot, we descend through puffy tumors that hang over Houston Intercontinental airport. When the plane turns to land you get a view of eight thousand patrol cars on the ground, lights flashing off recently wet concrete, and probably sirens and game-show buzzers running as well. All for little Vernon, Vernon Little. After landing, the plane turns toward some bleachers set up around an empty section by the airport perimeter. We slow and park sideways to the stands, and I'm drenched through the window by flashlight from crowds of media. You physically feel the jackrabbit pulse that says, *'There he is!'* It's Tuesday, exactly three weeks since hell's tumble-dryer went to work on our lives. Although it's four in the morning, you just know every household in the land is tuned in. *'There he fucken is!'*

The marshals handle me down the steps of the plane, and parade me in front of the bleachers. Behind the bleachers is a fence, and behind the fence you can sense hordes of angry people, the type that show up wherever angry people are needed. I'm lifted into the back of a white truck, where some men in lab

196

coats and helmets are waiting. They harness me into a chair, and we get escorted into town by half the world's police cars. All the world's helicopters ride overhead, beaming lights down like a Hollywood premiere, the fucken Slime Oscars, boy. One learning I can give you from here: patrol cars don't smash up everywhere. Not at all. Nor do you get any simple ideas about how to distract the cops while you make a break for it, and leave them smashing into each other, and driving off bridges and shit. What's more, as soon as you're in a patrol car, you're immediately visited by the certainty that it won't happen. They drive fucken straight, take note.

Everybody has their fucken fun tonight, showing some future impartial jury how innocent I must be. Then I get banged back up to hell. Not back home, but down here, in Harris County, where all the big stuff happens.

I close my eyes in the cell, and do a re-cut of my life. In my cut of the thing, I ain't even in shit at all. Instead, I'm the kid out there who hears about somebody *else's* trouble, maybe some *other* kid took his dad's assault rifle to class and blew away half his buddies, Lord knows it fucken happens. Maybe I'd be the kid just *hearing* about it. Hearing about some poor fuck, probably the quiet one, the wordsmith, the one with thoughts and shit, at the back of the class. Until the gun came to school. I'd be the guy just *hearing* about it, with the tickly kind of luxury of deciding whether to be sympathetic or devastated, or not even pay attention at all, the way people do when shit happens that doesn't involve them. That's the kind of day I re-shoot in my head. Still full of different melted things, and dogs and all, but with me the outsider, up the street getting ice-cream, ignoring my carefree years, the way we do, and just getting bored and ornery.

I'm trying to sleep when the other cons on my row are waking up. One of them hears me sigh, and tosses some words through his door. 'Little? You a fuckin star!'

'Yeah, right,' I say. 'Tell the prosecution.'

'Hell, youse'll get the *bestest* fuckin attorneys, hear what I'm sayin?'

'My attorney can't even speak fucken English.'

'Nah,' says the con, 'they dissed his ass, he history. I saw on TV he said he still workin on it, but that's bullshit, he ain't even hired no more. You get big guns now, hear what I'm sayin?'

The guy eventually quiets up, and I snatch an hour of shitty sleep. Then a guard comes to maneuver me to a phone at the end of the row. He marches me proudly past all the other cells, kind of parades in front of them, and everybody jams up to their doors to watch me pass.

'Yo, Burn! Burnem Little, yo!'

I get sat by the phone. The guard fits himself an earpiece, then dials home for me. The number's disconnected. I get him to dial Pam's.

'Uh-huh?' she answers through a mouthful of food.

'Pam, it's Vern.'

'Vern? Oh my Lord, where *are* you?'

'Houston.'

'Hell, that's right – we saw it on TV. Are they feeding you?'

The guard leans over and whispers, 'Egg and chorizo, half an hour.'

'Uh – egg and chorizo, we're having.'

'What, just that? Just chorizo and egg?'

The guard frowns. He makes the motions of a full tray of trimmings.

'And a whole bunch of stuff,' I say.

The guard shoots me a thumbs-up. Mom is already tussling for the phone, you can hear her in the background. She finally wins.

'Vernon?'

'Hi, Ma.'

'Well are you *okay*?'

'I guess so. Are you okay?'

'Well Lally dumped Leona, so that's one thing, not that we ever thought he wouldn't. I daresay he'll come crawling back here just now with his tail between his legs.' She gives an ironic kind of grunt.

'Ma, gimme a break.'

'Well you just wouldn't understand, he needs a strong woman around, with all that new responsibility – specially now he edged Vaine out of the picture . . .'

'Responsi-*bility*?'

'Well you must've heard, he bought the rights to your trial and everything. The company's in negotiations to buy the correctional facility at Huntsville too, and he's just stretched to the limit, without someone who really understands him, who really cares.' She listens to my stony quiet for a moment, then tries to pump some cream pie. 'So – did you have a nice birthday?'

'Not really.'

'Well I left the cake this year, I didn't know if you'd be in town. Anyway, if you showed up I could've grabbed one at Harris's, their opening hours are extended till ten every night now, although Marjorie isn't too comfortable with the new arrangement, not yet anyway. These things can take time, I guess.'

I'm still deciding if it's a bad or a good thing, this syndrome of loved-ones not talking about obvious shit. In a way it's kind of embarrassing, with this really obvious big maggot in my life, oozing and stinking in front of everybody. Nobody talks about it, though. I guess it speaks for itself.

A pretty good breakfast turns up after I finish the call, with toast, grits, and hash browns on the side of my egg and chorizo. Then my new attorney arrives, appointed by the State. They cast Brian Dennehy as my attorney, no fucken kidding, all burly and wise. Ole Ricochet Rabbit really did get fired, I guess. Another underdog replaced by overdogs. This Brian gives me some real hope, though, you know he always wins his cases. I'm damn hopeful, and I just know the jury will love him, they'll be wishing he was their dad, all crusty and benign. I have a long talk with ole Brian, and tell him the way things are stacked.

'You're saying you're innocent?' he asks. 'You weren't even there at all?'

'Well, I mean I was there at, like, the school, and I guess my body crossed the same ground as where Barry Gurie fell, but . . .'

He frowns and holds up a hand. 'Your testimony may not inspire a jury. You with me?'

'Uh – sure.'

'It's an important defense,' he says from the door. 'Let's not push our luck. It's important for you, and important for me.'

'Glad to hear you say it.'

'Oh sure,' he nods. 'Capital trials are the cutting edge of our justice system.'

'So, Mr Little, you'll be the first to trial the new system – excuse the pun.' The man from the court chuckles, and looks away. Whenever he smiles he looks away. And he smiles plenty, sitting here all cozy on the bunk in my cell.

'Before you decide, you should know there's no pressure whatsoever to press the buzzer, which will be prominently mounted in your, um – security enclosure. A camera will be trained on it at all times, to guard against accidents. But, if at any moment during the proceedings you should feel inclined to change your plea, or to in any way revoke the information given so far, the buzzer will give you recourse to instant and positive action, as well as providing a valuable visual aid in the interpretation of justice for viewers across the globe . . .'

'Is there a buzzer for being innocent?'

'Vernon, you *are* innocent. Until proven guilty – remember?' The man rolls my way and smiles into my face like I'm a very small child. 'I assure you every precaution has been taken in the system's design. Both the button and the lights it activates are green, thereby avoiding the more stressful implications of the color red. Also, although we jokingly *call* it a buzzer, the sound it makes is more of a *chime* . . .'

Act IV

How my summer vacation spent me

nineteen

Every forty-three blinks, the flashing lights on the police cars that follow my van into Houston synchronize. They flash separately for a few turns, then start flashing in series, like leading-in lights. Then, for a second, they all flash at once.

What I learn as I'm driven into Houston under low, still clouds, and choppers, for the first day of my trial, is that life works the same way. Most of the time you feel the potential for synchrony, but only once in a while do things actually synch up. Things can synch good, or synch bad. Take me, for example. I stand accused of just about every murder in Texas between the time I left home and when they hauled my ass back. With my face all over the media, folks started seeing me everywhere, I guess. Recall, they call it. Watch out for that sucker. And I'm still accused of the tragedy. Everybody just forgot about Jesus. Everybody except me.

So the whole summer has passed since I last troubled you with my talkings. Yeah; I spent summer locked up, waiting for trial. Jesus kept me company, in a way. I just couldn't talk. Life got real, I guess. Maybe I just plain grew up. Watch out for that sucker too, I mean it.

I turn to the bitty side-window in the van and watch fence posts slide by. An October damp has taken the landscape and wrung out the shine. Maybe it's better wrung out. That's what I think when I look back at the last weeks. For instance, my ole lady attempted suicide. Pam called secretly to ask me to be more encouraging about Lally, and the fridge and all. She said Mom closed up the house one day, turned the oven on full, and sat by its open door. Apparently it's still a Cry For Help, even though our oven's electric. Now Pam is feeding her up.

As for me today, I'm like a refrigerator myself, stale, empty, not even plugged in. My body has realized it doesn't need sensory applications anymore, it just needs a real focused band of logic to survive. Just enough to play checkers and watch TV, that's how smart the human body is, cutting back on things like that. And wouldn't you know it – I needed glasses. The state discovered I have real bad eyesight, so it kindly got me these new glasses. I was none too sure at first, on account of they're kind of big, and thick, with these clear plastic frames. But, with my head shaved clean, and all polished up, I have to admit they look okay, once you get used to them. The whole outfit's kind of cool really, this pale blue pants suit, and my glasses with an elastic strap to keep them around my head. The strap was meant to hang around my neck, but I tightened it up to my head on account of it used to block my cross. Yeah – Mr Abdini gave me this crucifix on a chain. I couldn't believe it, he was so nice and all. Ole Abdini drove all the way over here just to bring me this cross, with the little dude on it. Well, not even just a little dude, like – that's Jesus on the cross. I mean, it's hard to see all the details, but you just know it must be Jesus.

I had a talk with the psychologist here, told him I didn't have any human qualities, like any skills or anything. But he said it wasn't true, he said I had fine higher perceptions and sensitivity toward my fellow beings. In a way, I guess I do have those talents. I could sniff trouble before all this started, I say that must be a talent. It has to count for something. The other big news is that I quit cussing, believe it or not. I guess I've just used some of this time to, you know, watch TV, and not dwell on the bad side of things. Dwelling on the bad side of things has been identified as a problem area for me, that and being anal-fixated, if you'll excuse me saying it, where all my thoughts end up relating to human waste matter, and undergarments, and what have you. Big problem area, but the psychologist says realization is the first step to change. I can't even conjure tangs anymore, really. I'm just watching plenty of ole TV-movies, I guess checking back where I went wrong. The other day, a movie even brought a tear to my eye.

A lynch-mob crowds the streets around the courthouse, throwing things, screaming, and hammering on the van as I drive through. I see them through this tiny window, them and the cameras watching them. One thing, though, at the back there seems to be a crowd of supporters as well. The front of the courthouse has turned into the Astrodome, with camera and light towers, and live studios with National Personalities on them. Then there are catering wagons, hot-dog stands, power trucks, make-up trucks. T-shirt stands, lapel-pin stands, balloon sellers.

I don't get taken straight to the courtroom, but into a make-up room behind the building; apparently on account of its being 'Bathed in succulent, diffuse light,' as the dude explains who sits me down and strokes my head. Some other court folks are here getting blush on their faces. They smile at me as if I was a colleague from the mailroom in their office, and talk about today as if it was a ball game. I notice my make-up is kind of pale. Pale and gray.

I'm finally walked up a long corridor, like the barrel of a gun. Bright light cuts the outline of a door at the end, and I'm led through it into the courtroom. Here we go. I enter this court an innocent man, I have to say, and I believe I'll leave it via the front door, once they hear my story. Truth always wins out in the end, see. I look around at the cast of my whole life, who sit waiting in the smell of finger-paintings and popcorn glued onto cut-outs of shepherd Joseph's lambs. Cameras whir on swivel mounts, people's heads turn with them to watch me being locked into this kind of zoo cage, with a microphone, and a big green button mounted on the front. The cage has shiny black bars set four inches apart, and stands three feet taller than my head when I stand. One guard unlocks a door at the back, while a second man handles me inside. A plaque on the cage door says it's made from a new alloy that no man alone can destroy. I cast an eye around the room and see my mom there with her mouth all tight across, like a Muppet or something. Her wrists are bandaged, I guess from her Cry For Help. Pam sits next to her with a face that tells you they're full of some plastic motel breakfast, of the kind where the ingredients come in matching shapes, like out of a clay mold. They just love hospital food, and motel breakfasts and stuff. Today Mom has her own camera position. No knife turning, though, you know it. My knife turns by itself these days, now that I'm all grown up. My *conscience* is what the knife ended up being, according to the psychologist. A knife is the greatest gift your folks can give you, according to him.

My new attorney looks real positive, ole Brian, real confident about things. He stops for a moment to wink at me, then unloads a box of files onto his desk. There's a whole set of shiny new prosecutors too. The head prosecutor even wears baggy pants, if you don't think it's too vulgar to say, if it's not too regressive into my problem area. That's how damn funny he thinks today's going to be. At the bench on high, an ole judge clasps his hands together, and nods to the attorneys. Silence erupts.

'Ladies and gentlemen of the jury,' says the prosecutor. 'Today we open one of the most cut-and-dried legal cases this state has ever seen. A person stands before you, having extinguished the lives of thirty-four decent citizens, many of them children – friends of his, even. A person who openly admits attending the scene of a high-school massacre, and who has been positively identified by eyewitnesses at the scenes of sixteen other capital crimes. A person whose childhood fantasies revolved around bloodshed and death. A person whose perverse sexual leanings link him inextricably to the other gunman in the high-school shooting. Ladies and gentlemen – today you will meet a person – and I use the term loosely – who, at the tender age of sixteen, has supplanted the notorious John Wayne Gacy, for the depth and boundlessness of his disregard for the most basic rights of others.'

He sweeps a hand across the crowd to my cage. Faces turn to

take in my shiny head, my huge swimming eyes through the glasses. I stay impassive. The prosecutor smiles, as if remembering an ole joke.

'And you know,' he says, 'like Gacy – the boy cries innocence. Not of one crime, where maybe his identity could've been mistaken. But of thirty-four vicious slayings across this great state.'

Parts of my body have retracted by the time Brian takes the mound. He paces slowly around the open space of the court, nodding quietly to himself. Then he stops to lean on the jury bench, and looks into the air, reminiscing.

'Lord knows,' he says, 'it's a fine thing to relax in front of the TV after a hard day's work.' He rubs his chin, and strolls into the clearing. 'Maybe watch a movie.' A frown takes his brow. 'Must make life a little hard for the stars of that movie, though, having everyone recognize them on the street. Why do I mention it? I mention it because four-point-three murders happen every week across the region supposed to be my client's stomping ground. Four-point-three murders happened before the crimes of which he stands accused – four-point-three happened during his supposed reign of terror. And four-point-three are happening this week, while he's here with us.' He turns and stares at each jury member in turn. 'What we will discover, ladies and gentlemen, is that no allegation of murder existed against my client until the day his picture appeared on our TV screens. From that moment forward, virtually every murder in Central Texas and beyond has been attributed to him. That means *all the regular murderers* took a vacation, and Vernon Gregory Little fulfilled nearly the *whole published quota of murders*, some of them occurring almost simultaneously, with different weapons, at opposite ends of the state. Please ask yourselves: how? By remote control? I don't think so.'

My attorney takes a walk to my cage. He looks thoughtfully at me, grabs one of the bars, and turns back to the jury.

'What I propose to show you during the course of this trial, ladies and gentlemen, is the breadth of human suggestibility. Media arrive at the scene of every murder, with a picture of one suspect alone: the defendant. And not just any media. Media under the direct employ of the man who most stands to gain from these proceedings. A man who has built an industry – no, a virtual *empire* – on the relentless persecution of this single, hapless youngster. A man who, before the tragic events of May twentieth, was nobody. A man you will meet, and judge for yourselves, during this trial.'

Brian saunters over to the jury, pulls his sleeve cuffs up a little, and leans intimately over their railing. His voice drops. 'How did this happen? Simple. Under the glare of camera lights, a confused and grieving public was offered the chance to be part of the biggest prime-time bandwagon since O J Simpson. "Is this the suspect?" they're asked. The face rings a bell. They've certainly seen him somewhere, recently even. Result? Even *black* witnesses to *black* murders in *black* neighborhoods recognize this sixteen-year-old white schoolboy as the suspect.'

He scans the jury, narrows his eyes.

'Fellow citizens, you will see that this meek, shy young man, with no previous record of wrongdoing, had the misfortune of being a *living victim* of the Martirio tragedy. Events overwhelmed him at a crucial point in the delicate unfolding of his manhood. He was unable to properly articulate his grief, couldn't assimilate the fragmentation around him. I'll show you that the boy's only mistake – and it was a big one – was not crying "*Innocent!*" quickly or loudly enough.'

The prosecutor spreads his legs wide for that one, if it ain't too smutty to mention. But I like what Brian said. I look around the room, and I get to marveling that justice will visit here, just like it's supposed to, just like Santa. This is a special place, reserved for truth. Sure everybody's smug, but that could be on account of the confidence they have that justice is coming. Take the court typist woman – the *stainographer* I heard somebody call her, don't even ask me why they need her – is her head thrown back with confidence that justice is coming, or just because of the stench of the words, the stains she has to punch into her sawn-off machine? And why is her machine sawn-off, why can't you have the full alphabet in court? You wonder if she likes being close to the slime, or even loves it. Maybe she tells her buddies about it after work, and they all tighten their lips together. Sigh, 'Oh my God,' or something. And maybe the attorneys wear these kind of half-smiles all the time, even at home. Maybe they *became* attorneys because of this overdeveloped skill of making hooshy little laughs that suggest you're the only person in the world ignorant enough to believe what you just said. Maybe they let a hooshy laugh slip when they were babies, and their folks said, 'Look, honey, an attorney.'

The wonderment of it all wears off by lunchtime on the first day. After that, I sit like a zombie for days of maps and diagrams, footprints and fibers. Jesus' sports bag comes out, with my finger-prints on it. It keeps all the world's scientists busy for a week. I just sit, impassive, I guess, with all these illogical thoughts in my head, like how the hell does anybody know whether a fiber was found on a shoe or a sock? The jury dozes sometimes, unless it's a new witness from the make-up room.

'Can you identify the person you saw around the scene of the crime?' the prosecutors ask. One by one, the witnesses, strangers to me, cast their eyes and fingers my way.

'That's him in the cage,' they say. 'The one we saw.'

And like in all courtroom dramas, everybody turns up from the first part of the show, one by one, to tell their stories. You wait to see if they're going to help you out, or put you the hell away. By the time a November chill calls blankets to my jail bunk, proceed-ings have thawed their way down to the bone.

'The State calls Doctor Oliver Goosens.'

Goosens walks to the witness stand. His cheeks swish like silk bulging with cream. He takes the oath, and exchanges a tight little smile with the prosecutor.

'Doctor – you're a psychiatrist specializing in personality disorders?'

'I am.'

'And you appear today as an impartial expert witness, without reference to any professional contact you may have had with the defendant?'

'Yes.'

The judge holds out a finger to the prosecutor, which means stop. Then he turns to my attorney. 'Counsel – has your objection been lost in the mail?'

'No, your honor,' says Brian. He stands motionless.

'This is your client's own therapist. Am I to infer you'll ignore the conflict?'

'If you wish, sir.'

The judge chews the inside of his mouth. Then he nods. 'Proceed.'

'Doctor Oliver Goosens,' asks the prosecutor, 'in your professional opinion, what kind of person committed all these crimes?'

'*Objection!*' shouts my attorney. 'The crimes aren't proven to be the work of a single person.'

'Sustained,' says the judge. 'The State should know better.'

'I'll rephrase,' says the prosecutor. 'Dr Goosens – do these crimes suggest a pattern to you?'

'Most certainly.'

'A pattern common to your area of expertise?'

'Traits associated with antisocial personality disorders.'

The prosecutor strokes his chin between thumb and forefinger. 'But who's to say these traits belong to one person?'

Goosens chuckles softly. 'The alternative is a localized epidemic of antisocial disorders, lasting precisely six days.'

The prosecutor smiles. 'And what makes sufferers of these disorders different from the rest of us?'

'These personalities thrive on instant gratification – they're unable to tolerate the least frustration of their desires. They are

210

facile manipulators, and have a unique self-regard which makes them oblivious to the rights and needs of others.'

'Am I correct in thinking these aren't mental illnesses as such, they don't involve any diminution of responsibility on the sufferer's part?'

'Quite correct. Personality disorders are maladjustments of character, deviations in the mechanisms of reward attainment.'

The prosecutor drops his head, nods thoughtfully. 'I hear you mention *antisocial* personality disorder. Is there a more common term describing sufferers of that disorder?'

'Antisocial personalities are, well – your classic psychopaths.' A muffled gasp shifts through the court. My glasses grow thick and heavy.

'And known manifestations of the disorder include murder?'

'Objection,' says Brian. 'Most murderers are not psychopaths, and not all psychopaths commit murder.'

The judge's eyes fall weary on the prosecutor. 'Counsel – *please*,' he says. You can tell he wants to say stronger words, but he just says 'please'. The difference between what he *wants* to say and what he *can* say is what makes his eyes all cowy, I guarantee it. The prosecutor tightens up the bitty sinews that pass for his lips, and turns back to Goosens.

'So Doctor – sufferers of the disorder you mention, am I right in thinking they're *impassive* to the results of their actions – they feel no remorse?'

'*Objection!* Lack of remorse is consistent with innocence!'

The prosecutor turns to the jury and smirks. I just stay impassive. 'Overruled,' says the judge. 'Your client is not being referred to.' He nods for Goosens's answer.

'Sufferers have a much higher threshold of arousal than you or I,' says Goosens, swishing his cheeks at the prosecutor. 'Their appetite for thrills can drive them to ever-greater risk, without regard for the consequences.'

'Thrills such as murder?'

'Yes.'

The prosecutor lets that one sit awhile, on the floor of the court. The stench of it wafts jurywards. He turns to look at me for his next question to Goosens. 'And tell us – does sexuality play a part in such behavior?'

'Sex is our most powerful drive. Naturally, it's a primary conduit for behaviors directed toward the acquisition and maintenance of power over others. And in the antisocial mind – death and sex are common bedfellows.'

'And how might these traits arise, in layman's terms?'

'Well, a fixation can develop in childhood . . .'

'A fixation for, let's say – a woman?' The prosecutor lowers his face, but swivels his eyes up to the witness stand.

'Well, yes, the object of male fixation is most often female.'

'A sociopath might kill a woman for thrills?'

'Yes, or he might – kill *for* her . . .'

'No further questions.'

Macaroni cheese for lunch today. And bread. Later, it curdles high in my gut as my attorney steps up to the witness box, smiling.

'Oliver Goosens, how are you today?'

'Just fine, thank you.'

'Tell me, Doc – do these antisocial disorders worsen with age?'

'Not necessarily – to be classified, the characteristics must have been in place by the age of fifteen.'

'Is the condition still treatable at fifteen?'

'Most disorders remain treatable at any age, although with true antisocial personalities the results are questionable.'

'You mean they can't be successfully treated?'

'That's the prevailing evidence.'

My attorney takes a little walk around the court, head down, thinking. Calculating Pi, probably. Then he stops. 'In your report to the Martirio Local Court, you recommended my client attend outpatient treatment with you, rather than be detained?'

Goosens looks up at the judge. The judge nods for him to answer. 'Yes,' says Goosens.

'Kind of a light-handed approach for an untreatable psychopath – don't you think?'

Irritation skips over the doctor's face. 'These cases can be hard to diagnose in one session.'

'You didn't have a problem implying it for the jury just now.' Brian gives a hooshy little laugh. 'And, Doctor, in terms of the sexual connotations you mention – would it be equally possible for an antisocial mind to fixate on a man, or – boy?' He starts to pace a narrowing circle around Goosens.

'Of course. Jeffrey Dahmer is a good example . . .'

'But what would distinguish regular homosexual desire from pathological fixation?'

'Well, um – consent. A pathological deviant would trick or force his targets, without reference to their wishes.'

'So, a person who forced his desires on boys – would be a psychopath?'

'Certainly could be, yes.'

Goosens doesn't look so smug anymore. My attorney finishes his circling, then nails him with an eye that says, 'Let's play ball'. 'Oliver Goosens,' he muses. 'Ever hear the name "Harlan Perioux"?'

Goosens turns white.

Brian turns to the jury. 'Ladies and gentlemen – Judge – please excuse my language here.' He moves to the witness stand, and leans into Goosens's face. 'If not, perhaps you've heard of an internet site called *Bambi-Boy Butt Bazaar*?'

'Excuse me?'

'A man named Harlan Perioux was indicted in Oklahoma for procuring and corrupting teenage boys for that website – tell us please, under oath – is there something you know about it?'

'I don't have to answer that.'

Brian smiles a lazy smile. He lifts some documents off his table, and hoists them into the air. 'I have exhibits showing that you,

Oliver Goosens, previously went by the name of Harlan Perioux.' A sharp murmur breaks through the court. 'I put it to you, Doctor, that five years ago you were indicted under that name, on four charges relating to the corruption of boys for your pornographic website.'

'Charges were never proven.'

'And I further suggest to you, Doctor, that you own and operate that site still, under the name *Serenade of Sodom*.'

Somebody in the back stifles a snort of laughter. The judge scowls.

'Am I right, Doctor?' Brian says it slow and clear. 'Yes – or – no?'

Goosens's eyes jackrabbit to the judge. He nods for him to answer.

'No. Not entirely, no.'

'My last question: is it true you also treated Jesus Navarro Rosario, around the time of the school tragedy, in May this year?'

Goosens's eyes fall to the floor.

'And that you presented him with these ladies' undergarments, a charge for the purchase of which has been traced to your credit-card?'

Brian holds up a plastic bag. Inside are the panties Jesus wore on his last day alive.

twenty

I sit on a jail toilet feeling a little hopeful, to be frank, just letting my worldly pressures crackle through my lower tract. I
know I shouldn't say it, but exercising your tract is one of the
greatest hits, boy. It's another thing you're never taught about
life. In fact, it not only doesn't get taught, but they teach you
the opposite, like it's the Devil's Work or something. It's like my
mom invented all the damn rules of the world, when you think
about it.

But I don't think about it at all. It's morning, and the air in
the shade has that hazy, wet crispness you get in winter. I have
some time before they load me into the wagon for the trip back
to court, so I hang here in the bathrooms nearest to the prison
yard. I even have a Camel to smoke, a brand-spanking-new
Camel Filter, from Detiveaux, who's on trial for grand theft.
He's feeling generous on account of his girlfriend brought their
new baby to visit. I told him the kid looks just like him, which
it kind of does, even though it's a girl. Now here's me sucking
wads of blue smoke, and trying to ash between my legs without
burning my reproductive apparatus. All my troubles jump out
of my tract like rats from an airplane, and I just get lighter and
clearer every second. Making plans like crazy. Tracts, boy,
damn.

The journey into court is gray and regular. From the make-up
room, I hear helicopters thumping over the courthouse, in case I
escape, or something. Ha. Like: yeah, right. They *wish* I'd escape,
just so's they can avoid the hard core of regret they have coming
when my innocence struts out. They're going to have to eat that
ole dish cold. I sit stiff with this kind of righteous optimism

during make-up today, eating fries. They must whiff that ole truth around the corner, to suddenly feed me fries. Only problem is they cuff me extra-tight for the walk to my cage, and I have to hunch my shoulder up to my cheek, where I smeared ketchup. As I try to clean the ketchup, I watch a shaft of sunlight swivel slowly over the courtroom floor, until the witness stand is lit up like Mount Sinai. The sound of tattered leather scuffles up the stairs towards the back. Without even looking, you know it's Mom, leaving. She gets her picture took arriving each morning, but she can't handle the guts of the day. Pam'll be outside in the Mercury, both feet on the pedals.

The judge arrives, nods to everybody, and I sit back to watch my Fate played out before me.

'The State calls Taylor Figueroa.'

Taylor steps through the crowd in a gray business suit with short skirt. She throws back her hair, fixes the cameras with a girl-next-door smile, then stands tall like a majorette to take her oath. Goodness but she's pretty. A taste crawls through me of how things could have been. I kill it.

'Ms Figueroa,' says the prosecutor, 'please state your age and occupation.'

Taylor bites her lip, like she's thinking about it. When she speaks, her inflection rises, then dips, then rises again at the end, like a car changing gear. The school smell effect.

'I just turned nineteen, and like, I was a student, but now I'm kind of, trying out for a career in media.'

The prosecutor nods sympathetically, then frowns. 'I don't want to cause undue distress, but you'll appreciate these proceedings demand that some delicate questions be asked – please, hold up a hand if this becomes too uncomfortable.'

Taylor scrapes a tooth over her lip. 'It's okay, whatever.'

'You're very brave.' The prosecutor hangs his head. 'Ms Figueroa – have you ever been – stalked?'

'*Stalked?*'

'That is, has a disproportionate interest ever been shown toward you by a stranger, or a casual acquiantance?'

'I guess so, yeah, one guy.'

'What made you think this person's interest was unusual?'

'Well like, he just turned up out of the blue, and started confessing to all these crimes and whatever.'

'Had you known him previously?'

'Uh-huh, kind of, I mean – I think I saw him outside a party once.'

'*Outside* a party?'

'Yeah, like, he wasn't invited or anything.'

'Was anyone else outside this – party?'

'No.'

The prosecutor nods at the floor. 'So – this person was alone, outside a party he couldn't attend. And he talked to you?'

'Uh-huh. He helped me into the back of this car.'

'He *helped* you into the *back* of a car? What happened next?'

'Like, my best friend turned up, from inside the party or whatever, and this guy went away.'

My eyes move over the jury members, revising their age up to where they all have daughters like Taylor. Their eyebrows show a new slant.

The prosecutor waits for it all to sink in. Then he asks, 'So where did you next see this person?'

'In Houston.'

'Did he reside in Houston, or in Harris County somewhere?'

'No. He was on his way to, like – Mexico.'

'From where?'

'Martirio.'

The prosecutor shoots a meaningful glare at the jury. 'Martirio to Mexico via Houston is quite a detour.'

'Yeah, like, I couldn't believe it, he just came to see me, and he confessed to all this stuff and whatever . . .'

'And then what happened?'

'My cousin turned up, and he ran away.'

Taylor drops her head now, and everybody holds their breath, in case she cries or something. She doesn't though. The prosecutor waits till he's sure she ain't, then he lets go the cannonball. 'Do you see that person in the courtroom?'

Taylor doesn't lift her head, she just points at my cage. I lower my face to try and snag her gaze, but it's glued to her shoes. The prosecutor tightens his lips, and launches himself, business-like, into nailing the rest of my cross.

'Let the record show that the witness has identified the defendant, Vernon Gregory Little. Ms Figueroa, you will have heard the defense claim that Vernon Little was in Mexico at the time of the most recent murders. They say you knew he was there. Did you know he was there?'

'Well, like – he was there when I arrived.'

'How long can you definitely say the defendant was in Mexico?'

'Three hours maybe, tops.'

'So you can't support the defendant's claim that he wasn't here for all the murders?'

'I guess not.'

The prosecutor moves to the witness box, rests one arm on the railing, and smiles caringly at Taylor. 'It's nearly over,' he says softly. 'Just tell us, in your own time – what transpired during those hours in Mexico?'

Taylor stiffens. She takes a breath. 'He tried to, like – make love to me.'

'Was this when he confessed to the murders?'

'Uh-huh.'

Breath is intaken across the room, across the world, probably, followed by a buzz of murmurs. My soul screams out with the sting of it, but my attorney nails me quiet with an eye. The green buzzer in my cage starts to look inviting as, ever so slowly, the room, the cameras, and the world, turn to study me in greater detail. The prosecutor just smiles, moves to his table, and presses a button on a machine there.

'Yeah,' my voice scratches through the court. 'I did it for you.' It plays over and over. 'I did it for you, for you, for *you*. I *did it*.'

Brian puts on a real hooshy face for the cross-examination. He puts his hands in his pockets, and stands in front of Taylor, like her dad or something. He just stares at her, as if what she's about to say is the dumbest excuse he ever heard. Her eyes flick down a little, then widen like, '*What?*'

'You saw the defendant for three hours in Mexico?'

'Uh-huh.'

'So, as far as you're concerned, he could've been anywhere in the world, outside those three hours?'

'I guess so.'

'Why did Vernon Little come to meet you in Mexico?'

Taylor rolls her eyes – a girl's hoosh. 'Well, to have sex, or confess, or whatever.'

'You paid him to have sex with you?'

Taylor recoils. 'No way!'

'So no money changed hands between you that day?'

'No, well like . . .'

'Yes or no answer, please.'

'See, but . . .'

'Yes. Or no.'

'Yes.'

'So you gave Vernon Little some money – three hundred dollars, in fact.' Brian turns to the gallery, raises one eyebrow. 'Darned boy must be good.' A chuckle scurries through the back.

'Objection!' barks the prosecutor.

'Sustained,' says the judge.

Brian throws me a bitty wink, then turns back to Taylor with his most fatherly stare. 'Did Vernon Little know you would be in Mexico that day?'

'See – but, like . . .'

'You surprised him, didn't you? You used a cash offer to entice him – a confused, innocent, desperate teenager – to a place where you appeared, out of the blue. Is that the truth?'

Taylor's mouth flaps emptily for a second. 'Yeah, but I was told . . .'

My attorney raises his hand to her, then folds his arms. 'I put it to you that you were employed to enact this stunt. You were employed to entrap the defendant, not by the police, and not necessarily with cash, but lured with promises of celebrity by the man behind this entire charade.'

She just stares at Brian.

'Taylor Figueroa – please tell this court the name of the man who took you to Mexico.'

'Eulalio Ledesma.'

'No further questions.'

Lally appears at the top of the stairs, dressed all in white. His face is waxy. Angry puckers squirm on each cheek as he grinds his teeth inside. The crowd turn to look at him as he steps down the aisle, into the light. I turn to look at the crowd. You can tell they love him. The prosecutor is first to examine.

'Eulalio Ledesma – you've been in a unique position to observe the defendant, first as a close family friend, and later, I'm sure, as a concerned citizen . . .'

'Tch, excuse me,' says Lally, 'I have a meeting with the Secretary of State – will this take long?'

'I can't speak for the defense, but I'll keep it brief,' says the prosecutor. 'Just tell us, please – if you could characterize the defendant in a word, what would it be?'

'Psychopath.'

'Objection!' shouts Brian.

'Sustained – the jury will ignore both question and answer.' The judge rotates a hard eye to the prosecutor. 'And Counsel will remember a young man could well be executed as a result of these proceedings.'

220

The prosecutor gestures to the jury like his hands are being tied, but the judge quickly scowls him out of it. He skulks back to Lally. 'Perhaps you'll tell the court, Mr Ledesma – did the defendant say anything to you, privately, about the school tragedy?'

Lally draws his lips tight, the way your best buddy does when he has to tell his mom you ate the last cookie. 'Not as such,' he says.

'Did anything he do suggest his involvement?'

Lally takes a deep breath. He looks at me with black, swollen eyes, and shakes his head. 'He talked in his sleep some nights.' His bottom lip starts to bounce. 'Growled in his sleep, more like it – "Boom," he would say. "Take that – booom . . ."' A sob breaks free from his throat. Deathly hush spreads over the world.

The prosecutor bows his head, and waits a respectful moment. Then he says, 'I'm sorry to put you through this . . .'

Lally raises a trembling hand, cuts him short. 'Anything to bring peace upon those wretched souls.'

Sniffles break out in court. There ain't a trace of hoosh about the prosecutor anymore, not within a hundred miles of him. After eight centuries, he just asks, 'Did you also see the defendant kill Officer Barry Gurie?'

'From the ground where I lay, injured, I saw the defendant run towards Officer Gurie. I heard a scuffle, then three shots . . .'

The prosecutor nods, then turns to my attorney. 'Your witness.'

Brian straightens his tie, and steps up to the box. Silence crunches like lizard bones.

'Mr Ledesma – how long have you been a TV journalist?'

'Almost fifteen years now.'

'Practicing where?'

'New York mostly, and Chicago.'

'Not Nacogdoches?'

Lally frowns. 'No-ho,' he hooshes a little powerdime-booster.

'Ever visit?'

'No-ho.'

Brian shoots him a knowing smile. 'Ever told a lie, Mr Ledesma?'

'*Tch* . . .'

'Yes or no.'

'No-*h-ho*.'

My attorney nods and turns to the jury. He holds up a calling card. 'Ladies and gentlemen, I am about to show the witness a calling card. It reads, "Eulalio Ledesma Gutierrez, President & Service Technician-In-Chief, Care Media Nacogdoches."' He glides it through the air to Lally's face. 'Mr Ledesma – is this your business card?'

'Oh *p-lease*,' hooshes Lally. He's like an ole-fashion train all of a sudden.

Brian gives him his hardest stare. 'A witness will testify that you presented this card as your own. I ask again – is this your card?'

'I said *no*.'

'Your honor, if I may be allowed to append a witness to this examination, for the purpose of identification . . .?'

'Go ahead,' says the judge.

My attorney nods to the back of the court. The double doors creak open, and two orderlies guide a little ole Mexican lady into the room. Brian waits until she's tottering at the top of the stairs, then he closes in on Lally.

'Mr Ledesma – is this your mother?'

'Don't be ridiculous,' growls Lally.

'Lally! My *Lalo*!' cries the lady. She breaks free of the orderlies, but her foot catches a railing in the aisle, and she tumbles to the ground. The judge rises out of his seat, frowning as the lady is helped to her feet. She bawls, and tries to pinpoint Lally's voice. He stays quiet. His cheeks pucker double-time.

Brian lets the hush return before calling to the ole lady. 'Mrs Gutierrez, please tell the court – is this your son?'

'It's him.'

She pulls her helpers down the aisle, then her foot misses another step, and she dangles suspended in their arms. The judge pulls back his lips like he just stepped on a spleen. He squints at the ole woman, then shakes his head.

'Ma'am – can you point to your son?'

Breathing is canceled across the world. 'Lalo?' she calls. 'Eu-*lalio*?' He doesn't answer. Just then, one of the attorneys folds his arms, and at that nano-rustle of his sleeves, the ole woman flinches and points to the prosecutor. 'Lally!'

The prosecutor throws out his arms in despair. The judge's eyes fall to my attorney. 'Time out – am I to understand this witness is visually impaired?'

'Every woman knows her child's voice, your honor.'

'Lalo?' sniffs the woman, now reaching for the stainographer.

The judge sighs. 'Just how in God's name did you figure to get a positive identification?'

'Your honor,' starts Brian, but the judge slams down his glasses and spreads his hands wide.

'Counsel – the good lady can't *see*.'

A good night's sleep doesn't happen for me tonight. I twist and buck with the horrors of Jesus, knowing I'm in a lottery to join him in the flesh. When I'm locked in my zoo cage next morning, everybody's attention hangs on me. Sure, Brian gets up and argues, says it's entrapment and all. But you get the feeling everybody kind of knows Lally's was the final nail. Subtle changes in the room tell you they know; the stainographer's head sits back an extra notch, for instance.

While all this happens I feel a vibe from Jesus. It says to cut my losses, forget about my family secrets – it says I've been loyal above and beyond the call of duty, I just have to let them find the gun. It says to tell them about the bowel movement I had outside school that day. I mean, shit must carry a lot of evidence about a guy. Probably you could clone whole other guys from it, then just ask them why they did it. One of my fingers touches the green button in the cage, feels its surface. Cameras whirr close. You just know crowds on the street, people in airports, folks in the comfort of their own smell at home, men in barber shops in Japan, kids skipping classes in Italy, are tuned in, holding their damn breath. You sense a billion cumulative hours of human life just got shortened by raging blood-pressure. Power, boy. I purse my lips, and trace a gentle line around the buzzer, toying with it, pretending to have hefty options. The sudden hush in the room makes Brian spin around. When he sees my hand over the buzzer he scrambles my way, but the judge hisses behind him.

'*Leave him be!*'

I don't hit the buzzer to change my story. I hit it because my story ain't getting told. I get an enlightenment about the ten years it feels like I've been listening to this whole crowd of powerdime spinners, with their industry of carpet-fiber experts, and shrinks and all, who finish me off with their goddam blah, blah, blah. And you just know the State ain't flying any experts down for me. What I learned is you need that industry, big-time. Because, although you ain't allowed to say it, and I hope I ain't doing The Devil's Work by saying it myself – Reasonable Doubt just don't apply anymore. Not in practice, don't try and tell me it does. Maybe if your cat bit the neighbor's hamster, like with *Judge Judy* or something. But once they ship in extra patrol cars, and build a zoo cage in court, forget it. You have to come up with simple, honest-to-goodness proof of innocence, that anybody can tell just by watching TV. Otherwise they hammer through nine centuries of technical evidence, like a millennium of back-to-back math classes, and it's up in there that they wipe out Reasonable Doubt.

With nothing to really lose, I hit the buzzer. It makes a sound like a xylophone dropped from an airplane, and I'm suddenly blinded by a firestorm of camera flashes. The last thing I see is Brian Dennehy's mouth drop open.

'Judge,' I say.

'*Shhh!*' chokes Brian.

'Go ahead, son,' says the judge. 'Shall we activate the recant procedure?'

'No sir, it's just that – I thought I'd get a chance to say how things really happened, but they're only asking stuff that makes me look bad. I mean, I have witnesses all the way back to the tragedy.'

'Your honor,' says the prosecutor, 'the State would hope to preserve the structure of this case, after all the effort that's gone into it.'

The judge stares blankly at him. 'And I would hope, Counsel, that the State, like this court, would seek to preserve the *truth*.' He smiles warmly for the camera, then says, 'Swear the boy in.'

'Your honor,' says Brian, holding out a helpless hand.

'Silence!' says the judge. He nods to me. 'Say your piece, Mister Little.'

I take a deep breath, and go through the routine with the Bible. Brian sits with his head in his hands. Then I quiver right to the heart of my concern. 'I never was in any trouble. My teacher, Mr Nuckles, knows it, he knows where I was. The reason I wasn't in class is because he sent me to get a candle for some teeter-totter experiment – if he'd talked earlier, none of this suspicion would've happened.'

The judge stares at the attorneys. 'Why has that witness not appeared?'

'He was judged unfit by his doctors,' says Brian. 'Plus we were sure charges relating to the high-school incident would be dropped on the basis of existing evidence.'

'I think we need to hear from your Mr Nuckles,' says the judge. He looks up at the cameras. 'I think the world will *demand* to hear from him.' He waves a hand at the court officers. 'Order him to appear – we'll travel to his bedside if necessary.'

'Thank you, sir,' I say. 'Another thing is . . .'

'You've made your point, son. In fairness now, I'll have to let the prosecutor ask you some questions.'

I think you can hear my attorney weeping. The prosecutor

adjusts his smile and wanders over. 'Thank you, Judge. Vernon Gregory Little, how are you today?'

'Okay, I guess – I just was going to tell . . .'

He holds up a hand. 'Your position is that you never saw the last sixteen victims – correct?'

'See, the thing is . . .'

'Yes or no answers, please.'

I look at the judge. He nods. 'Yes,' I say.

'And you never saw the victims at school, until they were dead or dying – correct?'

'Yes.'

'But you admit you were at the scene of those murders?'

'Well, yeah.'

'So you've sworn under oath that you were at the scene of eighteen deaths, although you didn't see all those deaths happen.'

'Uh-huh,' my eyes flicker, trying to keep up with the math of the thing.

'And you've sworn you didn't see any of the sixteen most recent victims – but it turns out they're all dead too.' The prosecutor runs his tongue around his mouth, frowning. It's an advanced type of hoosh, in case you didn't know. Then he smiles at the jury, and says, 'Don't you think your eyesight is starting to cause a little trouble around town?' Laughter bubbles through the court.

'Objection!'

'Leave it, Counsel.' The judge dismisses Brian, and waves me to answer.

'I wasn't even there, at the latest deaths,' I say.

'No? Where were you?'

'Mexico.'

'I see. Did you have a reason to be in Mexico?'

'Uh – I was kind of on the run, see . . .'

'You were on the run.' The prosecutor tightens his lips. He looks back to the jury, which is mostly station-wagon owners, and the like; some hard-looking ladies, and a couple of nervy men.

One dude you just know irons his socks and underwear. They all emulate the prosecutor's lips. 'So let's get this straight – you say you're innocent of any crime, that you never even saw half of the victims. Right?'

'Yeah.'

'But you admit to being present at the first massacre, and you have been positively identified at the scenes of the other murders. Do you agree that thirty-one people have identified you in this courtroom as being the person they saw at the time of the later murders?'

'Objection,' says Brian 'It's old news, your honor.'

'Judge,' says the prosecutor, 'I'm just trying to establish the defendant's perception of the facts.'

'Overruled.' The judge nods at me. 'Answer the question.'

'But . . .'

'Answer the question yes or no,' says the prosecutor. 'Have you been identified as the suspect by thirty-one citizens in this courtroom?'

'Uh – I guess so.'

'*Yes or no!*'

'Yes.'

My eyes drop to the floor. And once I'm aware of what my eyes are doing, the rest of me gets that first wave of panic. Heat rushes to the back of my nose. The prosecutor pauses, to give my body space enough to betray me on TV.

'So now, having had your presence established at the scenes of thirty-four murders – you tell us you were later *on the run*.' He makes googly eyes to the jury. 'I can't imagine *why*.' A chuckle bumps through the room.

'Because everybody suspected *me*,' I say.

The prosecutor tosses his arms out wide. 'After thirty-four murders, I'm not surprised!' He stands a moment, while his shoulders bounce with silent laughter. He shakes his head. He mops his brow. He wipes a tear from the corner of one eye, takes a deep breath, then stumbles the few steps to my cage, still vibrating with fun. But when he levels his gaze at me, it burns.

'You were in Mexico on the twentieth of May this year?'

'Uh – that was the day of the tragedy, so – no.'

'But you just told this court you were in Mexico at the time of the murders.'

'I meant the recent ones, you know . . .'

'Ahh I *see*, I *get it* – you went to Mexico for *some* of the murders – is that your story now?'

'I just meant . . .'

'Let me help you out,' he says. 'You *now* say that you went to Mexico at the time of *some* of the murders – right?'

'Uh – yeah.'

'And where were you otherwise, when you weren't in Mexico?'

'Right at home.'

'Which is in the vicinity of the Amos Keeter property, is it not?'

'Yes sir, kind of.'

'Which is where the body of Barry Gurie was found?'

'Objection,' says my attorney.

'Your honor,' says the prosecutor, 'we want to establish that all the murders took place before he ran.'

'Go ahead – but do feel free to find the point.'

The prosecutor turns back to me. 'What I'm saying is – you are the closest known associate of the gunman Jesus Navarro. You live mighty close to the scenes of seventeen homicides. You have been identified at all of them. When first interviewed, you absconded from the sheriff's office. When apprehended and released on bail, you ran to Mexico . . .' He leans into the bars, casually, wearily, and lets his face relax onto his chest, so just his heavy eyes poke up. 'Admit it,' he says softly, reasonably. 'You killed all those people.'

'No I didn't.'

'I suggest you killed them, and just lost count of all the bodies mounting up.'

'No.'

'You didn't lose count?'

'I didn't kill them.'

The prosecutor tightens his lips and sighs through his nose, like extra work just landed at knock-off time. 'State your full name, please.'

'Vernon Gregory Little.'

'And where exactly were you in Mexico?'

'Guerrero.'

'Can anyone vouch for you?'

'Yeah, my friend Pelayo . . .'

'The truck driver, from the village on the coast?' He ambles to his desk and picks up an official-looking document. He holds it up. 'The sworn affidavit of "Pelayo" Garcia Madero, from the village named by the defendant,' he says to the court. He carefully lays the paper down, and looks around the room, engaging everyone's attention individually. 'Mr Garcia Madero states that he only ever met one American youth in his life – a hitch-hiker he met in a bar in northern Mexico, and drove to the south in his truck – a hitch-hiker called *Daniel Naylor* . . .'

twenty-one

Life flashes before my eyes this fourteenth of November, bitty flashes of weird existence, like the two weeks of a mosquito's life. The last minute of that life is filled with the news that Mr Nuckles will testify on the last day of my trial, in five days' time. Observers say only he can save me now. I remember the last time I saw him. Twentieth of May this year.

'If things don't happen unless you see them happening,' said Jesus, 'do they still happen if you think they're gonna – but don't tell nobody . . .?'

'Sounds like not unless nobody doesn't see you not telling,' I say.

'Fuck, Verm. Just forget it.' His eyes squint into knife cuts, he just pedals ahead. I don't think he can take another week like last week. His lust for any speck of power in life is scary at times. He ain't a sporting hero, or a brain. More devastatingly, he can't afford new Brands. Licensed avenues of righteousness are out of his reach, see? Don't get me wrong, the guy's smart. I know it from a million long minutes spent chasing insects, building planes, oiling guns. Falling out, falling in again, knowing he knows I know he's soft at heart. I know Jesus is human in ways nobody'll spend the money to measure. Only I know.

Class is a pizza oven this Tuesday morning, all the usual smells baked into an aftertaste of saliva on metal. Rays of light impale selected slimeballs at their desks. Jesus is locked in his school attitude, lit by the biggest ray. He stares at his desk, baring his back, exposing his knife. You probably have a knife stuck in you that loved-ones can twist on a whim. You should take care nobody else discovers where it's stuck. Jesus is proof you should take damn good care.

'Yo Jaysus, your ass is drippin,' says Max Lechuga. He's the stocky guy in class, you know the one. Fat, to be honest, with this inflatable mouth. 'Stand clear of Jaysus's ass, the fire department lost another four men up there last night.' The Gurie twins huddle around him, geeing him on. Then he starts on me. 'Vermie – git a little anal action this morning?'

'Suck a fart, Lechuga.'

'Make me, faggot.'

'I ain't no faggot, fat-ass.'

Lorna Speltz is a girl who's on a time-delay from the rest of us. She finally gets the first joke. 'Maybe a whole *fire engine* is up there too,' she says with a giggle. That authorizes the she-dorks to start up. Hee, hee, hee.

School never teaches you about this mangled human slime, it slays me. You spend all your time learning the capital of Surinam while these retards carve their initials in your back.

'Find focus, science-lovers.' Marion Nuckles arrives in a puff of Calvin Klein chalk dust, all gingery and erectile. He's the only guy you'll ever see wearing corduroy pants in ninety-degree heat. Looks like he'd wear leather shorts without laughing.

'Who remembered to bring a candle?' he asks. Suddenly I find my shoe needs tying. Like just about everybody, except Dana Gurie who produces a boxed set of gold-leaf aromatherapy candles.

'Oops – I left the price on!' She waves the box around real slow. It even looks like she highlighted the price with a marker. That's our Dana. She's usually busy reporting who barfed in class. The careers advisor says she'll make a fine journalist.

Lechuga stands out of his chair. 'I think Jesus used his candle already, sir.'

Exploratory snorts of laughter. Nuckles tightens. 'Care to elaborate, Max?'

'You mightn't want to touch Jesus' candle, that's all.'

'Where do you think it's been?'

Max weighs up audience potential. 'Up his ass.'

The class detonates through its nose.

'Mr Nuckles,' says Dana, 'we're here to receive an education, and this doesn't seem very educational.'

'Yeah, sir,' says Charlotte Brewster, 'we have a constitutional right to be protected from deviated sexual influences.'

'And some people have a right not to be persecuted, Miss Brewster,' says Nuckles.

'That's *Ms* Brewster, sir.'

Max Lechuga puts on his most blameless face. 'Heck, it's just fun, y'know?'

'Ask Jesus if he finds it so fun,' says Nuckles.

'Well,' shrugs Charlotte. 'If you can't take the heat . . .'

'Get out of the car!' chirps Lorna Speltz. Wrong, Lorna. *Duh.*

Nuckles sighs. 'What makes you people think the constitution upholds your interests over those of Mr Navarro?'

'On accounta he's a diller-wippy,' says Beau Gurie. Don't even ask.

'Thank you, Beauregard, for that incisive encapsulation of the issue at hand. As for you, *Ms* Brewster, I think you'll find that our illustrious constitution stops short of empowering you to breach a person's fundamental human rights.'

'We're not breaching any rights,' says Charlotte. 'We, The People, have decided to have a little fun, with whoever, and we have that right. Then whoever has a right to fun us back. Or ignore us. Otherwise, if they can't take the heat . . .'

'Get out of the fire!' Wrong, Lorna. *Duh.*

'Yeah, sir,' says Lechuga. 'It's constitutional.'

Nuckles paces the width of the room. 'Nowhere in the papers of State, *Doctor* Lechuga, will you see written "If you can't take the heat."' He spreads the words out thick and creamy. It's a tactical error with Charlotte Brewster fired up the way she is. She won't tolerate losing, not at all. Her lips turn anus-like. Her eyes get beady.

'Seems to me, sir, you're spending a lot of time defending Jesus Navarro. A whole lot of time. Maybe we don't have the whole picture . . .?'

Nuckles freezes. 'Meaning what?'

'I guess you don't surf the net much, huh, sir?' Lechuga casts a sly eye around the room. 'I guess you ain't seen them – boy sites.'

Nuckles moves towards Max, trembling with rage. Jesus abandons his desk with a crash, and runs from the room. Class goddess Lori Donner runs after him. Nuckles spins. 'Lori! *Jesus!*' He chases them into the hall.

See Jesus' dad, ole Rosario? He'd never end up in this position. Know why? Because he was raised back across the border, where they have a sensible tradition of totally freaking out when the first thing gets to them. Jesus caught the white-assed disease of bottling it all up. I have to find him.

The class casually slips into character for the scene, the one where they're innocent bystanders at a chance event. Heads shake maturely. The Gurie twins swallow a giggle. Then Max Lechuga gets out of his chair, and goes to the bank of computer terminals by the window. One by one, he activates the screen-savers. Pictures jump to the screen of Jesus naked, bent over a hospital-type gurney.

I step up to Nuckles in the hall outside class. He ain't seen the computer screens yet. 'Sir, want me to find Jesus?'

'No. Take those notes to the lab and see if you can find me a candle.'

I grab the sheaf of notes from his desk, and head outside. Already I can see Jesus' locker hanging open in the corridor; his sports bag is gone. Nuckles returns to the class. I guess he sees the pictures, because he snarls: 'You cannibals *dare* talk to me about the *constitution?*'

'The constitution', says Charlotte, 'is a tool of interpretation, for the governing majority of any given time.'

'And?'

'We are that majority. This is our time.'

'*Bambi-Boy, Bambi-Boy!*' sings Max Lechuga.

*

Dew tiptoes down Lori Donner's cheeks, falling without a sound onto the path outside the lab. 'He took his bike. I don't know where he went.'

'I do,' I say.

I guess she feels safe, Jesus turning out the way he is. She's just real sympathetic. I'm still not sure how to handle the new Jesus. It's like he watched too much TV, got lulled into thinking anything goes. Like the world was California all of a sudden.

'Lori, I have to find him. Cover for me?'

'What do I tell Nuckles?'

'Say I fell or something. Say I'll be back for math.'

She takes one of my fingertips and kneads it. 'Vern – tell Jesus we can change things if we stick together – tell him . . .' She starts to cry.

'I'm gone,' I say. The ground detaches from my New Jacks, I leap clean over the school building, in my movie I do. I'm fifty yards away from Lori before I realize that the candle, and Nuckles's notes, are still in my hand – I don't want to ruin my Caped-Crusader-like exit, though. I just jam them into my back pocket, and keep running.

Sunny dogs and melted tar come to my nose as I fly to Keeter's on my bike. I also catch a blast of girls' hot-weather underwear, the loose cotton ones, white ones with bitty holes to circulate air. I'm not saying I catch a real whiff, don't get me wrong. But the components of this lathery morning bring them to mind. As Nuckles would say, the underwears are *evoked*. I ride this haze of tangs, dodging familiar bushes along Keeter's track. A sheet of iron creaks in a gust, somehow marking this as an important day, a pivot. But I'm embarrassed. The excitement of it puts me in a category with the ass-wipes at school, toking on the drug of somebody else's drama. Your neighbor's tragedy is big business now, I guess because money can't buy it.

I spy fresh tracks in the dirt. Jesus went to the den all right. The last bushes crackle around me as I squeeze into our clearing. But he's not here. It's unusual for him not to stick around and sulk, shoot some cans with one of the rifles. I throw the bike down and scramble to the den hatch. The padlock is secured. My key is back home, in the shoebox in my closet, but I manage to lever back an edge of the hatch enough to squint into the shaft. My daddy's rifle is still there. Jesus' gun is gone. I follow his tracks up the far side of the bunker, scanning the horizon all around. Then I catch my breath. There, in the far distance, goes Jesus – a speck away, standing up pedaling, flying, on the way back to school with his sports bag. I screech after him, catch myself running like the kid in that ole movie, 'Shane – come back!' But he's gone.

Blood circulation re-starts in my body. It's interpreted as a window of opportunity by my bowels. Thanks. My brain locks up over a crossfire of messages, but there ain't much I can do. Believe me. I grab Nuckles's handwritten physics notes from my pocket. They're all I have for ass-paper. I decide to use them, then ditch them in the den. Some bitty inkling tells me they won't be top priority when I get back to class.

On the ride back to school I'm followed, then overtaken, by a rug of time-lapse clouds, muddy like underfruits bound for the fan. You sense it in the way the breeze bastes your face, stuffs your sinus with dishcloth, ready to yank when the moment comes. Trouble has its own hormone. I look over my shoulder at the frame of a sunny day shrinking, vanishing. Ahead it's dark, and I'm late for math. It's dark, I'm late, and my life rolls toward a new alien world. I haven't figured out the old alien world, and now it's new again.

School has a stench when I get back, of sandwiches that won't be eaten, lunchboxes lovingly packed, jokingly, casually packed, that by tonight will be stale with cold tears. I'm bathed in the stench before I can turn back. I drop flat to the ground at the side of the gym and, through the shrubs, watch young life splatter through slick mucous air. When massive times come, your mind sprays your senses with ice. Not to deaden the brain, but to deaden the part that learned to expect. This is what I learn as the shots fire. The shots sound shopping-cart ordinary.

I find a lump of cloth tucked in the shadow of the gym. Jesus' shorts, the ones he keeps at the back of his locker. Somebody cut a hole in back, and painted the edges with brown marker. 'Bambi' it says above. A few feet away lies his sports bag. I grab it. It's empty, save for a half box of ammunition. I keep my eyes down, I don't look across the lawn. Sixteen units of flesh on the lawn have already given up their souls. Empty flesh buzzes like it's full of bees.

'He went for me, but got Lori . . .' Nuckles snakes around the corner on his belly, slugging back air in blocks. 'He said don't follow him – another gun, at Keeter's . . .'

One of Jesus' fingers betrayed him. He hit Lori Donner, his only other friend. I look up to the school's main entrance and spy him arched over her crumpled body, shrieking, ugly and alone. I never see his face in its likeness again. He knows what he has to do. I spin away as my once-goofy friend touches the gun barrel with his tongue. My arms reach for Nuckles, but he pulls away. I don't understand why. I stare at him. His mouth turns down at the edges, like a tragedy mask, and spit flows out. Then a chill soaks through me. I follow his eyes to the sports bag, and leftover ammunition, still tightly gripped in my hand.

twenty-two

Nuckles looks white and pasty stepping down the court aisle, his hair is reduced to clumps. You'd say he had something more than a nervous breakdown, if you saw him. He's bony and frail under his ton of make-up.

'Marion Nuckles,' says the prosecutor. 'Can you identify Vernon Gregory Little in the courtroom?'

Nuckles's sunken eyes worm through the room. They stop at my cage. Then, as if against a hurricane wind, he raises a finger to me.

'Let the record show the witness has identified the defendant. Mister Nuckles, can you confirm you were the defendant's class teacher between ten and eleven o'clock on the morning of Tuesday, May twentieth, this year?'

Nuckles's eyes swim without registering anything. He breaks into a sweat, and crumples over the railing of the witness box.

'Your honor, I must protest,' says Brian, 'the witness is in no state . . .'

'Shh!' says the judge. He watches Nuckles with razor eyes.

'I was there,' says Nuckles. His lips tremble, he begins to cry.

The judge flaps an urgent hand at the prosecutor. 'Get to the point!' he hisses.

'Marion Nuckles, can you confirm that at some time during that hour you gave some notes to the defendant, written in your own hand, and sent him with them on an errand, outside the classroom?'

'Yes, yes,' says Nuckles, shaking violently.

'And what happened then?'

Nuckles starts to dry retch over the railing. 'Scorned the love of Jesus – erased his perfume from across the land . . .'

'Your honor, *please*,' shouts Brian.

'Doused it all in the blood of babes . . .'

The prosecutor hangs suspended in time, mouth open. 'What happened?' he shouts. 'What exactly did *Vernon Little* do?'

'He killed them, killed them all . . .'

Nuckles breaks into sobs, barks them like a wolf, and from my cage in the new world I bark sobs back, pelt them through the bars like bones. My sobs ring out through both summations, spray the journey to the cells behind the courthouse, and continue through a visit from an officer who tells me the jury has retired to a hotel to consider the matter of my life or death.

Friday, twenty-first of November is a smoky day, tingling with a sense that solid matter can pass through you like air. I watch the jury foreman put on his glasses and lift a sheet of paper to his face. Mom couldn't make it today, but Pam came by with Vaine Gurie and Georgette Porkorney. Vaine is frowning, and seems a little slimmer. George's ole porcelain eyes roll around the room, she distracts herself with other thoughts. She trembles a little. You ain't allowed to smoke in here. And look at Pam. When I catch her eye, she makes a flurry of gestures that seem to describe us eating a hearty meal together, soon. I just look away.

'Mr Foreman, has the jury reached a verdict?'

'We have, sir.'

The court officer reads out the first charge to the jury. 'How do you find the defendant – guilty, or not guilty?'

'Not guilty,' says the foreman.

'On the second count of murder, that of Hiram Salazar in Lockhart, Texas – how do you find the defendant, guilty or not guilty?'

'Not guilty.'

My heart beats through five not guilties. Six, seven, nine, eleven. Seventeen not guilties. The prosecutor's lips curl. My attorney sits proud in his chair.

'On the eighteenth count of murder in the first degree, that of Barry Enoch Gurie in Martirio, Texas – how do you find the defendant, guilty or not guilty?'

'Not guilty,' says the foreman.

The officer reads a list of my fallen school friends. The world holds its breath as he looks up to ask the verdict.

The jury foreman's eyes twitch, then fall.

'Guilty.'

Even before he says it, I feel departments in the office of my life start to close up shop; files are shredded, sensitivities are folded into neatly marked boxes, lights and alarms are switched off. As the husk of my body is guided from the court, I sense a single little man sat at the bottom of my soul. He hunches over a card table under a naked low-watt bulb, sipping flat beer from a plastic cup. I figure he must be my janitor. I figure he must be me.

Act V

Me ves y sufres

twenty-three

On the second of December I was sentenced to death by lethal injection. Christmas on Death Row, boy. To be fair, ole Brian Dennehy tried his best. In the end, it doesn't look like they'll cast the real Brian in the TV-movie, I guess because he doesn't lose his cases. But my appeal will draw out the truth. There's a new fast-track appeals process that means I could be out by March. They reformed the system, so innocent folks don't have to spend years on the row. It can't be bad. The only news about me is that I put on twenty pounds since the sentence. It keeps out some of this January chill. Apart from that, my life hangs still while the seasons whip around me.

Taylor's eyes flicker brightly through the screen. TV makes them sparkle, but they move strangely, as if she holds them back on a leash. Her grin is frozen like it came out of a jelly mold. I watch her almost-but-not-quite staring at me, until, after a minute, I realize she's reading something behind the camera. Her lines must be written there. After another moment I realize she's reading something about me. My skin cools as understanding dawns.

'Then, when the big day arrives,' she says, 'everybody else, including witnesses, will assemble at five fifty-five in the lounge next to the visiting room. The final meal will be served between three-thirty and four o'clock in the afternoon, then, sometime before six, he'll be allowed to shower, and dress in fresh clothes.'

A stray, impassive thought bubbles up through my mind: that Pam will have to supervise my last meal. 'Oh Lord, it's getting soggy . . .'

'Right after six o'clock,' says Taylor, 'he'll be taken from the cell area into the execution chamber, and strapped down to a gurney. A medical officer will insert an intravenous catheter into his arm, and run a saline solution through it. Then the witnesses will be escorted to the execution chamber. When everyone is in place, the warden will ask him to make any last statement . . .'

The host of the show chuckles when she says that. 'Heck,' he says, 'I'd recite *War and Peace* as my last statement!' Taylor just laughs. She still has that killer laugh.

I've seen a whole lot of Taylor these last weeks, actually. First I saw her on *Today*, then she was with *Letterman*, talking about her bravery, and our kind of relationship together. I never realized we got so close, until I saw her talking about it. She came out in November *Penthouse* too, real pretty pictures taken at the prison museum. That's where they keep 'Old Sparky', the State's first electric chair. November *Penthouse* has these pictures of Taylor posing around Old Sparky, real fetching, if it's not too bold to say. I have one posted in my cell, not the whole body or anything, just the face. You can see a piece of the chair too, in back. I guess lethal injection wouldn't look so good for modeling, like with Taylor draped over the gurney or something.

On the bench in my cell I have one of those ole distractions with the metal balls that hang on fishing wire, in a row, and clack into each other. Next to it sits my towel, with my art project tools hidden under. Yeah, I still hide things under my laundry. Some habits are a real challenge to break. Then, next to my towel, is the baby TV Vaine Gurie loaned me. I reach up and change the channel.

'The Ledesma man is wrong, is criminel, they are many more fax hiden than come out in court.' It's my ole attorney, Abdini, speaking to a panel of ladies on local TV. Lookit ole Ricochet there, my man the underdog. He's dressed like for a Turkish disco.

'Vernon Little's appeal is in process now, isn't it?' asks the hostess.

'It is,' says another lady, 'but it's not looking good.'

'Police neber fine the other way-upon, for instants,' continues Abdini.

'Excuse me?' says one of the panel.

'I think he means they never found that other *weapon*,' prompts her colleague.

The ladies all laugh politely, but Abdini just scowls at the camera. 'I will fine it . . .'

I flick channels again, to see who else is on the gravy train. On another show, a reporter talks to Lally. 'But what do you say to those sectors of the community that accuse you of trash-mongering?'

'Tch, nonsense,' says Lally. 'First, the broadcast itself is a non-profit venture. Revenues flow right back to the State, instead of taxpayers' money flowing out to support some of the worst criminals in the land. Second, it upholds our basic right to *see* justice being done.'

'So you're effectively proposing to fund the State's penal system by selling broadcast rights to the prisoners' executions? I mean – isn't a prisoner's last hour a little *personal*?'

'Not at all – don't forget that all executions are witnessed, even today. We're simply expanding the audience to include anyone with an interest in the proper function of law.' Lally puts a hand on his hip. 'Not so long ago, Bob, all executions were public – even held in the town square. Crime went down, public satisfaction went up. Throughout history it's been society's right to punish delinquents by its own hand. It makes plain sense to give that right back to society.'

'Hence the web-vote?'

'Exactly. And we're not just talking executions here – were talking the ultimate reality TV, where the public can monitor, via cable or internet, prisoners' whole lives on death row. They can live amongst them, so to speak, and make up their own minds about a convict's worthiness for punishment. Then each week, viewers across the globe can cast a vote to decide which prisoner is executed next. It's humanity in action – the next logical step toward true democracy.'

245

'But surely, due process dictates the fate of prisoners?'

'Absolutely, and we can't tamper with that. But the new fast-track appeals process means prisoners' last recourses at law are spent much sooner, after which I say the public should have a hand in the roster of final events.' Lally lets fly a hooshy laugh at the reporter, and spreads his hands wide. 'In the tradition of momentous progress, it's blindingly simple, Bob: criminals cost money. Popular TV makes money. Criminals are popular on TV. Put them together and, presto – problem solved.'

The reporter pauses as a helicopter settles in the background. Then he asks, 'What do you say to those who claim prisoners' rights will be breached?'

'Oh *please* – prisoners, by definition, live in *forfeit* of their rights. Anyway, cons today can languish in institutions for years without knowing their fate – wouldn't you say *that* was cruel? We're finally giving them what the law has always promised but never delivered – expediency. Not only that, they'll have greater access to spiritual counsel, and musical choices to accompany their final event. We'll even craft a special segment around their final statement, with the background imagery of their choice. Believe me – prisoners will welcome these changes.'

The reporter smiles and nods at Lally. 'And what of reports that you're gearing up for a shot at the senate?'

I switch off the set. I ain't looking forward to cameras in here. We just have an open toilet, see? I guess that's where the money gets made. Internet viewers will be able to choose which cells to watch, and change camera angles and all. On regular TV there'll be edited highlights of the day's action. Then the general public will vote by phone or internet. They'll vote for who should die next. The cuter we act, the more we entertain, the longer we might live. I heard one ole con say it'd be just like the life of a real actor.

Before lights-out I sit up to play with the clacking metal balls, something I've been doing a lot of lately. Ella Bouchard mailed me a pome that I sometimes read too, about true hearts and what-all. I know it's spelled *poem*, but she don't, not yet anyway. I avoid the pome tonight, and just play with the cause-and-effect balls. Then Jones the guard brings the phone to my cell. The cell-phone is one good thing about Lally's operation. That, and cubicle doors in the shower block, and electronic cigarette lighters, even though they don't give a flame.

I take the phone from Jonesy. 'Hello?'

'Well,' says Mom, 'I don't know who's been talking to Lally . . .'

'Who *hasn't* been talking to him, more like it.'

'Well don't get snotty Vernon, God. I'm just *saying*, that's all. People came snooping about your father, and they've been hassling the gals as well. You'd think Lally'd be busy enough, what with everything. Meantime I have to scrape up the money to do something about that damn bench, it sinks more every day . . .'

'Snooping?'

'Well, you know, asking why they never found your daddy's body and all. Lally's been so antsy since he dumped Georgette – even Pam and Vaine noticed it.'

'Vaine's in your club now, huh?'

'Well she's been through a lot, what with Lalicom pulling out of the SWAT team. The sheriff's taking all his home troubles out on her, and she's under real pressure to prove herself – you just don't *empathize*, Vernon.'

'There ain't a whole lot I can do, Ma.'

'I know, I'm just *saying*, that's all. If he'd only come home, things'd be different.'

'Don't wait up for him.'

'Well there's *love* at stake, a woman *senses* these nancies.'

'Nuances, Ma.'

'Oops – I have to run, Pam and Vaine just arrived, and I haven't finished the zipper on Pam's pants. Harris's is floating the e-store today and there are specials galore. Promise me you'll be okay . . .'

'Palmyra's wearing *pants* . . .?'

She hangs up. Taylor's voice oozes out of a TV in the next cell, so I go back to clacking the balls, just watching them. I have too much pain right now to work on my art project. Maybe later.

'Jeezus, Little,' screams a con up the row. 'Fuck up with yer cunted fuckin noise!'

He's an okay guy, the con. They're all cool, actually. They all planned a beer together, with ribs and steak, when they get to heaven. Or wherever. I still plan to have some here on earth, to be honest. The truth's still out there, virginal and waiting. Anyway, I don't take much notice of the row. That's one thing about these balls, once you set them clacking. You focus right in. Drop two balls, and an equal two clack off the other side; just this one metal ball in the middle passes on all the shock.

'Burnem Little you motherfuckin scroted cunt-ass shitsucker,' screams the con.

'Je-sus Ch-*risst*,' hollers Jonesy, 'keep it down, willya?'

'Jones,' says the con, 'I swear I'm gonna waste my fuckin self if he don't quit clickin them fuckin balls.'

'Chill out, the kid's entitled to a little diversion,' says the guard. 'Y'all know what it's like with an appeal pending.' He's actually okay, ole Jonesy, though he's none too smart. Stops by my cell sometimes to tell me my pardon came through. 'Little, your pardon came through,' he says. Then he just laughs. I laugh too, these days.

'Jonesy, I ain't kiddin,' calls the con. 'That fuckin click, click, click goes on day and fuckin night, the kid's losin his sense – fix him a little time with *Lasalle* for chrissakes.'

'Oh yeah, like you give the orders around here. Gimme a fuckin million dollars and I'll think about it,' says Jones. 'Anyway, he don't need Lasalle. He don't need no Lasalle at all, now shut the fuck up.'

'Little,' screams the con, 'fuck your goddam appeal, I'll ream your ass with a fuckin Roto-Rooter if you don't quit them balls.'

'Hey,' barks Jones. 'What am I now tellin you?'

'Jonesy, the kid's bended up, he need some *Lasalle* to help him face his God.'

'Take more'n damn Lasalle to straighten this boy out,' says Jones. 'Git some sleep now, go on.'

'*I have some goddam basic fuckin human rights in this fuckin joint!*' screams the con.

'Git to sleep goddammit,' barks Jonesy. 'I'll see what I can do.'

I go real quiet. Who's Lasalle? The idea of facing my God sticks in my brain like a burr.

A guard comes for me after breakfast and takes me out of my cell.

'Yeah, yeah,' go the cons as I shuffle along the row.

We go down some stairs into the lower tract of the building, which is like the bowels, if it's not too rough to say, and end up in a dark, wet kind of corridor with only three cells running off it. The cells have no bars or windows, just these bank-vault kind of doors, with reinforced peepholes.

'If you wuzn't who you wuz, you wun't even be comin down here,' says the guard. 'Only you celebrity killers git to come down here.'

'What's down here?' I ask.

'Think of it as a chapel.'

'The pastor's down here?'

'Pastor *Lasalle's* down here.' He stops at the last door, and unlocks it with a set of keys.

'You lock the pastor in there?' I ask.

'I lock *you* in there.'

The guard flicks a switch outside the door, and a pale green light glows into the shadows of the cell. It's empty except for two metal bunk frames that fold out of the wall on each side.

'Siddown. Lasalle be along just now.'

He steps back into the corridor, throwing an eye into the gloom of the stairwell. After a minute you hear clinking and shuffling, and an ole black man appears in a beat-up mechanic's cap, and regular gray shirt and pants. He wears a bemused kind of smile. You sense it's been around awhile.

'Knock when you want out,' the guard tells him, locking the door.

The ole black man unfolds the opposite bunk, and squeaks down onto the bare springs, as if I wasn't here. Then he pulls his cap down low, folds his hands in his lap, and shuts his eyes, real comfortable.

'So – you're a preacher?' I ask.

He doesn't answer. After a minute you hear a gentle wheezing from his nostrils, and see his tongue laze around his mouth. Then his face nods onto his chest. He's asleep. I study him for about six decades, until I get bored of the shadows and the damp, then I slide off the bunk, and step away to knock for the guard.

Lasalle stirs behind me. 'Crusty young outcast,' he says, 'all brave and lonely, older than his years . . .'

My feet weld to the floor.

'Lopin away to hop another bus outta town.' I turn to see a yellow eye pop open and shine at me. 'Only one bus leaves these parts, son – and you know where it's goin.'

'Excuse me?' I stare at his ole slumped form, watch his lip hang dopey from his jaw.

'Know why you down here with me?' he asks.

'They didn't say.' I sit back down on the opposite bunk, and slouch to see under the shadow of his cap. His eyes glisten through the dark.

'Only one reason, boy. Becausen you ain't ready to *die*.'

'I guess not,' I say.

'Becausen you spent all these years tryin to figure things out, and in figurin them out you got tangled up worse'n before.'

'How do you *know*?'

'Becausen I'm human.' Lasalle creaks to the edge of his bunk. He takes a big pair of glasses from his shirt pocket, and puts them on. Huge moon eyes swim through the glass. 'How you feel about us humans?'

'Heck, I don't know anymore. Everybody's just yelling their heads off about their rights, and stuff, and saying, "Nice to see you," when they'd rather see you in the river with your neck cut. I know that much.'

'Boy, ain't it the truth,' says Lasalle with a chuckle.

'Ain't it just? Folks lie without even thinking about it, like every day of their lives, "Sir, I woke up with a fever," then they spend the whole *rest* of their lives telling *you* not to lie . . .'

Lasalle shakes his head. 'Amen. Sounds to me like you plain don't want to associate with those people no more, you rather not even be around.'

'You're right there, Pastor.'

'Well,' he says, eyeing up the cell. 'You got your wish.'

That kind of hits me sideways. I sit up.

'What else did you wish for, son? I bet you wished you could shut your mama up once or twice before, I bet you dreamed of quittin home.'

'I guess I did . . .'

'Presto,' he says, opening out his hands. 'You lookin more and more lucky.'

'But, wait – that ain't the right logic . . .'

His eyes bore through me, a hardness comes to his voice. 'Ahhh, so you a *logical* boy. You all strung out on everybody else's lies, and everybody else's habits that you hate, becausen you *logical*. I bet you can't even tell me a thing you *love*.'

'Uh . . .'

'That cos you such a big man, all crusty and independent? Or wait, lemme guess – it's probably cozza you ole lady – I bet she the type of lady makes you feel guilty about the leastest thing, the type who probably gives the same dumb ole cards on you birthday, with puppy-dogs, and steam trains on 'em . . .'

'That's her.'

Lasalle nods, and blows a little air through his lips. 'Boy that woman must be one stupid cunt. Must be the dumbest fuckin snatch-rag that ever roamed this earth, probably is so butt-spastic . . .'

'Hey, *hey* – you sure you're a *pastor*?'

'Boy, she one selfish fuckin piss-flap . . .'

'*Wait, goddammit!*'

There's a noise at the door, the peephole darkens. 'Keep it down,' says the guard.

I realize I'm on my feet, with my fists clenched tight. When I look back to Lasalle, he's smiling. 'No love, huh, kid?'

I sit down on the bunk. Velcro maggots crawl up my spine.

'Lemme tell you something for free – you'll have a honey of a life if you love the people who love you first. Ever see your ma choose a birthday card for you?'

'No.'

He laughs. 'That's becausen there ain't the hours in a boy's agenda to watch her stand and read every little word in those cards, turn every feeling over in her soul. You probably too busy hiding the thing in you closet to read the words inside, about rays of sunshine the day you came into the world. Huh, Vernon Gregory?'

Heat comes to my eyes.

'You messed up, son. Face it.'

'But I didn't mean for anything to happen . . .'

'Stuff needed to happen, kid. Different stuff from this. You just ain't faced your God.' Lasalle goes to his pants pocket and pulls out a rag for me to wipe my eyes. I use my sleeve instead. He reaches over and wraps a wrinkly hand around mine. 'Son,' he says, 'ole Lasalle gonna tell you how it all work. Lasalle gonna give you the secret of this human life, and you gonna wonder why you never saw it before . . .'

As he says it, I hear movement in the corridor outside. Footsteps. Then Lally's voice.

twenty-four

'The key to this first public vote', says Lally, 'is not to give too many choices. We need to pick a shortlist of prisoners, advertise them well, then open the voting lines and see who performs.'

It sounds like he's with at least three other men. The guard knocks urgently on our door, but doesn't open it, like he just wants us to shut up.

'We have a hundred and fourteen ready to go,' says another man. 'You mean put up three dozen or so, for the first vote?'

'Tch, no way. I mean put up two or three, at most. Flesh-out their characters for the audience, show interviews, reconstructions of their crimes, tears from the victims' families. Then give the candidates web-cam access for the last week, live to air – a head-to-head battle for sympathy.'

'I see,' says the guy. 'Kinda *Big Brother*, huh?'

'Precisely, just how we sold it to the sponsors.'

'But how do we select the first two?' asks a third man.

'It doesn't really matter, provided the crimes are strong enough. I heard a concept the other day that kind of interested me, though, I think it was on a game show or something – *"The last shall go first,"* it said. Has a ring to it, don't you think?'

'Nice,' says the fourth man. 'Top-of-mind recall.'

'Precisely.'

Their footsteps slow as they approach the cell, you hear the guard clink to attention.

'Any reason for you to be down here, Officer?' asks Lally.

The guard shuffles on the spot, then a shadow passes over the peephole. 'Open this door,' says Lally. The key turns, and he looks inside. 'What have we here?' He turns to the guard.

'Aren't the men supposed to be segregated?'

'Oh sure, sure,' says the guard, fidgeting with his keys. 'It's just like, therapy, you know? A little counseling makes the living easier up on the Row.'

Lally frowns. 'This boy is a mass-murderer – surely it's a little late for counseling. Anyway, these cells are out of bounds, we're installing sound post-production down here.'

'How's your mama?' I ask Lally. The words skim from my lip like spit. 'Motherfucker.'

'Jesus, kid!' chokes the guard.

Lally stifles an impulse to lash me, his business cronies keep him chilled. I stare slow deaths at him. 'There ain't prayers enough in heaven to stop me paying your fucken ass back,' I hear myself whisper. Even Lasalle recoils.

Lally just smirks. 'Break them up.'

'Yes, sir,' says the guard. He straightens, and waves an angry hand at Lasalle and me. I try to catch Lasalle's eyes, but he just shuffles away.

'Lasalle – what's the secret?' I hiss after him.

'Later, kid, later.'

Lally smiles at me as I leave the room. 'Still trying to figure things out, eh, Little man?' He gives an asthma laugh, then his voice folds into echoes as he leads his men away. 'So, February fourteenth we launch the first vote.'

'You mean Valentine's Day?' asks another man.

'Precisely.'

Guess what: you can receive junk-mail on Death Row. The week before the first vote I get a sweepstakes letter that says I definitely won a million dollars; at least that's what it says on the envelope. I think you have to buy encyclopedias to get it or something, or to maybe get it. I also find a *Bar-B-Chew Barn* token entitling me to a *Chik'n'Mix* for two, at any of their branches across the State. Yeah, they're across the State now. Tomorrow the world, I guess.

I'm working on my art project when I hear Jonesy making his way down the Row towards me. Banter from the other cells lets you know where he is. He's bringing the phone. I stiffen, and stash away my art stuff. As it happens though, the big news reaches me before Jonesy arrives with the phone. I hear it from a TV up the Row.

'. . . The body of the American will be flown home today. Forty refugees also died in the skirmish,' says the news. 'After the break – the end of the road for serial killer Vernon Gregory Little; we'll have the latest on that failed appeal, and also – the duck and the hamster that just won't take no for an answer!'

Jones doesn't look at me, he just passes me the phone. 'Vernon, I'm sorry,' my attorney crackles through the receiver. 'I don't have the words to tell you how I feel.'

I just stay quiet.

'There's nothing more we can do.'

'What about the Supreme Court?' I ask.

'In your case, I'm afraid the fast-track process puts that option out of our reach. I'm sorry . . .'

I put the phone down on my bunk, hearing every crease of the blanket like gravel in my ears.

Tonight they install cameras in my cell, and remove all the TVs and radios from the Row. We ain't allowed to see how the voting's going, that's why. I just sit quiet in the darkest corner and think about things, I don't even play with the clacking balls. Eight squillion valentines turned up for me, from sickos all over the world. Somebody in the mail room was kind enough to just send up the one from Ella Bouchard. I left her on my mail list, don't ask me why. I don't open it, though. The Row is extra-quiet tonight, out of respect, I guess. They're called the worst in the land, but my Row mates know something about respect.

I need another date with Lasalle. As the first public vote gets underway, I find myself thinking hard on some of that stuff he said. Not that it made a whole lot of sense, back when I had a chance to live. But it laid an egg in my mind that started growing.

Face my God. In between trading junk-mail, the other cons get talking about this week's public vote, laying bets who'll be first to go. That's what they do in between griping for their TVs and radios. They don't bet on anyone from this Row, but you know the feeling of being the last one in the dentist's waiting-room? That's me right now. The problem with the voting is that you don't get to hear if it's you until the last day. You have to stay prepared. Sometimes I get grand schemes to be wacky for my execution, wear socks on my ears or something, or say something bizarre for my last statement. Then I just bawl a little. These days I'm bawling way too much really, for a man, I know it.

By the last day of voting, I can't bear it anymore. In an hour the world will know who's going to die. I bitch to Jonesy about some more time with Lasalle, but he ain't interested. He argues with another guard over who gets to mind the governor's phone-line in the execution chamber, for the first executions. Occasionally he snaps down the Row at me.

'*Mr Laid-his-ma* ordered no more visits,' he says. 'Anyway, in a while you mayn't have to worry about nothin no more.'

In the end I take up clacking the metal balls again, until the other cons join in griping. All it does is ruffle Jonesy's feathers. 'Which one a you fucks got a million bucks to pay for special favors?'

'Git outta here,' yell the cons.

I just sigh. The swirl of musty air rustles a paper on my bench. An idea rustles with it. 'Jonesy,' I say, grabbing the sweepstakes letter. 'Here's your million.'

'Yeah, *right*,' he says.

'I ain't fooling – look,' I hold up the envelope.

'You think I was born yesterday?' snorts Jonesy. 'I just about have to shovel that mail-order fuckin bullshit off my driveway every mornin.'

I try a hooshy laugh on him. 'We-ell,' I hoosh. 'O-kay – but this is a legally binding promise for a million bucks – you know they can't say it unless it's true, and they say it right here in red and white.'

'Hey, Little!' calls a con. 'You sayin you got the latest sweep-stakes letter?'

'That's right.'

'Does it have black writin on it, or red writin?'

'It's the red one, all right.'

'God, Jesus in Heaven – I'll give you two hundred for that letter,' he says.

'Lemme see that,' Jonesy snatches the letter through my grille. He studies it a second, then says, 'It's got your name on it, that ain't no good to me.'

'Officer Jones,' I say, like a schoolteacher or something, 'my execution-kit has a last will and testament in it – I can *leave* it to you, see?'

'Little, wait!' yells another con. 'I'll give you three hundred for that letter.'

'Fuck that,' hollers another, 'I'll make it *five*!'

'Pipe the fuck down,' shouts Jonesy. 'Didn't y'all hear he gave it to *me*?' He checks his watch, then points through the grille at my slippers. 'Get ready.'

When the clinking of his keychain is out of earshot, a giggle flutters along the Row. 'Hrr-hrr-hr, fuckin Jonesy,' go the cons.

'Little,' says the con next door. 'You finally learnin how to git along.'

Officer Jones personally marches me along the Row, and down the stairs to find Lasalle. We have to sidestep a porter pushing a trolley loaded with TVs and radios on their way back to the cells. That means the vote is over. Behind the appliances struts the dark-suited man with the execution papers. It's his job to deliver the papers to the head warden of a Row, so that he can deliver them to the condemned man. As the suited man passes, I see Jonesy flash him an eyebrow, almost imperceptibly. The man just as imperceptibly shakes his head, and walks right on by.

257

'None of my boys dyin today,' says Jones. My gut relaxes. I live again, for now. When we reach the floor below, a different floor this time, Jones sticks his head into a regular-looking room, but nobody's there. He calls to a guard up the Row.

'Lasalle around?'

'In the cans,' says the guard, 'takin a dump.'

Jonesy takes me to the shower block on the floor below, and marches me right inside.

'Ain't we gonna wait for him to come out?' I ask.

'No time – it's execution day, I have to get downstairs. You got five minutes.' He casts a shifty eye around, then he leaves me with this echoey drip of brown-sounding water, and goes to stand outside the door.

I crouch on the wet concrete floor, and scan under the cubicles for evidence of life. Two cubicle doors are shut, not that you can lock them or anything. Under one door hangs a pair of jail slippers, and regular jail pants. Under the other is a pair of polished black shoes, and blue suit pants. I knock on that cubicle.

'Lasalle – it's Vern.'

'Aw Jesus. What you think I can do for you from a prison fuckin toilet?'

'Uh – help me face my God.' I hoosh it ironically. I guess it's ironic, hooshing when you're in the prison shithouse on some poor bastard's execution day.

'*Shit*,' he gripes.

Everybody's tense today, see. Tension even buzzes through this can door, like we just met in the freezer section of *Death-Mart* or something. Waves rise to engulf me.

'Really wanna meet you God?' says Lasalle. 'Then git on you damn fuckin knees.'

'Uh – it's kinda wet out here, actually, Lasalle . . .'

'Then make a fuckin wish to Santa. Ask for what you most want in this damn world.'

I think for a second, mostly wondering if I should just leave.

Then, after a moment, I hear Lasalle's clothes rustle inside the cubicle. The toilet flushes. He opens the door. His ole turkey neck appears, poking out of a collar and tie. His bottom lip juts dumb.

'Well?' he says, looking around. 'You a free man?' I look around, like a dumbo, while he straightens his tie, and raises a polite hand to the door. 'Officer Jones,' he calls, 'any news on the boy's pardon?' Jonesy just laughs, a real dirty laugh. Lasalle glares at me. 'So much for fuckin Santa.'

'Some preacher you are,' I say. I turn for the door but he grips my arm and spins me around. One tubular vein stands out from his neck, throbbing like it lives on a reproductive organ.

'Blind, dumb *shit*,' he spits, his breath like hot sandpaper in my ear. 'Where's this *God* you talk about? You think a caring intelligence would wipe out babies from hunger, watch decent folk scream and burn and bleed every second of the day and night? That ain't no God. Just fuckin *people*. You stuck with the rest of us in this snake-pit of human *wants*, wants frustrated and calcified into *needs*, achin and raw.'

The outburst takes me aback. 'Everybody needs something,' I mutter.

'Then don't come cryin to me becausen you got in the way of another man's needs.'

'But, Lasalle . . .'

'Why you think the world chewin its own legs off? Becausen the goodies are right there, but we can't fuckin get 'em. Why can't we get 'em? Becausen the market for promises need us not to. That ain't the work of no God. That's human work, animals who dreamed up an outside God to take the heat.' Lasalle pokes a trembling lip at my face. 'Wise the fuck up. Intermingling needs make this world go round. Serve that intermingling, and you needs can get fulfilled. Ever hear say, "Give the people what they want?"'

'Sure, but – where's that leave God?'

'Boy you really missed the boat. I'll make it simple, so's even fuckin *you* can understand. Papa God growed us up till we could wear long pants; then he licensed his name to dollar bills, left some car keys on the table, and got the fuck outta town.' Water rushes to his eye-holes. 'Don't be lookin up at no sky for help. Look down here, at us twisted dreamers.' He takes hold of my shoulders, spins me around, and punches me towards the mirror on the wall. 'You're the God. Take responsibility. Exercise your power.'

Four men appear at the door: two guards, a chaplain, and the guy in the dark suit. 'Time for the final event,' says the suit.

My eyes snap to the cubicle where the other prisoner takes a quiet dump, but the men walk right past it and grab hold of Lasalle. His lip juts dumb again, his shoulders droop. Through the corner of my eye I see Jonesy calling me out.

'Lasalle? You a *con*?' I ask.

'Not for long,' he says softly. 'Looks like not for long.'

'C'mon, Little,' calls Jones from the door. 'Lasalle won the first vote.'

'But Lasalle, was that like – the secret of life?'

He tuts and shakes his head as the group march him to the door.

'I mean – what's the practical . . .?'

He holds a hand up to the guards. They stop. 'You mean, how do you *do it*? Big yourself up – watch any animal for clues. As for us *humans* – check this . . .' He pulls a lighter from his pocket, and motions us to hush. He clicks the lighter once, softly, then cranes an ear toward the toilet cubicles, where the other con still sits out of sight. After a moment, you hear rustling in the cubicle. Then a lighter clicks inside. We watch a puff of smoke rise up, as the con drags on a cigarette he didn't even know he wanted. The power of suggestion. Lasalle turns to me with a smile, and clicks his lighter in the air. 'Learn their needs, and they'll dance to any fuckin tune you play.'

Jonesy grabs my arm as the group turns to the corridor. I wrassle free, and pounce a couple of steps after Lasalle, but Jonesy threads his arms through mine, headlocking me from behind. It's what he needs. I don't struggle.

'*Thanks, Lasalle,*' I holler.

'No sweat, *Vernon God,*' comes the voice.

'Boy,' says Jonesy, when he gets me to the stairs, 'you really bought his bullshit.'

'Somebody told me he was a preacher.'

'Yeah, *right.* Clarence Lasalle, the fuckin axe-murderer.'

I lie awake on my bunk tonight as Lasalle's execution buzzes from the TVs along the row. I expect to hear Taylor's voice, but one of my fellow inmates says she left the show to try and be a roving reporter. She has all the contacts now, I guess. Just needs that one big story. Anyway, we only catch the last hour of the show. Lasalle doesn't make any final statement, which seems kind of cool. He chooses 'I Got You under my Skin' for his final tune. What a guy.

This view of my ceiling grows familiar over the rest of the week, I even work on my art project, underneath a towel, lying here on my back. The entertainment appliances disappear again, right after Lasalle's event, and I get to thinking about his last talkings. It all sounded too simple, like a TV-movie or something, like just any ole thing they'd run violin music to. It gets me thinking though, about my wasted ole damn life. They don't even have job descriptions for the kind of talents I have. I guess the tragedy is that I should've been up there as the prosecutor, or even Brian Dennehy – I'm the one that can sense stuff about people, and situations and all. Sure, I'm not a great student or anything, or athlete or anything, but I have these talents, I'm sure I have. I guess the way their powerdimes mount up against mine, the final tally of dimes in the power system means they go through, and I don't. One learning, though: my big flaw is fear. In a world where you're *supposed* to be a psycho, I just didn't yell loud enough to get ahead. I was too darn embarrassed to play God.

Watch any animal, said Lasalle. Give them what they want, and watch any animal. I can understand the giving thing, but I spend nights all the way to the Ides of March, I survive two, then three more execution votes, trying to place the animal clues. I end up watching these useless brown moths that thwack around the light in my cell, felty splinters torn from nighttime, lost and confused. I guess they're animals. I hear moths are actually programmed to fly a straight line, steered by the moon. But these supermarket kind of lights mess up their navigation. Now look at them. I watch one snag behind the light cage, spanking dust off its wings in puffs. Then, 'Thp,' it spins to the floor, broken. The light just buzzes on. So much for the moon. I can relate to moths, boy.

Fantasy animals start to infect my dreams, linen spaniels that romp with Jesus, but in daylight I struggle to make sense of Lasalle's concept. I guess the only permanent animal I know is Kurt the dog, and I ain't sure he counts when it comes to the Secret of Everything. Ole Kurt, who drives himself crazy with the smell of next door's barbecue, who props up his self-esteem by being president of the barking circuit. You know he wouldn't be president of anything, if the circuit knew how damn measly he was. He would've been laughed out of town, if they knew. But they don't.

I sit up on the bunk. Kurt gets by with the bark of a much bigger dog.

twenty-five

'Well but, Vernon, are you using the bathroom every day?'
'Heck, Ma.'

'It's just that this week you're up against that sweet cripple who supposedly killed his parents. And he cries all the time. *All* the time.'

'You sayin I look guilty?'

'Well on camera you always just lie staring at the ceiling, Vernon, you can be so *impassive*.'

'But I didn't *do* nothin.'

'Don't let's start that again. I just don't want the day to arrive and you not be – you know, *ready* – it's March twenty-eight tomorrow, I mean, that'll be another vote under the bridge . . .'

Death Row always hushes when my ole lady calls. I guess it's like that in TV-land too, you know how entertaining she can be.

'Did you get the thing I sent for Pam?' I ask.

'Well yes, and thank you very much, from both of us. You know, we were even saying . . .'

'Mom – I think you should use it at the, you know – the time . . .'

'Well that's what we were saying . . .' I wait while she gives a bitty sob, and blows her nose. My eyes mist up too. She leaves the receiver for a second to compose herself, and returns with a sigh. 'Then we can just remember you the way you were – just imagine you're out on your bike . . .'

'Sure,' I say. 'That's why I sent the token – you can use it at any branch y'know.'

'Well we're very grateful, specially if you saw the price of a *Chik'n'Mix* lately. Pam and I will use the token, and Vaine can pay for her own . . .'

'And Ma – tell Nana she don't have to come up here either.'

There's a pause on the line. 'Well – Vernon, I haven't told your nana about, you know – the trouble. She's old, and she only watches Shopping anyway, she won't have seen the news – I think it should just be our little secret, okay?'

'And when I don't show up for lawnmowing this spring?'

'Oh hell – Vernon, the gals just arrived and I haven't finished Vaine's skirt.'

'Vaine's wearing a *skirt*?'

'Listen baby, we're canvassing votes for you, so don't worry – some people end up waiting years on drrth rhrw . . .'

After the call, I lay back on the bunk and plough things over in my mind. Needs, boy, human needs. Mom once said Palmyra was into food because it was the only thing she could control in her life. It wouldn't run from the plate, or stand up to her. I think about it, and see Leona sucking attention like sunrays; ole Mr Deutschman savoring his mangle-headed tangs. Sympathy dripping giddy into the aching sponge of Mom's life. Melted cheese and Vaine Gurie. Give 'em all what they want, I say.

I know the *Barn* token is a good want to give Palmyra, but I should think of something especially for Mom, even though another death in the family will probably fix her true need, like for sympathy. Shame it has to be me, though. And, know what? Who else I'd like to fulfil before I go is ole Mrs Lechuga. She's had a hard time of things, and I regret the stuff I said about Max. I guess I'm just pumping cream pie about it all, this giving of wants and whatever, but – what the heck. You only die once. Strangely, I even feel I should grant something for the ole jackrabbit media. You can only guess what they really want.

Then there's Taylor. Oh Tay. She's tight with all these media types now, reporters and all, with helicopters and stuff, so it won't be easy granting a wish for her. What she really wants is a big new story to launch her career. Maybe just a real nice call or something would do the trick. Maybe that could solve all the more difficult wants, a nice phone call.

I work my way through the list of wanters, until I hit Vaine Gurie. She seems to have fallen in with Pam now, don't even go there really. The only thing I can think she wants is a homicidal maniac for her SWAT team to practice on. She ain't easy. To be honest, though, I think I only linger on Vaine to avoid working on Lally's want. I know the Godly thing, the forgiving thing to do, is to give a want to Lally, even though he has just about everything. Just some bitty token, y'know?

The appliances return early this Sunday morning, giving the day a brisk feel. March twenty-eight. Execution day for somebody. Engineers set the TVs up permanently this time, and install a system to shut them down during the vote. Emotions howl like pack-dogs in my soul when a bunch of paperwork arrives with my breakfast tray. First is a brochure about how to act for the cameras, and what not to say or do. The whole Row must've got that one, on account of everybody's saying and doing the wrong thing. Under the brochure is a glossy page showing some cartoon convicts, with arrows on their clothes and all, giving hints for your last statement. Then another form has a list of musical choices for the Final Event: you get to choose one tune before the witnesses come into the chamber, and one for the Event itself. It's mostly real ole music on the list. I know I'll regret my choices when the time comes. I'll just have to be brave to that wave.

As I digest things, the regular Sunday quiet falls over the Row. You hear some papers rustle. Then a con calls out, softly.

'Burnem – you okay, my man?'

I turn over the last sheet of paper on my pile. Under it lays an order for my execution, effective six o'clock tonight. I look at it like it was a napkin or something. Then I fall down on my knees, bawl like a storm cloud, and pray to God.

twenty-six

Folks are friendlier to me on the afternoon of my death. The cons are friendlier by not hassling, especially the one I gave my clacker-balls to. Everybody else quietly avoids the issue. It's a busy-feeling day, like one of your mom's urgent baking days gone wrong, with feelings left unattended, a sense that somehow I forgot something, left the oven on, didn't lock the door. A sense that I can do it when I get back.

When my belongings are neatly folded on the table, and my bunk is stripped clean, four executives arrive with a cameraman. My row-mates wave fingers through their grilles, and holler good wishes as I shuffle down the row. 'Yo, Burnem – fuck 'em up man, *piss* on those muthas . . .'

Bless them. We pass down the hallway Lasalle disappeared from, not for the ride to the Huntsville unit, but to the new Events Suite here at Ellis, right downstairs. It's a one-stop shop now, carpeted and all, with artwork on the walls. I miss the chance of a last drive, but at least the Suite has windows. It seems gray and cool out, with just a few bugs clicking. A part of me is disappointed there ain't tornadoes and firestorms for the night of my death, but then – who do I think I am, right?

Just like she promised, Pam supervised my last meal. *Chik'n'Mix Choice Supreme*, with fries, rib-rings, corn relish, and two tubs of coleslaw. How smart she is – she had the kitchen people stuff bread in the tub, to absorb any excess steam, and keep the bottom pieces crisp. You figure the coleslaw ain't Pam though – that'll be Ma, on account of it's healthy. Those gals will be eating the same thing this evening, when I'm on the gurney. It's what they want, to imagine I'm just out and about on my bike, instead of being put to death.

At four-thirty I get to evacuate my tracts in a private restroom. They even give me a copy of *Newsweek* to read, and a Marlboro to suck on. I'm numb, like anesthetized or something, but I still appreciate these little touches. *Newsweek* says Martirio has the fastest economic growth rate in the world, with more new millionaires than even California. The cover shows a bunch of Guries throwing banknotes into the air and laughing. It ain't all roses, though: if you read farther down it says they're getting sued by the California tragedy, over the use of their statistics. Typical Martirio, I have to say.

An hour before my execution, I get to make some private phone calls. First I try home, then Pam's. There's no answer, I must've missed them already. Ma's been through a lot, and so's Pam, I guess. Bless them. They don't have answering machines, so I can't just say 'I love you' or something. In a way, though, it gives me the courage to make some other calls.

First I try Lally, to get it over with. His secretary almost hangs up, until I tell her why I'm calling. Lally's in a meeting at the new Martirio mall. She connects me to his phone. 'Big man!' he says when the phone answers. I give him what he wants, and tell him where my gun is stashed. He seems to accept the gesture gracefully.

Next I call Mrs Lechuga. Boy is she surprised, she even tries to change her voice so I'll think it's a wrong number. 'Oh my God,' she says.

'Yes?' I answer. She's been through a lot, bless her. In the end I think she's glad I called. Knowing her love of information, and her ole position as president of the douche-brigade, I'm sure she just loves the want I grant her. In a way, I designated her the command center for this evening's wants.

The next brainwave is to call Vaine Gurie, on her way to meet Mom and Pam at the *Barn*. I give her just what she really wants – just what she really needs, actually, if you think about it. She ends up being real touched to hear from me, and promises to pass my love on to the gals. I guess it *is* love after all, in that zany way we humans have.

Finally, for my last call in the world, I try Taylor Figueroa. She answers her phone personally, and her voice immediately takes me back to another time and place – a moist, fruity place, if it's not too smutty to say. And guess what: I give her the break she's been waiting for. She squeals with delight, and says to look after myself. Sounds like she means it too.

When I hang up the phone, two guards appear with a chaplain, and escort me to the make-up suite.

'Don't you worry darlin,' says a make-up lady, 'a little blush'll perk you up.'

Another lady whispers, 'You want toothpaste, or you think you can make it on your own?' I snort when she says it, and she looks at me, confused. Then she kind of gets it, and laughs along too. Not everybody gets the irony of things, that's what I learned.

Next, a girl with a clipboard arrives and makes me sign a waiver for my final statement. I'm going out quietly, just like Lasalle. I ask her one special favor in return. She calls a producer to check it out, then says it's okay. I can take my shirt off for the Event. She leads the pastor, the officers, and me down a bright hallway to the execution chamber. My knees go weak with the kind of swooniness you get from hospital smells; the pastor even takes hold of my arm when I hear the tune playing down the hall.

'*Galveston, oh Galves-ton – I am so afraid of dying . . .*'

We pass the broadcast control room, and guess what: they must've licensed the TV weather theme for the show. I hate that theme. I close my ears until we reach this simple white room with a window along one wall, and theater-like seats beyond.

'*Before I dry the tears she's crying . . .*'

I take off my shirt. My skin is mostly healed now, from my art project. Tattooed in big blue letters across my chest are the words '*Me ves y sufres*' – 'See me and suffer.' A medical orderly helps me climb onto the gurney, which is kind of person-shaped, like the hole left after a cartoon character crashes through a wall. I catch a glimpse of Jonesy in a room at the back. He must be manning the governor's phone. The governor is the only man who can stop this now. He'd need some damn convincing evidence to do that. Jonesy just turns away when he sees me. He doesn't stand near the phone.

Guards secure me to the gurney using thick cowhide straps with metal buckles, then the orderly raises a vein in my arm, and gives me a tiny shot, of anesthetic I guess. He fixes a long needle onto a tube that runs through the wall from the back room. I look away as he slides the needle into my vein. After a moment, cool solution begins to flow.

An usherette appears behind the glass that separates me from the witness area, and people start filing into their seats. Fragile Mrs Speltz is the only person I recognize. Aside from the wave of sadness I get from her haunted eyes, I actually feel relieved that she's the highlight of the witness area. Nothing in there suggests I'll be missing any parties when I'm gone. Then, just as I'm thinking that, the darnedest thing happens: a tall, beautiful young woman in a pale blue suit squeezes along the back row to her seat, kindling my groin out of retirement. Even the guards turn to watch as she sits, modestly tugging down the hem of her skirt. Then she looks at me. It's Ella Bouchard. Boy did her equipment arrive. Bluebonnet eyes call to me through the glass.

'Sailing' starts to play now, because when Fate opens up, it opens up with both barrels. I try to swallow, but my mouth is woody. A terminal learning comes to me: that for all the sirens, game-show buzzers, and drum-rolls of life, it is the nature of men to die quietly. I mean, what kind of life was *that*? – a bunch of movies, and people talking about movies, and shows about people talking about movies. Still, I guess I asked for it. By being negative, destructive. I remember once calling my daddy to collect me from a place, but was sad when he came because I'd since grown to love the place. Death takes me like that.

I feel an itch around the needle, and close my eyes. Voices in the chamber soften, and I feel myself slipping away, up and over the gurney, into a reverie. I look down on myself, but instead of panic, instead of sudden death, I float out of the chamber, and over the landscape outside, where my senses are filled with the scent of lawn-clippings. I'm transported, clear as day, back home to Beulah Drive. There's Mrs Porter's, and there's my front yard. It's today, it's right now. The mantis pumpjack beats with my soul as a black Mercedes-Benz sweeps into my driveway. Mrs Lechuga's drape twitches. Mom ain't home this evening, which is unusual. She's eating out with Pam. I watch Lally climb out of the car. Bless the motherfucker to hell. Bless his bones smashed and stuffed through the ligaments of his puking fucked eyes, bless his mouth to suck me off, take my bile so it kills him dead to a place where he stays conscious and fucken broken and cold, shivering fucken worms and slime from organs that pop and fucken waste as I laugh.

He seems excited by the want I granted. I know the question of the second firearm always plagued him. He lets himself into the house through the kitchen, and moves to my bedroom closet, where he finds the shoebox containing the padlock key, just like I told him. Next to it lays a bottle of ginseng. You can't even see the LSD pearls I stuffed in it all those moons ago. He smiles, and picks it up.

An unmistakable sound draws me back out of the house. It's the Eldorado, idling up the street. For the first time in Leona's life, she parks at the unfashionable end of Beulah Drive. Neither she nor George or Betty talk, or adjust their make-up. They don't even breathe. They sit parked under a willow and wait. Nobody, but nobody, overrides Nancie Lechuga's instructions. I watch with the ladies as Lally climbs into his car and drives away. They follow at a discreet distance. Mrs Lechuga's drapes twitch shut behind them. She's back in charge of the brigade, bless her.

Mom and Pam are fretting over the chicken by now, as Muzak boils the life out of some ole song. A two-inch pile of napkins sits soggy with their tears, under a sprinkling of salt and crumbs.

I'm touched that my spirit is with them, just like the ole days, when hanging out together was like playing a favorite ole disc, reliving the tickles you got when you first heard it. Neither Pam nor my mom is saying anything relevant, that's the beauty of it. I don't know if it's on purpose, or if it's like a genetic kind of thing that folk just cruise into comfortable, meaningless ole routines when the shit hits the fan.

Mom just says, 'Well but they've moved things around since last time.'

Pam says, '*Lord*, you're right, the cashier used to be over *there*.'

All I can say is they must've moved it in about five seconds, for the time these gals spend out of the joint. But where's Vaine? She's usually so *punctual* when it comes to *chicken*.

I race like a breeze over my ole stomping grounds, through Crockett Park towards Keeter's. Lally can't help chuckling when he reaches Keeter's corner. He can't stop laughing as he bounces up the track, and he's positively howling by the time the den comes into view, as the elephant dose of hallucinogens starts to warp his perception. His last steady action is to fit the key into the den padlock, pull back the hatch, and haul out my daddy's rifle. My ole lady bequeathed me that rifle, on condition I never bring it near the house. I had to act fast the day Daddy disappeared. Mom was real antsy. She got over it by shopping for garden furniture – go figure.

Thunder from an approaching helicopter nudges the acid in Lally's bloodstream to a peak. The vista starts to liquefy before his eyes. He's a drug-crazed, homicidal maniac, loose in our community. He turns his back on sunlight beaming low over the escarpment, only to find a spotlight pinning him from the other side.

'Drop it!' barks a voice. It's Vaine with her SWAT team. She shields her eyes against dust from the settling chopper.

Lally reels in a wild circle, confused, caressing the rifle, erasing Mom's fingerprints, and her worries, forever. As Taylor Figueroa ducks out of the helicopter with a news cameraman, Lally raises the rifle and cries in an unearthly tone. '*Ma*-mi,' he bawls, finding the trigger with both hands. '*Mamá!*'

Watch out Taylor, like – oh my *God*!

'*Open fire!*' Vaine screams to her team.

Lally's face is a mask I fucken adore, suspended in time forever as slugs whistle and pierce the evening sky. He dances mid-air as chunks of his body pelt down like rain, before the bulk of him thuds twitching to the ground. Leona Dunt's Eldorado has to swerve off the track to avoid him.

'Wow, but is it supposed to be hidden, like – *in* the shit?' asks Leona, pouring out of the car in a cloud of tobacco smoke.

'I think Nancie means the *story* about the shit is what's valuable,' coughs Betty, ashing a cigarette into the dust. 'Just the *evidence* of the shit, the *story* rights . . .'

'Honey,' says George, 'a bonanza is a bonanza, whether it's *in* or *on* or *about* the shit, now hand me that flashlight . . .'

'Golly,' says Betty, scraping through the bushes around my den. 'Looks like somebody's been here already . . .'

My vision dissolves, my mind shimmers back to the gurney and I find myself still alive, teeth clenched into a smile. That's some fucken anesthetic, boy. I look over to see the guards nod to each other in readiness. As the day's first thunder crackles outside, I turn to wink at Ella through the glass. Then I close my eyes. I wait for the deep to claim me, for the cool in my arm to turn icy, or not to turn at all, to just vanish through the glare with everything around, including lumpy ole asshole me.

Sailing
Takes me away
To where I've always heard it could be
Just a dream and the wind to carry me
And soon I will be free . . .

Suddenly, a cannonade of noise swells through the windows and cracks, down the stairs and ducts of the jail, a thousand voices and fists and feet triggered by some invisible cue. My eyes pop open to see if God, or the devil, has come to claim my slimy soul. Instead, Abdini bursts into the witness area, followed be a horde of cameramen. The whole jail must be watching it live on TV. Abdini has a dirty brown ball of paper in one hand, and a melted candle in the other. He holds them up to the glass, singing, jumping. It's Nuckles's notes, the ones I used to wipe my ass that fateful day. 'Test prove it!' he cries.

A phone rings out back. After a moment I crane to see Jonesy toddle into the chamber, shaking his head. He leans over the end of the gurney, cups his hands to his mouth.

'Little – your pardon came through.'

twenty-seven

The ladies study the envelope like it was the body of a dead baby.

'Definitely one of those Italian cars, a *Romeo and Juliet* or whatever,' says George.

'I know,' says Betty, 'but why send the brochure to Doris's?'

'Honey, it doesn't say *Doris* on the front, it says *Leona*. Just the *address* is Doris's.'

'But *why*?'

George shakes her head. 'Loni wants us to know she's getting one of those sports cars, I guess.'

Betty tightens her lips, and tuts awhile. 'I *know*, but why doesn't she just come over, like always, or even just call? Maybe she went to have the implants after all . . .'

George blows a plume of smoke, finishing with a ring that travels up and over the *Central-Vac* box on the rug. 'Betty, don't piss me off, okay? You know damn well why.'

'Oh *Lord*,' scowls Betty. 'But that's her *ex-ex*-husband, the tragedy was nothing to do with *her* . . .'

George rolls her eyes. 'I know, I *know*, but some people might question the quality of a marriage that left a man chasing teenage boys for kicks – you have to admit that's *out there* even for *Marion Nuckles*, never mind the phony shrink he hooked up with. And goddammit to hell, Betty, now you've got me saying "I know."'

'I *know*.'

George clicks her teeth. Then their eyes meet, and they start to froth with helpless laughter.

'Girls, it's here!' calls Mom through the kitchen. 'It's the side-by-side!' She tries to keep her mouth pointed down, in mourning for Lally, but her eyes give her away. My ole lady just loves being in mourning. It's one of her needs, I guess. Bent ole kitten.

I hear Brad hollering up the hall, so I slink into the kitchen where a pile of media paperwork sits on the bench, along with some contracts from my agent. On top of the pile is a faxed cover of next week's *Time* magazine – the headline reads: 'Stool's Out!' The picture shows the dried remains of my crap, wrapped in Nuckles's class papers, sitting in a scientific laboratory. Behind it, Abdini proudly holds up the note Jesus left in the den, for Nuckles and Goosens, the lovers and internet entrepreneurs. 'You sed it was love you batsards,' reads the note, in his ole baby scribble. My eyes drop for Jesus. One thing, though: his note inadvertently granted a big ole want for Nuckles and Goosens. Now they'll have all the boys they could wish for, up there in prison. Somehow you sense they might be doing a little more receiving than giving, though. But hell. As Nuckles himself would say – 'Beggars can't be choosers.'

Farther along the kitchen bench lies a copy of today's paper, with the headline: 'Old Familiar Feces.' The picture shows Leona out at Keeter's, holding lumps of shit in her hands. Farther down still is an article about Taylor. She'll be fine. Just maybe not filling her panties the way she used to. Maybe they can implant a silicon butt-cheek or something, who knows?

Mom bunts me over the porch and down to the wishing bench, where the man from the morgue hovers. 'Let me shake your hand, son,' he says, 'your daddy would've been mighty proud.'

'Thank you,' I say, breathing in the clear blue day.

'Yessir, that was some turnaround. What's your secret?'

'I went down on my knees and prayed, sir.'

'Mighty fine,' he says, turning to Mom. 'And ma'am – I think we can process that earlier insurance matter just now – the body clearly can't be found.'

'Well thank you, Tuck,' says Mom, running a hand over her wishing bench.

'Mr Wilmer!' calls George from the porch. 'See what you can do for that poor woman in Nacogdoches . . .'

'Be my pleasure, Mrs Porkorney – you take care now, y'hear?'

After he turns away, Mom frowns at the fridge box being wheeled up the driveway. She frowns extra-hard, not just on account of being a double widow, but because Leona taught her not to show too much joy over new goods. You have to pretend they don't matter, that's what she taught her, that and how to throw her head back when she laughs. Doesn't fool me, though.

I lean over the bench and soak up Mom's clammy warmth. When the ladies join us, Mrs Lechuga comes to her window across the street. She sends a little wave, and I realize who's missing, for the full set of dice in my life – Palmyra. But, hey – I guess it ain't every day you get to play pinball on *Oprah*.

'Vern,' says Betty, 'Brad's just desperate to show you his birthday present.'

I try to nod politely, but my eyes snag on some dappled pink flesh behind the willows up the street. It's Ella with her suitcase. She wears a wool sweater over a loose cotton dress that swishes full of honey breeze. She grins when she sees me watching her. I told her I'd send a car, but she insisted on taking one last walk through town, crazy girl. Anyway, we'll be back. Mexico ain't so far.

'Kurt, *stay*!' Ole Mrs Porter bangs through her screen, and struggles down the lawn with a table full of knitted toys. Then, as I cross the driveway to meet Ella, Brad thumps onto the porch behind us.

'B-ooom! *Suck shit muthafucka!*'

'That better not be loaded,' says Betty. '*Bradley Pritchard!* Don't you point that thing, or it'll go right back to the store!'

I ignore him by rubbing lips with Ella. Then we both turn to watch Mrs Porter stand her toys by the roadside. She's setting up a fucken stall for chrissakes. We just swallow giggles.

'Ma'am,' I call over the road. 'Mrs Porter!'
She cocks her head, in a kindly way, and flaps a little wave.
'Everybody's gone, Mrs Porter. Everything's back to normal . . .'

THE END

Acknowledgements

Give me a spirit that on this life's rough sea
Loves t'have his sails filled with a lusty wind,
Even till his sail-yards tremble, his masts crack,
And his rapt ship run on her side so low
That she drinks water, and her keel ploughs air.
  George Chapman

Love to Katz for gently stitching and filling such fine new sails; to my parents and family for this taste for the sea; and to all whose faith opened space beneath a ragged keel.

To the Burnbury Court of Miracles: Strawberries to Dawn & Mark, who practiced friendship with the stealth many reserve for crime; Lisa for energy and chocolate; Bubbles & Frog, who didn't put me up in Hong Kong; Val Wilson, Martinez, and the Cavendish milieu for enlightenment and vodka; to the CWs – Hawker Siddeley!
  May the Watras be with Hog, Hildegard, and all Bara crew; *Abrazos pa Toño y los cuates – ora si verda carnales*; to Junius and family for longevity of faith; Lynn Pearce & family for mindful encouragement; to all whose shores remain littered with my sins – this could be the handle of a mop . . .

Special thanks to Clare Conville, of Conville & Walsh, Lee Brackstone and all at Faber and Faber, for the vigor with which they hoisted this sheet to the breeze, and to Grant Stewart, whose keen eye first sighted the craft approaching.

P.S. Gumby – still want that assassination?